FOOTSTEP

FOOTSTEPS ON THE PATH

Mona Callister

Published by Levens Publishing

A CIP catalogue record for this book is available from the British Library.

ISBN 978-1-9989923-0-0

Book layout and cover design by Clare Brayshaw

Prepared and printed by:

York Publishing Services Ltd
64 Hallfield Road
Layerthorpe
York YO31 7ZQ

Tel: 01904 431213

Website: www.yps-publishing.co.uk

*I will walk the path that our
Fathers have trod before us*

St. David

AUTHOR PROFILE

MONA Callister was born in Blackpool with Manx ancestry, has three sons, seven grandchildren and still lives near the Fylde coast.

She is a retired primary school teacher and a keen amateur painter.

Since she was a child, taking ferry trips from Fleetwood to Douglas, she has been fascinated by the Isle of Man and its history, especially its folk lore and fairies. Perhaps it is because she is named after the island, also known as Mona's Isle, that she feels a strong sense of belonging whenever she visits.

The Isle of Man and the Fylde coast of Lancashire feature in most of her writing.

To my son Mark,

who has encouraged and supported me from day one.

PART ONE

ISOBEL

CHAPTER ONE

SOMETIME during the night my sister left home. She had crept out of the house without disturbing any of us so we were shocked, the next morning, to find that her bed had not been slept in and that her drawers and closet had been emptied. Although I shared her secret about the young man she had met at our church, there had been no hint of what she was about to do, so I was not only shocked, I felt abandoned. Martha, my older sister, was my only source of family affection and now, by her night flight, she had slipped free from a life stifled by the rigid confines of Victorian society and ruled over by strict unloving parents, leaving me alone with them. Suddenly my bleak life had become yet more bleak. I was desolated.

Father's immediate reaction was rage at being defied rather than concern for his daughter.

'Did you know about this, Isobel?' he barked at me. I shook my head. It was safer to say nothing.

'I'll find her.' He grabbed his coat and hat. 'She can't have gone far. Someone must have seen her. I'll bring her back.'

Someone had indeed seen her and when he was told that she and her lover had taken the night coach to London and would now be beyond pursuit, he returned home white faced with fury, and through gritted teeth told my mother and me that my sister's name was never to be mentioned again. Then he marched into his study, still wearing his hat and coat, and slammed the door. I had never seen him so furious. My heart sank as I watched his display of temper. Neither of us had ever dared defy him before and now that Martha had gone, I knew his grip on me would be tightened. He had lost one daughter, he would not risk losing another.

I couldn't turn to my mother for comfort. To her, my father's word was as the word of God, so she neither made any protest nor showed any distress at the loss of a daughter. The only tears that were shed were mine, but they were not for my sister, they were for me, because now I was trapped.

Father was a parson, but our parsonage had nothing of the welcoming rose-covered country home the name usually evokes. We lived in an uninviting, oppressive house which even the sun could not warm. Our door was not open to visitors. All meetings were held in the cold, gloomy church, and from a very young age, my sister and I had learned the art of daydreaming in order to endure the long arduous sermons my father preached. Mother would dig us sharply in the ribs if either of us dared to fall asleep.

'Sit up straight and pay attention,' she would hiss. 'Show some respect.'

How we envied those children whose parents not only allowed them to sleep but also provided a comforting arm to lean against.

I never knew whether my mother had succumbed to this joyless way of life after marrying my father, or if it had been a meeting of two like minds, but either way she was as entrenched as he in their rigid, parsimonious routine. Even the poor people of the parish, whom Martha and I visited on behalf of our mother, had a brighter blaze on their hearth than we did. Fortunately, our maid was a very good cook who could produce a tasty meal even from the cheap cuts of meat our mother ordered, so although we were always cold, we were never hungry. Meals were eaten in silence, apart from the Grace intoned by Father, often long enough for our food to grow cool. Although he liked the sound of his own voice, the only words Father spoke to Martha and me were instructions on our duties and counsel on our behaviour, with mother's endorsement of 'Quite right too' punctuating every sentence.

Luckily, I had found a box of books tucked away in the corner of the attic where I had my bedroom, presumably left behind by the previous parson. These, and the fact that neither parent could climb the steep stairs to invade my privacy, kept me sane. I could hide away in my sanctuary and read of a world outside this cold prison, for that is what it seemed. I even managed to sneak some books down to Martha who shared my dream of escape. Lots of our conversations began with 'One day…'

Now that my sister had found her 'one day' and escaped, it seemed that all those dreams had vanished for me. My parents would never let their only remaining child leave home. Prison bars were my horizon. I would be kept at home to look after them in their old age, tethered to a life that was as limited as it was useless. It was a prospect that filled me with dread since, never having been shown any love, I had little affection for either of them. I was nineteen years old and desperate to escape as my sister had done but, with no lover on the scene, elopement was not a way out for me. I could see no hope ahead.

* * *

The letter arrived one morning, several months later, and recognising the handwriting as that of my childhood friend, Sarah, my father passed it to me unopened. I took it to my room to read, and what a good job I did because the first few lines caused me to leap up and prance about the room in delight, Sarah was inviting me to visit her for a few weeks at her home in the Isle of Man! Perhaps God was answering my unspoken plea – for I had certainly not prayed to him – but it was the godsend I needed. Now, somehow, I had to persuade Father to let me go.

'Father, Sarah has invited me to stay with her for a few weeks in the Isle of Man.' I handed him the letter. 'I would very much like to see Sarah again.' I spoke as casually as I could then held my breath while I waited for his reply. I had to be careful not to appear too eager, he must be convinced it was his own decision because if he sensed my desperation to leave, it would be a definite no. There was a faint glimmer of hope though. Sarah's parents were his devout parishioners, so he would very likely assume that their daughter would run a similar establishment to the ones that both he and they reigned over. Eighteen months ago, Sarah had married a doctor, Stephen Corkish, and because of his profession, her parents had been approving. Of course, neither they nor my father knew that Sarah had shared the same dreams of escape as Martha and me. They had both achieved that dream and this was my chance, probably my only chance, and I had to take it because now, thanks to Sarah, I had somewhere to go. Since Martha had left, I had been the model of an obedient daughter. I knew my parents were both watching me for signs that I might follow my sister so I had to allow time to dispel their suspicions. I hoped that I had succeeded enough to be able to persuade them now.

Surprisingly, it was my mother who swayed his hand. 'I think a visit to Sarah would be quite useful, Edward,' she said. 'I want to move Isobel Ruth into the room at the end of the corridor so it would be a good opportunity to have the room cleared and cleaned ready for her things to be brought down.'

She didn't say, but we all knew, that this room had been my sister's, who had been required to attend my mother whenever she decided she was in a delicate state. Obviously, that job was now to be mine.

I crossed my fingers as I waited. I felt sure that, to him, the thought of my being on hand in the next room to care for my mother, would carry more weight than would the fact that a visit to a friend might do his daughter some good, and I was right. It did. He took his time to read the letter then looked at me over the top of his glasses.

'I suppose that could be arranged,' he said slowly. 'She might visit for a week or two, provided we can find an escort for her on the journey.' He smiled smugly, obviously pleased by this rare show of magnanimity.

Desperately anxious not to do anything that might make him change his mind, I bowed my head, feigned humble gratitude, and murmured, 'Thank you, Father.'

I made sure my letter of acceptance to Sarah was in the next post.

* * *

Our home was in a market town in Lancashire, a few miles from the coast, so to reach the Isle of Man I would have to drive to the fishing port of Fleetwood and take the ferry across to Douglas. It would be the furthest I had ever travelled and the thought of the long journey made me feel nervous but until I actually set foot on the Isle of Man,

I would not feel free, so whatever had to be faced to get there – I would face.

Sarah wrote back saying that her husband would meet me off the boat and that by sheer good luck, or God's good grace, he had a patient who would be returning to the island the following week after a business trip and who would be willing to act as my escort. Sarah knew my father!

I would have agreed to any conditions in order to leave, so even though we had little time to make arrangements, due to needing to fit in with my escort's plans, by the end of the week I had my bag packed and my travel documents booked. My father even gave me two sovereigns, the first money I had ever had of my own, and this time I didn't need to feign gratitude. I was truly grateful.

Father travelled with me to Fleetwood. The dock was busy with trawlers unloading their catch, and there was a strong smell of fish. The boat I was to sail on was at the dock side and there were already people on the gangplank going aboard. A middle-aged gentleman introduced himself as Mr Lane, my escort, and luckily my father approved of him because if he had not, I wouldn't have put it past him to change his mind, even at this late stage.

My mouth was dry with excitement as I looked up at the big boat I would be sailing on. I had never been on water before and there was just a little fear mixed in with the anticipation and I had to swallow hard to contain it. I must not let anything stop me from boarding this boat. Even as we were walking up the gangplank, I kept looking back to make sure my father was not following to prevent me from leaving. Not until there was water between us would I feel sure I had escaped. I could have wept with relief when we finally pulled away from the dock. Unless my father was prepared to swim for it, he could not stop me now.

Mr Lane found a seat for me in a quiet corner of the saloon and I sank down, squeezing my eyes tightly together to check the tears that were brimming at my eyelids, but I was unable to stop them. Mr Lane opened his paper and tactfully left me to weep. It was silent weeping, no sobs or catches of breath, just hot tears sliding down my face and dripping off my chin. Why was I weeping when I should be laughing with joy? I was free.

CHAPTER TWO

STEPHEN was waiting to meet me at the dock side in Douglas, but if Mr Lane had not been there, I would have failed to recognise him, having seen him only once at Sarah's wedding. I was greeted with a warm smile by a tall, handsome, well-dressed man.

'Welcome to Douglas, Isobel,' he said. 'Did you have a good crossing?'

'Yes, we did, the sea was very calm. Thank you for arranging for Mr Lane to escort me. I don't think Father would have let me come otherwise.'

He laughed. 'Even though I am sure you think you are quite old enough to take care of yourself.'

He had a carriage waiting and I stuck my head out of the window for most of the ride, excited to see the town where I would be living for the next few weeks. I was also very much looking forward to seeing Sarah again, but I tried not to think beyond that. I had already experienced a miracle in fleeing the miserable prison I had called home, so for the time being that was enough, but three little words kept chanting inside my head, matching the clip-clop rhythm of the horse's hooves – I am free, I am free, I am free.

Sarah and I were delighted to see each other again. 'Oh, Isobel, how lovely to see you.' She held out her arms and

I perched beside her on the sofa eager to embrace her but was surprised to feel how thin she had become.

'It is lovely to see you too,' I said. 'How did you know I needed rescue?'

'I began to plan when I had your letter telling me about Martha,' she said. 'I knew you would be feeling bereft.'

'I was. It was such a shock. She had kept it secret even from me, and we have heard nothing from her since, although if a letter had arrived father would have intercepted and confiscated it.'

'Anyway, she's free and I'm sure she will be happy, just as I am, and just as you will be now you are here.'

'Well, I'm certainly looking forward to not having to sit through my father's sermons for a while,' I said and we both laughed. Sarah leaned forward on her elbow.

'Do you remember how your father would say, "And in conclusion…" and we would all heave a sigh of relief that the end was nigh, only for him to carry on for at least another ten minutes?'

Even though it was a miserable reminder, we both giggled, and I saw the delight in Stephen's eyes as he watched his wife's happy face.

We chatted while we took afternoon tea, but I could see that Stephen was keeping an eye on Sarah, and after a while he suggested that Mrs Berry, the housekeeper, show me to my room, and what a delightful room it was. Sarah had made every effort to make me feel at home. There were many thoughtful little touches: flowers on the dressing table, a pile of books by my bedside, and the room carried the scent of lily of the valley from the block of soap on the washstand. My window had a view across fields where golden oats flickered in the breeze. It was perfect. I stretched out on the comfortable bed, spread my arms wide and my head sang its little song – I am free, I am free, I am free – because come what may, I was never going back.

* * *

I soon understood why Sarah had invited me. She had become very frail and though I did not yet know the cause, I could tell that she was ill. Neither she nor Stephen mentioned her debility, so I didn't ask. It was my company she needed, and I was happy to give it. I was very fond of Sarah.

Because she quickly tired, I found I had plenty of time to myself, and I developed the habit of taking a walk every day, sometimes across the fields and sometimes along the beach. I especially loved to walk on the shore when a strong breeze was blowing. The salt spray stung my cheeks and the wind blew my hair free from the severe bun I wore, but I didn't care. My boots sank into the soft sand, leaving a trail of footprints, and I laughed with joy – they were the footprints of a girl who was free. I would return to the house exhilarated, my cheeks glowing and my eyes bright from time spent in the fresh air.

'Our Manx air is doing you good, Isobel,' Stephen said. 'How I wish Sarah could benefit as you are doing.'

'Perhaps on a warmer day she might be able to sit in the garden for a while,' I suggested. 'I'm sure she would feel better in the fresh air.'

Stephen shook his head. 'Sarah is not as strong as you are, Isobel. She has not left the house for the last six months.'

'Yet she is always so cheerful when we talk, she never complains.'

'No, she doesn't and because of that I am hopeful we may overcome this sickness. I think she will find the strength to fight it in time. You have already made such a difference to her since you came. I think talking about your childhood memories has given her something to cling to. I hope you will be able to stay with us for some time yet.'

I was on the point of telling him about my escape and how I was never going back, when it occurred to me that I would be putting him in an awkward position. In telling him that I had left home for good it could be seen as taking advantage of an invitation which had only suggested a few weeks. Instead I just answered, 'I hope so too.'

Every day made me realise how much Sarah relied on me. I wrote to my parents telling them she was not in the best of health and that I would be extending my visit for as long as I was needed. Their reply consisted of a very brief, but very terse, order to take the next boat back to Fleetwood. They did not express any concern for Sarah. I deliberately waited several days before answering, then I told them I was sorry but I could not possibly leave, and I hoped they would understand that, since my friend was dependent on me, I would not be returning in the foreseeable future. This time there was no reply.

As I watched the tender way in which Stephen cared for Sarah, I saw, for the first time, how loving a relationship could be between a man and his wife. Now I understood why Martha had left the house so secretly. She couldn't risk anything jeopardising the happy future she would share with her husband. Alone in my room at night, I couldn't help but wonder what it must be like to have a man love you like that, to have a husband and to be a wife. I tried to imagine myself with a beau, but I could see no hope of romance for me and drifted off to sleep still wondering.

* * *

'ISOBEL – ISOBEL.' It was the middle of the night yet Stephen was knocking urgently at my bedroom door. I hurried to open it to him. 'It's Sarah, she has collapsed. Can you come?'

'Yes, of course.' I grabbed my robe and followed him quickly down the corridor to Sarah's room. 'What's happened?'

'She has haemorrhaged. I've managed to stabilise her but she needs attention. Will you help me?'

Sarah was in bed and I stared at my friend who was so pale and still that she could have been dead. Stephen had asked Mrs Berry for warm water and towels to wash Sarah but did not want such a personal service to be carried out by a servant, so I set about removing her stained nightgown and between us, with Stephen lifting her when needed, we made her as comfortable as we could.

She opened her eyes and smiled at me. 'Thank you, Isobel.'

I could barely hear her voice she was so weak. Stephen put a glass to her lips and she managed to take a few sips of the concoction he had prepared, and after a while, although she did not gain colour in her cheeks, for she had always been pale, she looked recovered enough for Stephen to dim the lamp and leave her to sleep.

We went down to the kitchen, where Mrs Berry had brewed a pot of tea, and we sat by the fire in need of recovery ourselves after such an alarming and distressing incident.

'You were so good with Sarah, Isobel,' Stephen said. 'Thank goodness you were here. Thank you.'

'Don't thank me, Stephen. I would do anything for Sarah.' I meant it with all my heart. She was my friend, I loved her and I had thought we were losing her.

In the following weeks, Mrs Berry and I prepared nourishing delicacies for Sarah while Stephen kept a daily watch over his wife, and we were all rewarded on the day she felt strong enough to get out of bed and sit in the chair. A month later she was well enough to come downstairs and join us at the dining table. She was still not strong and needed lots of rest, but we had our Sarah back and we were thankful.

Now that she was doing so well, I began to think about my future. I was aware I could not stay with Sarah forever. I had to start earning a living, and with no skills apart from domestic ones, a post as a companion seemed my only option. Soon I would start to make enquiries.

* * *

Unable to sleep one hot sultry night, I got up and walked barefooted in the garden. It was bliss. Dewy grass bathed my feet and a soft breeze cooled my skin, which still held the heat of the day. A full moon cast its silver light across the lawn, stealing the green from the grass, and all the scents of the garden were on the air. The moon seemed close enough to touch and as I gazed into its brightness it was easy to believe in the Little People that Mrs Berry had told me about and in which, as a born and bred Manx woman, she firmly believed. Perhaps they had cast a magic spell, or perhaps it was the ancient pull of the full moon, but a strange potency tingled through me, as though I had been endowed with my own magic power. I had a strong feeling of belonging – as if I was part of the night and the night was part of me. I plucked a stem of sweet lavender and rubbed it on my arm to share its fragrance and, enchanted by the beauty of the night, lines remembered from my girlhood studies floated into my head.

'The moon shines bright in such a night as this when the sweet wind did gently kiss the trees and they did make no noise.'

I sniffed the lavender and remembered more. 'In such a night Medea gather'd the enchanted herbs.'

'In such a night did young Lorenzo swear he loved her well—'

The voice came from behind, startling me. I had not realised I had spoken aloud. It was Stephen. He was dressed and had obviously returned from a night call. I finished his quotation.

'—stealing her soul with many vows of faith and ne'er a true one.' I smiled at him. 'I would out night you,' I said.

Stephen laughed. 'I see we both know our *Merchant*.'

He was standing by the hedge, moonlight illuminating his face while shade hid the rest of his body, creating a strange disembodied image that added to the haunting magic of the night. He moved towards me and I held out the lavender. He reached to take it, but instead took the hand that held it and that was all that was needed. My already heightened senses soared. An overwhelming excitement took my breath and my whole body tensed. I waited, not knowing what I was waiting for, only aware that some mysterious power held me in its grip and wherever it led me, I would go.

Stephen pulled me to him, and I went into his arms to be held in the tenderest embrace I had ever known. There was no fear as I lifted my face for my first kiss. He kissed my mouth, my eyes, my neck – and the garden started to spin.

Held tight in his arms, our bodies pressed together, I lost all awareness of the garden. Dark space swirled round me, then wet ground was beneath me and I gasped as the first touch of a man's bare skin against mine sparked a fiery tingle in my stomach and I clung to Stephen, astonished and excited by his body. We rolled in a twine of legs and arms, and when he pushed into me my body instinctively knew how to rock to his rhythm. I had not known such joy and pain could be felt at the same time. I wanted it to go on and on, like a flower that goes on opening and opening until the last petal falls, but a final violent spasm wrenched a long moan from me and I fell back on the grass, exhausted.

Clouds drifted across the moon and took the silver light, and as the darkness came it took the magic. With the fever gone I lay in Stephen's arms, breathless and dazed and tingling from the thrill of what had just happened. Although he still held me, he didn't move or speak. I could hear his heavy breathing and listened as it slowed, hearing what I thought sounded like a sob, then the cool night air and the damp grass chilled me and I began to shiver. Stephen immediately lifted me away from him.

'You're cold. I'm sorry, I should have been more thoughtful.' He wrapped his jacket round me. 'Let me take you in and get you warm.'

'Stephen–' I began but he stopped me.

'Isobel, please let me apologise now before we go inside. I should never have let this happen, please forgive me. I didn't realise just how innocent you were, but you came to me so willingly I thought… I promise it will never happen again.'

'But Stephen–' He stopped me again.

'No, please listen to me, Isobel. You have a life ahead of you that cannot include me. This was a moment of madness, for both of us I think, and I am sorry it cannot be more.' He looked up as the moon appeared again from behind the clouds. 'The full moon can do such strange things – and we must leave it there.'

I was still shivering and shaking from the night's coolness and too amazed by what we had just done to fully take in what he was saying. I wanted to stay in the arms that had held me in my first discovery of love, but instead he took my hand and led me back to the house, slipped his jacket from my shoulders, briefly touched my cheek, then turned and walked into his study and shut the door.

I stared after him. He had left me. His silence and the closed door told me, without doubt, that he had left me. It was all over. I don't know what I had expected but this sudden change, this sudden rejection, frightened me. I felt lost. Unsure of what to do next, I waited for a few minutes, but the door stayed shut. Miserably, I crept back to my room.

Was that all there was to love, just that one out of this world joining together, ending in an explosion of physical frenzy that left me longing for more? How could I know? I knew nothing of men except that I had been at first shocked and then on fire at the touch of his body, especially that part for which I had no name.

My nightgown was wet from the grass and, still shivering, I pulled it off to find a clean one, but as I tossed it into a corner, I noticed bloodstains, then with a stab of alarm I found smears on my thighs. Had I been hurt? I had certainly felt pain and I ached all over. Too overwhelmed by misery to think further, I burst into tears, washed myself, then crawled into bed and fell into an exhausted sleep.

It took all the courage I could find to face Sarah the next day, because now I understood just what had happened. I had betrayed her by taking her place with her husband. I was racked by shame and remorse. What a way to repay the friend who had been so kind to me. Yet even in the midst of this dreadful guilt there was a tiny part of me that did not truly regret what had we had done. It had been my first experience of love and I had responded like an eager puppy to a kind hand, and something in me had changed forever. As if I had shed my old skin, a new Isobel had replaced the innocent and ignorant girl I had been, and I had become a woman. But I had no idea what I was going to do next.

At first, I waited for Stephen to give me some sign that the relationship between us had shifted. Surely that night had made a difference, but as he continued to behave in exactly the same way as before, it gradually dawned on me that the man I had loved that night was gone. He had meant what he said, it would never happen again. I was left to live with a very guilty conscience and the daily struggle to behave in a normal manner towards Sarah. In an attempt to atone for the wrong that I had done her, I doubled my efforts to help her regain her health and strength, then once she was well again, I would leave, for there was now no way that I could stay.

As she grew stronger and her need for me lessened, I told her of my plan to apply for a post as a companion, an idea which she instantly dismissed.

'You can't, you are *my* companion, Isobel, you already have a post here.'

'I can't stay here forever, Sarah,' I said. 'I need to be able to pay my way.'

'But you more than earn your keep. Wait, let me talk to Stephen, I'm sure we can make you an allowance. I can't part with you. You have helped me so much. I feel far better now than I have done for a long time and that is all thanks to you.'

'No, no, I can't take money from you, Sarah,' I began. Then seeing the look of panic that had come into her eyes,

I changed my words. 'So, let's just carry on as we are, shall we? It was only a thought, that was all.'

That night in my room I took stock of my situation. I most certainly could not accept money from Sarah and definitely not from Stephen, but I had been with them for six months now and staying here was not the future I had planned. It had always been intended as just the first step towards independence. I needed to do more with my life, or the whole escape from home was wasted. Marriage was not part of my plans, especially now, feeling as I still did about Stephen, because although I had accepted that he would never be part of my future, the memory of that night in the garden remained vivid. The surprise and joy of my first experience of love was sadly tainted by the guilt of deceiving Sarah and it was a hard secret to keep, especially since I seemed to be the only one deeply affected. Stephen continued in his old way, caring tenderly for his wife, and although I was glad that Sarah had been spared unhappiness, it was slighting to have been cast off so abruptly.

I remembered the night when we had thought we were losing her and my shock on seeing the amount of staining on her nightgown where she had haemorrhaged, and that reminded me of the lesser shock when I had found blood on my own body after that moonlight meeting with Stephen. Then memories turned to questions as it dawned on me that my monthly cycle had not occurred. Could that physical act have brought on my time too early, disrupting the natural rhythm of my body? There had been blood, but I had not suffered any injury as far as I could tell, nor had any pain since, so I decided to wait and see.

Waiting and seeing did not mean forgetting, and when there was still no sign after another two weeks, I began to think perhaps I might have been injured after all. Although I was embarrassed, I decided to speak to Stephen. There was no one else I could talk to. He was a doctor and I needed help, and after all he was the only one who would know the reason why I was worried. I stumbled my way through my explanation and waited for his answer. When he didn't speak, I looked up and was alarmed to see his face was white.

'Is it serious?'

'Not serious as an illness, but it is serious. Isobel, I am almost sure you are going to have a baby. I'll need to examine you, but every sign tells me I am correct.'

I stared at him. 'What do you mean have a baby? How? I don't understand.' What on earth was he talking about? I was an unmarried girl of nineteen, how could I possibly be going to have a baby?

A look of surprise flitted across his face then he spoke very slowly.

'My dear, do you really not know how? It is because of that time we were together. That is how procreation takes place, not just in people but every other animal species. It's a natural process, but in this case, for you and me, it is a very bittersweet one. The fact that you may be carrying my child fills me with joy, but what it means for you, Isobel, fills me with sorrow.'

I had still not fully understood. I was somewhere in a little world of my own trying hard to make sense of his words. What he had just said seemed impossible. How could just one brief occurrence, breath-taking though it was, have such a profound consequence?

I remembered my Father's words in church during a marriage ceremony. 'Duly considering the causes for which matrimony was ordained. First, it was ordained for the procreation of children.' They were solemn words, so to me marriage and children had always been firmly linked as one and the same, but I had never had any knowledge of the process involved in producing such children.

Stephen stood up and took both my hands. 'Oh, Isobel, my dear child, you have never been told, have you? You are much more innocent than I realised.' He let go of me. 'You mustn't worry. I will make sure you are safely taken care of. At the moment I don't know how, but I will look after you, I promise.'

His eyes held tears and at the sight of them I suddenly understood the gravity of my situation. My stomach somersaulted and I vomited on the floor.

* * *

I waited for Stephen to tell me that he was mistaken but the morning sickness I soon began to experience shattered any hope that he was wrong. I couldn't bear to think about the baby. I could only think in horror of my own situation. How could I possibly take care of a child when I had no money and no home to offer? Stephen was worried, but at least he had joy in his heart at the thought of a child. It was what he had always longed for but feared impossible, while I was living in a nightmare from which I could not escape.

He had promised he would look after me and I had to put my trust in him. There was no way I could return to my parents now, even had I wished to do so. Their silence had sent a message just as clearly as the written word. Like my sister, I had been disowned, so when he told me about the arrangements he had planned, I listened and agreed. With no other way to turn I didn't know what else to do. I certainly agreed to his plea that Sarah must never know.

Being unable to have a child herself, it would kill her and I would have her death on my conscience as well as guilt.

It seemed Stephen had confided in a close friend in Ireland, Fergus O'Mahoney, who had been at medical school with him, and he had agreed to help. Fergus had a very forward-thinking wife, Clodagh, who was a strong advocate for the improvement of women's welfare. They would both welcome me and take care of me until the baby was born, and since Fergus was a doctor, Stephen knew I would be in safe hands when the time came. His plan was to invite them both over for a short stay and they would suggest taking me back with them for a supposed holiday. He had already prepared the ground by suggesting to Sarah that I might need some respite soon, after all I had done for her, and she had instantly been remorseful that she had burdened me. I hated the deceit of all this scheming, and I had never been so afraid in my life.

CHAPTER THREE

FERGUS and Clodagh arrived, bringing a much-needed ray of light. They were a couple in their late thirties, both chatty and cheerful, and the rare sound of laughter echoed round the house. Sarah was delighted when they invited me to visit them in their castle in Ireland and urged me to accept. I went carrying a life that was just four months old, facing a future I could not envisage beyond the birth of the child.

It would have taken a very committed zealot not to be influenced by the free and easy way of life enjoyed by Clodagh and Fergus. Each day was lived, not as if it was their last, but as the very first of an exciting journey. Even a rainy day was greeted with joy, 'Whatever this day has in store for us we can make room for it.'

They did not keep to a regular routine and we ate when it fitted with Fergus's duties. Mrs Byrne, who helped Clodagh and who was not treated as a servant but as a friend, made nourishing stews from a plentiful supply of fresh vegetables, and delicious boiled puddings from fruit and berries, served with lashings of thick cream, because Fergus was often paid with what people produced on their land rather than with money. He accepted all these offerings as if he had been given a gold sovereign. 'Now, won't we be having a fine feast tonight, Mrs Doyle,' he would say. 'I never saw such a fat rabbit. Thank you.' Then

Clodagh and Mrs Byrne would work their magic and a fine feast we would have.

Sometimes Fergus picked up his fiddle and played for us. He and Clodagh would sing together, his rich Irish tenor harmonising perfectly with Clodagh's soft contralto. They mainly sang old Irish ballads, but occasionally Fergus struck up a jig and Clodagh and I would dance around the room, the beat going faster and faster until we collapsed into chairs with me laughing as I had never laughed before.

From the very first moment Clodagh took charge of me, like a hen keeping her chick safe under her feathers. She was a mother figure and a tutor and certainly my salvation in those early weeks. Everything about her blew away all the petty, stuffy restrictions of my parsonage upbringing. She was a woman with strong convictions and not afraid to express them. Words I had never heard flowed from her tongue as easily as the words of endearment which were part of almost every sentence. I had never been so 'Darlin'd' or 'Dearie'd' in all my life.

Clodagh's cause was to let women have a voice in a world that was not yet ready either to let them, or to listen. I think she saw in me, with my sad situation, a case she could take up and influence. I was like a clean page she could write on. She gave me the mother's love I had never known, taught me to value myself and claim my place in the world. I blossomed in her care.

'First of all,' she said, as she helped me to undress on that first night, 'we are going to get rid of this.' She unlaced my stiff boned corset and dropped it on the floor. 'God never intended a woman to be shaped like an hourglass. That corset was so tight it was squashing all your insides together, and we are certainly not going to let it squeeze the life out of the little baby that is growing in there.'

Free from the restriction, I took a deep breath and promptly belched.

'There you are you see, there wasn't room for the air to get either in or out properly – you'll feel better for that. Now the little fellow has got space to kick his legs when he has a mind to.'

She talked about my pregnancy openly as though there was no shame in it. Through her, I began to see my situation in a new light.

'You were a naïve young girl, Isobel, and you were taken advantage of. I'll say no more. Fergus and I do not see eye to eye on this, but then he is not a woman.'

There was no way I could keep the baby, even Clodagh knew that, but again Stephen had it all worked out. He wrote with the suggestion that after the birth I would return to Douglas, bringing the child, who would be said to have been born to one of Fergus's patients and orphaned when only a few months old. Stephen would offer to adopt the baby, but he did not say how he would persuade Sarah, nor how he would explain the length of my 'holiday' to her, but that was up to him. I could not think so far ahead other than to be thankful that the baby would be loved, and by its own father. Before all that I had to face a growing child, a changing body and the unknown business of giving birth, but again Clodagh took charge.

She was rubbing my hair dry after I had washed it, and since I was wearing only my chemise, she took the opportunity to enlighten me about myself. I learned that every part of my body had a name and that there should be no more embarrassment in talking about my nipples and vagina than there was in talking about my hair and teeth.

'Everything has a name and we should use that name.' She picked up my brush and started to disentangle my curls.

'I have no patience with euphemisms or hidden meanings. Where does that lead except to misunderstanding and ignorance?'

Nevertheless, I had to keep my gaze fixed to the floor when she started talking about the male body, even if I did learn the name for that part of Stephen of which I had been so ignorant. Much as I admired Clodagh and her freedom of spirit, I still had enough of my parsonage background inhibiting me to be able to throw it all off just yet.

She told me about intercourse which, I learned, was what I had experienced with Stephen.

'Sure, and didn't you enjoy it while it lasted?' she asked, shocking me into a deep blush. I couldn't look at her because, yes, I had enjoyed it.

'How did you know?' I whispered, making her roar with laughter.

'Well, although you were shocked about the baby you didn't seem traumatised by the actual experience, and indeed why should you be? 'Tis one of the blessings of this world, so it is, the love between a man and a woman.' She paused for a moment. 'Although in your case it maybe came at the wrong time.' Then she laughed again. 'But look what you have been given. You will be a mother like the Blessed Mary.'

In likening me to the Blessed Mary she made it seem as if, in a way, I was being absolved of my sin. She was ignoring the fact that we had apparently arrived at motherhood by completely different paths, but her words comforted me. Blessed was a word I could apply to Clodagh as well as Mary.

'I still feel dreadful about Sarah, though.'

'You are bound to, but this is not your fault and you must never for a moment think so.' She hesitated as if she had been about to add more, then gave my hand a little pat. 'Sure, Nature has her own way of keeping the human race going and no matter what some people may say, we are all Nature's children.'

Clodagh, with her corset-free figure, was certainly a child of Nature, a woman at odds with the illiberal social conventions of the Victorian 1870s we were living in. Her mission in life was to improve the lives of working girls, of worn out mothers with large families, and even the lives of the rich ladies who appeared to have so much in their privileged way of living, yet had no rights of their own. At that time, there was little that could be done by a lone woman, but there was a murmuring among some of the more educated ladies, and Clodagh had her ear to the ground.

CHAPTER FOUR

ONE day Clodagh decided to take me swimming, and the idea horrified me so much that I protested that it would not be good for me in my condition.

'Nonsense, quite the contrary, it will be valuable exercise for both of you. We have a lovely little lake here. I used to swim there with my brothers when I was a girl and I still swim regularly. It is quite safe and no one else ever goes there so we will have it all to ourselves.'

'But I can't swim, Clodagh, and I'd rather not try if you don't mind. I don't like deep water.'

'Sure, the water is not deep where we will swim and you needn't worry at all, I shall take care of you.'

She left no room for argument. The lake was part of the grounds of Clodagh's home, an old castle which must once have been impressive but was now crumbling for lack of money. She and Fergus lived in the small part of it that was safe for the time being but they both knew they would have to leave one day. Clodagh had enjoyed an idyllic childhood there running wild with her four brothers across acres of land which stretched down to the rocky seashore. Apparently, her father had been sole heir when his own father had died, but he was never equipped to take on the running of such a large estate, nor had he wanted to. He was a poet who spent his days wandering the countryside, filling his head with verses he never managed to finish, and spending money he never managed to replace. It was her mother who had kept the family going, even after they had had to let the last of the servants go.

All Clodagh's brothers had moved away, so it had been left to her to do what she could to keep her widowed mother in her home until she died. Fergus had joined her there when they wed in the false hope that they could work a miracle and bring the place back to its glory days, but he had soon decided that the best it could offer them was a temporary roof over their heads in a small wing almost buried in the glories of the wild, overgrown grounds.

'You find Paradise where you look for it,' said Clodagh. 'And here it is.'

Despite my reluctance, a few days later I found myself by the lake in a glorious little hollow where the water was shallow enough to be able see the lakebed for quite a long way out. It did not seem at all threatening and I was soon paddling barefooted and, to my surprise, enjoying it.

'Didn't I tell you there was nothing to fear?' Clodagh tried to splash me. 'You should have seen your face when I suggested a swim, you would have thought I had suggested swimming the English Channel.' She laughed in the loud lusty way she had. 'I think paddling is as far as we will go for today, just to get you used to the water, but I can't be by the lake and not swim in it.'

She began to take off her clothes.

'Sit on that rock and watch me. This is how you will be swimming by the time I have finished with you.'

I watched, both embarrassed and fascinated, as she removed every item of clothing and walked naked into the lake then, when she reached deeper water, dived under. She surfaced much further out and began to swim. I had never seen anyone swim like that. She darted and swooped on and under the surface, totally at one with the water. Her display was impressive but if she hoped that one day, I would be able to swim like that, then I feared she would be very disappointed.

She joined me on the rock to allow the sun to dry her body but her long red hair was still damp as she dressed so she left it hanging loose as we walked back to the house. With her green eyes sparkling from the exercise and her bright hair flowing round her shoulders she was beautiful, a mature woman in all her glory.

'Goodness, Clodagh, that was wonderful, but I could never swim like that and I certainly couldn't take all my clothes off.'

'You can swim in your chemise then, but I promise you I will have you swimming before the summer is over.'

I was terrified the first day that she made me venture deeper into the lake, but Clodagh was firm. She coaxed me into a position where I was held in her arms, my back against her chest, and then she began to walk backwards so that I lost my balance and my feet floated up. I panicked and screamed.

'Please, please don't let go of me,' I begged.

I struggled to stand up, grabbing her arms to try to get control of my body but she just laughed and carried on pulling me backwards and when I realised that my head was still above water and that I could breathe, I calmed down a little.

'Keep tight hold of me, Clodagh, don't let go.'

'I won't, but even if I did the water would hold you just as well as I can if you just let it. Don't fight it, lie back and let yourself float on the surface. You are floating now really – I am only holding you so that you don't become hysterical again. Good heavens, I never heard such a palaver in all my born days. Would you just look at yourself? You are in no danger whatsoever and all you are doing is frightening the baby. Stop it.'

We went to the lake almost every day after that and, as Clodagh had said, no one ever came there. I learned to swim in my chemise, and she swam unhampered by clothes just as she had always done.

'Does Fergus know you swim naked?'

'He does not – or if he does, he makes a good fist of pretending that he doesn't, for he knows it would not make a scrap of difference. He did not grow up by the water as I did so he doesn't love it as I do.'

I grew to look forward to my time in the lake, especially when my body began to swell and I carried the weight of a growing child. It was a relief to let the water take some of the strain and eventually Clodagh did manage to teach me to swim. Not like her of course, I would never reach her standard, but enough for me to benefit from the exercise, just as she had known I would. We even swam in the rain.

'We will get wet anyway, so what does it matter?' said Clodagh. 'A soft day never did anyone any harm.' A soft day was what she called a day with very fine rain that floated, rather than fell from the skies. No wonder she was so clear skinned.

I was swimming gently along one day when I suddenly gasped and stood up clutching my stomach. 'Oh!'

'What is it?' Clodagh was instantly at my side.

'I think the baby just kicked me.'

Clodagh grinned. 'He did not, the wee imp! Sure, he's having his own swim in there, so he is. You can expect more of that from now on. Tis nothing at all to worry about.'

Nothing to worry about or not, I decided that I would restrict my amount of time in the water from now on. I was more cautious than Clodagh.

* * *

Sarah and I wrote to each other every few weeks. I told her all about the castle and its beautiful wild grounds and about how I was learning to swim, but I had to be very careful what I wrote. I had become so relaxed living with Clodagh and Fergus that a careless sentence, or even one word, could stir unwelcome curiosity. Sarah's letters were much shorter, mainly because she had nothing to tell me. Nothing was happening in her life and I could tell she was slipping back into her old depression. I had been the one to lift her out of it and now, by leaving her, I was most likely the one responsible for her relapse, but in my circumstances, there was nothing I could do about that. I tried not to think about what the future might bring. I was so happy living in the bright bubble of loving care that these two people had provided, that I wished I could suspend time so that the bubble couldn't be burst. But no one can suspend time. Eventually, the cold weather put an end to our bathing days and I settled down to await the baby's birth.

The bubble burst on the day my waters broke. Clodagh had prepared me well so I was not too alarmed, but she had also warned me that there would be pain, and *that* I was alarmed about. I had never been tolerant of pain, whether a headache or my time of the month, but I had always suffered in silence, preferring that to the lecture on self-discipline which my mother would certainly have delivered, sympathy not being part of her nature. Luckily, I had Clodagh.

'I shall be by your side every minute, mi darlin', so there is nothing to worry about. You are young and in good health, you will be fine.'

I was in good health thanks to her. My skin had the ruddy glow of time spent walking in the fresh air, I was strong in my limbs from the gentle exercise of swimming and I had not put on a lot of weight other than that of the growing baby. I had even begun to wonder whether I would have a son or a daughter, for the first time showing an interest in the tiny life that was part of me.

When the pains began Clodagh was there to keep me calm.

'It's only the baby on the way out, mi darlin',' she said calmly. 'Just thank the Lord you are not a cat – they give birth to four or five.'

Even as the agonising waves of knife-sharp pain tore at my stomach, she made me laugh.

'Remember, your little baby is going through this just as much as you are. What you are feeling is him trying to find his way into this world, and you will help him by letting each contraction flow down through your body without trying to stop it. Breathe deeply and blow the pain away.'

She made me walk about as the pains came and went, and when it was time for Fergus to take over, the baby was so ready to be born that I barely had time to lie on the bed. Nothing could have prepared me for the overwhelming flood of love which swamped me when I first saw the tiny body of the child who had just caused me the worst pain I had ever known.

'You have a healthy little boy, Isobel.' said Fergus. 'Well done.'

Clodagh handed him to me after Fergus had tended to his immediate needs and I pressed him against my breast as if I would never let him go. I looked down at his little red face just at the moment he first opened his eyes.

'There now, aren't you the very first person he has seen in this world and won't he always know that you are his mother.'

One thing I did know was that he would always be my son. I looked up at Clodagh and both of us were smiling and crying at the same time.

'You clever little darlin', you have done it, so you have.'

I had done it. I had given birth. My child was healthy and there was no one else in the world with whom I would have wished to share this wonderful moment than these two.

For the next few days Clodagh made me rest, but she did not try to keep me in bed. Her methods went against the usual confinement customs of the day, but she based them on witnessing the births she had attended in the cottages and cabins of the women who lived in the surrounding lanes. Most of them were used to bearing a child almost each year and she had seen how they took birth in their stride and were soon back on their feet again. Few suffered any ill-effects.

'It is not an illness to be recovered from, it is a natural process and the body will heal itself,' she said.

We did not discuss the day, now looming, when I must leave Ireland and return to the Isle of Man and hand my son over to his father and Sarah, but it was a day I would have to face and I needed to prepare myself for the greatest pain of all. Just as I had taken her place with her husband, now Sarah would take my place as the mother of my boy. My father had preached divine retribution – I wondered if this was it.

Fergus wrote to Stephen to tell him of the baby's birth, and within a few days he had a reply. He didn't show the letter to me, but as he read out details of the plan which Stephen had suggested, I noticed Clodagh keeping her lips pressed together. I left the room to see to my baby, and shortly after I heard the rare sound of raised voices. I could not hear what was being said but it was Clodagh who seemed to be doing most of the shouting. Then the sitting room door opened and she ran upstairs to their bedroom. I didn't know what to do. I wanted to offer my help, but I knew she would not welcome any intrusion until she was ready.

I took the baby out into the garden and wandered between the overgrown borders where wild flowers had taken over. I was miserable for the first time since I had come to Ireland. Clodagh found me there and I was relieved to see she was smiling again.

'I hope there is nothing wrong, Clodagh?'

'Not at all, don't look so forlorn, Isobel, there's nothing to worry about. It was just me letting off steam. It's all over now.'

'Was it about me?'

'Yes, it was in a way. It was regarding that letter Stephen sent. I read it and it made my blood boil. That selfish man was full of his own delight at having a son, but only briefly asked how you were. He outlined every little detail of the plan he has made. It seems to me that he is very free with his plans, and all contrived to protect him and his role in this. You were taken advantage of, Isobel, and he should be ashamed of himself for the way he has manipulated you.'

'But he didn't manipulate me,' I protested. I couldn't tell even Clodagh how willingly I had responded. I had come to realise that this willingness had played a part in what had happened, even though it had been due to my ignorance. 'He explained why he could not do more for me. We had Sarah to consider.'

'Yes indeed, but it is a pity he did not consider Sarah when he came across you in the garden. Fergus does not feel as strongly as I do, because naturally he has some loyalty to his friend, but you know where my loyalties lie, I am always on the side of downtrodden women.'

She took the baby from me and began to sing, a beautiful lilting melody with the same few words repeated over and over again – loo-la-loo-la-loo-la-li. Although I knew she was singing to the baby, her clear low voice soothed me after the distress I had felt when I heard my two dear friends arguing. If Clodagh was happy again, then so was I.

CHAPTER FIVE

CLODAGH and Fergus decided to escort me back to Douglas so that it would be they who would hand the baby to Sarah. I knew this would have been Clodagh's idea. It meant I would be able to stay in the background and hide any distress that might show in my face.

Sarah was delighted to see me again, but more delighted to see the baby. She took him in her arms and looked up at Stephen with such joy in her eyes that it was like a stab to my heart, and even though I had tried to prepare myself, I had to leave the room. That look should have been mine.

Clodagh found me in tears in my room. She and Fergus were returning that same day and had to catch the ferry soon.

'I can't help you to live through the next few weeks, my love, but hard as they will be, you will find a way. You are strong, but don't punish yourself, Isobel, and if ever it all becomes too much for you just remember, we are only across the water.'

She hugged me, kissed me, and left me.

* * *

Watching Sarah with my son was painful, but it was harder to watch Stephen. He could openly show his deep love, whilst I could only show as much affection as was appropriate for my position as Sarah's friend. There were many times when I was holding the baby and had to hand him back to Sarah, that I felt an urge to snatch him back again. The longing to keep his little body in my arms was overwhelming.

'We must choose a name for him,' said Sarah. 'What about Edward?'

My heart sank. Not Edward, I wanted to say. I had no wish for my son to carry the same name as my father.

'I had thought Philip,' Stephen suggested. 'We could have Edward as his second name.'

'No, I want Stephen to be his second name.'

I was so relieved to have two other names in the offing that before I could stop myself, I blurted out, 'Philip Stephen sounds lovely, doesn't it?'

'Philip Stephen? It sounds perfect,' Sarah smiled.

'Perfect.' Stephen glanced across at me, and in that brief eye contact, just for a moment, we were linked – him and me and our son.

Sarah still needed to rest during the day so there were many hours when I had him all to myself, when I could hold him, feed him and talk to him as I had in Ireland, as a mother. Sarah not only allowed me to share in Philip's care, she seemed to take it for granted. There was no reason why I would leave, especially since I had supposedly just returned from an exceptionally long holiday, so I stayed and acted as nursemaid to my son, sharing those precious early days. It was more than I had hoped for, but I could not see how it would last.

I was back where I had started, living as a guest and facing the prospect of one day needing to earn my own living. I could hear Clodagh's voice in my head, 'Take each day as it comes and whatever it brings, make room for it.' That is exactly what I did.

* * *

Sarah and Stephen were planning Philip's christening. Stephen had asked his youngest brother William, to be godfather, and Sarah asked me to be godmother. This was certainly a day I needed to "make room for" but how could I refuse, she was honouring me and couldn't know that she had just put up the price I was paying. I accepted. Godmother – mother – what difference did the name make? I knew which I really was.

Because it was a family gathering, Clodagh and Fergus were not invited so I had to face what would be an ordeal, on my own without the support of my friends. This was my child's christening and somehow, I had to get through it. As I stood at the font holding Philip, I looked down into his blue eyes and remembered the first time I had done this. I also remembered Clodagh's words, 'Won't he always know you are his mother?'

Do you, Philip, I wondered, do you know I am your mother? Then, aware that I was holding him far too closely and looking at him far too lovingly, I turned my gaze to the font. I did not dare look at the vicar because I knew he would see in my eyes a look he would recognise – that of a devoted mother.

After the christening all the guests came back to the house for a party, Philip's first. I was standing by the table holding a plate and hesitating over the food when Robert, Stephen's older brother, approached me.

'The salmon is very good would you like to try some? We have met before, haven't we? It's Isobel, isn't it?'

'Yes, I wasn't sure if you would remember me.'

'Of course, I do. Would you like to take my advice and try the salmon?'

I had actually only just eaten a portion, but I nodded, thanked him and accepted his offer to serve me. He found a chair for me by the window and I watched him as he returned to the table for the salmon.

He was very like Stephen. The same fair hair, the same height and handsome face, but it lacked Stephen's warm smile. Robert Corkish was a serious man. He lived near the mine that he had run since their father had died, had never married and did not often visit Douglas.

He drew up a chair and joined me. We chatted but I found the conversation a bit stilted and hard work, then Sarah came over to us with Philip in her arms.

'Can I leave Philip with you for a few minutes, Isobel? I really must lie down for a while.'

My arms were reaching out before she had finished speaking. 'Of course, you can.' I turned to Robert. 'Have you met your nephew?'

'Today for the first time, he's a sturdy little fellow, isn't he?'

I had to squash any pride in my voice as I agreed.

'And he is also very lucky,' he added.

Stung by what I took to be a reference to Sarah and Stephen's offer to adopt Philip, I immediately bristled and said coldly, 'I think Sarah and Stephen are the lucky ones.'

He seemed a little taken aback. He looked at the baby then at me.

'I meant that he was lucky to be in the arms of such a charming young lady.'

Now it was my turn to be taken aback. I had not only jumped to the wrong conclusion I had received a compliment from this rather stern looking man and had more or less thrown it back in his face. I was saved by a cousin coming across to ask if she could hold Philip and, in handing him over, I covered my embarrassment.

* * *

'Robert is coming to dinner tomorrow, Isobel,' Stephen told me the next week, 'and he specifically asked if you would be here.'

'Oh.'

'I think you have an admirer. Have you been keeping a secret?'

'Not at all, there is nothing to be secretive about I can assure you.' I was uncomfortable with the conversation but Stephen wanted to pursue it.

'Isobel, you know that you can do whatever you wish. I can only be glad for you if you find a new life for yourself.'

'How can I find a new life away from Philip?' I kept my voice low, but I could not disguise a tone of resentment.

'I apologise, I spoke out of turn.'

I sighed. 'No, Stephen, you didn't, it is just that it is all so hard for me.'

'I know,' he said as he turned away.

They seated me next to Robert at the table and there was no doubt about it, I definitely had an admirer. He was very attentive to me, he even smiled, and the next day he called at the house to invite me to visit the mine. His carriage was waiting and because I could not think of an excuse to refuse, and also because I was really interested in seeing the mine, I accepted.

He showed me round and was very knowledgeable about every function in the mining of tin. I was not at all bored. I accepted his invitation to go back to his house for tea. Although it was a not a large property, it was well furnished and immaculately kept, thanks to Mrs Gale, his housekeeper. I had a lovely afternoon. We walked in the garden which had views over the hills and was full of flowers. Robert picked a large bunch for me including the ones I had especially admired. I could tell this was not something he usually did when he handed me a rather untidy bouquet.

'I suppose you will be able to do something with them,' he said laughing. 'I'm afraid I am too used to heavy machinery to be able to be artistic.' I was pleasantly surprised to find how well we got on, but not as surprised as I was when, on the drive back, he asked for my hand in marriage.

'Well?' he asked when I hadn't answered.

'I am taken by surprise.' I told him. 'You don't really know me.'

'I knew I would ask you from the moment I saw you nursing Philip. I saw what a gentle soul you are. You held him as tenderly and lovingly as a mother.'

He could not know how accurate he was.

'Will you think about it?'

I nodded. 'I will. I'll write to you with my decision.'

When I thought over that conversation later in my room it struck me how formal it had been. The only mention of love had been when he talked about the loving way in which I had held Philip. There was a lot of thinking to be done, and right at the heart of it, of course, was Philip. I needed advice but there was no point in writing to Clodagh, because I knew full well that her first words would be, 'Do you love him?' and my answer would have to be 'No'. She would then paint a picture of the kind of life I would lead in a loveless marriage, but I would take no heed because I could only live a life that would include Philip, as this one would do.

Instead, I spoke to Stephen and his response destroyed any last trace of the love I once felt for him. As soon as I told him about Robert's proposal, his face lit up.

'Why, that would be the answer to everything, Isobel.'

He sounded excited. 'It will be the perfect solution for you. You will have a new life and a respected place in society as Robert's wife.'

So, I was a problem that could be solved, and solved in a way which suited him. As a married woman I would be off his conscience.

'I have not told Robert of my decision yet.' I said, coolly. 'There is a lot I would need to say to him first.'

'Surely that won't be necessary?' I saw the worried look on his face.

'Can you really think I would allow myself to start a new life with the dark shadow of deceit between us?'

'But we agreed no one else would know, didn't we?' Now his face showed panic. 'Neither Robert nor Sarah need be troubled if we keep our promise.'

That was the moment when I saw him as Clodagh had always seen him, a charming but shallow man who could condone deceiving his brother as well as his wife without showing any sign of the torment that I was struggling to cope with. His response made me more ashamed of what had happened between us than any amount of moral guilt had done. But he was right. I had promised and to save unhappiness, I must keep that promise, although apparently, I would have to wrestle with my conscience alone.

In the end I had to write to Clodagh. Even though I did not tell her of my dreadful dilemma, I needed to hear from her, to read her loving words and to feel reassured by just having contact with her.

And Clodagh came.

'Clodagh, I can't believe you are here. What made you decide to come?'

'Sure, and didn't you tell me you needed me? Of course, I came.'

'But I didn't say a word about needing you, I'm sure I didn't. I was very careful not to sound desperate.'

'Ah, I don't read the words you do write, I read the words you don't write and I knew you were crying out for help. Aren't I right?'

We went into the garden and I told her everything, including Stephen's reaction.

'God in Heaven, the crassness of that man – and him a doctor too – thank goodness you sent for me.'

'I didn't actually–'

'Yes, you did,' she interrupted, 'or at least your heart did. It's all one and the same, but I am here now, and we will sort this out before I go back.'

She had come over for the day on the ferry, and after paying her respects to Sarah, she suggested that we walk along the beach on the pretext that she had messages from the friends I had met in Ireland.

'I hate to say it, but Stephen is right,' she said. 'This marriage would be the best way forward for you, Isobel. I know you don't love Robert, and normally I would be telling you not to sacrifice your life, but this is different because it involves Philip. You have told me you cannot live a life away from him, so the sacrifice you will have to make is to be able to live with your conscience, and this you must do if you are not to destroy other lives.'

It was partly the answer I wanted and partly a cause for argument because I was still making a pretence of struggling with my decision, but with her usual wise understanding, she left me alone to think while she collected shells from the sand.

Philip was, and always would be, the overriding force in any decision I might make, so, although I attempted to give weight to the morality of keeping my secret, I knew what I had already decided in my heart. I had just needed Clodagh to tell me it was all right, that there was no choice and never had been right from the moment Robert proposed. He was offering more than marriage – he was offering the only path I would be able to follow. I would be near my child, not as his mother of course, but as a loving aunt, and I would have to pay for this by carrying the guilt of taking a decent, honourable and unsuspecting man as a husband and deceiving him for life.

'It will be the cross you have to bear.' said Clodagh.

By the time she left to catch the ferry home, I had already steeled myself for the role I must play, probably forever, and I knew I would never need her so urgently again. She had taught me lessons I would never forget, brought me to adult womanhood and prepared me to take my place in the world and accept my responsibilities. I was ready to stand on my own two feet. I wrote to Robert accepting his proposal.

* * *

No one from my family would attend my wedding. I did not know where my sister was, there had been no word from her before I had left home and I understood her wish to sever all contact with our parents. It had taken courage for both of us to escape the strong grip they had held over us throughout our childhood, and now, like my sister, I too wanted to be safely married before they could intervene, so our wedding was quiet with just a few of Robert's family members present. He asked Stephen to be his best man and I asked their youngest brother, William, to give me away. I didn't know him well but since he was coming over from Liverpool for the wedding anyway, it seemed appropriate.

Most of the ceremony passed in a tormented daze for me. There were moments when I wanted to blurt out the truth about Philip and only knowing that Sarah was sitting behind me, holding him, prevented me from an outburst. It would not help Philip, and would probably either send Sarah spiralling back into depression, or kill her and I would have murdered her. These wild thoughts were, thankfully, swiftly followed by lucid ones. I could not harm the good man who was at this very moment, taking vows to become my husband. The vicar's words came and went and I struggled to concentrate on what he was saying. 'Man and wife together as long as you both shall live.' I was now Robert's wife so I must have said 'I do.' I could not remember. But one strong thought was foremost. My promise to honour and obey this man to the end of my days. It was a pledge that I would keep.

* * *

We went back to the house near the mine to start our married life, and on that first night I realised I would not find the same passion that I had known with Stephen. Although at the age of thirty-two Robert was ten years my senior, he was as inexperienced as I had been, and after some awkward fumbling, it was over. I remembered that moonlit night in the garden and was glad that I had found such magic in that first time. Clodagh was right, the love between a man and a woman is one of the joys of life, but if my wedding night had been my first experience, I would not have agreed with her.

This time, I knew at once when I became pregnant. Robert was ecstatic, he hoped for a son and he began to take extra care of me straight away.

'I'd like you to be nearer a doctor and midwife when the time comes, so I am thinking of buying a house in Douglas. Would you like that?'

I would have agreed even if I did not, for I wanted to please him, but I did like the idea, very much. I would be nearer to Philip. I had accepted the gnawing ache of having to live with my conscience, feeling it was what I deserved, so to now have so much joy given to me made me feel that there must be a second Isobel living alongside me, one the sinner and one the blessed. I could only think that Isobel, the sinner, would pay a terrible price for the happiness of Isobel, the blessed, on the day of reckoning. In the meantime, I would have my two babies near to each other, brought up as cousins of course, but I would make sure they were as close as siblings.

* * *

To keep myself occupied while I waited for the move to a new house, I began to reorganise one of the flowerbeds in the garden. I was used to being active and, remembering my other pregnancy when I had swum almost every day and taken long walks with Clodagh, I did not want to let myself stagnate.

'Should you be doing that?' Robert asked. 'Daniel can do whatever you need to be done.'

'Don't worry, I'm not doing anything that will harm the baby, I promise. Anyway, Clodagh said it is best to keep active...' The words had just slipped out and I was horrified. Why on earth would Clodagh be advising me on activity during pregnancy when, at this early stage, we had told only one or two people that I was with child? Desperate to deflect his thoughts from what I had just said, I hurried on. 'I've planted pansies and forget-me-nots for the scent. I hope you like them.'

'I shall like anything that you have planted.'

Yet again I had had to resort to deceit, and when Robert looked at me in the way that he was doing now, with eyes full of love, it almost broke my heart.

The house he chose was way beyond my expectations and I was awed when he took me to see it. It was a large three storey stone house on the outskirts of Douglas, standing in its own grounds and within walking distance of Sarah – and Philip.

'I have asked Mrs Gale and Daniel to move with us but we shall need extra staff for the new house.'

Both Mrs Gale and Daniel had been with Robert's family since he was a boy and he would need his housekeeper and his coachman in Douglas, but I felt a slight panic at the thought of hiring new servants. It was not something I had any experience of so it was a relief when he continued, 'Mrs Gale and I will see to that of course. I want you to take all the rest you need at the moment. Just concentrate on the baby. You are the most important people in my life.'

Robert's care for me proved that I had married the right man because the care was not only because I was carrying his child, he loved me for myself. Robert was not a man to display his emotions in company but when we were alone, his tenderness to me was more than I deserved. In giving him a child, I would be repaying him in the only way I could.

We moved to Douglas two months before the baby was due and it was strange at first living in such a big house, but once Sarah had brought Philip to see me it suddenly became a home. It had welcomed two people I loved dearly, and they had left their presence in the atmosphere.

'What a beautiful house, Isobel, and so near to us. I had no problem with the walk. We shall be able to see each other every day.' Sarah looked round the room, delighted.

'I would love that,' I answered. 'We shall be as close as sisters, and our children will be like brothers, or brother and sister if I have a girl.'

Sarah was still maintaining her health, though she would never be very strong, and I saw Philip regularly. If I let myself lay down the burden of guilt, I could enjoy this pregnancy and look forward to giving Robert a much-wanted child.

I remembered all Clodagh's instructions when it was time to give birth and I had to defy the midwife, who wanted to put me into bed at the start of the first mild pains, and insist on following the same birthing methods as before. I walked about, though only in the room, which was as far as I dare push the midwife's reluctant compliance, and if she had any suspicions that this was not my first pregnancy, she gave no sign. My labour was quicker and less painful than my first and she delivered another little boy. Again, I was swamped by that instant powerful love when I held him in my arms. I was so proud to present Robert with his son, and this time I could exchange that special look with him and share the joy as new parents.

Sarah brought Philip to see the baby and I thought I would die of happiness as I watched him patting his 'cousin' on the head. They looked very much alike and the one feature they shared, and which everyone commented on, was the blueness of their eyes. They were forget-me-not blue like my own, but because both Robert and Stephen also had blue eyes it was put down to traces of the Viking features which still appeared among the people of the Isle of Man, Ireland and the north west coast of England. There were many flaxen-haired, blue-eyed children in the area I had come from. Sarah called them, 'Our two little Norsemen.'

Robert was such a proud father. Like Stephen he had the son he had always wanted, and we all settled down to family life with Sarah and me now sisters, as well as friends. I was happy for Robert to name our son and he chose John, after his own father, and William after his youngest brother.

John was a placid baby from the start and I took care of him myself, refusing all Robert's offers of a nurse maid. Mrs Gale was all the help I needed, and she gave me the same support that Clodagh had given over a year before. I could not help comparing these two loving, motherly women with the one who had given birth to me. Since becoming a mother, myself, and experiencing that instant love for one's child, I was unable to understand how she could have been so cold and unloving. How different my life would have been had she only been more like these two lovely ladies.

Robert felt that my parents should be told they had a grandson, so I wrote to tell them of John's birth, but there was no reply. I had to assume that, as with my sister, my page had also been turned and the book closed, but I couldn't help thinking how much my parents had missed by not having the joy of a grandchild, or possibly even grandchildren, for Martha may also have a child.

Now that I was a member of the Corkish family, there was one important thing I needed to do. I had to establish an acceptable relationship with Stephen. I spoke to him regularly, of course, as I must as his sister-in-law, but I felt that he was assuming a friendship that I would never feel. I had never been able to condone how easily he had put the past behind him, with no sign of a conscience that I could see, and I would never regard him as a brother, as he seemed to expect. I managed to contrive a civil but dispassionate form of communication between us that was conducted as if through a pane of glass, and he soon understood. It was a situation we could both maintain and subtle enough for the family not to notice.

Watching John and Philip play together gave Sarah and me so much joy. Despite Stephen's fear of a relapse, Sarah was still maintaining her comparatively good health but due to her weak heart, she would never be strong enough to play the robust games I enjoyed with the boys. I was proud to be able to teach them to swim. Instead, she had other skills to offer and she taught them both to read and write and count. Between us we gave them an idyllic childhood.

Despite the contentment however, there were times when I disliked myself intensely. I abhorred the deceit which permeated my relationship with the ones dearest to me – the two boys, and Robert and Sarah. Like the time when I had carelessly mentioned receiving advice from Clodagh regarding pregnancy, when she had not yet been informed of my condition; then the fear I had felt when the blueness of the eyes of both boys had been commented on, and I had had to quickly introduce Viking ancestry to deflect further curiosity. It even touched my friendship with Clodagh because she had, from the first, sworn to keep my secret thus involving her in my deceit, but it was in those moments of deepest gloom that her voice seemed to echo the strongest.

'You were a naïve young girl, Isobel, and ignorant of the power within a woman's body. You didn't know what you were doing. But you know now and that knowledge is a shield. It puts you in charge of that power. It gives you choice.'

They were the words of a woman who wanted equal rights for women and as such they were non-judgemental and helped me to find a balance between guilt and the need to secure my place in my new circumstances.

* * *

Once John had learned to read, Robert began to educate him. There was a large globe in the library and Robert showed him how to locate all the different countries that were part of the British Empire. Listening to Robert's deep patient voice answering John's childish piping questions, I could not believe the way my life had changed. Watching them, with their two fair heads close together, pouring over maps on the big table, golden sun streaming through the windows, I felt as if my whole life had turned golden. Whatever may come in the future, nothing could take away these precious days, and I treasured them.

* * *

A letter arrived, addressed to me, and bearing a Lancashire post mark. Robert handed it to me. 'It looks as though your parents have made contact at last,' he said.

'I doubt it.' I answered, but I was curious. I took out a typed letter. It was from a firm of solicitors informing me of the death of both my parents.

'What is it, Isobel?' Robert must have seen the surprise on my face.

'Both my parents are dead.'

'Oh, my dear, I am so sorry.' He put his arm round me. 'How did it happen?'

I handed the letter to him. I couldn't read any more because I felt numb. To hear so suddenly, that they had both gone, was a shock. Robert read the rest of the letter. Apparently, they had both contracted flu during an epidemic and it had proved fatal for them. He paused for a moment while he read the rest.

'It goes on to say that you and your sister, Martha, have inherited their estate. Your father did not leave a will so you and Martha are next of kin.'

I supposed that my father had not left a will because he had not expected to leave this world so suddenly, and just as my mother had followed him so obediently in life, she had dutifully followed him in death. There had been no time for her to inherit. I was still numb and I needed to wait for that numbness to fade before I could know what my feelings were. I hoped I was suffering from delayed shock because if I had been a loving daughter, surely, I would have been distraught at the loss of two parents at the same time. As it was, I could feel nothing. Not loss, not regret, not even sadness and I was dismayed at my coldness. Robert was still speaking.

'Your parents did not leave a great deal of money but it is enough to give you a nice little nest egg of your own. I will contact the solicitor for you, if you wish, to finalise everything.'

A thought occurred to me. 'Does he give Martha's address?'

'No, but I can ask for it when I reply. He must have it.'

The numbness faded and all I could think of was that at last I might be able to make contact with my sister. The emotion that had been lacking for my parents, brought tears of excitement for my sister. Now I had to wait, but I would wait in hope.

* * *

It was six months before I heard from Martha. She was living in Wisconsin in America, had five children and was happily married to a farmer. Her first husband had died soon after they had reached New York but she had been introduced to her present husband within the year. It was obvious from her letter that she had put all thoughts of Lancashire behind her, and although she seemed pleased to hear from me, I did not recognise her as my sister Martha. I doubted we would correspond very often.

I did not conceive again, and Robert, content with his one lovely son, never mentioned any hopes he may have had for a larger family. It was an easy life and one that I had never thought to have in the dark period before Philip's birth. I owed everything to Robert, and I was grateful. If my life was dictated by his, it was only the same as that of many other wives in my position, and I remained true to my pledge to honour and obey, but deep inside, I still carried enough of Clodagh's influence to know that if I had not made that vow, I would probably have joined her campaign for the rights of women. Instead I concentrated on being a loving wife and mother and acting as a devoted aunt to Philip.

* * *

When John was eight Robert brought those carefree days to an end.

'I have put John's name down for my old school in Lancashire.' he told me. 'He will start after his birthday.'

'But I expected he would go to school here on the island as Philip does.' Stephen had sent Philip to a school further down the coast near Castletown, where he was a boarder but still within easy reach of home, and I had automatically assumed John would follow in his footsteps when the time came.

'I know you would probably like to keep him here with you, my dear, but I want him to get the same good education that I did and learn to be independent. The Lancashire coast is not all that far away, and he will be home for holidays. I'm hoping he will take over the mine one day and this will prepare him.'

I tried to think of the right words to dissuade him without actually defying him, but there was nothing I could say. Everything he had said made sense. John was pleased and excited when Robert told him about the school, but he had never been away from home before and I worried how he would fare once he was on his own.

A few months later, just after John's eighth birthday, Robert took him to board the ferry to sail to Fleetwood, where a teacher would be waiting to take him to his new school. He was still excited when we said goodbye, and I managed to keep the tears away until he was gone.

With both boys at school it was lonely for Sarah and me and we missed them, but each time they came home for the holidays it was obvious that they were both thriving, and I had to admit that Robert had known best.

CHAPTER SIX

I WAS writing a letter to John when I heard a commotion downstairs. Snatches of raised voices, bumps and bangs. I went to the gallery and looked down into the hall. The stable boys were carrying Daniel, the coachman, into the house and Robert was clearing a table to lay him on. Mrs Gale was in tears. I hurried downstairs.

'What is it – what has happened?'

'Daniel has been kicked by a horse. I've sent for Stephen.'

Robert was placing a cushion under Daniel's head, who I could see was unconscious.

'What can I do?'

'There is no bleeding, but he has a large bruise and a swelling just here on his right temple. I don't know what we can do until Stephen comes.' Robert was very distressed.

'Loosen his collar,' I said. 'Is he breathing?'

'I don't know.'

'Shall I get some water and bathe his head?'

'No – yes, I don't know – what else we can do?'

Mrs Gale and I brought warm water and a cloth from the kitchen and I sponged the ugly purple swelling. There was no reaction from Daniel, no flicker of the eyes as I touched his temple, and all I could do was remove the mud which the horse's hoof had left as it kicked him.

'We should get his wife.' said Mrs Gale. 'Shall I send one of the maids?'

'Yes, of course, I should have thought of that.'

Robert was rubbing Daniel's hands in a frantic effort to revive him when the doctor came. It was Stephen's colleague.

'Stephen was out on a call, so your man came to me,' he explained.

We all moved aside as he examined Daniel, but it was only the briefest of time before he turned to Robert.

'I'm very sorry but I'm afraid he has gone. He was killed outright. Nothing could have saved him.'

Daniel and Robert had been young boys together and his death was a great shock to Robert. I saw him stagger and hurried across to help him to a chair. I had to take over. Daniel had married Esther, one of the maids who came to work for us after we moved to the house in Douglas, and they had started a family. Mrs Gale knew that Esther was carrying their fourth child and since the maid had not yet left to fetch Esther, I sent Mrs Gale instead, to break the dreadful news.

'Find out what help we can give please, Mrs Gale. Anything we can do, we will – promise her that.' Then I turned to my husband to take him away from the distressing scene and into the drawing room, where I tried to comfort him. He wept in my arms. It was my first experience of death, and though I was distressed, I was not as upset as Robert. I saw a caring and compassionate side to the serious and sometimes stern man that I had married, and for the first time I felt love rather than affection for him.

Robert made sure that Daniel was buried with dignity. He attended the funeral and took care of all the costs, while I did my best to enable Esther to provide for the family

Daniel had left behind. Through Mrs Gale, I arranged for her to take in our light laundry, which she could do at home and, also through Mrs Gale, I paid her rent until after the child she was carrying was born. We made sure she could survive.

The boys were doing well at school and I saw more of Philip than I did of John, because being on the island, he was able to come home for weekends from time to time. He had decided that he did not want to be a doctor like his father, but showed an interest in mining.

Although disappointed, Stephen accepted this and encouraged his son, and Robert was more than pleased when Philip asked to be shown how the mine functioned. He gave him his own hard hat and handed him over to one of his older miners to take under his wing and introduce him to the rules which had to be learned before he would be allowed to join the men deep in the mine. John sometimes joined him when he was home from school but he didn't share Philip's enthusiasm.

'It seems strange that it should be Philip, and not John, who is interested in the mine,' Robert said one day. My heart missed a beat.

'How do you mean?'

'Well, it is John who was born into a mining family, Philip was only adopted into it, yet he is the one who has shown interest, right from being a child.'

Yet again, I had to quickly divert his train of thought into a safer direction.

'Oh, there's plenty of time yet, John has a few more years before he needs to make up his mind. His head is full of all sorts of different ideas at the moment. Let's just wait and see.'

'I suppose you are right.'

I took a deep breath. A secret had not only to be kept, it had to be guarded, and the deception involved at those times made me hate myself. This had been such a moment.

* * *

One morning, when John was home for the Easter holidays, he wandered into the small study where Robert and I were finishing our morning coffee.

'Father, there is a little cart in the stable – have you any use for it?'

'Not so far as I know, why?'

'Because if you haven't, then I can find a very good use for it. The little girl who collects and brings back our laundry has to carry a very big basket. The cart would be so much easier for her.'

'I can't think which cart you mean, but so long as you check with the stable lad then yes, take it by all means.'

'Thank you, Father.'

John wandered out again and Robert and I smiled at each other. Not only was our son clever, he had the most thoughtful of natures, the perfect son.

Robert and I were very happy together. Daniel's death had created a loving bond between us and I was content, even though I noticed that Robert was beginning to neglect his matrimonial duties. I did not mind because I had never experienced the same thrill I had shared with Stephen. When I thought about that night in the garden, it dawned on me that Stephen had only ignited that spontaneous fire in me because I had been so very ignorant and so very much in need of love, and there had been no fear because his first touch had been so gentle. I had thought I loved him but in truth I had only responded to my awakened sexuality or, as Clodagh would say, 'responded to Nature.'

In fairness, I had also begun to understand more about Stephen's part in that night. As a married woman, I could now understand something of the strain he must have been under, living with a wife who could not be a wife in the true sense. The magnetism of a young girl in her first arousal, combined with the innocence which led her so willingly into his arms, had been too hard to resist. That much I understood. It had been his behaviour since, that had been hard to accept. For him to so easily put everything behind him, without showing any sign of self- reproach, or none that I could see, disappointed and disillusioned me. It even made his continued care of Sarah seem like a charade. How lucky I was that I had married the brother I could respect as well as love.

CHAPTER SEVEN

IT seemed incredible that the time had come for the boys to leave school. The golden years had slipped by so peacefully that I seemed to have left my early trauma behind me in the mists of the past. As we all expected, Philip took up a position in the mine, but John had taken more than a year to choose his path before deciding to study law. He was now waiting to go to university. Robert was happy with John's choice because he was still hoping his son would eventually take over the mine, perhaps in partnership with Philip, and felt his studies could be usefully applied to the management.

Sarah and I loved having the boys at home again and watching the closeness between them. They had both grown into such handsome young men and, since we had brought them up as closely as brothers, I did not need to hide my pride in Philip as well as John, because Sarah felt the same pride in John as well as Philip. We could not have been a closer little group. Clodagh's words rang true at this time, "You find paradise where you look for it," and I had found mine. Did I really believe my debt had been paid in full?

* * *

I heard angry voices coming from Robert's study one morning and I went into the hall, fully intending to eavesdrop, but the door opened suddenly and John rushed out. He was visibly upset. I reached out to him but he brushed past me. When I went into the study, Robert was standing by the fireplace, red in the face and obviously furious.

'Robert, what is it?'

'Our son has taken leave of his senses.'

'Why, what has he done?'

'Taken leave of his senses, that's what he has done.' He banged his fist on the mantlepiece. 'I can't talk any sense into him. He is defying me, Isobel, and I will not allow it.'

'That doesn't sound like John.' I tried to placate him.

'I can't believe what he has just told me.' Robert paced round the room. 'He has just said he intends to get married.'

What? John had not been home from school long enough to have established a relationship, and in any case, as far as I was aware, he didn't know any girls. At twenty, John had yet to make his way in the world, he could not afford to keep a wife. It had got to be a misunderstanding.

'Not only that, he tells me there is a child on the way.'

Shocked, I sat down on the nearest chair. This was no misunderstanding. It was worse than I could possibly have expected. I stared at Robert. No wonder he was in such a state. I feared for him. 'What are you going to do?' I asked quietly.

'Forbid it of course. He is not yet twenty-one, he needs my consent. Well he won't get it.'

'Yet he is very nearly twenty-one, Robert, and then you won't be able to forbid it.'

'We must hope he comes to his senses then. He just wouldn't listen to me, Isobel.'

I had never seen Robert so upset and cross. I had to do something to try to calm him down.

'Will you let me try, please?'

'If you think you can succeed where I have failed, then by all means, please do.'

'I'll do my best.'

My best was not good enough. I failed as Robert had done but after talking to John, at least I understood a little more. The young woman was the little girl for whom he had arranged the hand pulled cart so many years ago. Her name was Grace and they had been meeting since he finished school. Now I was aware of how he had been spending his time while resisting his father, but I could tell that this was not just some tawdry affair. Our son had fallen deeply in love with the girl. I was also aware that she was the daughter of two of our former servants and I dreaded to think of Robert's reaction when he found out. He would be even more enraged than he was now, even though she was Daniel's daughter.

Since there was a baby to be born, John was adamant he could not consider waiting to marry, and I knew I was the only member of the family who could relate to their situation, for it was one I shared. Despite being upset, I couldn't help but feel proud of my son for protecting the girl, especially when I remembered my own fear and despair when I had been faced with having to give birth in secret, and with strangers, which Clodagh and Fergus had been at first. It was going to take every bit of persuasion I could muster to try to get Robert to change his mind – but I had to try.

Over the next few weeks Philip, Sarah and Stephen all tried to help, but no one could even engage Robert in conversation about the matter, let alone try to change his mind. He would not budge. John also stood his ground, even when Robert told him he would withdraw all financial support and that he must leave the house if he persisted in his lunacy. He left without saying goodbye to any of us. I was devastated.

I knew that Mrs Gale had kept in touch with Esther, and shortly afterwards, through her, I learned that John had married Grace as soon as he had turned twenty-one. Apparently, Grace's mother had been as disapproving as Robert, being well aware of the class difference between them, but she told them about an empty cottage which belonged to her family where they would at least have a roof over their heads while they awaited the birth. Since John was now penniless, it was all that was available to them. They moved to the rough little cottage in a small bay further down the coast and my heart ached when I thought of the way my son was now living, especially when Mrs Gale informed that I had a grandson.

John wrote to his father to tell him about the child, but although I saw the letter, I was not allowed to read it. Robert returned it unopened. I thought my heart would break.

I had to do something for my son. I did not dare tell Robert, but I sent some money and a few things to make the cottage a home, including the wooden cradle in which I had rocked John as a child. Since I could not hold my grandson in my arms, it was the only link I could forge with him. Loyalty to Robert prevented any further contact, but now that his initial anger had cooled, I could tell he was very unhappy. All his hopes for his son had been taken from him, and although I wanted to comfort him, I was too miserable myself to offer much help. I had watched my son walk out of my life, through no fault of my own, and I was desperately unhappy.

Philip was my only comfort during those weeks. He did what he could to help John in a way I could not – he appealed to William in Liverpool.

'I have written to Uncle William and asked for his help in finding work for John. No one round here dare help him because of Uncle Robert's stance, but I am sure Uncle William will. Don't worry, Aunt Isobel, it's just a matter of time. Uncle Robert will come around eventually, I'm sure.'

How I wished I could be so certain. I badly needed Clodagh. I wrote and she came with her open arms. Being hugged by Clodagh was like being wrapped in a soft warm blanket. I could feel the tension seeping away.

'Will I ever stop needing you, Clodagh?' I asked.

'Will I ever stop being there when you do?' she answered. 'What is it?'

'I feel as if I am walking on shifting sand. Everything seems to be sliding away from me. When I first came here, to the Isle of Man, I remember walking along the shore, leaving deep footprints in the wet sand, and I was full of joy. I remember how it felt to be free, to know that I had escaped at last from my old life. Now I have found that escape does not always mean freedom. Not the freedom that you embrace. I seem to be trapped in a vortex that will never let me stop spinning. Life shifts and changes just when I think I have a grip on happiness.'

'Nothing stands still, mi darlin'. Even the stars in the sky must spin in their courses. You know my philosophy, take each day that comes and make room in it for what you must do, because the sun will always rise on a new day altogether. Let's take a walk, there is something I want to say to you.'

We went for a long walk across the sands and she gave me one piece of advice about a matter to which I had never given any thought, even though I recognised the importance of it.

'I know you intend to go to your grave with your secret, Isobel, but you must leave the truth behind for the sake of both Philip and John. They are brothers and they should know that at some point in their lives. Also, Philip has a right to know that you are his mother.'

'But you know I made a promise, and I can't break that, it would destroy the family.'

'I said you must leave the truth *behind*. It will not involve breaking any promises. This is what I think you should do. Write a statement or a letter telling what happened and secure it away somewhere to be opened after your death. It will be cathartic for you, get rid of all your demons, but then you must forget about it and concentrate on the life before you. Allow time to heal the estrangement between Robert and John, for it surely will in the end so long as love is still there, and you've said that much of Robert's heartache and unhappiness is due to his enduring love for John. And, sure, isn't time something you have plenty of?'

No one could soothe me like Clodagh. I could always rely on the wisdom of her words. Writing everything down, almost as a confession, was like opening a dam to let static water flow, and knowing that no one else would read it while I lived, enabled me to write from my heart. My pen scratched across the paper as I wrote line after line, scribbling as fast as I could, words tumbling from my mind as I poured out all the unhappiness and fear that had blighted my younger years. Tears wet the paper as I worked out all the resentments, bitterness and insecurities that I had suppressed from my childhood, and later the burden of keeping that terrible guilty secret which must still be kept. When I threw down my pen I was drained.

Then, with my rant over, I read through the scribbled pages and found I was looking at the outburst of an unhappy, unloved child and the torment of an ignorant young girl.

I was neither of these now. I was a mature, sensible woman, who was able to reason through her problems in a way those two young ones had been unable to do. But now they were gone, and I had replaced them. I tore up the pages, threw them all on the fire and watched as they burned taking much of the trauma with them. As Clodagh had said – it had certainly been cathartic. Then I wrote again, this time as the adult Isobel, giving just a factual account of Philip's birth, the decision to marry Robert and the birth of John. No agonised feelings, no recriminations to sully memories, just the plain facts so that my boys would know the truth. Then I placed the pages in an envelope and hid it away in a cupboard among a pile of old household papers which needed to be kept but were no longer used. Where, one day, they could be found. Now I must face my present life and sort out its problems.

There was a lot to sort out. Although my family was divided at the moment, I drew comfort from the fact that everyone was alive and well. I could look to the future with the hope that, one day, we would all be together again as the happy family we had been. And Clodagh was right about the healing power of time. As she said, we had all the time in the world. Didn't we?

PART TWO

GRACE

Grace shivered as a blast of icy wind found the narrow gap at the top of the door and gusted through, whipping her hair across her face. She pulled the shawl further over her head and snuggled her sleeping baby closer, protecting him from the freezing draught. The storm was close, battering her cottage, the little cove and their part of the island. In the face of the gale racing in from the west, the brightly coloured rag rug in front of the fire and the cushioned rocking chair, where she was sitting nursing her son, offered a semblance of cosiness, but there was no comfort for her. The vivid images she was fighting so hard to hold at bay were flying way out to sea, and every rock of the chair seemed pitched to the same pulse as the gigantic rolling waves tossing a small struggling ship to-and-fro, until one powerful swell was finally destructive enough to smash it into driftwood and right now her John could be on that little boat.

CHAPTER EIGHT

ON the 1st of October 1895, the people on the Isle of Man awoke to a spectacular sunrise which seemed to herald a glorious sunny day, but all around the coast the Manx fishermen knew better. "Red sky at morning, sailor's warning." They had learned this old saying from their fathers, so like them they took heed, hauled their boats well up above the high tide line and made ready for the foul weather they knew was to come.

The storm blew for three days. Three days and still the wind shrieked and raged, flinging its mighty force against the island's coast. The sea pounded and crashed, sucking down heavily on the shore, stirring the coarse loose shale in a constant grinding motion, rolling and building before spewing it back in a shattering spray as the waves hit the jutting rocks with which the island braced itself. Rain lashed across the land in stinging torrents and crops lay flattened where the furious gale had laid waste a path. Heavy, sulphur coloured clouds closed in on the treetops and roofs as if to swallow them into the belly of the tempest. The whole island strained against the battering but it was the east coast which bore the brunt. It was the worst storm in living memory.

In a small bay down the coast from the town of Douglas, a cluster of pebble cottages huddled together on the sandy shore, set above the high tide line and sheltered by the horseshoe shaped cliff that curved around behind them. Grace's home was the last in the row, set with its back to its neighbours and tucked up in the crook of the sweeping arm of the cliff. Her one roomed rough stone cottage had been built into the rock face, making use of it as a fourth wall, and a fireplace had been cleverly constructed round a crevice that created a natural flue. Warmed by the turf fire, the extra heat from the rock wall kept the windowless room snug, making up for the sombre shadow of the cliff, while the ever-burning fire and usually wide-open door provided all the light that was needed, but tonight the door was shut tight and lashed securely to its frame.

Grace had seen no one during the three days. None of her neighbours had ventured out except to tighten their roof ropes, whipped loose in the ferocious battle with the wind. Well protected by the cliff, Grace was more comfortable than most, and her ropes held tight, though in the face of this deluge, water leaked from the sodden turf roof, making pools here and there where the sandy earth floor could no longer absorb the water.

Yet safe as she and the child were, Grace was in torment. Her husband could be anywhere. Surely, she hoped, surely he would have waited for the storm to pass, but lurking behind that hope was the sickening fear, heightened by the howling violence of the wind, that he might already have sailed and was somewhere out there now, somewhere in the watery hell that was the Irish Sea.

She shivered again and reached forward to throw on another turf to keep the fire burning steadily. Heat from the flames helped to strengthen her flagging spirits, and she needed that strength because she had a child who depended on her so, swaying from side to side, she rocked her son and hummed a wordless lullaby. It was the tune her mother had crooned to her when she was a baby. It had soothed her then and it soothed her boy now.

Potatoes and herring were bubbling gently in the big black pot hanging over the fire and soon they would be ready, then she would have to force herself to eat to provide nourishment for the child she was nursing. John had built the turf stack high before he left and she still had a full sack of potatoes. Hanging from the rafters under the cockloft, were several strings of herring which they had bought from their neighbours. She was as well provided for as was possible.

All the other cottagers in the cove were fishermen, and each family had its own small open boat going out to fish the herring. On the top of the cliff were the crofts where they grew vegetables and crops, making them mainly self-sufficient, except when crops failed, then they pooled what they had and helped each other to survive. They collected driftwood for their fires, built their cottage walls with pebbles from the beach and covered their roofs with thick turf, held in place by long ropes made from twisted straw. Mussels, cockles, shrimps and crabs from the rocks and sand, as well as the fish they caught, provided an iron rich diet, which made them the hardy seafaring folk they were, and hardy they needed to be because life was spartan in the little bay. Fishing was a dangerous industry and the people lived side by side with hardship and hazard. Boats could be lost out at sea. A man could fall overboard in the swell and be washed away. At those times they relied heavily on each other because only as a community could they survive.

Not having a boat or croft of their own, Grace and John relied on buying supplies from their neighbours. Although they were both islanders, and Grace was kin to the old aunt who had lived there, she and John were not known to the folk in the bay. After a first brief interest, the cottagers had not been curious about them. Having realised that the newcomers were not fishing folk and would be no threat to their hereditary fishing rights, the little community had accepted them.

The reason for their coming now lay sleeping in his mother's arms. Robert John Corkish was just six months old, blue-eyed and flaxen-haired like his father, an innocent child who, like Grace herself, had unwittingly been the cause of John's split from his family. She laid him gently in his wooden cradle and covered him with a thick shawl before turning to the simmering pot over the fire, fanning the billowing smoke away from her face. A blue and white dish and a silver fork were placed ready for the herring and potatoes and she ladled every drop of liquid over, so as not to waste any nourishment. John had brought these fine things with him – the knives, forks, spoons and pots; the wooden cradle which had been his as a child; the rocking chair and the small wooden cupboard where they kept the food. His mother had done her best.

* * *

Grace started as the door rattled loudly, suddenly buffeted by a strong blast of wind. Brief flashes of white light flared through the gap in the door and lit the room as lightning forked and fizzed across the sky. Thunder banged so close overhead that she shrank down and leaned over the cradle to protect her baby, fearful for the roof. If only John was here. If only she could know where he was now and put an end to the night-mare she had lived with for these last three days, yet it was just four days ago that they had both been so full of hope.

'I've had a letter from Uncle William in Liverpool,' John had told her. 'He has heard about my father's reaction to our marriage and he's offered to help. He says he'll find a place for me in his firm.'

Grace had listened anxiously, wondering what it might mean for her. She assumed the invitation was intended only for John, since Uncle William was John's father's youngest brother and he would hardly welcome the woman and child who had been the cause of the rift between father and son.

'What about Robert and me?' she had asked.

'He says he has a house we can rent. I don't suppose it will be very big, but at least it will be a home and we can – what is it, Grace, what's the matter?' John had suddenly seen the tears she tried to hide.

'Nothing.' She had pressed her hand against her mouth to stop her lips from trembling. 'It's just such a relief to know that everything is going to be all right, I've been so worried.'

John had put his arms about her and held her tight as they both looked down at the beautiful child they had created, then laughed as their son burped loudly from a belly full of milk.

'Then stop worrying, love.' He had kissed the top of her head. 'I'll have to go across to Liverpool for a few days to sort things out, but then I'll come back for you and Robert. You've never left the island, have you?'

'No, never.' Grace had felt a flutter of alarm. She had led such a simple life until these last few months when so much had changed. The quiet marriage in the little chapel, the move to the cove, the birth of her son, and she had coped with them all so well. Yet now, it seemed she would have to face even more changes. A move to Liverpool would be challenging, but with John beside her, she would manage. He'd made sure she had all she needed before setting off for Ramsay to find a ship.

But that had been before the storm had come.

Grace glanced down at her dish and saw that it was empty. She had swallowed the food without tasting it. She rinsed her bowl out with water from a large ewer and threw the dregs into a small crack in the rock, where it would seep through to the sand. Usually, she filled this ewer each day from the small waterfall that trickled down the cliff behind the cottage, but the trickle was now a torrent, swollen by the continuous rain, so the water must be used sparingly until she could venture outside again.

The fire flickered moodily as the wind swept down the crevice, sending flying sparks and billowing smoke around the room. Her child still slept soundly, his cheeks rosy and his hair almost silver in the firelight, and she stooped to kiss his forehead before moving his cradle to a corner away from the smoky fire. She wrapped her shawl around herself, lay down on the blanket covered straw pallet which was her own bed, and giving in to exhaustion, finally found the rest she had denied herself for the last three days. Mother and son lay by the smoke blackened rockface, each gaining strength from deep sleep, while outside, the wind howled on and rain lashed against the roof and walls. But the storm was losing its fury, and before dawn it had passed on to tear itself out across the Atlantic Ocean, leaving the island battered but silent. The calm had come.

It was the silence that woke Grace. She lifted her head and listened but there was only the soft swish of the sea as it slapped on the rocks. The fire glowed dully, but the room had held its heat and the floor was steaming as it dried out. The storm had gone. It was over.

She stretched and pushed the shawl aside. Robert was snuggled deep in his cradle, still sleeping soundly, and she stirred the embers with a fire-hardened stick, throwing on the last piece of wood, which cracked at once, promising a good blaze. Untying the door, she pushed it wide open and pegged it with a short wooden stake dug into the earth floor. It would stay open all day now the storm had gone. The sweet tang of the sea wafted in, sweeping the cottage clear of the smoky pall which had stung the eyes and irritated the throat.

The sudden light and his mother's movements woke the baby and he turned his head to look for her, pushing his chubby little fists up to his mouth and sucking noisily. Grace laughed, lifting him high into the air, smiling at his bright face. 'Hungry?' She brought him down to her shoulder and stepped outside, taking deep breaths of the fresh salty air, glad to be out of the cottage at last.

Over on the horizon the sun was rising and glinting on the gentle swell of a sea now so calm it was hard to believe there had ever been such a storm. Lacy little waves fanned up the sand before trickling quietly back to the smooth water. Gulls called harshly as they circled above before dropping down to float in the sunshine, water drops glistening on their white feathers. The sky was a pale turquoise with wisps of white cloud hovering high in the peaceful air.

Yet all along the cove, the high tideline told a different story. From the deep sea had rolled pieces of metal encrusted with barnacles from the ocean bed – parts of ships lost in other storms in other years. Broken planks of wood, smashed branches and tree trunks had been torn from the soil elsewhere and flung onto their shore. Rubbery seaweed had twisted itself round bits of old fishing net, and remains of dead fish were tangled in the knots. The sea had left gifts. Already her neighbours were out picking over the flotsam. One of the older men stopped as he carried an armful of wood back to his cottage. 'Your man's not here?' he asked.

'No, he's away to Ramsay,' Grace answered. 'He's taking a boat to Liverpool, but I expect he'll have waited for the storm to pass. No one would sail in such weather, would they?' She looked at him hopefully.

'Not if they knew what they were about, they wouldn't.' He nodded towards the wood he held. 'Better have this then, before it all goes.' And he stacked the large pile against her cottage wall where it would dry out in the sun.

Grace smiled and nodded her thanks, knowing he would not welcome anything more. To these people, helping each other was just part of their way of life, and she knew she could rely on any one of them if need be. Their kindness was balm after the harshness of John's family.

Robert turned his head and began to push against her breast, so she brought out the little stool and sat in the doorway to nurse him. The warmth of the sun and the calmness of the sea soothed away most of the deep dread that had clung about her every hour of the last three days and, as she looked out on the gentle sway of the water she relaxed, and hope replaced the fear. If John has waited for the storm to pass and gets a ship today it will be a smooth crossing, she comforted herself.

For the rest of the week the sun shone, the sea stayed calm and each day brought more hope. Now John would come home. Grace took Robert to the water's edge and held him so that he could dabble his feet in the frothy waves that rippled up the sand. His chubby little legs jerked and kicked as the cold water tickled his toes and he gurgled, excited by the sudden thrill.

'Is that nice?' His mother swung him back and forth, in and out of the water, her own bare feet wriggling in the soft wet sand. They both laughed as they paddled, then Grace turned to look up along the cliff path as she had so often done in the last few days in case John was at last making his way home. There was no sign of anyone.

'Come on, time for some dinner.' She lifted Robert, holding his back against her chest to let his wet feet drip away from her skirt, and turned for one last glance at the cliff. She stopped and looked harder. Someone was moving slowly down the top of the cliff path. Tall clumps of grass hid the first few steps so she couldn't see who it was, but then the figure moved on and she saw that it was her sister, Ellen.

'It's Aunty Ellen,' she told Robert. 'She must have changed her day off. Let's get the kettle boiling.'

Smiling, she carried the baby into the cottage and laid him down on the rag rug to kick. She filled the ewer from the waterfall, once more gently cascading down the cliff, poured water into the big black kettle and set it on the trivet over the fire. The brown teapot was warming by the hearth, and she spooned in the tea leaves then stepped back to look through the doorway to see how close her sister was.

That was odd. Usually Ellen ran the last few yards across the sand, her face beaming, but not today. Today she seemed to be dragging her heels, walking almost reluctantly. Something was wrong. Grace hurried to meet her.

Ellen kept her head down as she walked and only when Grace called her name, did she look up and meet her sister's eyes.

'What is it Ellen? What's the matter?' Grace put her arm round the thirteen-year-old girl's shoulder.

Ellen waited until they were in the cottage and she had put down her basket before she spoke.

When she did, her voice shook. 'Mam has sent me Grace. I've got to tell you there's been a shipwreck. It's John – he went down with the boat.'

'What?' Grace stared. What had she just said?

'John's mother sent word to Mam. They heard from the uncle John was going to see. He said the boat went down with all hands in Liverpool Bay. It was the mail-boat, Grace, he'd got a passage on that. It was the only boat that went out.'

'But he could swim!'

Bewildered and unable to make sense of what she had just heard, Grace clutched for hope. Unable to offer any, Ellen remained silent. Grace half-laughed as if she was being teased, looking hard into Ellen's face, willing her to deny the words she had just said, but the misery in her sister's eyes told her the truth.

Shock swamped her. Blood drained away from her face and she swayed as her legs seemed unable to support her; her mouth was dry and she struggled to breathe. The thudding and throbbing of her heart echoed the pounding inside her head. From far, far away she could hear Ellen's voice, but the person her sister was talking to and whose hand she was holding, was someone else, not Grace. She was someone who was watching from a remote corner, detached from the nightmare that was building at the dark edges of a room which suddenly started to spin. Her body began to shake violently as panic clawed at her. Frightened, Ellen pulled her across to the bed. She rubbed Grace's hands between her own, tears running down her cheeks in silent sorrow for her sister.

Grace stared numbly through the door. The sun lit the sand, glinting little flashes of silver where it caught the quartz grains. She could hear the voices of her neighbours, the mewl of a cat as it waited for a fish-head, the harsh call of gulls from high above the sea – all normal everyday sounds, but now intensified and vibrating through her ears with a banging beat as if to join in with the drumming already thumping in her head.

They sat side by side, Grace numb with shock, unable to stop the shaking and gasping as she tried hard not to scream, Ellen quietly sobbing as she watched her sister's grief, until little Robert, growing tired of kicking, began to whimper for attention. Ellen picked him up and cuddled him, soothing and shushing until he fell asleep, then laid him in his cradle. She brewed the tea that Grace had begun to prepare and held the cup while her sister tried to sip through chattering teeth. The hot amber liquid cleared some of the dream-like trance and Grace took the cup in shaking fingers and drank. Slowly, as the strong brew coursed down her throat, her spinning senses swung back into the room.

'I'm sorry, Grace,' Ellen, still trembling, sat down beside her and sipped her own tea. 'Shall I stay with you tonight?'

Grace made a huge effort to focus. 'Can you?' she managed to ask. 'Won't you have to be back?'

'Not till tomorrow dinner time. They've given me my day off because they know John's family and heard what has happened.'

For the rest of the day Ellen took charge. She passed Robert to Grace to be fed then took him back to see to his other needs. She made a stew from the meat and vegetables she had brought with her and persuaded Grace to eat a bowlful. She kept the fire burning brightly, even though there was no need for the extra heat, but she hoped her sister would draw comfort from the flames and the crackling of the wood, and gradually, as the long, long day wore on, Grace began to move about, helping Ellen with the many little jobs which, though unnecessary, held the shock at bay. The bed was straightened many times, the cupboard was tidied, and the wood re-piled neatly in the corner. The teapot was filled again and again, each time with weaker brews, using the tea sparingly, until at last the sun set and the two girls lay down on the bed and slept from sheer exhaustion.

It was not a long sleep for Grace, but it was enough to restore sufficient strength for her to realise that taking care of Robert was the only thing that mattered now. Leaving Ellen still sleeping, she got up and stirred the fire, adding wood to get a blaze before tempering it with turf. When her baby woke, she lifted his warm little body and held him close to nurse him, each of them needing the other equally, and in the flickering firelight, swaying together in the old rocking chair, the two of them started a new day.

CHAPTER NINE

FOR the first five days Grace haunted the water's edge, prowling to-and-fro across the sand, staring out to sea, as if by keeping a vigil she could still keep a hold on John. She tormented herself by imagining the horror of his last hours, trying to re-live and so share them, as though by so doing she could even try to save him, yet she knew full well that the sea had taken him.

Her neighbours tried to help, bringing food and offering to look after the baby, but they could not ease her mental anguish. At first, they kept a careful watch as she paced the shore, unsure of her intentions, but then they noticed that she never allowed the water to reach her feet and they understood. The sea would not take her – it had become her enemy. Then Ellen brought a message from their mother. It said, 'Tell Grace she can come back home and I'll take care of the baby. She'll need to find work.'

Still in shock and in great need of help, Grace packed up her belongings, and with her two brothers and Ellen lending a hand, carted them all to her mother's small house, cramming everything into the tiny room she and Robert would share. There was scarcely enough space, but they were all the possessions she owned, and they mattered.

Back in her old home, laid in bed with her son sleeping by her side, she tried to find some way get past the horror of the last two dreadful weeks when her world had come to an end. Everything was still too raw to heal, but she had to face the new life she must now lead as a widow with a young child. Her grief had to be put, not behind her but to one side, where it would wait its turn, because she would carry it as an extra limb for the rest of her life. Robert was the only anchor she could cling to now, but her love for him was strong enough to give her the will to hold on tight. No prayers were said that night and would not be ever again. When it mattered, they had not been answered.

* * *

It was hard to believe that everything could come crashing down so suddenly. The last six months had been the happiest she had known, married to the love of her life and the mother of their son. She let her mind seek back to those early days when she had hope in her heart, although she had been well aware of the sacrifice John had made by marrying beneath him and angering his father. She had tried to persuade him not to go against his father's wishes, but John loved the beautiful girl he had been secretly seeing since leaving boarding school, and once he'd known about the baby, there was no way he would abandon her – not even when his furious father had cut off his funds and severed all communication. In the face of her husband's determination, there was little John's mother could do, but Isobel Corkish had quietly done what she could and it had helped. Grace's own mother had initially been harsh.

'Oh, Grace, you young fool, what have you done?' she had said. 'What do you think will become of you now? He'll not marry you. His family won't let him. You've ruined yourself. Well, you've made your own bed and now you must lie in it. There's nothing I can do for you.'

Yet it was she who had come to their aid by telling them about the old cottage further down the coast that had belonged to her aunt. Since no one else in the family wanted the primitive little house down on the sand, it had stood empty since the aunt had died, so she had sent Grace to look at it. Most of the men in Grace's family worked in the mine and had no interest in living in a fishing cove but, spartan as it was, it had been a godsend to the homeless and penniless Grace and John awaiting the birth of their child. John had hoped it might make a difference when his father knew he had a grandson, and he had written to tell him, but there had been no reply.

Although Grace heard nothing from her own mother, Ellen had often come on her afternoon off, and through her she had learned what Esther had to say.

'When I tell Mam I've been here,' Ellen told her, 'She says, "I suppose you found the child starving and no decent clothes to his back?" She only says that so I'll tell her, "No Mam, he's fat and bonny and sleeps on a feather bed in a fine wooden cradle." That way she finds out what she wants to know without really asking. She asks about you too, Grace, in that funny roundabout way of hers, but when I asked her if she had thought about coming to see the baby, she said, "There are younger legs than mine able to run up and down cliff steps." I think that means she is hoping you'll take the baby to see her.' They had both laughed knowing their mother's odd ways.

'I'm glad you come anyway, Ellen,' Grace had said. 'It's a bit lonely here when John is off looking for work. The trouble is, people have heard about the break with his father and they don't want to go against someone as important as he is by helping his son.'

As the son of a mine owner, John had been born to comfort. Both Grace's parents had worked as servants for the family so, when her father Daniel had been killed in a stable accident while Grace was still a child, Mrs Corkish had arranged for Esther to launder their fine linen. It was hard if not heavy work, but it enabled her to care for her four children and as soon as Grace was old enough, she began to help her mother. That was how she had met John. Four years older than her, John was away at school, but once, when he was home, he had seen her hefting a heavy basket of clothes as she collected the washing and he had arranged for a little hand-pulled cart to be made available, making it so much easier for a small girl. Grace had adored him from that day.

As the only son, John was the family heir, so with everything resting on him, Robert Corkish had been bitterly disappointed when his son had told him, at the young age of twenty, that he wanted to marry. When he learned that the girl was the daughter of two of their former servants, he had been furious. It was not what he had planned for his son's future, neither indeed for the family's future, so there had been a rift which no one could mend.

All of this had unbelievably happened to her in such a short time and was why she was in her present situation because now, with John's death, it seemed all chance of reconciliation had died with him. There had been no word from his family. Grace had hoped that shared grief might mend the breach but if the tragedy of losing a beloved only son could not bring about the acceptance of an only grandson, she had to face the fact that she must bring up Robert on her own.

Her most pressing need was to find work and build a new life for herself and the child who would carry the name of a family to which he did not belong, even though he shared their blood. Grace knew she would not be able to offer him the kind of life which John would have provided once he had made his way, but her own family were decent working-class people. The values she could offer might be different from those of the Corkish family, but they were still values, one of which was the willingness to rally round as a family in time of need. As her mother was doing, as her sister had done and as her brothers had done, and that was the value that mattered most. Robert would be brought up in a way that would have made John proud. She had to quell the bitterness she couldn't help but feel when she thought about John's family. What kind of parents could reject their only child? Even though John's mother had provided some of their essential needs, and they had been grateful, she had still obeyed her husband in his harsh decision and, as a mother herself, Grace found that hard to understand.

Grace also felt bitter about the public way in which she and Robert had been slighted. Everyone in Douglas knew of the Corkish family, even if they did not work for them, and Grace was aware that a few of her neighbours were muttering behind their hands, the unkindest of them calling her and Robert 'castoffs'. Cruel words always found their way back to the target. She hated this slur, especially to her son, but carrying such a well-known name, there was no hiding away, so she held her head up high and feigned indifference.

Finding work was essential and, after walking round Douglas looking at vacancy notices, she found a position as an assistant in a drapery shop, working long hours but bringing home enough money to provide for her and Robert as well as make a contribution to the family housekeeping. It was a bonus to find that she was allowed to buy remnants quite cheaply so, with the help of her mother, she stitched a set of smart working clothes.

Grace was taller than most women and, as if her name had bestowed a gift on her, she possessed a natural grace that flowed through her every movement. Her eyes were the soft grey of a sea fret rolling ashore bringing rain, and her hair, though fair like her son's, was pearlier, blending in with the grey of her eyes. It shone like silk and in the sunshine little flashes of silver enriched the pearl so that, lifted and rippled by the wind, it was as flecked as the sea itself. She took pride in her appearance and wore her clothes well and it didn't take long for her boss to realise what an asset that could be to the shop, and to place her on the counter selling the most expensive bolts of cloth where she served the wealthiest customers.

* * *

One evening, just before closing, an elegant well-dressed lady came into the store and made her way over to the counter. Grace glanced up and knew at once that she was looking at John's mother, Isobel Corkish. The brilliant blue eyes, the fair hair, the expression – John had inherited them all. For a moment the two women faced each other, and Grace's heart skipped a beat as she went from puzzled surprise to hope. Why was she here? Was she bringing a message from John's father at last?

John's mother spoke first. 'Hello Grace.'

Shyness made Grace answer rather awkwardly with a quiet 'Good evening' and at once she felt it was the wrong thing to say, that it had sounded too formal. 'Hello' back would have been better.

'I wonder if I could talk to you for a moment.' Mrs Corkish didn't smile, but her tone was not unfriendly.

'Yes, of course.' Grace glanced across at the other girls who were hovering curiously nearby. 'But perhaps we could talk outside? I shall be leaving in a few minutes.' She didn't know what it could be about, but whatever it was she did not want it to be overheard.

'Thank you, I'll wait at the corner for you.' said Mrs Corkish. It was then that she smiled, and again Grace was struck by the heart-lurching likeness to John.

They were both rather hesitant when they met. Although Grace's mother, Esther, had met Isobel Corkish when she had worked at her house, Grace had not seen her before. When she had carried the washing to-and-fro as a child, she had always gone to the back of the house and only spoken to the servants. Isobel, however, had seen Grace. She knew that she was living with her mother and she knew where she was working. From a distance, and from the inside of her carriage, she had been able to watch the girl her son had married. It had had to be done secretly, since her husband had not changed his mind, but it had helped Isobel to make up her mind that this was a respectable young girl whose son was her grandson. Although he might never be an heir, he was a Corkish, and Isobel wanted to be sure he would not be a pauper.

'I have come to see you because I want to help you.' she began. Grace remained silent. John's mother hesitated. She had obviously been expecting a reply but at that moment Grace could not think of anything to say. She was still waiting to hear the words that would mean the world to her, that her son was wanted. Faced with silence, Mrs Corkish hurried on.

'I think you know that it is difficult for me to do what I would really like to do, but I have a sum of money of my own – no, please listen…' She stopped Grace's protest with a hand on her arm. 'It is money I inherited from my own family and it was always intended to be for John.' Her voice faltered and Grace felt her hand tremble where it still rested on her arm, 'Now, I want it to be for his child.'

She didn't use the baby's name, and Grace wondered if she knew that he had been named Robert, for his grandfather.

John's mother took a sealed brown paper package from her bag and held it out to Grace. 'You will need some of it to buy a house of your own to live in, I know, but I hope you will put the rest away for the child's future.'

She phrased it as a request rather than an order, but even so Grace could tell that the older woman was expecting her to accept the money gratefully, and though, of course, she was appreciative, Grace was proud and still smarting from the family's rejection. She was determined to show that she was quite capable of providing for Robert herself. After all, her son was obviously not being accepted into the family, was he? That seemingly was still being denied him. She made an effort to answer politely but disappointment at Mr Corkish's continued intransigence out-weighed any gratitude and made her sound defiant.

'John and I were grateful for the things you sent and I know it wasn't easy.' She tried to smile but her lips were stiff. 'We have both lost John, and that's been hard for each of us, but you are left with all your memories of his childhood, you have his past. I am left with his son, so I have his future, and I promise you I will do everything I can for our child, perhaps not in the way John would have been able to do, but he will have the very best I can provide. So, thank you, but I can manage.'

John's mother looked down at the packet in her hands. 'There is a considerable amount of money here. I am not imposing conditions because I believe you to be a sensible, hard-working young woman who will use it wisely, but as I said, this is my own money that the baby would have inherited from John if – well if things had been different.' She held the packet out again, and seeing Grace still hesitate, she softened her voice. 'Please take it.' It was almost a plea.

Grace took the thick parcel and slowly placed it inside her jacket. 'I will take it, but I will put all of it away for Robert, and I will buy a house for us when I have saved enough money myself. However long it takes.'

For a few tense moments the two women stood facing each other.

'I'm sure you will do what you think is best for both of you.' John's mother gave a sad smile and briefly, Grace thought she might ask to see the baby, but then she saw that the meeting was over. A smile, a nod, and Isobel Corkish crossed the road to where a carriage was waiting, and drove out of their lives.

CHAPTER TEN

GRACE had not had even the slightest thought of buying a house until Mrs Corkish had inferred that she expected her to use some of the money for that purpose. No one she knew owned their own house. Most people, like her neighbours and her family, rented their home, expecting nothing else. Even among the more well off it was rare to find a woman owner, so for a working girl like herself it was way beyond anything that she could possibly aspire to. She felt sick with horror when she thought about the way she had blurted out that rash defiant reply, 'I will buy a house when I have saved enough money myself.' The unexpected meeting with John's mother had triggered a defensive attitude that was boosted by bitterness and pride, so she had spoken more defiantly than she would have done if she had had time to prepare herself.

What on earth had she done? What had she been thinking of? Having said that she would put all the money away for Robert, meant that now, she had no alternative but to try to save what she could from the low wage she earned. It would take a lifetime of saving before she could even think about looking at a property, even one of the poorest. But now she felt committed by that proud, senseless remark. Not for a moment did it occur to her that she could simply ignore those words, just forget about them. For Grace, the fact that she had said them to John's mother had set them in stone, as though she had sworn an oath that tied her, honour bound, to something that was unachievable – and all because of that stupid, stupid pride. She could have wept.

The only thing she could do now, was to start saving every penny that could be spared. That meant that if they wanted anything which could not be bought from the housekeeping money, they went without until it could be afforded. Nothing would make her dip into those savings and gradually, frugality became second nature to her and saving, an obsession.

As a child, Grace had always been accepting of her life. It was much the same as that of her neighbours and most of the other people around her, lots of hard work and never much money, yet she had never considered her family to be poor. Esther, having worked in the well-to-do Corkish house, had picked up the high standards required there and when she married, had brought some of those standards into her own home, teaching her children good manners and providing them with a respectable upbringing. There was always food on the table and a good fire to warm them and Grace was quite content with her own self-worth, so it had been slighting to be dismissed by John's family without a single meeting, but her mother had been right – they did not welcome her. At first, she had been happy just to have John, and she had wanted nothing more, but then she had had her son and lost John, and that had made all the difference. Now she had something to fight for.

Under the pressure of her self-inflicted commitment to buy a house and aware of the all too slowly growing amount in her savings book, she decided to look for more work. It had to fit in with her hours at the drapers of course, but she found a part-time job as a waitress in one of the guest houses on the Promenade, serving suppers. Although it was only seasonal work it brought in extra money and, with good tips, it all added to the pot. She had to start work at seven o'clock, and since she didn't finish at the shop until six o'clock this meant she had to go straight to the guest house. Her mother was still looking after Robert, who was nearly always in bed by the time Grace got home from work, and sometimes still asleep when she got up in the morning. It was one of the sacrifices that had to be made, but on Sundays, Grace's day off, she often took him to the park for a picnic of jam sandwiches, to give her mother a rest. It was the highlight of the week for Grace.

'Can we go on the sands today, instead of the park?' Robert asked one Sunday. 'I want to swim in the sea.'

'No.' Grace answered sharply. 'You can't swim.'

'But I want to learn.'

'Not today, the tide is in.' Grace knew that she was denying her son the pleasure she had known as a child, that of playing on the sand, splashing in the water and collecting shells, but she could not bring herself to go near the sea. It was something she would have to overcome eventually, since they lived on an island, but it would take a great deal of courage for she would be stirring up vivid memories, and she was not yet ready to face those.

'I'll tell you what, though, we'll buy ice creams when we have our sandwiches, shall we?' she offered, and Robert instantly perked up.

'Can I have a wafer?'

'You can.' She had diverted him this time but he would ask again and she must be prepared.

* * *

She watched with pride as her son started school. He had his own room now that her brothers and Ellen had left home, and was becoming a big, strong boy, able to help around the house, but, as he was growing stronger, his grandmother was becoming frail. Grace, now the sole breadwinner for her mother and son, and working long hours, didn't notice just how frail.

After he had done his chores, Robert usually went out to play with his friends, a group of boys who met in the small park at the end of the road. One or two he knew from school, but there were older boys who had already started working. None were more than thirteen or fourteen years of age but to Robert, at eight, they seemed to be very grown-up and exciting. They smoked, and if they were a bit boisterous at times, well, it was easy enough to keep out of the way and watch from the side-lines, as he was doing now.

'My mum would kill me if she knew I was here,' his best friend Eddie confided. 'She's told me to keep away from this lot.' He nodded towards the older boys who were having one of their rough arguments. A lot of shoving and squaring up was usually involved, and sometimes a bit of swearing, but tonight the banter had spilled over into actual fighting. Two of the boys were rolling on the ground, egged on by their jeering mates. Robert and Eddie watched in fascinated horror from behind the safety of the hedge, ready to run for it if need be. Robert knew his mother would react in exactly the same way as Eddie's if she knew he was here, but that was the thrill – *feeling* part of it yet not actually *being* part of it. Too young to really join in, but happy to laugh at the coarse jokes he didn't understand.

Now Eddie had had enough. 'It's late, I'm going, are you coming?' He began moving gingerly away. Robert nodded. Things had gone too far this time and he was feeling rather scared. They turned and ran down behind the hedge towards the park gate. Once outside, they ran faster. It was getting dark and they were very well aware that they should have been home by now. Both boys were from respectable families, but Eddie had a father as well as a mother waiting for him and he risked a good telling off. Robert knew his grandmother would be nodding off in her chair by the fire and that he could easily let himself into the house and go up to his bedroom without disturbing her. He'd done it many times.

'See you tomorrow,' he called as Eddie sprinted away.

Once home, he went around to the back of the house as he always did, quietly lifted the latch and let himself in. He took off his boots, washed his hands and face at the sink, and as he was taking the towel from the hook behind the kitchen door, he noticed that the lamp wasn't lit. The fire was burning and cast a bright glow about the room, but it was odd because his grandmother always lit the lamp as soon as the daylight faded.

He looked across to her chair and there she was, asleep as usual. He wondered if he should light the lamp. She'd obviously been asleep for quite a while and not noticed the growing dark. In the firelight his Gran looked peaceful, head lolling against the back of her chair, her hands folded across the shawl she always tucked round her knees to keep the draught away – so still and quiet.

Still and quiet? This wasn't right. Gran was a snorer, and she usually had a twitch in her hands as if they couldn't rest, even in sleep, yet there she was – *still* and *quiet!*

Frightened now, Robert moved nearer. 'Gran?' he whispered. Then. when she didn't move, louder to try to rouse her, 'GRANNY!' It was a yell, but she still didn't move. In terror, he realised he was looking at death. He spun round, ran from the house leaving his boots where they were and raced barefoot down the road to Eddie's house. He banged on the front door, gasping and trembling and almost fell into the room as the door was opened by Eddie's father.

'Robert—whatever's up?' Mr Cowley stood back to let Robert through. 'What's happened?'

'My Gran is dead.' Robert was wide-eyed with fear.

'Dead? Are you sure?' Eddie's mother led him to the fire. 'Where is she?'

'She's in the chair in the kitchen, but the lamps not lit, and she's not snoring like she usually does, and everything's very quiet, and I thought she was asleep but she's...' Robert's babble dried up as he stopped to draw a deep breath.

'I think we'd better make sure first.' said Eddie's mother. 'You go and see, George, make sure.'

'Aye, keep him here. He's had a shock. I'll go and have a look.' Eddie's father pulled on his boots and went out. Eddie was sitting at the table staring at his friend, Robert's teeth were chattering and he couldn't stop shaking. Mrs Cowley sat him down in her own chair by the fire and found a pair of Eddie's socks to put on his cold feet.

'Where's your mother, Robert?' she asked.

'She's at work.'

'Yes, I know, but *where* does she work?'

'At the Marine View. She finishes at nine o'clock.'

'Well, she'll have to finish earlier tonight. I'll get George to go for her when he comes back – ah, here he is now. Well?'

'She's gone all right, no doubt about it. Died in her sleep by the look of it.' He looked sympathetically at Robert, 'It's the best way to go.'

Eddie left the table and came to sit on the little stool by the hearth, near Robert.

'You can have my supper if you want,' he offered, handing Robert a slice of bread and dripping from which he'd already taken a bite.

'Ta.' Robert took it and began to eat. With his mother's budgeting, they ate adequately but rather frugally, and supper was not on the menu in his house. He could not afford to miss this chance.

'His mother works at the Marine View on the front,' Mrs Cowley said. 'You'd better go and fetch her home, George, before we decide what to do next.'

'Right.' George wrapped his scarf round his neck and patted Robert's head. 'You'll be all right once your mother's here lad. It's been a shock for you, it has, but you'll be all right when she comes.'

It was an hour before George returned with Grace. She put her arms round Robert and held him close, both of them silent, both trembling.

'I've made some tea.' Mrs Cowley poured out two cups. 'Here, drink this, it always helps.' She handed Grace a cup and gave one to Robert, and the hot liquid warmed his cold stomach.

'You can leave Robert here while you go home and sort things out. I'll go with you and George can go and tell the doctor.'

Esther lay in the chair just as Robert had found her. Tears filled Grace's eyes as she looked at her mother's silver streaked hair, her lined face with white hairs sprouting from her chin, at her gnarled blue-veined hands still clutching her shawl and wondered when it was that she had become this old woman. All her life she had been strong and hardworking, and although she could sometimes be harshly spoken, Grace was aware of how much she had relied on her these last few years. Now, as she saw the limp body sagging down in the chair, she was also painfully aware that due to her strict way of living she had imposed frugality on her mother too. The old shawl was threadbare in places; the thick black bombazine skirt had been part of her mother's clothing for as long as Grace could remember, summer and winter alike, and her leather boots were cracked with worn down heels. Even though she had always appreciated what her mother had done for her and Robert, there had been no little treats, no little comforts that might have made the days a bit sweeter at the end of a hard life. Instead Esther had taken on the care of a grandson and brought him up without a word of complaint. Had her mother known she was ill and that she was nearing the end of her road? Was there anything her daughter could have done for her? Grace searched her conscience and knew that there probably was.

A flood of mixed emotion engulfed her, regret, guilt, loss, love and most of all a deep sadness. Grace bit her lip to prevent her mouth twisting into the stretch of a long howl she would not be able to stop once started. She wept quietly for a moment then, remembering the woman who was standing quietly by the door, she took a deep shuddering breath and turned, ready to take the first sad step in the order of things to be done.

* * *

Esther had a good funeral. All the family had contributed and even after Grace's share of the costs had been taken out, her savings book showed a reasonable balance. Esther's house had been rented and Grace was offered the tenancy, but she looked at her savings, the most money she had ever had in her life, and began to consider the possibility of looking for a small cottage to buy. It was an enormous undertaking and it scared her when she thought about it in bed at night, but it had been her aim for so long and so much effort had been put in that to waver now would diminish all the sacrifice that had been made. It would do no harm to make enquiries.

There was a little terraced house she had seen and liked in a quiet street on the outskirts of Douglas. She asked the price, and although it was quite cheap it was still far more than she had available. Disappointed, she sat down to weigh up her options, and at the back of her mind, and definitely influencing her thinking, was the thought of the money put away for Robert. Either she took up the tenancy on her mother's house and carried on saving for a few more years, or she did what she had once sworn not to do, which was to use some of the money that was still untouched in the bank and still available to her. It was this that provided the safety net without which she could never have pursued her dream of ownership.

She remembered John's mother's words. 'I know you will do what you think is best for both of you.' It was almost as though Mrs Corkish had foreseen the present situation and was giving her permission. Perhaps she had been far wiser than Grace had realised, in making sure the money would be there when needed and not tied up in a trust fund.

Grace had never asked for advice from anyone, preferring to rely on her own common sense, so although this must surely be the biggest decision she would ever make, she felt it had to be hers and hers alone. At eight years of age Robert was too young to be taken into her confidence even though it would affect him just as much as it would her.

Looking at her savings again, she made calculations. If she withdrew the shortfall out of Robert's account, leaving the bulk still invested, she could buy the house and then simply pay the amount which she had been saving each week back into his account to build up the balance again. Surely that made sense? Then Robert would have a house *and* a nest egg to give him a good start in life when he was older. Was this the time to take advantage of the security the money provided? To swallow that prickly pride and act practically? Grace made her decision.

CHAPTER ELEVEN

TWO months later, Grace and Robert were living in their new home. It was a two up and two down terraced house with a washhouse, coal shed and a lean-to lavatory in the flagged yard. Her furniture fitted and she made some new curtains using remnants from the shop. Grace looked round her little house with deep satisfaction. It was theirs. She had done it. John would have been proud of her. Now she and Robert could start to build their future.

It took longer to get to work from the new house, meaning she had to leave earlier and was home later, but now that they owned their own home, she had achieved her aim, and the pressure to continually save had been lifted. She handed in her notice at the guest house and looked forward to spending more time with her son. But Robert had grown into the habit of going to the park most evenings to meet the older boys he now considered his pals. Eddie had been forbidden by his parents to mix with these lads and did not go quite so often, but one evening he arrived sporting a new bicycle, new to Eddie anyway. Robert was envious.

'When did you get this?' he asked, touching the handlebars and ringing the bell.

'Today. It's my birthday,' Eddie told him proudly, swerving his bicycle away from Robert. 'It didn't take me long to learn to ride it. I fell off a couple of times, but I've got the hang of it now.'

'Can I have a go?' Robert tried to put a foot on the pedal.

'No. I've not to let anyone else have a ride. You might fall off and damage it.'

'I won't!'

'You might. Anyway, my father says I mustn't. I'm off now. See you at school tomorrow.' After a slight wobble, Eddie pedalled off.

Robert looked after him wistfully. It was just what he wanted and he had his own birthday coming up. Birthdays had never been much celebrated in his family; sometimes a special cake for tea, and once, one of his uncles had made him a wooden boat with canvas sails and he had taken it down on the sands to launch it in the rock pools. That had been a really good present, but a bicycle was something else.

'Mum, Eddie's got a bicycle,' he announced when he got home. 'He got it for his birthday.'

'Did he? That was a good present, he's very lucky.' Grace had a feeling about what was coming.

'It's just what I could do with,' Robert continued. 'I could ride it to school. Think how much quicker it would be.'

'Well, there won't be many boys going to school on a bicycle, I can tell you,' Grace smiled. 'And you know I won't be able to afford one now I've bought the house.'

Robert had known it would be useless. He'd known that in spite of owning their own house, things were going to be just the same, never spending a penny unless it was necessary, always eating sensibly, dressing sensibly, making clothes last. But no treats. No surprises. No bicycles!

He had to walk through his old neighbourhood now to get to the park. The older boys there had accepted him as part of their group, nicknaming him Snowy because of his fair hair. He had become more confident and no longer hid when things got a bit rough. Although he was too young to be really involved, he sometimes joined in the jeering banter from a sense of bravado, egged on by his mates. It was a time of experiment. Pushing against the boundaries of his respectable upbringing, and putting guilt to the back of his mind when he thought about what his mother would say if she knew what he was up to.

He was walking home one evening, past the corner of Eddie's street, when he noticed Eddie's bicycle leaning against the wall of his house. It was almost dark and lights were shining from the windows. The street was empty. This would be a chance to have a good look at it. He lifted it away from the wall and turned the handlebars as if he was riding it. He was sure he would be able to ride, it seemed easy enough and he was good at balancing. He could walk along the wall at school easily, whereas Eddie always had to jump off halfway. No wonder he couldn't ride a bicycle!

He glanced at the house and then down the street. All quiet. Perhaps he could have just a little ride. If Eddie came out and saw that he really could ride, Robert felt sure he wouldn't mind him having a go. He threw his leg over the crossbar, gripped the handles and put one foot on the pedal, balancing himself with his other foot on the ground as he wobbled, but then he found that the harder he pushed down on the pedals, the easier it was to balance. When he had wobbled to the end of the street, he realised he didn't know how to stop, so he turned the wheel and rode on around the corner and soon he began to pedal properly. He laughed. Just as he had thought it was easy, he *could* ride a bicycle.

The road sloped downhill making the pedalling easier and the more the road sloped, the more speed he picked up. Wind rushed past his face as he sped faster and faster, away from the street and on down the hill, loving the new experience of speed. Gaining confidence, he followed a bend, automatically leaning in to the curve. The bicycle was flying along without the need to pedal and he had to concentrate hard to keep his balance. Then the road began to swerve uphill and to put in the extra effort needed, he had to push down hard on the pedals. Soon, the pain in his legs slowed him down and made him grit his teeth. He stopped for a moment to relieve his aching muscles and looking back, he suddenly realised how far he had come.

In a panic he turned around and began the long haul back up the steep hill that he had just skimmed down, needing to climb off and push the bicycle for most of the way. The machine was heavier than he had thought and he was puffing and red in the face by the time he had struggled to the top, so it was a relief to reach flat ground. Just around the corner, then he could put the bike back with no harm done.

Just around the corner, in a group outside the house, stood Eddie, Eddie's mother and father and the local policeman. The front door was wide open and light was streaming out onto the road. They all turned as Robert rode up.

'That's *my* bicycle!' Eddie snatched it from Robert, catching one of the pedals on Robert's shin as he pulled it away. It hurt!

'What do you think you're playing at?' shouted Mr Cowley. He was furious and Robert quailed back from him. He tried to speak but he was still gasping from the ride, his leg was stinging like mad and he didn't know what to say.

'Didn't I tell you?' Mrs Cowley's angry voice made Robert even more afraid. She turned to her son. 'I told you he was going to the bad. Now you know. And he's supposed to be your pal.' She glared at Robert.

Robert found his voice – he needed to stick up for himself. 'I only had a little ride,' he said, and even to his own ears the words sounded cocky.

'You took this bicycle without permission, disappeared for nearly an hour, and now you say you only went for a little ride?' The policeman took out his notebook.

An hour! He'd been gone for an hour? Robert was horrified. 'I didn't damage it–'

'A good job too,' spat Eddie's mother.

'What on earth did you think you were doing?' Mr Cowley was still furious.

'I just wanted to see if I could ride it.' Robert knew he still sounded cocky.

'These people reported the bicycle missing nearly half an hour ago. They looked all over the place.' The policeman frowned at him. 'You've caused a lot of upset. You know stealing is a crime, don't you?'

Dumbstruck, Robert looked from one to the other of the Cowley family.

Eddie was straddling his bike and inspecting it for damage, but Mr and Mrs Cowley's faces were hard and unrelenting. Could these be the same people who had been so kind to him when his grandmother had died? Frightened and not knowing what to do next, he looked up at the constable, who was the only adult not in a rage.

'Right.' He put his hand on Robert's shoulder. 'You'd better come with me, my lad, then I'll be having a word with your mother.'

The Cowleys ushered Eddie and his bike inside the house and, with a final glare, slammed the door with a bang.

CHAPTER TWELVE

GRACE lay in bed, head throbbing and eyes swollen from weeping. It was one of the worst times in her life, nearly as bad as losing John, this dreadful fear for Robert. Sometimes she hoped she was dreaming, that it was all a nightmare and she would wake up to find everything was normal, but it was not a dream and nothing was normal any more. Her son, her darling child, had been accused of stealing! The Cowleys had made it clear to Grace that they considered Robert had become a 'wrong 'un'. It seemed they knew more about her son than she did. They knew about the lads at the park, they knew about the coarse jokes and the odd rough and tumble and they knew that Robert was in the thick of it. How could they know what she did not?

Grace racked her brains again and again, searching for signs of a change in Robert's behaviour, but there were none. He had certainly seemed to be growing rapidly, becoming a strong boy, but at home there was nothing to show any difference in him except, and she had to admit this, Robert spent very little time at home. She had to face the fact that for the last seven years she had been so busy concentrating on scraping together her nest egg that she hadn't really known what Robert did when she was at work. In her mind he had stayed her fine young son. How could he have become this boy they described whom she didn't know? Whatever had been going on, Robert was not the hard lad anymore. He was a terrified young boy who cried himself to sleep while his mother lay sleepless in the next room. The threat of birching hung over them both. It was the punishment meted out to young boys on the island for petty larceny. Six stinging strokes with a spray of birch twigs were administered to a bare backside by the police sergeant and it was considered a very effective deterrent, not least because of the humiliation involved. Boys rarely offended a second time. The officer had told Grace it all depended upon what the Cowleys decided to do.

Grace went to see Ellen, now married with a family and her husband a clerk in a shipping company. She was indignant on Robert's behalf and immediately took his side.

'He *borrowed* it, that's all. That's not stealing.'

'But he took it without asking,' Grace wept. 'The policeman gave him a good telling off. He warned him what happens to boys accused of stealing, and we know what that means.'

Ellen nodded. Everyone dreaded the shame of the birch. Added to that, they were both aware that already the malicious tongues were wagging again due to Grace's connection to the Corkish family, and because of this Grace felt stigmatised. If John's father heard what had happened, he would feel justified in the decision he had taken nine years ago. Most of her neighbours sympathised with her but there was that churlish few who did not, and those were the tongues that wagged the most. The thought of her son being the object of this spiteful gossip inflicted a pain like a stab to the heart, and for the first time, Grace felt crushed. She lost the determined self-possession that had enabled her to hold her head high when faced with rejection by John's family. The shock of having Robert accused of theft, even though he had not actually stolen the bicycle and had not been charged, had drained all her strength and her will to fight.

'I've had enough, Ellen, I can't take any more. I'm tired of constantly trying and then having the rug pulled from under my feet. It's so unfair.'

'I know.' Ellen took her sister's hand. 'No one could have tried harder than you have. You couldn't have done any more.'

However, she did have a suggestion to make. Why didn't Grace take the boat across to the main land? It would get Robert away from the bad influences and Grace away from the gossip.

'Why not go to Blackpool?' Ellen urged, 'You'll be able to find work in a shop or a hotel, you've done both, and you can rent a couple of rooms for the time being. Don't you remember how John was going to take you to Liverpool? You were ready to go away then, weren't you? And you're older and more experienced now. At least go for the time being, until everything has calmed down. Think about it. Grace.'

Grace did think about it, night and day. It would be such a relief to get away from the town where she had always been in the shadow of the family who had slighted her. She had really struggled to prove her worth as she raised their grandchild, but all that effort been in vain, because it was very obvious that John's father had no intention of doing anything for Robert. Without the pressure of trying to attain what was virtually an unattainable goal, she would not have spent long hours away from her son which had left him to his own devices. Without the obsession to save, save, save, she would have probably been able to afford to buy him a second-hand bicycle for his birthday and the whole incident would never have happened. The Corkish influence on her, even if it was of her own making, had been disastrous and the thought of that shadow now falling on Robert, together with the stigma of gossip, both of which could follow him through life if he stayed in Douglas, was too much to bear. The town where she had been born, had now become the scene of heartache and she just wanted to run away. To leave it all behind would be to release all the stress and strain. She talked to Robert and was surprised by his reaction.

'Can we do that?' he asked eagerly. 'Can we go away and never come back? Let's go soon, Mum.' His lips trembled, 'I can't face the birch.' He was a frightened little boy who had never been hit in his life and was terror-stricken at the thought of the stinging lash and the shame of exposed bare buttocks.

They had still heard nothing from the police, which meant that the Cowleys had not pressed charges, but to Grace, fleeing now seemed to be the answer to her despair. A new life would give her new strength because she still had a son to raise. She went to see Ellen again. Could they possibly just go, leave everything behind and get away from it all?

Ellen talked to her husband, and together they made a plan. Grace would hand in her notice at the shop then she and Robert would take the boat to Fleetwood, leaving Ellen to see to the sale of the house and furniture.

The little home that Grace had built such dreams around meant nothing to her now compared with the awful thing that had happened to Robert. All the effort in proving that she could raise John's son by herself was wasted because she had failed in the way that mattered most, in guiding his moral character and teaching self-discipline. It was Robert himself, even though he had always been at the heart of everything she had done, who had needed all her attention, but she had lost direction in her obsession with trying to live up to the Corkish name. They would make a new start and she would never make the same mistake again.

* * *

Ellen's husband arranged an early sailing and sooner than they had expected, and taking very little luggage, Grace and Robert were on the Irish Sea heading for the fishing port of Fleetwood in Lancashire. Neither of them had been on the ferry before and the boat seemed enormous once on board. Grace also had to face the alarming thought that she was taking her son on a voyage across the same sea that had taken his father. It was the first time she had been on the water since John had drowned, and although the sea was not rough, there was a grey sky which seemed to threaten her. Everyone who had grown up on the island knew that the sea was unpredictable, and she had to keep a tight control over the fear that knotted her stomach.

She tried to make sense of the last forty-eight hours when so much had needed to be done so quickly, and of the last two weeks when her world had fallen apart for a second time. Both of them were nervous about the journey, and they sat huddled together on a bench on the spray-wet deck, sheltered from the wind by the funnel stack, with the sea a shining path before them, taking them away from everything they knew.

Grace put her arm round her son. 'It's only across the water, Robert, we are not going very far away. It will be a new life for us, but we'll manage. I can find work in a shop or a hotel.'

'I can work as well, Mum,' said Robert. 'I'm big for my age, I can say I'm older.'

'No, you won't, Robert, you'll go to school. Learn as much as you can. It's what will give you the kind of future your father would have wanted for you.'

Robert knew only what he had heard from his mother about the father who had been lost at sea, but she had told him about the money put by for him before they left the island, because she felt he was now old enough to understand. They would need it to pay their way until they found their feet, she told him, but once Ellen had sold the house and the furniture, the money would be put back. Robert, used to scrimping and scraping, had been impressed.

* * *

Once safely docked at Fleetwood, they were told they could get a train to Blackpool, but they discovered the trams also ran there and were cheaper. They had heard a lot about Blackpool and the famous Tower that had opened there ten years ago, in 1894, and they were excited at the thought of seeing it for the first time.

The tram stopped opposite the Tower and they stood on the promenade gazing up at the big iron structure pointing way up into the sky, so very much higher than they had imagined. They had to crane their necks to see the top. Little cages were running up and down inside the girders and it made Grace feel dizzy to think of soaring to such a height.

Robert gasped. 'It's so big!' he said. 'What if it fell down?'

'Oh, it won't do that. We'll go and have a look inside one day, shall we? Once we've got ourselves sorted out.'

The promenade was busy, much busier than Douglas. With the country experiencing a booming economy Blackpool was attracting visitors from the mill towns by the trainload and noisy crowds streamed in both directions all about them. Grace had no idea which way to go. Further along the promenade, a pier stretched out over the sea. There were a lot of people gathered there so Grace decided they should head towards it. There was a large square opposite the pier and Grace could see a row of shops, all very busy, and she led the way towards them.

'I'm hungry, Mum.' Robert's stomach rumbled loudly.

There were several cafes, most already quite full, but they managed to find one where they were shown to a table shared with an older lady. Grace felt too tired to eat, a cup of tea was all she wanted, but Robert was famished, so she ordered plates of meat and potato pie and asked for a pot of tea to be brought straight away, to revive her.

'We'll have to start looking for somewhere to stay after this, even if it's only for one night.' She poured them both a cup of tea.

'Don't worry, Mum, we'll find somewhere.'

The smell of food had perked Robert up, and he looked round to see what other people had on their plates.

'I just wish we knew where to start looking, though.' Grace gave a little tired sigh.

The lady opposite them was preparing to leave and she watched as the waitress brought their food. 'Excuse me,' she said, 'but did I hear you mention looking for somewhere to stay?'

'Yes.' Grace looked up hopefully. 'Actually, it's lodgings we're after. We've just moved here so we're looking for somewhere for at least a few weeks.'

'Well, in that case, I might be able to help you. I know where two rooms have just come empty, and it's only a ten-minute walk from here. I live opposite so I can recommend the landlady. I can give you the address if you like.'

'Yes please. We don't know Blackpool at all, so we didn't know where to start looking.'

'Try here, then.' The woman wrote an address on the back of an envelope.

Grace looked down at the paper in her hand. MRS THOMAS. WESTHOLME. GEORGE STREET. 'How do we find it?'

'Walk straight on down this road,' The lady pointed out of the window. 'Take the second right and it's on the left. You'll see the street sign but you can always ask if you get stuck. I have to go back to work, or I would take you there myself. Good luck,' She moved away to pay her bill.

'Well, knowing that there are rooms available is certainly better than trudging round streets we don't know.' Grace had brightened at the possibility of finding accommodation. 'That lady seemed respectable, and at least we have made a start. It's worth a try.'

'I'll carry your bag, Mum.' Robert reached for it as they left the café. 'You must be tired.'

'No more than you.' His mother picked up the bag. 'Thank you, Robert, but I can manage. She said it was only a short walk, so it won't be long now. Let's just hope the rooms are still free when we get there.'

The food had cheered them both up, and after they had passed the railway station, the crowds thinned out and they felt less hustled.

'Do you think it's much further?' Robert was tired. They'd been up early that morning and the day seemed to be going on forever.

'It can't be far. We've been walking for nearly ten minutes now so we should be almost there – and look, here it is.' Grace pointed to the sign on a large terraced house.

All the houses looked respectable and neatly presented and Grace was hopeful when she looked up at Westholme. A paved path led to the front door and there was a small lawn to one side enclosed by a low brick wall over which dahlias peeped their brightly coloured heads.

Robert was doubtful. 'It looks a bit grand, Mum.'

'It's bigger than I was expecting,' Grace admitted. 'But now we're here we may as well see what the rooms are like and find out how much the rent is. I certainly like the look of it from the outside.' Grace rang the bell.

A dark-haired, middle-aged lady wearing a floral print dress, answered the door. 'Hello.'

'Mrs Thomas?'

'Yes, that's me.' Mrs Thomas's dark eyes flicked from Grace to Robert.

'My name is Mrs Corkish,' said Grace. 'And this is my son. We were given your address by a lady who said she lives opposite.'

'Oh yes.' Mrs Thomas smiled.

'She said you had two rooms to rent. We're looking for lodgings for a few weeks. We've just moved here.'

'That's right, I have. These rooms have only recently become available, just last week actually. I take lodgers not weekly visitors, so you've come to the right place. Come on in and I'll show them to you.' Mrs Thomas stepped back to invite them in. Grace and Robert followed her into a large lobby with a big oaken coat stand pressed against one wall. 'Leave your bags here,' she pointed to the coat stand, 'then come this way.'

A wide carpeted staircase led up two flights of stairs, and as they followed her up to the top floor, Grace had the sinking feeling that they were way out of their price range. This house had the air of well-kept comfort and there was sure to be a rent to reflect that.

They were shown into what was obviously a living room because it was dominated by a green plush sofa. A small table and two chairs were tucked in one of the recesses at the side of the chimney breast, while a built-in row of shelves, the top one fitted with a gas ring, filled the other. Although there were no curtains at the window and the small fireplace had an empty grate, the room had a welcome feel to it, but Grace's heart sank. Pleasant though this was, they did not need a sitting room, it was two bedrooms they wanted.

Mrs Thomas opened a connecting door to a smaller room. 'This is the bedroom.'

A made-up bed pushed against the wall, a large wardrobe, a small chest of drawers and a wooden chair filled the room.

Grace sighed. 'It's very nice, Mrs Thomas, but I'm afraid it's not what we are looking for. It's two bedrooms we need. We'll both be out during the day, so we really have no need for a living-room.'

'The rent is four shillings a week,' Mrs Thomas continued ignoring the negative reaction. 'Downstairs it's another shilling a week but this is cheaper because of the stairs. This last flight is a bit steep – some people can't manage them.'

Grace was surprised by the rent, she had expected more, but it was still only one bedroom. It wouldn't do.

'I'm afraid it's still two beds we need, Mrs Thomas. Thank you for showing us though.'

She glanced at Robert. He was standing by the window looking pale and tired. If he felt anything like she did, trudging the streets again was the last thing they needed. Mrs Thomas was eyeing up Robert.

'Your son is a big lad but I would think he is no more than ten. If he would share a bedroom, he can move into my grandson's room just below here. Jim's nine, a bit younger than your boy; he's used to sharing a room and he gets on with anybody.'

'Robert's nine as well.' Grace turned to her son to read his reaction to the suggestion, and he surprised her by nodding.

'Is that all right, Robert? Are you happy to share?'

'Yes, I don't mind.'

Grace thought quickly. Robert looked as though any bed, any floor in fact, would be welcome. They both desperately needed a good night's sleep, the house was clean and comfortable, the gas ring meant that they would be able to cook their own food, which would save money, and if things didn't work out, once she found a job they could always move.

'We'll take the rooms, Mrs Thomas. I have got the money to pay you until I find work, so you needn't worry about us not being able to pay the rent.'

'I ask for the rent in advance, paid weekly.' Mrs Thomas nodded and smiled. 'Oh, and I'm just washing the curtains for in here. I'll put them up later, then it will look more homely.'

Grace took five shillings from her purse and held them out.

'It will be another sixpence for your son, of course, for a child's half-share of a room.'

For a moment Grace was slightly put out, then she remembered the prices at the guesthouse where she had worked in Douglas and had to admit that this was, in fact, a fair charge. She handed over the required sixpence.

'Right then, I'll leave you to settle in, but when you are ready, come down to the kitchen, the door at the end of the hall passage, and I'll give you a nice cup of tea by the fire. You both look tired out.'

How nearly I misjudged her, thought Grace. She was a landlady, used to people coming and going and her manner was business-like, as it had to be, but there was kindness there too, something they both needed just now.

As soon as Mrs Thomas closed the door, Grace flopped down on the sofa and Robert went into the bedroom and flung himself, spread-eagled on the bed. They both rested silently for a few minutes.

'I think we've done the right thing,' Grace called through the door. 'But if you don't get on with – what's his name, Jim? – we can always leave. At least we've got somewhere for tonight.'

'I like it,' Robert called back. 'I like being right up at the top of the house. Look how far down the street seems. Just imagine what it's like at the top of Blackpool Tower. I bet that's scary.'

Grace laughed. If Robert felt like this then it made everything so much easier. All they had to do now was meet Jim and see how the boys got on.

They went downstairs to collect their bags and bring them back to what was now their room. Grace shook out their clothes, spreading her skirt and a dress over the bed to get rid of the creases. She put their few personal things, brush and comb, soap, flannel and a pair of towels, on top of the chest of drawers alongside a wash bowl and a large jug of water.

'We'll keep all your clothes in here,' she told Robert. 'You'll only be going downstairs to sleep so you'll be up here with me most of the time.'

It didn't take long to put everything away, and after they had washed their hands and faces and tidied their hair, they went down to the big kitchen and knocked on the door.

Mrs Thomas was ironing. 'Come in, I'm just doing your curtains.' She stood the iron on its end and went across to the stove where the kettle was simmering. 'I'll just go through the routine.' she said, handing them their tea. 'I've got four other lodgers so you will be sharing the bathroom.'

Bathroom! Grace and Robert looked at each other, pleased. This was luxury. They had never had a bathroom before.

'If you want to do your own washing, you'll have to see me. I wash for my other lodgers so you'd have to fit in with that, or I can do it for you, just let me know.'

'What about water, Mrs Thomas? I didn't see a tap. Where do we get water for the kettle or to drink?'

'Oh, you can come in here any time for that.' Mrs Thomas obviously didn't see any problem, but now Grace understood why the rent was reasonable. Two flights of stairs to climb every time they needed water- it was a good job she was strong. They would have to buy a very big jug as soon as they could to save on trips.

'Ah, here comes Jim now.' Mrs Thomas looked out of the window as a young boy opened the back gate and walked up the yard. He came into the kitchen and glanced across at Grace and Robert then sat down at the table, obviously used to having different people around the house.

'Jim, this is Robert, he's going to share your room. He's nine as well so it'll be nice having someone of your own age, won't it?'

Grace saw a small curly-haired boy rather warily eyeing the boy who was a good head and shoulders taller than himself, but Robert was grinning at him, so Jim grinned back.

'Why don't you take Robert to your room and show him where the bathroom is at the same time?' said Mrs Thomas. After they had left the room, she added, 'They'll get on like a house on fire, I can tell. Now, let me tell you about our shops. If you go down to the next corner, we have a nice little parade of local shops. We have a butcher's, a baker's, a green-grocers, a newspaper shop, a hairdresser's, and a fish and chip shop.' Then, obviously thinking to impress, she added, 'We've even got a bicycle shop.' But Grace froze at the mention of the bicycle shop. She had almost lost the sense of doom that had hung over her since Robert's escapade but now it returned with a sickening thump, as though a lead weight had suddenly been dropped in her stomach. She got up quickly.

'Thank you for the tea, I was ready for it after such a long day. I'll find Robert and then we'll go and do some shopping.'

'You'll need your keys then.' Mrs Thomas took the two keys from the board behind her. 'You can come and go as you please, of course, but this is a quiet house and we ask you to respect that.'

'We will.' A quiet house was just what Grace wanted. 'We won't be any trouble, Mrs Thomas, I can assure you.'

Mrs Thomas smiled. 'I knew that, Mrs Corkish, as soon as I saw you. You get a sense for these things when you've been a landlady for any length of time and I've been one for over twenty years.'

Grace's stomach was still quivering and all she wanted to do was crawl into bed, but first there was shopping to be done, something which would help to lift the dark mood that had been triggered by an innocent remark.

CHAPTER THIRTEEN

TWO weeks later, Grace came home from the shops and found a letter waiting for her. She recognised Ellen's handwriting. Robert was not home from school yet, and she climbed the stairs quickly, glad to be able to read whatever the letter contained without him seeing any reaction she might have.

As soon as she could she had written to her sister, sending her new address and asking about the house sale. Ellen had replied that the house was about to be sold, and that she had managed to get a reasonable price for most of the furniture, especially the cradle, and as soon as Grace had a savings account, the money would be paid into it. They were still waiting to hear from the police. Ellen had given them her own address for a contact with Grace, but she had heard nothing. That had been last month so this second letter, not sent in reply to one from Grace, must have the news she was dreading. Her fingers trembled as she opened it.

Ellen's writing was spidery and the large words seemed to float on the page as Grace's eyes filled with tears, and she had to brush a hand across her eyes before she could read.

Dear Sister,

You will be glad to know that the Cowleys never intended to bring any charges, so there will be no court case. When they heard you had gone away (I've not told anyone where you are) they were very sorry it had come to that and said they didn't want to make it any worse for you. They had just hoped the fright would teach Robert a lesson, but it's a pity they didn't think of telling us that sooner. I know you will be relieved to hear this news and hope that you will be able to sleep better now. The house has sold and all the money is waiting for you when you send me your bank details. Tom is dealing with it, he's much better at this sort of thing than I am. I hope this letter finds you both in good health as is your loving sister, Ellen.

Grace leaned back on the sofa, her shoulders sagged and her body sank into the cushions. She stopped trembling. Relief poured through her like a great wave draining her of physical power and she sat there unable to move. She was still there when Robert came home.

'What's for tea?' he asked as he took off his boots.

Grace stirred and regarded her son with mixed emotions. If only he hadn't taken the bicycle in the first place, he must have known it was wrong. The consequences had been dire, a complete upheaval triggered by one thoughtless act. Irritation pricked at her, but as he looked up when she didn't answer, she saw the fair hair, the blue, blue eyes and was overwhelmed with protective love. She knew she would kill for him if needed. This is how John had looked as a boy, she remembered, that time he had arranged for the little cart. In this son, who was so very much like him, she still had a part of John, and she would make sure he grew up to be a good man like his father.

Looking back, she thought again of how she had allowed a taxing sense of guilt and overwhelming responsibility to engulf her, leading her to set her sights on the wrong target. It had been at a cost, and the price had been too high because she had been unfair to herself in assuming that guilt. All she and John had done was to marry and have a much-loved child. Why should there have been a price to pay for that? The hope that, in time, they would be accepted back into the Corkish family, had ended with John's death, and yet she had still carried on paying. Ellen's letter now freed her of any ties to Douglas and therefore to that family. She would let go of the negative emotions swirling round her, that had been holding her back, and she and Robert would move on unfettered. Now she knew where her priorities really lay. She stood up.

'Well, we *were* having stew, but I'm afraid it's not even started yet, so, I'll tell you what, why don't we have fish and chips instead?'

'Fish and chips, yes please!' Robert's face lit up at the treat, not one that often came his way, and he didn't ask why.

Grace decided to wait until they had eaten before telling him the good news. She didn't want him to think of it as a celebration because there were things that needed to be said before they could this behind them, but for now, they would enjoy the treat.

* * *

Once Robert had settled into his new school, Grace began to look for work. At first, she tried to find employment as a chambermaid in a hotel. It would mean working mornings, fitting in with her decision to be there for Robert as much as she could, but although she made enquiries at several of the Promenade hotels, she was told by all of them that she needed experience.

She tried the boarding houses next, but it was late in the season and there were no vacancies. It was while she was walking down one of the town centre roads, lined on each side by boarding houses, that she noticed a sign in the ground floor window of a detached building.

VACANCY FOR AN OFFICE WORKER. APPLY WITHIN, it read, followed by the name of the firm. There was no mention of specific skills and Grace hesitated for quite a while, mentally going over the answers she could honestly give if she was asked whether she had any office experience. She thought about her work at the drapers and decided that if she described the work that she had done there, writing out the invoices and receipts, without actually calling it office work, it wouldn't be untrue.

The brass plate bearing the name of the company told her this was an insurance firm. It would be a good job if she could get it, that was if she even dared to walk through the door.

She boosted her courage. Surely anyone who could buy a house, then pack up and move to Lancashire to start a new life, could take finding a job in her stride. Grace knew she was a good worker, but she was also discovering that finding work was not as easy as she had hoped, and her confidence was slipping. Yet one way or another she simply had to find a job. Taking a deep breath, she climbed the steps and walked through the door into a glassed reception area. A young woman sat facing her.

'May I help you?'

'I've come about the vacancy.'

'Oh.' The receptionist regarded her for a moment. 'Please wait here.'

Grace stood nervously while the girl went through to an inner office, reappearing almost instantly with an elderly gentleman, neatly suited and wearing glasses.

'Good morning,' he said pleasantly, 'I'm Mr Hall. I understand you've come about the vacancy?'

'Yes, I saw the notice in the window.'

'Please come through to my office.'

He held the door open for her, indicated a chair, and seated himself at his desk.

'May I ask your name?' He pulled forward a pad of paper.

Grace wasn't sure whether to say Mrs Corkish or Grace Corkish, and in the end, she said, 'Mrs Grace Corkish.'

'Can you tell me something about yourself, Mrs Corkish? Where you have worked before, for instance, and what experience you have?'

Grace looked down at her hands. They were gripped together making a single fist, and she deliberately unclenched them and spread her fingers out on her knees and took a deep breath. She needed to be calm.

'I've only recently moved to Blackpool,' she said. 'I am from the Isle of Man and I am a widow with a young son. I worked in a drapers' shop in Douglas for nine years, and I also had a part-time job in a hotel there.' That had sounded all right. She hadn't been dishonest with any of that.

'Did you work in the office in these jobs?' Mr Hall asked, getting straight to the point.

'In the hotel I worked as a waitress in the evenings, and just for the season, but at the drapers I did a variety of duties.' She crossed her fingers – this was the tricky bit. 'I wrote receipts and prepared invoices, general work really.'

'You have good writing skills then?' Mr Hall made a note on his pad. 'Have you done any typing?'

Grace cast about for a noncommittal reply and found none. 'No, I haven't. I'm very good at picking things up, though. If I were shown I would learn very quickly.'

He made another note and looked up. 'You've worked in a hotel and a shop, so you are used to dealing with people. How did you get on with them?'

Grace felt on safer ground. She knew she had been popular, both at the shop and at the hotel, and she had developed a confident way of speaking, with more formality than her normal speech at home, enabling her to communicate easily with everyone. She could answer this one without any subterfuge.

'Talking to the customers was an important part of both jobs, and I always really enjoyed it.' She needed to make a good impression, so she added, 'I was the senior assistant at the shop, and I trained the new girls. The hotel offered me permanent work but as I already had my job at the shop I had to refuse, but they were obviously satisfied with me.'

'May I ask why you left the Isle of Man?'

This was another direct question. She hesitated and looked down at her hands – they were clenched again. She looked up at Mr Hall and he must have noticed her unease.

'If you can assure me that it was for, say, personal reasons and not for anything untoward...' he suggested, giving her an opening.

Grace thought quickly. No charges had been brought so it was a clean slate. She had no need to tell this man anything about the last month, especially since they had come here to leave all the past behind them, and she needed the job.

'It was for personal reasons,' she said quietly. 'I am a widow as I said, and I want to give my son a new life. There are more opportunities here on the mainland. I've moved here for his sake.' That was quite true. The whole move had been because of Robert.

'The job is in our Reception office. It's the one Miss Pearson is doing at the moment. It means welcoming clients, dealing with the post, doing the filing and helping out with the typing.'

Grace mentally ticked off three out of four and waited to see what he would say next. He studied his notes.

'Miss Pearson will be able to show you our filing system and how to deal with the post, but what about typing? You say you have not done any.'

'I'm afraid not but I'm very willing to learn.'

'It's mainly typing letters of acknowledgement and addresses on the envelopes, but you would be required to assist my secretary at times. I'm afraid Miss Pearson won't have time to teach you to type before she leaves us. She is getting married and we have been finding it hard to replace her.' He paused. 'Would you be prepared to take typing lessons?'

Grace was taken aback. Lessons cost money and since it would have to be at night school, that would mean leaving Robert alone in the evenings, even if only for a few weeks.

'I'm not sure I could afford lessons.' She knew she was reducing her chances.

'We haven't talked about money yet of course. We pay seven shillings and sixpence a week for a trial month and then, if everything is satisfactory, ten shillings. The hours are from half-past eight to half-past five. Saturday is a half day.'

He looked at her for a moment.

'I think you will represent our firm very well in Reception, Mrs Corkish. You will be the first impression our clients have of us and it's important that we get it right, so I am prepared to offer you the post but on two conditions. First, I will require testimonials from the two places where you have worked, and second, I would need you to learn to type. The ten shillings will depend on your ability to take on typing work.'

He waited for Grace to reply. Her throat had gone dry and she swallowed.

'Thank you, Mr Hall. I can assure you I will do my best.'

'I hope so, Mrs Corkish.' He stood to show her out. 'Will you please leave your name and address with Miss Pearson, also the names and addresses of the persons we will need to contact in Douglas. As soon as I receive the testimonials, subject to them being satisfactory, I will write to you confirming your appointment and giving you the starting date. Good morning.'

He didn't offer to shake hands, but he held the door for her to leave his office.

She'd done it, she'd got a job and a good one at that. She couldn't wait to get home and tell Robert.

Two weeks later she received a letter telling her the job was hers and that she was to start on the following Monday. Bearing in mind what Mr Hall had said, she had made enquiries about typing lessons and had already enrolled at night-school and had her first lesson. As she had thought, she found it easy to manipulate the keys and she copied the keyboard sequence on to a piece of paper so that she could study it at home. Things were looking up at last.

She had sent her bank details to Ellen but the money from the sale had not yet arrived and she was worried about the money she was taking from Robert's inheritance. Looking back over the last couple of months, Grace could hardly believe how much her life, and consequently she herself, had changed. From somewhere she had found the deep strength needed to take the decisions she had had to make, in order to protect her son. He was ten now and wanting to leave school. Because of his tall, strong build, he felt he was ready to start work, and indeed, some children did leave at that age, but Grace hoped to keep him in school until he was fourteen. Robert was a reluctant scholar though. He could read well enough and he could manage arithmetic, but writing was a chore to him, possibly due to his thick fingers. The pen often deposited a large blot on his paper, and he was always having a ruler laid across his knuckles by the teacher. Robert did not like her. Miss Ratcliffe was a strict lady in her fifties and, having met her when she took Robert to join the school, Grace did not like her either. She had been spoken to as though she was a pupil herself, and there had been no warmth in the woman's eyes.

'We all call her, Miss Ratbag,' said Robert. 'Not to her face, though.'

'I should hope not!' Grace turned her head away to hide the smile she could not keep from her face. Children could be very knowing. Perhaps next year she might start thinking about an apprenticeship for him, but first she needed to settle into her new job and gain her typing certificate. At the moment she had quite enough on her plate.

* * *

Miss Pearson greeted her on her first morning and introduced her to some of the other staff in the main office. 'This is Miss Watson, Mr Hall's secretary.' Grace received a brief nod. 'And this is Mr Collins, the Chief Clerk.' This time she was offered a warm handshake. 'And this is Miss Price, our Accounts Clerk.'

Grace stared. She knew that face, it was the lady from the café.

'Oh hello, I know you, don't I? You are the lady who told me about Mrs Thomas. What a coincidence.'

Miss Price nodded her head and smiled. 'I thought I recognised you when I saw you come in for your interview. How are you settling in? I heard you had taken the rooms.'

'Very well, thank you–' Grace began, but before she could say any more Miss Watson's cool voice cut in, 'When you are ready, Mrs Corkish, there is work to be done.'

Miss Pearson raised her eyebrows and led the way into Reception.

By the time Miss Pearson left at the end of the week Grace had mastered the filing system, was already handling the post and greeting visitors, and making good progress with her typing at night-school. She was determined to make a good impression.

The money arrived from Tom, and to Grace's relief the amount the taken from the inheritance was safely replaced. Although they were managing well on the money she earned, Grace was finding old habits die hard and they were still living quite frugally. They had still not been to the Tower, as Robert sometimes reminded her.

Unexpectedly, Mrs Thomas shattered the peace. She told Grace that she needed the bed Robert was using.

'My son Harry is coming back. He's been working in Liverpool but now the job's come to an end and he's moving back. He's a widower, is Harry, so he'll be living with me. I'm sorry, but I have no choice. All my rooms are taken, as you know.'

Grace was dismayed. 'When is he coming back?'

'On Friday next week.'

'So, we will have to start looking for somewhere else then?'

'Well, it's up to you,' Mrs Thomas answered, 'But I'll tell you what I could do. If you like I can take the sofa out of your sitting room and put a small bed in its place. You'd still have the two chairs to sit on. I'd be very sorry to see you go.'

Grace considered this. They had both enjoyed sprawling out in the evenings in front of the fire, Grace hearing Robert read and listening to his stories about his day at school and his battles with the dreaded teacher. They would miss that sofa, but if it saved her having to look for other rooms it might be the best way. It was nearing Christmas and the colder weather had already arrived, now was not a good time to be upheaving themselves. Besides, they had both begun to feel at home here. Mrs Thomas was a reliable presence, someone who was becoming a friend as well as a landlady, and at the moment, when Grace was making every effort to adapt to a new life, she needed the comfort of this house to help her sustain her energy.

'We'd both be sorry to go too. We'd much rather stay so, yes please.' The frugal side of Grace prompted her to add, 'And I shall be glad to save the extra sixpence.'

'Well, of course,' Mrs Thomas answered rather stiffly. 'Your rent will be just the four shillings. I'll have the bed moved in next weekend.'

Grace realised she had piqued her landlady and tried to placate her. 'I think Robert will miss Jim. They get on so well together, don't they?'

'Well, Robert's only moving out of the bedroom – not out of the house!'

* * *

Harry moved back to his mother's and Grace and Robert settled into their new sleeping arrangement. Grace met

Harry when she went down to the kitchen to fill the big water jug. She took a good look at the man who had disrupted their life merely by coming home to his son and mother. The faint resentment she had felt when she had first been told he would need the room, disappeared when she found herself looking at an adult version of Jim. He was washing his hands at the kitchen sink, but hurriedly swilled them and moved out of the way when he saw Grace with her jug.

'Sorry, I'm in your way,' he said, picking up a towel. 'You must be Robert's mother?'

'Yes, that's right, and I suppose you are Jim's father – Harry?'

'Yes. I'm sorry Robert had to move out of the room. Are you all right up there?'

'Oh yes, we're fine.' Grace assured him. 'Is it nice to be home again? You must be pleased to be back with Jim.'

Harry nodded. 'Yes, I missed him, but I knew he was all right with my Mum looking after him. He seems to have grown about six inches while I was away.'

'They shoot up at that age,' Grace agreed. 'One day they are little boys and the next they are young men.'

'That's true. Your Robert's a grand lad.'

'So is your Jim,' Grace countered swiftly. 'They have become really good pals.'

'I hope we will all be good friends,' Harry smiled.

Grace returned the smile, filled her jug and left the kitchen.

It was usually on Sundays when she saw Harry. They passed on the stairs or met in the kitchen, and occasionally sat at the kitchen table having a cup of tea with Mrs Thomas, but one Sunday Harry followed her as she was about to go up the stairs. Grace was aware that he was there and was irritated. They were friendly enough, but if Harry was about to try to move their relationship on a bit further, Grace didn't want to know. She would have to rebuff him and she didn't want to spoil the harmony they had established.

'Can I talk to you, Grace?' he called.

Trying not to show her irritation, Grace turned to face him.

'It's about Robert,' he said, sending irritation flying. Had something happened? The familiar dread tightened her stomach. She waited for whatever he had to say.

'He talks to me a lot when he's with Jim and he's been telling me he wants to leave school. He says you are thinking of an apprenticeship for him – is that right?'

Relief swept the tension away. 'I had thought about it, yes, but not until next year perhaps. Why?'

'I like Robert, he's a good lad and if you were interested, I'd be glad to take him on as an apprentice. I've got two men working for me, and we need a lad. He'd get a good training.'

'But what about Jim?' asked Grace. 'He's the same age as Robert, there are only a few months between them, won't you be taking him on?'

Harry looked embarrassed. 'Well, the thing is, Jim's a very bright scholar and his teacher wants him to sit the scholarship for the grammar school. It's what he wants to do and I'm going to let him try for it. He says he wants to be a doctor, though I don't know where he got that from. Robert has said he doesn't want to do anything like that. He says he wants to work with his hands. I'm just going by what he said.'

'I see. I know Robert doesn't like school,' admitted Grace. 'But I was hoping he would stay on for another year at least.' She paused and thought about what Harry had said.

'Have you talked to Robert about this?' she asked.

'Oh no, I wouldn't do that without speaking to you first,' said Harry.

Grace smiled. She liked Harry. He was a good man and he was right they had all become good pals.

'Can I think about it and talk to Robert?' she asked. 'It's not what I had in mind just yet, but I can see it would be a good opportunity for him. Robert's not likely to get a scholarship, so perhaps it is time to decide what he is going to do.'

'Just let me know when you decide.' Harry turned to go back to the kitchen.

Grace climbed the stairs with a slight flush to her cheeks, embarrassed by her thoughts. So much for the sin of pride! Fancy thinking Harry was going to ask you out. She was laughing to herself as she entered their room.

Robert was excited when she told him what Harry had offered and, because there was not a lot of building work on in the cold months of January and February, it was arranged for Robert to leave school at Easter. Harry wanted to wait until work began on a big house that was being built at Thornton, a village to the north of Blackpool, where he had the plaster and cement contract.

At work, Grace was puzzled that she had yet to be given the typing she hoped for. She had shown her certificate to Mr Hall after she had completed her course and he had congratulated her, so she had expected to be assisting Miss Watson by now, especially since she was being paid the ten shillings she had been promised. She often found herself with spare time on her hands and was keen to be more involved in the firm's work. Grace didn't have a lot of contact with Miss Price because apart from discussing office business, the older lady didn't indulge in chitchat. She was a serious lady in her fifties who always wore grey, which matched her hair and made her look like a shadow.

Miss Watson was quite different. She was a very striking looking woman with thick, curly auburn hair which she usually wore coiled in a bun at the nape of her neck. She had green eyes and dark lashes. Grace thought her beauty was wasted in an office. It was difficult to know how old she was, she could have been thirty or she could have been forty, but she had certainly been with the firm for quite a long time. It was perhaps because of this that she took a rather superior attitude to Grace, not in a hostile way, she was perfectly civil, occasionally even bordering on friendly, but she always made Grace aware that she must not overstep the mark.

CHAPTER FOURTEEN

MR Hall stopped by the Reception desk most days, to check the appointments book. He was a quietly-mannered man, a gentleman, and everyone liked him. It was his firm, started and built up by him. In his office was a rowing oar mounted on the wall behind his desk, which Grace glanced at when she took in his tea or coffee. There was some wording below it which she never had time to read because, obeying Miss Watson's instructions, she always left the room as soon as she had put down the tray.

Shortly before Easter, as she set Mr Hall's coffee down on his desk, he looked up and spoke to her. 'Are you looking forward to your Easter break, Mrs Corkish?'

'Yes and no,' she replied. 'My son leaves school at Easter and starts an apprenticeship. It will be very strange to think of him as a working man.'

'What kind of an apprenticeship?' Mr Hall seemed interested.

'He's going to be a plasterer.'

'It's a good trade. Will he be leaving home?'

'Oh no, he is too young to leave home. He will be apprenticed to my landlady's son, a master plasterer with his own firm.'

'Apprenticed to your landlady's son? He lives in the same house as you, then?'

- 135 -

'Yes, that's why Robert won't need to move away.' She was stopped from speaking further by Miss Watson entering the room with letters for Mr Hall to sign. She looked at Grace, nodding slightly towards the door. Grace took the hint and left.

Encouraged by the conversation with her boss, Grace decided to look for a chance to ask him about the typing. When she took in his tea a few days later he looked up as she entered, and she seized the opportunity. 'May I have a word, Mr Hall?'

'Yes, of course.' He gestured to a chair at the other side of his desk. 'Please sit down.'

Grace sat and immediately wished she hadn't. She hadn't wanted to be sitting down, as if at an interview, she'd intended to broach the subject quickly, in a bright, confident manner before she lost her nerve. Now, sitting eye to eye, she felt at a disadvantage and wondered how to begin.

'What was it you wanted a word about?'

'I was wondering about the typing you mentioned at my interview,' she began. 'I have my typing certificate now, as you know, and I was hoping to be given more work to do. I know that I can...'

'But you have been given extra work by Miss Watson surely?' Mr Hall interrupted her. 'After you showed me your certificate, I had a word with her.'

Grace was taken aback. She had certainly not been given any typing.

'Erm, no.' How she could answer this without putting Miss Watson in an awkward position? 'So far, I have only been typing the envelopes, I've not been given any other work – yet.' she added, hoping she wasn't causing trouble.

Mr Hall sat back with a sudden sharp movement. He swivelled his chair first one way and then the other; he picked up his pen then put it down again, clearly agitated. It was a moment before he spoke, but when he did his voice was calm.

'Leave it with me, Mrs Corkish. I'll have another word with Miss Watson. There has obviously been a misunderstanding. I encouraged you to take tuition with the promise of extra typing work, and I intend to keep that promise.'

Later that day, Miss Watson brought her two letters to type. They were standard replies, simple acknowledgements of enquiries, and at the end of the day, she had been given four more to type. Miss Watson had given no indication of what had gone on between her and her boss, and Grace was happy to leave it at that.

The next morning, Miss Watson sent a message to say she was unwell and would not be at the office that day. Grace took the note to Mr Hall, who read it then put it in his desk drawer.

'Would you be able to cover her work for today, Mrs Corkish? Miss Price will help you. She has stood in for us on previous occasions. Do you think you can manage?'

'Yes, of course.' Grace was eager to show what she could do.

Miss Price proved to be very efficient. She told Grace what to do and answered all her queries in such a clear, precise way that it was obvious she had the job at her fingertips, and at the end of the day, Grace thanked her for all the help she had been given. 'I've learned more today than I have in all the weeks I have been here.'

Miss Price paused for a moment then closed the office door.

'Mrs Corkish, there's something I feel I must say.' She paused again. 'I know you must have been puzzled by Miss

Watson's abrupt attitude at times. She has been here for many years now, but so have I. I see what goes on, even if I don't say a great deal, and I feel I must warn you. I've noticed that Miss Watson seems to be preventing you from moving forward in your job. Sometimes she has been at great pains to make sure that there is as little contact as possible between you and Mr Hall, as if she is deliberately preventing you from taking on more responsibility, but you mustn't let her hold you back. You must watch out for yourself.'

'Oh!' Grace couldn't think of anything else to say. She didn't want to become involved in office gossip.

Miss Price seemed to sense this because she added, 'Of course I speak in the strictest confidence, you understand.'

'Yes certainly.'

Grace was confused. Miss Price obviously felt strongly enough about Miss Watson's behaviour to feel the need to warn her, but what was the point? What on earth was she supposed to do? She could hardly confront Miss Watson when she had been warned in confidence, so she decided it would be best to leave well alone until there was a need to do otherwise.

A few days later, as she stayed behind to reorganise one of the files, Mr. Hall popped his head round the door and looked round the office. 'Has Miss Watson left?' he asked.

'Yes, about five minutes ago – can I help?'

'I have two urgent letters which must catch tonight's post. Do you think you could type them for me? I'm afraid it means keeping you late.'

'Yes of course, and it doesn't matter about keeping me, I have already told my son I will be back a bit later tonight.'

Grace was pleased to have the opportunity to show what she could do and took great care to produce two perfectly typed letters. Mr Hall signed them and offered her a ride home to make up for delaying her.

'I shall be going in your direction anyway, to drop the letters at the Post Office. We mustn't keep your son waiting any longer than necessary.'

Grace felt rather nervous about accepting a ride in his car, especially since it would be the first time that she had ever ridden in one, but it would certainly mean she would be home sooner. When she first climbed in, she sat upright, keeping her back stiff, but the leather seats were soft and comfortable, the car smelled pleasantly of leather and polish and Mr Hall chatted as he drove, so she began to relax and enjoy the luxury. He asked how she and her son were getting on with their new life in Blackpool, but when he went on to ask if she missed her old life in the Isle of Man, to her horror Grace found herself bursting into tears. He immediately drew in at the side of the road, clearly distressed at upsetting her.

'I'm so sorry.' Grace dabbed her eyes, making an effort to pull herself together. 'I didn't mean to do this.'

'It's my fault for prying into your personal life, Mrs Corkish. I have obviously triggered unhappy memories for you.' He patted her arm gently.

His kindness brought another flood of tears, and before she could stop herself Grace began to tell him all about John and the treatment they had received from his family. Even as she was letting the words spill out, she was appalled at her sudden outburst of emotion and the unstoppable way in which she was telling someone, who was to a certain extent a stranger, all about her private life.

Mr Hall sat quietly and let her sob her way through her story. Finally, the spate ebbed away and Grace sat there, drained. After a moment he started the engine again. 'Let's take the long way around, shall we? You will be able to face your son with a smile on your face by then.'

Grace turned and began to speak but he stopped her. 'No, don't say anything, Mrs Corkish. What needed to be said has been said, and it stays in this car. You have my word. Please do not feel embarrassed or worry about it any further.'

Grace knew that he would keep his word.

A few days later he opened his door. 'Could you come into my office please, Mrs Corkish?'

He had gone back to his desk by the time Grace looked up from her work, and as she entered, he stood up and walked over to the window.

'Would you close the door please?' he said without turning around.

Grace closed it quietly and waited. When he turned to face her, she could tell he was about to say something important, and she tried frantically to think whether she had done anything wrong. Had she been too forward with that outburst in the car? She had felt ashamed, afterwards, by such a lack of self-control, and he had told her to forget about it. But perhaps he could not. She couldn't read the look on his face and stood there nervously waiting. He didn't ask her to sit down and he himself, remained standing.

'What I am going to say may surprise you.' he began. 'After you spoke to me about the typing the other day, I thought long and hard about the situation. I had given Miss Watson very definite instructions to delegate some of the work to you, she could not have misunderstood. I'm afraid that when I spoke to her it became apparent that she has been harbouring some resentment towards you.'

Grace was shocked. She had given the older woman no cause to do so, but this appeared to confirm what Miss Price had been trying to warn her about.

'On the other hand,' he went on, and there was an uncertain look on his face, 'I have been developing quite an attachment towards you.' He hesitated when he saw the startled look on Grace's face, then he rallied and hurried on.

'I have been quite concerned for you since our talk in the car, and I've thought about it a lot. I have been quite lonely since my wife died and I have been looking for a suitable companion for some time now, someone to share the comfort of my home. I know I am a lot older than you, my dear, and I hope I am not being too presumptuous, but I have been thinking very carefully and I would like to make you a proposal of marriage.'

Grace gasped and grabbed the back of the chair in front of her with both hands.

'Let me explain. I am offering you and your son a comfortable home in return for companionship. Since you told me of your experience in the Isle of Man, I have been unable to stop thinking about the injustice you had to face. You were not treated as you ought to have been, and certainly not in the way you deserved. I know you have found life hard and what I am offering could make things so much easier for you both, as well as making life more pleasant for myself. I hope you will seriously consider what I have said, even though I have plainly shocked you.'

Grace stared at him, dumbfounded. She was more than shocked, she was in a state of total disbelief, and completely unable to speak. She could see he was waiting for a reply of some sort but her head was spinning and she was holding her breath. No words would come.

Mr Hall, her sedate, elderly boss, was asking *her*, his receptionist, to marry him. Her heart raced and her stomach quivered with queasiness.

'Take all the time you need.' he said. 'I know this has been very sudden, but please consider it carefully. I have a large house and you would be able to have all the privacy you wished. You would have security and I would do everything I could to make you happy. Think of the difference it would make to your life, and of course to mine. I hope you can see how it will benefit us both. It is a big decision to have to make I know. As I said, please take your time, then perhaps we can talk again, when you are ready.'

Grace let go of the chair and swayed dizzily as she turned to leave the room. She still couldn't speak. How she managed to get back to her office she didn't know. Her stomach was still churning as she walked home that evening. There was no one she could talk to. Ellen was too far away, and it didn't seem right to discuss something so confidential with Mrs Thomas. Grace had always made her own decisions, but this time she badly needed some advice. She didn't know where to begin. In one of her more friendly moments, Miss Watson had mentioned a large house and servants, so she knew vaguely what her employer was offering. She couldn't help but think of the enormous difference it would make to her life, something Mr Hall himself had been at pains to point out to her as a deciding factor. He was a kind man, the experience in the car had shown her that, so she had no fear of him, yet she had no love for either. How could she? He was old enough to be her father. Then she remembered that he had said he was offering marriage and security in exchange for companionship, and that made a difference. It meant he was not expecting a traditional marriage. In that case, was marriage necessary? The more she thought about this, the more she realised that it probably was. Mr

Hall's gentlemanly code of conduct would not allow him to compromise the reputation of a young woman, who was not a servant, by allowing her to live in the same house, even though there were already other people living there. Her heart softened. She would be safe with this man. All she had to do now, was be sure that she would not be using him for her own purposes. The thought of someone else taking over some of her responsibilities was tempting in the extreme. Even though they were managing to live a decent life now, she still felt committed to do more for Robert, and to be honest, if she looked into the future, all she could see was a long hard grind ahead. Weighing her security against loving companionship – was it enough? Mr Hall obviously thought so. She went to bed still undecided.

That night, in bed, she thought the conversation through again and again, seeking guidance, seeking an answer, and suddenly it came. If she was wrestling so hard with his proposal it meant that she was certainly considering it as a possibility, otherwise she would already have rejected it out of hand. She liked him, everyone at the office did, and by specifying a loving companionship, he was telling her he did not expect her to be a wife in the true sense of the word. Remembering the uncertain look on his face, she knew what it must have cost him to propose to her like that. He had put his dignity in her hands. She would keep it safe.

No man could ever replace John, of that she was sure. Her heart ached as she thought of those wonderful days together in the little cottage at the foot of the cliffs. She had wanted no other husband after John, had wanted no other hands to touch her body. A marriage such as this would leave all those unspoilt memories safely locked away, bitter-sweet memories that filled her eyes with tears. She turned over in bed, pulled the blanket up under her chin and, drawing up her knees in a throwback to childhood, rocked herself to sleep.

* * *

In the darkness she found him – he was here, he had come back! Joy sang in all her senses as she welcomed him to her arms, feeling his weight pressing against her stomach and breasts, smelling the tang of the sea as damp skin stuck to damp skin, tasting his cold salty lips, looking into his water brimmed blue eyes, hearing his long sigh as she clung to him, laughing and sobbing, delirious with happiness at the miracle of having him back.

Oh John, John, you've come back to me.

Her fingers roamed over all those well remembered places, eagerly tracing the square jaw to find his lips, touching the scar on his shoulder from a childhood accident, stroking his strong, muscular back. Her beloved John had come back, he was here.

She tried to pull his arms more tightly around her, but as she reached out, he slipped through her hands and she couldn't hold him, he was slithering and sliding away from her, she was losing him. She clutched frantically for the body she had held only a moment ago, but a sudden heaviness pressed hard on her throat, choking her, and she couldn't breathe. Gasping for air she twisted on to her side, grabbing and pulling as she tried to move the strangling weight round her throat, crying out in panic as a last frantic jerk finally freed her and she sat up dazed, the echo of that last desperate cry ringing inside her head. Had she called out loud? Had anyone heard? She strained to listen for sounds, but all she could hear was her own rasping as she dragged air back into her lungs. Wincing at the grinding emptiness in her loins, she stared into the darkness. John was gone. It was all over.

Her hands were still gripping the bed shawl that had twisted itself round her neck as she had reached for John, and screwing it up into a ball, she pushed it hard against her stomach to take away the dull ache, but she couldn't ease the agony of losing her beloved husband yet again. There had been many times over the years when she had missed John, but never before had she dreamed of, and actually recaptured, the excitement that had been part of their lovemaking. If only she had not woken before she had been able to relive, even in dream, the thrill of fulfilment. It seemed desire was still alive in her, perhaps more passionate for having lain dormant for so long. For Grace, the act of sex had never been just an animal instinct. She had needed to love wholeheartedly before giving herself to John and her passion had only been awakened now because the thought of a new marriage had triggered this vivid memory of her husband.

All her energy was sapped. She felt completely drained and overwhelmed by the fire that had been lit and the searing pain of coming back to a world without John. Burying her face in the pillow she curled up and wept. The first pale light of dawn glimmered through a chink in the curtains and slanted a faint grey stripe across the counterpane, before she fell into an exhausted sleep.

Both Robert and Mrs Thomas noticed how pale she was that morning.

'Are you ill, Mrs Corkish?' Mrs Thomas eyed her anxiously as Grace filled her water jug in the kitchen. Grace knew she looked hollow-eyed and washed out.

'It's just a bad headache. I'll be all right after a cup of tea.'

'You will be better after something to eat as well as a cup of tea.'

'I'm making porridge.' Grace tried to divert Mrs Thomas's concern. 'I just had a bad night, that's all.'

Mr Hall was out of town on business, much to her relief, and after managing to get through the day, Grace made her way home and back to the mental whirlpool that swirled her thoughts round and round, making it impossible for her to think straight.

After they had eaten, Robert went down to the kitchen to talk to Jim and, seeing the state of his mother, he offered to do the washing up for her while he was down there. Glad to avoid Mrs Thomas again, Grace went to lie down and think. Last night had shown her one vital thing. Even if she missed making love, and until last night she had not realised that she did, she now knew she could never make love to any man after John. That helped her to reach her decision. Mr Hall had said he was expecting nothing more than companionship, and Grace knew she could give him that. There was an affinity between them that she had obviously sensed that time when she had blurted out all her troubles to him in the car, because it had been so unlike her, and since there was no other kind of marriage she could ever contemplate, this would suit them both, just as he had said. She would accept his offer and make sure he did not regret it.

Relieved to have come to a decision, she decided not to say anything to Robert until she had given Mr Hall her answer, then she hoped the three of them would discuss the future together. Now that she had made up her mind, as with every other decision she had ever made, Grace committed herself. There would be no going back.

She felt unexpectedly shy when she went to see her boss the next day. He knew why she was there and helped ease her awkwardness by asking if she had considered his proposal. Grace looked at him and saw an elderly man watching her with the eyes of a young man and her shyness left her.

'I've thought about your offer and I shall be very happy to accept.'

He came across to her and she thought he was going to embrace her, but he simply took her hand in both of his and raised it to his lips. It was the first time in her life that Grace had been kissed on the hand, and it was such a gentle, respectful gesture that a warmth flooded through her and her eyes met his, answering the affection she saw there.

'Thank you, Grace, my dear.' He smiled. 'And I am Richard.'

For a while they talked tentatively, trying to come to terms with this new relationship between them, then Miss Watson knocked on the door, bringing letters to be signed.

'Say nothing yet,' Richard managed to murmur before she came in.

Grace sat at her desk. It was done. She had given her promise and she would keep it. Now she faced breaking the news to Robert and her sister Ellen back home. Home was still the Isle of Man, she reflected ruefully.

CHAPTER FIFTEEN

TELLING Robert was not as hard as she had expected. She began by explaining how kind her boss was and how all the staff liked him. She built a picture of an elderly, well-educated man, leaving out the fact that he lived in a house with servants. When she got to the part about the proposal, she tried to explain that it would be for companionship and that no one would ever replace his father, but Robert was so surprised that she was actually getting married that he wasn't bothered about her reasons. He had no memory of his father, knowing only what his mother had told him, so there was no problem there. His main concern was that his mother was a bit old to be getting married, but if it was to an even older man perhaps it didn't matter.

'Will you be having a wedding?' he asked. 'When will it be?'

'We haven't decided yet, we haven't really decided anything other than that we are going to marry. I wanted to tell you first, I hope you'll like him, Robert.'

'I've never been to a wedding before. Wait till I tell Jim!'

'No, you mustn't tell Jim yet,' Grace said hurriedly. 'You are the only person who knows and Mr Hall – I mean Richard – wants to tell people in the correct way, with an announcement, so until then it must be our secret.'

'Oh!' Robert looked disappointed. 'He'd have been flabbergasted.'

* * *

The local paper carried the announcement. Mrs Thomas read it then read it again. Mrs Grace Corkish? Our Mrs Corkish? The name of the man Grace worked for, followed by the name of the firm, confirmed that she was marrying her boss. She showed it to Harry and Jim.

'What do you make of this? She kept that quiet, didn't she? There wasn't even a hint. What a dark horse.'

Jim went to find Robert. He wanted to know all about the wedding and Robert, making the most of the reflected limelight that the news had cast upon him, airily promised to get him an invitation. Jim had never been to a wedding either.

At work, things were a bit different. Miss Price, Mr Collins and the male clerks all expressed their good wishes, but Miss Watson was icy. She offered her congratulations with barely concealed anger, and as Grace looked at the tight, strained face, it dawned on her that the animosity Miss Watson had been harbouring was jealousy. Not of Grace's work, but of the relationship between her and Richard. Miss Watson had seemingly spotted something in her boss's attitude to the new receptionist that Grace had not noticed. Obviously, this was what Miss Price had been hinting at and was what had been behind the withholding of the typing and the attempt to keep Grace limited to the Reception area? It explained a lot but there were more important things to think about at the moment. She let it go.

The first thing Grace needed to do was to arrange the meeting between Robert and Richard. She felt she couldn't bring Richard to their small rooms in a lodging house, but nor did she want to take Robert to Richard's home just yet. Bringing the two of them together was a big enough step for now. Whitegate Park was neutral ground and since it was close to Richard's house, they arranged to meet there on Sunday. Grace had already been to see her new home on the previous Saturday. The 'servants' she had heard about from Miss Watson turned out to be just a husband and wife team of housekeeper and chauffeur/gardener, and she had been made so welcome by the friendly couple who had looked after Richard for twenty years, that she knew she would be happy there. The house was impressive, and it would certainly take some getting used to, but she had no real fears. It was a large brick and stone detached house on Whitegate Lane, but it was not the sort of grand house that John had come from and where her mother had worked as a housemaid. It was a home, a superior one, but still a home. She looked forward to living there.

On Sunday, Richard was waiting by the gates of the park and as they walked towards him, Robert suddenly drew back, half hiding behind his mother.

'Is that him?' he whispered.

'Yes, don't worry, you'll like him.'

Robert, however, found that he was looking at a man who reminded him strongly of the two men he had seen at the police station in Douglas, when he had been taken there by the policeman on that dreadful night. When his mother had collected him, he had asked who they were and she had told him they were solicitors. Now Richard, in his smart grey suit and tie, reawakened his fear of that evening.

'This is my son, Robert,' Grace gently pushed him forward. 'Robert, this is Mr Hall.'

'I am very pleased to meet you, Robert.' Richard shook hands with him. 'Your mother has told me a lot about you.'

'Good morning, Mr Hall.' Robert displayed his best manners for his mother's sake. Crikey! How old he looked, even older than Robert had expected. His hair was grey and the neat little moustache on his top lip was white. He wore silver rimmed glasses on a wrinkled face and, even in the smart suit, he looked a little hunched. Robert stared at him. If he had been aware of Robert's summing up of him, the fit and healthy Richard, who carried his fifty-eight years well, would not have recognised himself.

They strolled round the park. Richard bought Robert an ice-cream and tried to make conversation, but the childless Richard was not used to young boys, and Robert was still wary of him. Then Richard suggested they take Robert to see his new home. Robert stood still. It had not occurred to him that he would be leaving George Street. He hadn't thought that far ahead and no one had talked to him about it. Seeing the startled look on his face, Grace realised her mistake. She put her arm around his shoulders and pulled him to her.

'Can we leave that for today, Richard?' she said quickly, trying to indicate with her eyes that this was the wrong time. 'We'll arrange it later, but Robert has promised his friend he will go on the sands with him this afternoon – in fact we really should be getting back now.'

'Yes of course.' Richard grasped the situation. 'I look forward to seeing you soon then, Robert.'

Grace nudged Robert. 'Good morning, Mr Hall,' he managed again.

'I'll see you tomorrow.' Grace smiled apologetically at Richard. He raised his hat as they parted.

Nothing much was said on the way home, but back in

their room it needed to be sorted out. Grace made a pot of tea before speaking.

'I know we haven't talked about this, Robert, but you must have realised we would be moving after the wedding?' Robert didn't reply so she tried again.

'Richard has a nice house, you'll have a room of your own, and there's a big garden. It's nearly as pretty as the park.' She laughed, trying to jolly him up.

Robert was thinking hard. Of course, now he came to think of it, he should have realised there was no space for Mr Hall in their two rooms.

'A room might come empty here, Mum,' he said hopefully.

Grace's heart sank. She had a lot of explaining to do. It had all happened so quickly and she had been so completely taken by surprise herself that she had not fully told him how great a change it was going to be. Not wanting to flaunt their new status, she had underplayed it, making it all the more difficult to explain now. How could she tell him that Richard would never fit into their present way of living? How could she say this without demeaning what they had? She had always tried to aim for the standards they might have had if John had lived, but everything had needed to be tailored to the practicalities of her situation. She had never had the money to indulge in the fine living which should have been Robert's birth-right. This move would be another big change for them both.

'The thing is, Robert, the house is quite big and Richard has lived there for a long time. It makes more sense for us to move there.' She wondered whether to tell him about the housekeeper and the chauffeur. She didn't want to make it sound too grand, but then she decided there mustn't be any further misunderstanding, she needed to be totally honest with him now.

'Richard has a lady who keeps house for him, and her husband drives the car and takes care of the garden. They live at the house and they are both very nice. I think we will be happy there, love.' Robert was silent.

'I'm sure you'll feel better once you've seen the house. It's hard to picture something you don't know anything about, isn't it? We can go one evening next week, if you like.' She waited for his reply.

'Can I go down to see Jim now?'

Grace sighed. 'Yes, if you want to.' She felt flat. That hadn't gone very well.

The visit was arranged, and Robert was shown his room as well as the rest of the house. He met Mr and Mrs Wignall and he stroked their cat in the kitchen. Grace was proud of his manners, he was polite and answered as pleasantly as he could when spoken to, but he didn't ask any questions and there was no excitement in his eyes as he looked around. Grace knew she was the only one who could spot this. He perked up a bit when Richard insisted on driving them home.

'Is this the car you rode in?' he asked his mother as they waited for Richard to drive it out of the garage. 'I never thought my first car ride would be in one as posh as this. I hope Jim sees us.' His luck was out, the road was quiet and as it was almost dark, not many people saw the big black Rover draw up at Westholme.

* * *

Richard took charge of the arrangements for the wedding, but he took care to go over every detail with Grace before finalising anything. He regularly attended a church near his home and, as they were both widowed, there was no objection to their wedding being held there. Grace was not religious. At school she had been taught to say the Lord's Prayer and to recite the 21st Psalm, and at home she had been brought up to thank the Lord for what they had been about to receive at mealtimes, and they had all wished each other 'Goodnight and God bless' at bedtimes, but they had not attended Sunday school or church mainly because, in their house, Sunday was not a day of rest. It had to be a working day, because that was when they cleaned the house and baked the bread. Tasks that had to wait until the washing and ironing that kept a roof over their heads, was done. She knew it was losing John that had turned her against her childhood faith, but it was not a strong faith that she had rejected. She told Richard she would prefer a quiet ceremony and he agreed.

'In view of the fact that it is a second marriage for both of us, I think just a few friends would do nicely. You have a sister, of course, don't you?'

'I have a sister and two brothers, but they all have families – they wouldn't come.' She didn't mention that they would not be able to afford to, in case Richard offered to pay their fares. It was something he would likely do. 'But I would like to invite my landlady and her family if I may, just three of them, is that all right?'

'You must invite any of your friends, Grace,' he answered.

Grace was slightly downcast as she realised that these three people were the only real friends that she had made in the two years she had lived in Blackpool.

* * *

On the day of the wedding, which came two months later, Grace went to Richard's house where Mrs Wignall had offered to help her dress. The pale blue gown she had chosen fastened at the back with a long row of tiny covered buttons, needing a second pair of hands to manipulate them into their small loops. Her bonnet was trimmed with a bunch of pink rosebuds and she carried a matching posy in her gloved hands. The mirror reflected a tall, elegant lady of whom Richard could be proud.

Mr Collins was to give her away. She had thought about asking Harry, but Richard had suggested his chief clerk, who had been with Richard since he had started the firm, so she had agreed. Robert's neatly pressed suit and a crisp white shirt had been left on his bed, shiny new shoes on the floor. He was to arrive with the Thomas family, and she had arranged for him to stay with them while she and Richard spent a few days in the Lake District. When they returned Robert would move to his new home and they would settle into their new life. For one moment Grace felt a pang of sorrow that they would be living the life she had always wanted for Robert but without the man who was his father, then she switched her thoughts to the ceremony and the dear man who had offered them this life and who was waiting for her.

Grace had been married in a small chapel when she had wed John, and as she made her vows to Richard, in the beautiful church, she was aware of the commitment she was making. "And to cherish." Cherishing was what this marriage was all about, and she meant those words. But they were not the same as the ones she had vowed to John. "Keep thee only unto him, so long as ye both shall live." Only one of them still lived, but the vow remained.

They went to a hotel for the wedding feast and Robert and Jim had their first taste of wine. It made them both lightheaded. When Richard made a speech, praising his beautiful bride and promising his everlasting devotion, Robert and Jim, their wine glasses empty, had to press their knuckles hard against their mouths, as they tried not to giggle. Mrs Thomas poured water into their glasses and made them drink it before they disgraced themselves.

Later, as the newlyweds travelled to Windermere by train, Robert walked back to George Street with the Thomas family, he and Jim still in high spirits. Mrs Thomas made cocoa and then sent the boys to bed.

'You've had a good day but now it's over, up you go.'

Neither of them got into bed, they were both too wound up to sleep. Jim stood on his bed and struck a pose, mimicking Mr Hall and imitating his voice, "My undying love and devotion," and they both doubled up with the laughter they had tried to hold back at the reception. Mrs Thomas came in.

'Come on now, settle down.' They both dived into bed. 'That's enough for one day.' She tucked each boy in and gave him a goodnight kiss. Robert looked up as she leaned over him.

'Mrs Thomas, this has been the happiest day of my life,' he said seriously.

She looked down at him for a few moments then smiled. 'Sleep tight,' she said.

While his mother and Richard were away Robert came to a decision, he would not be moving to Mr Hall's house. He was sitting at the breakfast table and Mrs Thomas was pouring his tea.

'I want to ask you something, Mrs Thomas.' he said.

'Ask away.'

'Can I stay here with you? I've decided I'm not moving to Mr Hall's. If I give you all my wages, will that be enough?'

Mrs Thomas put down the teapot. 'Oh. Robert, this is not something you can decide on your own just like that.

You're feeling unsettled, that's all. Wait till your mother comes back tomorrow.'

'It won't make any difference. I'm not moving. I've decided.'

'This isn't something we can talk about, Robert, it's for your mother to sort out, not me.'

'Well, if I can't stay here, I'll find somewhere else, 'cos I'm not moving there.'

Harry came through from the scullery. 'It's time we were off, Robert, are you ready?'

Robert nodded and picked up his work sack. Over his head, Harry and his mother exchanged a significant look, but later that night, when the boys were in bed, they talked.

'It's obvious he's made up his mind,' said Harry. 'I've seen that look on his face before. When he is determined he seldom gives up.'

'But there's nothing we can do.' said Mrs Thomas. 'I wouldn't dream of going behind Grace's back on something like this.'

'We won't go behind her back, but we can try to offer a solution if it is needed.'

Between them they came up with a plan that they would put to Grace on her return, if Robert persisted. Harry would move up to the two top rooms and Robert would share with Jim again.

'She won't like it,' warned Mrs Thomas.

'I don't suppose she will but we are only trying to find a way to help. It's up to her and Robert to sort it out.'

Grace couldn't wait to see Robert the next day. She had to stop herself from running as she neared George Street. Robert was happy to see her and they sat drinking tea with Harry and Mrs Thomas, but Grace was waiting eagerly for the moment when she would leave with him and take him to his new home. She finished her tea and stood up.

'Right, are you ready, Robert? Have you got your bags?'

'No, I'm not coming. I'm staying here.'

Grace misunderstood. 'But I thought you were coming now. Mrs Wignall is cooking a special lunch for you. It will give you time to settle in properly.'

'No, I mean I am not moving to Mr Hall's, I'm staying here with Mrs Thomas.'

'Now hold on, Robert,' Mrs Thomas interrupted. 'Nothing has been arranged.' She turned to Grace. 'You know I wouldn't agree anything without talking to you first.'

Grace stared. 'What do you mean agree anything? What has happened?'

Harry spoke. 'Robert has been talking to us, Grace, he says he doesn't want to move. We've not talked to him about it, obviously. As Mum has just said, we wouldn't do that.'

Grace took hold of Robert's hand. 'You are bound to feel a bit nervous, love. It will be strange at first but you'll soon settle in. Your room is ready for you and I've left a present on your bed.'

'Sorry Mum, but I'm not coming.'

'Of course, you are. It's all arranged.' Grace began to panic. Like Harry, she had seen that determined, almost defiant look before. When he had wanted to leave school, for instance, after Harry had offered him an apprenticeship. She had known then that she would face a battle if she had insisted on keeping him there. He was still young enough for her to bring parental pressure to bear on him, but she did not want an argument. 'Richard is expecting you. He's looking forward to having you.'

'I don't know why everyone is making such a fuss.' Robert said. 'It's not as though I am going away. I'm staying here, that's all. I'll come and see you and you will come and see us, won't you? It'll be just the same really.'

Grace suddenly felt shattered. Four little words dropped like four little stones – *Come and see us*. Robert was already identifying himself with the Thomas family. There had been a shift in their relationship while she had been away and it was because of her marriage. Everything she had done had been for Robert, and now he was refusing to move with her. She had one last try. 'Richard will be disappointed.'

'I'm sorry, Mum, but I never know what to say to him, and when I do, I always feel I've said the wrong thing, or said it the wrong way or something.' Robert shrugged his shoulders. 'I always feel I ought to call him Sir.'

Grace gave in. He didn't want to move to Richard's and she must accept it. She would start her new life without the joy that she had expected. There was no way she would break her promise to Richard. She had meant it when she had agreed to be his wife, but if she had known what the outcome would be… she dismissed the thought before it could take shape.

Harry told her what he and his mother suggested and she agreed. It seemed that Harry had sufficiently understood the strength of Robert's feelings, to make him take steps to find a solution, so for the second time, someone else had seen a depth of character in Robert that she, so absorbed in being a mother, had missed. Perhaps Robert carried inherent traits from his father's family which she could not recognise. But John might have.

She returned to Whitegate Lane with a heavy heart. When she told Richard what had been decided, he was philosophical.

'He needs time, my dear. It's a big change for him and, if I may say so, he is at the age where he should be allowed his opinions. Within reason, of course. Let some time pass, then see how things are at the end of it.'

Lying in bed in her own room, Grace grieved for the loss of the relationship she had hoped to have with her new husband and her son. But no tears wet her pillow.

* * *

Grace and Richard often had guests to dinner and Mrs Wignall cooked the entire meal. The food was good, very good, and guests enjoyed coming to their house. At first Grace had been nervous and relieved to leave the cooking to someone who was more experienced, and later it had just seemed easier to let things carry on as they were. Richard's friends were all such pleasant people, and so kind to Grace, but they were all, without exception, elderly, and she missed the chatter of young folk. She missed the gossip which Mrs Thomas used to pass on over a cup of tea because, even though she called at George Street very often, Mrs Thomas was inclined to treat her slightly differently now, as though her new status had somehow replaced the old Grace and she felt she had lost the intimacy they had shared.

'I'm still me, Mrs Thomas,' she had wanted to say, 'I've not changed.'

But she didn't say it because she knew that in certain ways she had. The clothes she now wore were more fashionable and expensive, and her confidence was growing as she was treated with respect and courtesy by Richard. She was more serene now that the stress of struggling to make a living had been removed.

Robert, however, was making himself more and more at home in the Thomas household. He loved his work as an apprentice and was showing signs of becoming a skilled plasterer. Harry was pleased with him. They were so much in tune with one another that they were almost like father and son. Robert certainly looked up to Harry as a father figure.

* * *

For Robert's thirteenth birthday, Harry gave him a pocket knife and Robert found a piece of firewood and began whittling away at once. By the time Grace arrived to wish her son a happy birthday, he had already carved a very life-like shape of a fish.

'That's very good, Robert.' She was impressed. 'You must take after your Uncle Charlie. Do you remember that boat he made for you?'

Robert did. It was one of the few presents he had had as a child.

'Happy birthday, love.' Grace handed him a small wrapped packet. Inside was a velvet pouch and Robert held his breath, not daring to believe it might be what he hoped. But it was – it was a silver pocket watch.

'Oh Mum, thank you. I can't believe it. A pocket knife and a pocket watch! Now I really feel like a working man.'

Every spare moment he could find, Robert spent whittling away at pieces of old wood.

The thick fingers, that had struggled with copperplate writing at school, now showed the skill that lay within them as he progressed from whittling old wood to carving carefully selected pieces of driftwood from the beach. He carved beautiful sculptures of birds and fish and it was obvious that he had a talent. Harry suggested that he carve his own designs to make the moulds for the ornate ceiling roses and cornices for which his firm was renowned, meaning that he could offer original designs to his clients. The business was doing well and the future looked bright for both of them.

As time went by, although Robert still called round to see his mother on Sundays, he didn't stay for the whole day as before. A cup of tea and a slice of Mrs Wignall's sponge cake and he was off. Grace could see that her son was happy, but if she stopped to think about it there was just that little nagging thought that, if she had not remarried, she might have been more involved in his life. Not just living in the same house and cooking and washing for him, but knowing more about his working day, about his friends and his plans. Or was she yearning for something she felt she had lost but which would have changed anyway with the passage of time? All children grew away from their parents to some extent, didn't they? But that didn't fill the aching void as she watched him become a confident young man leading his own life with his own friends.

CHAPTER SIXTEEN

ROBERT was celebrating his eighteenth birthday and Jim was home from medical school for the weekend. He had fulfilled his early promise, gone to grammar school and gained the qualifications needed to train to become a doctor. They were meeting Harry and a few of Robert's workmates at their local for some drinks and a plate of Lancashire hotpot. It was the pub's speciality, and Robert was looking forward to it.

Although it was busy, they managed to play a game of darts which he won. 'You know we only let you win because it's your birthday,' his mates teased him. They pulled two tables together and ordered the hotpot.

'Birthday, is it?' the waitress asked as she took the order. 'Many happy returns.'

'Thanks.' Robert grinned back, embarrassed. The waitress was small, fair-haired and rather plump. Robert had seen her many times before, but since he'd only called in for a drink and she only served food, he had not spoken to her. She brought the hotpot and a dish of red cabbage for them to help themselves.

'There you are, boys, that'll put hair on your chest!'

'Just what you need, Bob.' One of the lads tried to open Robert's shirt. 'He's still as bald as a baby.' There was a lot of good-natured banter as they tucked into plates of steaming meat and onion layered with golden potato slices, then they ordered a last round of beer – they all had to be up early for work the next day. The waitress was serving at a table near the door as they were leaving and she called goodnight to them. Robert turned to answer, and for a short moment their eyes met and a smile was exchanged. No one else noticed and they all headed off on their separate ways.

A week later, Robert went to the pub with Joe, one of his friends. The waitress was there serving as usual, but this time, having already spoken to him, she came across to say hello before carrying on with her work. From time to time Robert cast a surreptitious glance across and Joe noticed.

'Have you got your eye on her then, Bob?'

'No, I don't fancy my chances there, Joe. I bet she's married or courting.'

'Is she wearing a ring?'

'Not so far as I can see, but she's always on the go, it's hard to tell.'

'Well, there's only one way to find out – ask her.'

'No. I've only said hello to her, she'd send me on my way.'

Robert glanced over again. This time he caught her eye and again there was that brief connection between them, then she smiled and moved away.

'How old do you reckon she is, Joe?'

'Older than you, my son. She's probably about twenty-three or four I'd say.'

'I bet she is married, then. Anyway, it doesn't matter because I'm not asking her out.'

'Well, perhaps not tonight!' Joe gave a knowing wink.

A week later, Robert was walking past the pub just as the waitress was leaving. It had taken a fair amount of hanging around for a couple of evenings to time it right, but here she was, and she was alone. As he had planned, Robert feigned surprise when he 'accidentally' bumped into her. She looked younger without her hair tied back. She spoke first.

'Hello. Just going in for a drink?'

'No, I'm on my way home.' Robert was rather flustered.

'Oh, I won't keep you, then.' She looked up at him, smiling.

'No, it's all right. I'm not in a hurry. I mean, I was only out for a walk.' He took courage. 'Can I walk you home? If you are going home, that is.'

'You can if you like,' she said, laughing, 'but I only live across there.' She pointed to a row of terraced houses on the other side of the road. Robert laughed as well, and it broke the ice.

'Would you like to go for a walk on your evening off, sometime?'

'Yes, I'd like that,' she said. 'I'm Elizabeth, by the way, but please don't call me Lizzie.'

'I'm Robert,' he responded. 'My pals call me Bob and I don't mind which you call me.'

'Robert it is, then. I'm off on Monday evening if you want to go for that walk.'

'I do. I'll call for you about half-past seven, will that suit you?' He felt more relaxed now and he was able to take a good look at her. She still looked older than him, but she had not turned him down. She nodded.

'It's the one with the blue curtains. Number seven.'

'See you on Monday, then.' Robert watched her cross the street and open the door of her home. She waved before going in.

Elizabeth told him her age on their first evening. 'I know how old you are because of your eighteenth birthday,' she said. 'But you don't know how old I am.'

'Does it matter?' Robert didn't say that he and Joe had already made a guess.

'I'm twenty-two. That's four years older than you.'

'I might be eighteen but I am a working man and have been since I was twelve.'

'It's not a problem, then?'

'As far as I'm concerned, there are no problems at all, and if and when there are, we'll sort them out.'

'If and when?' Elizabeth raised her eyebrows. 'That sounds as though you are looking into the future.'

Robert blushed. It was their first meeting and although he had already decided that he wanted to see her again, he did not want to presume, so he just laughed. 'I would need a crystal ball for that.'

They had decided to walk on the pier. The tide was in and there was a rolling swell. The waves slapped dully against the pier's iron stanchions and the cool evening breeze blew gently against their faces. The reflection of the pier lights twinkled on the dark water. Robert reached for her hand and Elizabeth clasped it.

Three months later they were still seeing each other and regarded themselves as sweethearts. Twelve months later, Robert asked Elizabeth to marry him. She was pregnant. There was no question of not marrying, that had always been his intention, it would just be sooner than he had planned.

The news about the baby brought mixed reactions. The Thomas family was delighted, many a child had been conceived out of wedlock but born in wedlock, but Grace was not so pleased. Elizabeth, with her fair hair, pale lashes and rather square, blunt nosed face, could not be considered a beauty, and although Grace could find no fault with her, she had hoped that Robert might find a younger, prettier girl in time. She also considered Robert too young to be married, ignoring the fact that she herself had been only seventeen and John twenty-one, when they had wed, and for exactly the same reason as her son. But she had the good sense to keep her thoughts to herself.

Elizabeth worried about how they would manage, once she had to finish working.

'You seem so happy about this, Robert,' she said, 'But how can we afford to raise a child on what you bring in? Even if I go back to work, we shall need to pay someone to look after the baby. We shan't be able to manage when I need to stop work. There is only one way I can think of and that is for me to go back to my grandmother's house in Pilling…'

Robert interrupted her with a big grin on his face. 'Yes, I am happy, and there is no need for you to go anywhere. I have always had a sum of money put away for me, given to me by the grandmother I have never known, and it is enough for us to buy a nice little house. There won't be any rent to pay so we'll be able to manage well enough on my wages, and if you can make hotpot like that you serve at the pub, we shall live like royalty.'

They bought a three-bedroomed terraced house, near to the Thomas family, and after marrying at the Registry office, they moved in to their new home in time to be settled in before the baby arrived.

They didn't decide on a name because Elizabeth said it would all depend on what the baby looked like, then she would choose, and when she gave birth to a beautiful girl, she chose Margaret.

'Yes, she does look like a Margaret. What about Margaret Grace?' suggested Robert.

'That's a lovely name.' Elizabeth nodded. 'And I think it will please your mother.'

Grace came to see her little namesake and her first thought as she looked down on the little wrinkled face was – Margaret Grace Corkish – so you are another child who carries the family blood and bears the family name but is not actually part of the family. Then she switched her thoughts as she held the baby in her arms and remembered the soft warm feel of a tiny body, and the special milky smell of a new-born, and it was just like holding Robert again. She put her cheek against the silky fluffiness on the top of Margaret's head, and let her heart speak to John. *This is your granddaughter, my love, and one day I will tell her about you.*

* * *

Robert was besotted with his little daughter. She was a happy, smiley, baby and he loved to feel the strong grip of her tiny fingers grabbing his thumb. He loved their little house and Elizabeth had been welcomed as family by Mrs Thomas who lived just round the corner. He and Elizabeth were happy and contented.

There was only one cloud on the horizon and that was the war that was being fought between Britain and Germany. Busy with their new house and preparing for a new baby, the declaration of war had not impacted greatly on Elizabeth and Robert, and in any case, everyone said it would be over by Christmas. A patriotic fever had swept the country, whipped up by a clever recruiting campaign, with posters of Kitchener's forefinger seeming to point directly and challengingly to a man. At first, thousands of men had rushed to volunteer but as the war continued beyond 1915, and the appalling list of casualties brought home the cruel brutality of this modern war, in 1916 conscription began for all men between the ages of nineteen and forty. Robert was among them. His papers arrived when Margaret was nearly eighteen months old and, like thousands of other young husbands, he had to kiss his wife and child goodbye and catch a train to the barracks where he received his basic training before being assigned to an artillery regiment as a gunner. In this new mechanised warfare, for the first time, the battles were being fought from the air as well as on the ground. As a gunner, they all knew Robert would be in the thick of it. For Elizabeth there was fear and heartache, for Robert there was fear and dread, but for Grace, there was all three. The war, already casting a shadow over the whole country, now darkened their lives.

CHAPTER SEVENTEEN

WITH her husband away, Elizabeth considered taking a lodger. She wrote to Robert to ask what he thought about it and he replied saying it was a good idea and why didn't she ask Mrs Thomas for advice. Due to her good reputation, Mrs Thomas received many enquiries and she had to refuse most of them since her rooms were almost always occupied, but she promised to keep an eye open for a single female who might suit Elizabeth.

A few weeks later she sent a young girl to knock on Elizabeth's door. When she opened it, Elizabeth saw a very pretty, dark-haired, green-eyed girl smiling up at her and she immediately smiled back.

'Mrs Thomas sent me. She said you had a room to let.'

'Yes, I have. Would you like to come in?' Elizabeth showed the girl into the kitchen and invited her to sit down.

'I'm Elizabeth, by the way, and I'd better tell you I've never done this before.'

'I'm Jessie. I am a nurse and I'm used to renting – I'm no trouble.'

They beamed at each other again and from those first few moments they both knew they were going to be friends.

The room was the biggest bedroom at the front of the house. Net curtains wafted in the breeze from two open sash windows and long pale green velvet drapes hung almost to the floor. The bed was covered by a green satin eiderdown and over by the wardrobe stood a small armchair and a little table.

'Oh, this is very nice.' Jessie seemed genuinely pleased. 'I'd like to move in as soon as possible, if that's all right?'

'Yes, of course, the room is ready, as you can see, but I haven't told you how much the rent is yet – it's eight shillings a week with meals, would that be all right?'

'It would,' Jessie hesitated, 'but I have to work shifts, not at night, but my hours do change. I'm just wondering if I would fit in with your mealtimes.'

Elizabeth had already decided that she very much wanted Jessie to take the room, so she quickly worked out how she could accommodate her needs.

'Oh, I'm sure we can work round that,' she said. 'If necessary, I can always leave your meal in the small oven to keep hot, but there's only me to consider and I am happy to eat when you do. Twelve o'clock midday or six o'clock in the evening, I don't mind. I have a baby girl, but she has her own mealtimes, so that's no problem.'

Jessie grinned. 'Right then – when can I move in?'

Their first week together confirmed how lucky each girl had been with this chance meeting. Jessie told Elizabeth that she had been brought up on a farm in the Bleasdale Fells.

'But even as a child I knew I wouldn't stay on the farm, I always wanted something more. Then, when the war started, I had my chance. I moved to Blackpool and was accepted for nursing training. It was exactly what I was looking for, and I wouldn't want to do anything else now.'

At the end of two weeks Jessie had already made herself at home. She had begun to cook the meal on her day off, and when she was on an early shift, she helped Elizabeth to bath Margaret and put her to bed. They soon slipped into a very comfortable routine and little Margaret flourished in the loving atmosphere.

One Sunday, Jessie's day off, Elizabeth's mother-in-law came to visit. Jessie was surprised when she met the beautiful, well-dressed lady and was rather in awe of her. Elizabeth introduced her as Mrs Hall, Robert's mother, but when Jessie said, 'I'm very pleased to meet you, Mrs Hall,' she was stopped by a laugh and a hand squeezing her arm.

'Oh, please call me Grace, everyone does. I've heard so much about you from Elizabeth that I'm sure we are going to be friends. I hope you will be happy here.'

'I will if these first few weeks are anything to go by. Elizabeth has been so kind to me.'

'And Elizabeth tells me you are wonderful with Margaret – ah, do I hear my little granddaughter?'

Grace hurried out to the yard, where Margaret was just waking up from her morning sleep in her pram. She stayed for a cup of tea and a cuddle with the baby before going home to get ready for a dinner party that evening. When she had gone Elizabeth filled Jessie in on Grace's story.

'She seemed so posh when she came in.' said Jessie. 'I wasn't expecting someone like that, but she is very nice, isn't she?'

'She has been very kind to us, and although she is comfortably off now, she's not always had things easy. Robert's father drowned when he was just a baby, so she has brought him up on her own. The Corkish family is from the Isle of Man and they were very wealthy, but apparently, she has never had anything to do with them. She has made her own way. Then she married her boss, and as you can see, she is leading a very different life now. I'm glad for her. She's always quite ladylike and I'm sometimes a bit in awe of her myself, she's not chatty like me, but, as I say, she's very good to us.'

Jessie sensed that although the two women seemed to get on well there was that special warmth missing between them which, even so early on in their friendship, she and Elizabeth already shared.

Later in the week Mrs Thomas called round, 'Hello, how are you getting on?'

'Oh, very well indeed,' Jessie was pleased to see her, 'And thank you for sending me to Elizabeth's, I'm so lucky to have found such a lovely place,'

'Well, I thought you might be just what she was looking for. Elizabeth will tell you that I am a good judge of character, I'm not often wrong.'

There were two more members of Elizabeth's circle to meet, Mrs Thomas's son, Harry, and his son Jim. Jessie met Harry when he called round to fix a blocked drain. He was a good-looking man in his early forties with a head of thick hair just going silver at the temples. He was friendly in a quiet way and Elizabeth obviously relied on him while Robert was away, rather than Grace's husband Richard, her stepfather-in-law.

She met Jim while she was mixing a cake at the kitchen table. He tapped on the back door and walked in. Both of them were surprised to come face to face with a stranger.

'Oh, I'm sorry, I thought Elizabeth would be in.' Jim paused in the doorway, looking at the pretty girl stirring a batter with a wooden spoon. Her cheeks were flushed and wisps of her hair had come loose from the upswept mass of curls pinned on top of her head.

'You must be Jessie, I'm Jim Thomas.'

'You're Harry's son!' Jessie gave him a dimpled smile. 'Elizabeth's just nipped up to the shop. She'll be back in a minute.'

She hesitated about asking him to sit down, after all he was more at home here than she was, but, as if he had read her thought, Jim said, 'I'll wait then. Has she taken Margaret with her? She wants me to take a look at her. I hear she has a bit of a cough.'

'Yes, she has, but I don't think it's anything to worry about,' Jessie suddenly remembered that Jim was studying to be a doctor, so added, 'Though of course you will know better than I do.'

'Elizabeth is a bit overcautious, especially with Robert away. It makes every little sneeze seem more of a worry than it is. Lots of mothers are like that with their husbands away. I see she's got you busy.' He nodded towards the bowl.

'It's a cake to send to Robert, she's making up a parcel.'

'He's a lucky man.'

'Not really,' Jessie answered, 'it can't be much fun where he is. I know she worries about him.'

'Yes of course, that was a stupid thing to say, but you know what I mean, a happy marriage and a beautiful baby, that is what I meant.'

Jessie nodded. That was what she wanted for herself in a few years' time.

She put the cake in the oven just as Elizabeth walked in and handed Margaret to Jim.

'I know you'll think I'm making a fuss over nothing, but she's been refusing her food and she's a bit hot.' She watched Jim take Margaret's temperature and then put the kettle on. 'You've got time for a cup of tea I hope?'

'I've always got time for a cup of tea, and this little girl is fine. It's just a summer cold. Keep her warm, make sure she drinks plenty and she will be right as rain in no time.'

Yet again Jessie felt she was among family as they sat round the table drinking tea and chatting while the cake browned in the oven.

* * *

The parcel was never sent. Instead a knock on the door brought the dreaded news which shocked the family into deep grief. Robert had been killed at Passchendaele.

As soon she opened the door when she arrived home from work, Jessie knew there was something wrong. There was an eerie silence. When she went into the kitchen, Elizabeth was sitting upright, stiff backed, in her chair near the fire, staring fixedly at the dull embers. Mrs Thomas was standing by the window clasping a sleeping Margaret close in her arms. Grace was on the sofa, leaning, almost collapsed, against Richard. He turned to Jessie.

'It's Robert,' he said quietly, 'they had a letter.' He didn't need to say any more.

Jessie had come home to a house of morning and a family shattered.

She went straight to Elizabeth and put her hand on her shoulder and although Elizabeth reached up and touched Jessie' hand, she didn't speak. Jessie went over to Mrs Thomas. 'Let me take Margaret, Mrs Thomas.'

Mrs Thomas just shook her head and held Margaret tighter.

'Then, at least sit down.' Jessie helped her to a chair. She left Richard to see to Grace.

Every face was white and all eyes were blank. Jessie recognised shock. She went into the scullery to make hot sweet tea. Harry rushed in at the back door. He had just found the note his mother had left for him. 'Jessie, is it true?' Jessie looked at another shocked face.

She nodded and took his arm. 'Harry, will you help me to make some tea? That's all we can do for them at the moment. Get the cups out, will you?' She wanted to keep Harry away from the others for a moment or two to allow time for his panicky gasping to slow down. It would do no good to unleash a distraught Harry on them. They needed calm right now. His hands were shaking but Harry managed to help her carry the tea through. Jessie took Margaret from Mrs Thomas and laid her in her pram. Harry tried to get his mother to drink her tea. Richard was still struggling with Grace, trying to get her to sit up.

'It's all right. I can manage,' he said when Jessie offered to help. 'See to Elizabeth.'

Jessie went to her friend and knelt down in front of her. Elizabeth turned her eyes from the fire and as she looked at Jessie, tears began to trickle down her cheeks. Jessie put her arms round her, now she could begin to help her.

Richard decided to take Grace home as soon as she was able to move. She had not drunk her tea. She had not spoken.

'I'll take her home and put her to bed,' he said. 'She needs a good sleep.'

'Give her a sedative.' said Jessie. 'Let me know how she is tomorrow.'

After they had left, the others sat silent for a long time drinking the tea that Jessie kept pouring for them, but gradually they began to talk to one another in low murmurs, sharing their grief. By the time Harry and his mother set off to walk back to George Street, although Elizabeth was exhausted by the strain of sorrow, she was recovered enough to be able to tuck the sleeping Margaret into her cot. Jessie helped her into bed, then lay down on top of the eiderdown beside her and waited for the tears to flow.

Although sorrow-stricken for her friends, Jessie had not known Robert, so out of all of them, she was the most able to take care of the household and an oblivious baby. Harry was at the house most days, doing what he could, but he was badly hit by the news and also had to look after his mother who grieved for the boy who had become like another grandson to her. It was a nightmare time, one which was being suffered in many homes all over the country. A cruel war indeed, and one which was to drag on for over another year, but for Elizabeth and Grace it seemed as if it had ended that day.

Elizabeth never ceased to bless the day Jessie had come into her life. She relied heavily on her in those first dreadful weeks, and could not have managed without her, especially since Grace seemed to have retreated into a twilight world of her own because although she still followed her normal routine as far as eating, sleeping and dressing were concerned, every action was automatic and there was no sign of emotion. As had happened with his father, Robert's body was not recovered. He was one of the many soldiers who had no known grave, so with no funeral to attend and no resting place to visit or lay flowers, Grace felt she was joining father and son in limbo and no one could get through to her. It was as if part of her was missing. She spent long hours sitting in her room, constantly tidying her drawers and re-arranging her clothes in the wardrobe.

Richard tried to persuade her to walk with him in the park, but she just smiled and said she had lots of little jobs to attend to. Mrs Wignall suggested knitting. She knew Grace had knitted for Margaret and she thought that perhaps giving her something to occupy her seemingly restless hands, other than the constant tidying, might help to calm her obviously troubled mind. Richard thought it was worth a try.

'I wondered if you would like to knit a pullover for Mr Hall, dear,' Mrs Wignall said. 'I have some spare wool and a pattern. He could do with something warm for this winter.'

'Yes, if you want me to.'

Grace took the needles and wool from Mrs Wignall and placed them on the little table by her chair, then ignored them. Richard sighed. The next morning, however, he was hopeful when he saw that she had started knitting, but he soon realised that she had merely replaced the tidying with the knitting. She was simply completing row after row of identical stitches with no pattern or shape. Shock had pushed her into her own little world and imprisoned her there.

'She'll work her way through this in her own way and in her own time,' Mrs Wignall said. 'I've always found knitting a very calming pastime, I'm sure it will help her.'

'I hope so,' said Richard.

* * *

With Jessie's help and the liveliness of a toddler daughter, Elizabeth fared better. Gradually she began to take back the reins and start running her household again. Often during the summer evenings, the two girls liked to take Margaret down to the sands to paddle in the shallow water and watch the last of the sun's rays glint a path of gold across the grey sea. Sometimes, on their way home, they called in on Mrs Thomas for a cup of tea and a chat while Margaret slept in her pram. Harry was usually there, and occasionally Jim was home from medical school in Manchester. He was nearing the end of his training and he and Jessie found they had a lot to talk about. They made each other laugh with tales about the student slip-ups they had both made. It was not long before Jim asked her out.

'I hope it works for them,' Harry said, as he and his mother watched Jim set off in his best suit, hair slicked down with Brylcreem. 'She's a grand lass.'

'She's right for Jim. He'll not find anyone better suited. Give it time and you'll see I'm right.'

Knowing his mum's pride in being able to sum up people accurately, Harry wondered if she had begun to speculate about him and Elizabeth. There had been a growing affection between them despite the age gap, and he hoped she didn't just look on him as a father figure. Of course, it was much too early to make any advances, they were all still grieving for Robert, but if he wasn't mistaken Elizabeth looked forward to seeing him as much as he looked forward to seeing her. As his mum had just said – give it time.

* * *

That autumn, Jessie and Jim began to make plans for their wedding, and because they had very little money, Mrs Thomas suggested they move into the two attic rooms at George Street.

'It means I will always have a doctor in the house,' she said.

They decided on a quiet wedding with only Mrs Thomas and Harry attending, because Jessie's mother had been suddenly taken ill with an unknown cause and the family were extremely anxious. After the ceremony they both went to the farm for a few days to give what help they could and were there when the doctor diagnosed gall stones. Relieved it was curable, they returned to George Street to begin their married life in their little nest up in the attic.

Margaret had started school and was becoming a chatty little person. Hoping to spark some response in Grace, Richard had suggested that they meet her out of school one afternoon a week and take her to their house for tea, and as she began to react to the demands of a lively five-year-old, Grace gradually emerged from the dark depression that had held her in its grip for so long. With little involvement in the daily chores of the household, Grace had had time to nurse her grief and so it had stayed with her longer. Everyone was relieved at the change.

Mrs Wignall was still taking care of the housekeeping, including the cooking, but she was growing older, and it dawned on the newly aware Grace, that she had sat back for far too long. How could she have allowed herself to become so lethargic when she had always been used to hard work? Had she tried too hard to fit into Richard's way of life, to adapt to the slower pace of life he provided? Had she lost something of herself along the way? If so, she could start to reclaim it now by taking over some of the household duties and give Mrs Wignall a rest. A new energy was coursing through her veins and she felt reborn. It was time to stop being a passenger and get behind the wheel.

CHAPTER EIGHTEEN

THE war finally ended on the 11th of November 1918, and there were great celebrations all over the country. Elizabeth and Grace, although thankful that hostilities had ceased, chose not to join in any of the euphoria, preferring to remember quietly at home like so many others who had suffered a loss. Life would go on and people could begin to pick up the pieces, but things would never be quite the same again.

As Britain emerged from the devastatingly brutal war, Blackpool soon began to flourish once more as a popular seaside resort. Boarding houses were regularly booked up, the Golden Mile flaunted gaudy attractions to tempt the holiday crowds thronging the Promenade, all determined to enjoy themselves, while in the quiet streets away from the seafront, local people got on with their lives, adjusted to changes and concentrated on making a living.

Grace and Richard had met Margaret out of school and taken her back to their home for tea. It had become a regular arrangement now and they both looked forward to it very much. They had tea in the garden and Richard played a knockabout game of tennis with Margaret until it was time for her to go home.

'It's a lovely evening. Richard,' said Grace looking at the pearly sky, 'let's walk Margaret home instead of driving.'

'Do you mind if I don't, dear?' Richard answered. 'I'm feeling a little tired. I may have a lie down.'

Richard was now seventy-two and lately he seemed to be tired quite often. He still went into the office two or three times a week, but he had handed the reins over to Mr Collins, who was now his partner. Grace had grown used to his slower pace of life and she smiled now and kissed his cheek.

'I'll be back soon and then we'll have supper and an early night.'

Margaret gave Grandad a kiss and set off for home holding Grace's hand and chattering nonstop. Jessie was there when they got to Elizabeth's and Grace was pleased to see her, she had grown very fond of her. As they talked, Harry arrived, and soon they were all laughing and joking and it seemed like the old days to Grace. She loved relaxing with these younger people, such a contrast to the staid company of Richard's elderly friends.

She walked home beneath a full moon and the garden looked beautiful in the bright light. White marguerites and yellow marigolds floated like stars among the dark reds and purples of the geraniums and stocks and the air was heavy with fragrance. The moon cast a pale frosting over the lawn, silvering the foliage garlanding the trees so that the garden seemed to be sleeping peacefully. She could hear faint rustles and snaps as little night creatures made their way down secret paths through the undergrowth. The garden was far from sleeping.

She let herself in and went into the kitchen to make a snack for Richard. Mr and Mrs Wignall were usually in their bedroom by this time, but tonight she could hear their voices in the sitting room. The lamps were lit and when she went in Richard was lying on the leather chesterfield. Mrs

Wignall was holding a glass of water and Mr Wignall was loosening Richard's tie.

'Hello, my dear,' Richard said, smiling towards her.

'Richard!' Grace looked from him to Mr and Mrs Wignall. 'What's wrong?'

Mrs Wignall answered: 'I came in to see if anything was needed before we retired for the night and I found Mr Hall struggling for breath. He seems to have recovered a bit now, but he has had a funny turn.'

'Richard, how do you feel now, dear?' Grace knelt beside him.

'I'm fine, don't worry. I was just overheated that's all. It's over now.' He patted her hand.

'Have another sip of water.' Grace took the glass from Mrs Wignall and held it to his lips. Richard obediently took two sips and smiled again.

'There, now you can see I'm all right.' He looked a little pale but Grace could see that he didn't want a fuss, so she stood up.

'He seems to be all right now, thank you, Mrs Wignall. I'll see to him. I'm sure all he needs is a good night's sleep.'

'Well, if you are sure.' Mrs Wignall looked at Richard anxiously. 'Call us if you need us.'

'I'm sure we shan't – but thank you.'

When they had gone Grace knelt down again and took Richard's hand. 'What exactly happened, Richard?' she asked gently.

'It was nothing really. I was just dozing, then suddenly I found I couldn't breathe. Mrs Wignall came in almost at the same time and I must have scared her. She went for some water and brought Tom back with her. I was fine once I had a drink.'

'Would you like a cup of tea, or some hot milk?' Grace noticed that his colour was returning.

'No, I think I'll just go straight up if you don't mind.' He moved his legs to sit up. 'Have you ever regretted marrying me, Grace? Have you been happy?'

'Regretted? Not for one moment, and yes, I have been very happy. I must confess I was a bit sad at first when Robert decided not to live with us, then I saw how well he was doing on the path he had chosen for himself and realised he had made the right choice. We each know our own potential better than anyone else, don't we?'

'I suppose we do, but that doesn't mean someone else can't spot it. I knew from our first meeting that you had a quality about you that was just waiting for a chance to show itself. Then, when you told me your story that time in the car, I felt real anger that your husband's parents could be so blind as to not see what a gem they could have had in their family if only they had welcomed you.'

'John's father never met me, so there was no chance to make an impression either for good or bad, but it doesn't matter now. Thanks to you a whole new life opened up for me and I am quite a different person to what I was then.'

'You are the bud that was waiting to flower, all you needed was the right soil to grow in.'

'You are leaving out love, Richard. I thought I would never know love again after John, but with you I found a different kind of love, one which has given me deep contentment. I know what I owe to you.'

'You owe me nothing, the debt is all mine. You made my life bright again. I could hardly believe it when you accepted my proposal. I thought you would find me far too old.'

'Just as you saw beyond my youth to the person I could be, I saw behind your years to the man I knew I could be fond of, but I didn't know then how much I would grow to love you.'

'If you only knew how much that means to me, Grace.'

'I do know,' Grace stood up. 'And I also know that it is time you were in bed. You need a good night's sleep, and so do I after our little scare. Up you come.' She pulled both his hands. 'Will you be all right with the stairs?'

'Oh yes, I can manage.'

Richard turned to Grace, and in the tender gesture which had first aroused her affection for him, he took her hand and raised it to his lips. Grace put her arms round him and laid her cheek against his, holding him gently to her. 'Goodnight, then.'

She watched as he moved away and walked steadily out of the room. He was very dear to her, even more so now as he aged. One day, she knew she would lose him – but not tonight, thank God.

* * *

Richard died in his sleep a month later. This time there were no warning signs. He had spent the evening playing chess with Grace and had gone to bed at about ten o'clock. Grace found him when she took in his tray at eight o'clock the next morning. There was no shock as such, the day she had been expecting had come, but there was a deep, deep sadness. Richard had left her as quietly and peacefully as he had lived with her – a dear, kind and gentle man.

Mr Collins was the appointed executor, and Grace discovered that she had been left the house, plus an annual income which was more than enough to live on, but that he had left the bulk of his wealth to the church he had attended most of his life. Mr Collins had been surprised but Grace was not troubled by it. Richard had told her he would make sure she was taken care of, and since she had never known exactly how much money he had, she had no fixed expectations. The only thing she knew for certain, was that she did not want to continue living in the house on Whitegate Lane. It was too big for her and it had never really felt like her home without Robert there.

Mr and Mrs Wignall told her they were retiring to be near their daughter, which made the decision easier for Grace. She asked Mr Collins to arrange for the house to be sold. The family was surprised when they heard about Richard's donation to his church, making them all realise he had been far wealthier than they had supposed. They were even more surprised when they learnt that Grace was putting the house up for sale.

'I thought she was happy there,' said Mrs Thomas. 'I wonder why she wants to leave?'

'Well, for one thing, Mr and Mrs Wignall are retiring,' Elizabeth told her. 'Apparently, they have already bought a house near to their daughter in Preston. I don't suppose she wants to live in such a big house on her own.'

'It's a shame, though,' Mrs Thomas said thoughtfully. 'It's a lovely house, but of course it would be better to have a family living there to make the most of it.'

Elizabeth and Harry listened in silence.

'I'll make some tea.' Mrs Thomas got up to put the kettle on with a sly smile on her face.

A few days later Harry went to see Elizabeth. For some time, they had been aware of their feelings for each other, but nothing had been put on a firm footing. Now, with a good offer to make, Harry had decided it was the time to speak out.

'You know I love you, Elizabeth, and I've hoped for a while that you felt the same way.'

'I think you know I do, Harry.' Elizabeth's face lit up in the warm smile that Harry loved, the smile that made her plain face beautiful to him.

'Now is the time, then. Elizabeth, will you marry me? I can provide a good home for you and Margaret. I think the world of you both, and Margaret likes me, doesn't she?'

'Of course, she does. You are part of her life, Harry, as you are of mine. Nothing would make me happier I'd love to marry you. In fact, I've been waiting for you to ask me for quite some time. I was beginning to think I would have to do it myself next leap year.'

They both laughed and shared their first kiss as lovers. Harry had more to say.

'I've been doing a lot of thinking. You know my business is doing very well, I'm financially secure now, and I've been considering buying my own house. Obviously, I had planned for you and Margaret to share it with me, but I've had an idea. What would you say to me buying Grace's house and asking her to stay on with us? There's plenty of room and we will be able to keep an eye on her. It would have to be your decision obviously, but we all get on so well, don't we? I thought it might be the answer. Grace could stay in her home and we would have the sort of house I have always wanted for you.'

Elizabeth was rather taken aback. 'It would be a lot of money – are you sure?'

'Only if you are and don't worry about the cost. It will be a good investment. I've talked to my accountant and there is nothing to stop me buying a good property, even if we don't buy this one.'

Elizabeth looked at him for a moment then beamed.

'I can't think of anything I'd like better,' she said. 'I love that house. I think I have always secretly been a bit jealous of Grace living there. I never for a moment imagined myself living in it. It is way beyond anything I'd ever hoped for. Marrying you and living there as well,

I must be the luckiest person in the world. Thank you, Harry.'

'We'll have to put it to Grace, of course, but I'll have a word with Mr Collins as soon as I can because there may be other interested buyers.'

In fact, there were two offers on the table and Harry had to make a firm bid right away if he didn't want to risk losing the house. He asked Mr Collins to tell Grace he had made an offer and to report back on her reaction, which was one of surprise that he was able to afford the asking price.

'He's offered the full price?'

Mr Collins assured her that he had, and was in a position to go ahead if she agreed.

'Then yes, tell him I'd be happy to sell it to him. I'm just surprised that's all. I'd no idea he was doing so well.'

Harry called round that evening and Grace told him she was happy about the sale.

'The thing is,' said Harry. 'I know you have been happy in this house and I think I've found a way for you to stay. How would you feel…?' He hesitated. Grace was staring fixedly at the fireplace. He wondered if she was beginning to regret selling the house, after all, but perhaps she might feel differently when she heard what he had to suggest, so he carried on, explaining about him and Elizabeth and the plans they had in mind, suddenly stopping again as Grace turned her head and looked at him, startled.

'I'm sorry, this is all much too soon for you, isn't it? Can I get you a drink?'

'Some water please.' Grace whispered. She shook her head, had she heard right?

Elizabeth? Harry was going to marry Elizabeth! She had had no idea. In fact, for a moment, when he had talked about a way of letting her stay here, she had thought Harry was actually about to ask *her* to marry him. Not that she could ever have considered it. But Elizabeth! She was so much younger than him, and – Good heavens! – he even seemed to be suggesting that they would be able to keep an eye on *her*, as if she were in need of care. She was about the same age as Harry, for God's sake, not some decrepit old woman.

Harry brought the water and Grace gulped the whole glassful. It was cold and helped to check the churning in her stomach that had been triggered by the shock of the unexpected news.

'Look, I'll get off now, if you are sure you are all right.' Harry picked up his hat. 'I've given you a lot to think about, haven't I? I hope I've not upset you, Grace.'

'No, not at all.' Grace managed to sound calm, and just as he left the room, she remembered to say that she hoped they would both be very happy. Then she poured herself a large whisky and soda, went to bed and slept like a log. It was the best thing she could have done. In the morning Grace woke knowing exactly what she was going to do.

After breakfast, she went around to see Mrs Thomas. Harry was at work, as she knew he would be, and the two women sat at the kitchen table with a cup of tea.

'Harry told you, then?' Mrs Thomas opened the subject, her shrewd dark eyes watching Grace.

'He did, and I am very pleased for them both,' Grace answered truthfully. 'Elizabeth is a good mother to Margaret and she has always been so kind to me. I think she'll make Harry very happy.'

'So do I. He's like a dog with two tails,' said his mother. 'She's knocked years off him.'

Grace stared at her teacup. How come she hadn't noticed that? She had taken so much for granted. All the help Harry had given her, the thoughtfulness of Elizabeth in making sure she saw her granddaughter every week, telling her what they had been up to, including her in their life. They had both been so loving, giving her so much of their time. How could she have been so blind as not to see what was in front of her? She leaned forward and confided in Mrs Thomas.

'I've had a think about what Harry suggested, about them buying the house and having me live with them, and I know they mean well but–'

'But you are not ready to be put out to grass yet,' Mrs Thomas interrupted, 'And I should think not either. I know you were happy with Mr Hall, but you seem to have put your life on hold these last years. You paused and sat back and let someone else make all the decisions. At first, of course, you had been through a lot and you were weary, but you are too young and too intelligent to retire from life. Well, now you've come through it, I've seen a lot of difference in you these last few weeks, and I think you are ready to get back to being yourself again. You've still got a lot of living to do, Grace.'

Grace was surprised at how accurately her old friend had summed her up. She reached across the table and put her palm on Mrs Thomas's old wrinkled hand.

'You are quite right. I am ready and I have come to a decision. See what you think about this. I'm not going to live with Elizabeth and Harry, but I am going to sell them the house. Then, with the money from the sale, I am going to buy Elizabeth's house and move in there to be nearer to you. I'm going to change my name back to Corkish, so that Margaret and I share a name, and then I'm going to find myself a job.'

Mrs Thomas raised her eyebrows. 'My goodness, you *have* had your thinking cap on, haven't you?'

Elizabeth and Harry had a quiet wedding, coming so soon after Richard's death. They had never been particularly close to him, although they both liked the man they had known, but out of respect for Grace and the memory of Robert, they married as simply and discreetly as they could. Like Jessie and Jim, they did not have a honeymoon. In their case, the fact that they would begin their married life in the house of their dreams was honeymoon enough.

Margaret was thrilled to be living in the big house she had enjoyed visiting to see her Gran. It was only a few minutes away from the grammar school she now attended, and just a short walk to the park where she could play tennis. Many of her new friends lived nearby.

Elizabeth made few changes to her new home but those she did made it a brighter, more modern house. She replaced the old velvet drapes with light floral curtains and pelmets and painted some of the dark woodwork white. She turned a small bedroom into a sewing room, installed her old Singer sewing machine and was in her glory.

Mrs Thomas also decided to make changes. Jessie and Jim were eating breakfast when she made an announcement.

'I've decided to stop taking in lodgers,' she said. 'I'm going to retire.'

'When did you decide this?' asked Jim. 'You've not given so much as a hint about retiring.'

'Well, I'm telling you now. I'm getting older and I'm beginning to find it hard work.'

'I never thought I would hear you say that,' said Jessie.

'You probably thought you would never hear me say this either.' Mrs Thomas beamed at them. 'I am making this house over to you, Jim. It will be perfect for you to start your own practice in. I can move up to the two top rooms and you will have the rest of the house to yourselves.

I've turned eighty so I am going to take things easy. My sister, Ginny, is always asking me to go to stay with her and I want to go now, while I can still travel.'

'I can't let you do that, Grandma.' Jim protested.

'It's what I want, Jim. I'd love to see you with your own practice – and your own family one day. The house is big enough for both, so you see, there's method in my madness.'

A few months later, a delighted Jessie and Jim moved down from the attic rooms and started to make the alterations needed to turn two of the downstairs rooms into a surgery and a waiting room. Busy with painting and hammering and sewing, Jessie conceived without noticing. They were delighted when she took stock later.

'Your grandma's prophecy has come true,' she said to Jim. 'She's always prided herself on her ability to weigh up strangers, perhaps she's added another string to her bow, the ability to tell when the Stork is on the way.'

Five months later Mrs Bailey, the local midwife, helped Jessie to give birth to a seven-pound baby boy. They were all delighted, especially Margaret, and it was she who worked out the complicated relationship. Harry was her step-father, Jim was her step-brother so the baby was her step-nephew and she had just become an aunty. Jessie asked her to choose the baby's name and she chose Christopher.

'Christopher James Thomas,' Jim chose the full name. 'Welcome to the world.'

CHAPTER NINETEEN

GRACE sat down to open her letters. The morning sun shone through the window, glinting onto the two silver-framed photographs standing on top of her bureau, one of Robert and Elizabeth on their wedding day, and one of Margaret as a baby. The bureau was where she kept all the paperwork concerning the properties she owned and rented out. Even after buying Elizabeth's house, Grace had been left with enough money to invest in another property, and she had found one in the same street with good sitting tenants. This had been the start of her new venture because finding a job had not proved to be as easy as she had hoped. One difficulty was that the woman she had become, was very different from the hard-pressed young mother who had been prepared to work at almost anything to bring in the money. During her years with Richard, she had gained a sharper intellect and picked up a broad range of knowledge, and she had also acquired the confidence that security of money in the bank could bring, so whatever she did, it had to be something that would make use of her new talents and suit her personality. It was Mrs Thomas who had made the suggestion.

'I've always had a good living from this house, renting out rooms, but it has meant a lot of hard work. Why don't you become a different kind of landlady and invest in houses to rent? You'd be your own boss, be able to plan your own hours, and you've worked in an office so you will know how to handle the accounts, records, rent books and so on. All you need to do is make sure you get good tenants. Always ask for a reference but rely on your own impression as well. You are like me, Grace, a good judge of character, which is a big help.'

Grace had heard about the house down the road from Jessie, who knew the good family living there. They kept the house clean and tidy and paid the rent without fail, so encouraged by this easy introduction to the renting market, Grace had searched for her next property. Now she was the owner of seven houses, was running her own successful business and leading a pleasant, happy life. She smiled at the photograph of Margaret as a baby. That baby was now at university and about to graduate. It was hard to believe her grand-daughter would soon be twenty-one.

She slit open an envelope and the letter startled her. It was from Mrs Corkish! Grace had heard nothing from John's family since the day she had been handed the money for Robert, so many years ago. She had not even known if Mrs Corkish was still alive. It was clear it had been written for the old lady but presumably dictated by her. The letter did not address her by name and began almost abruptly.

You will perhaps be surprised to hear from me after so long, but although we have not been in contact, I have always been aware of the direction your life has taken. I was truly sorry to hear of the loss of your son. I know that he has a daughter who is now nearly twenty-one years of age, and it is because of her that I write to you.

I am now very old and not in good health. My husband has recently died, leaving the house to me. The mine he left to his brother's son who runs it.

I wish to leave the house and an income to your daughter who is, after all, my rightful heir. To this end I would like to ask if you would be kind enough to bring her to see me fairly soon, there are many things I would like to say to her and to you.

I would be most grateful if you could feel able to indulge me in this sincere request.

A spidery signature followed which was only just legible.

Grace leaned back in her chair, letter in hand, stunned. After all this time. So many memories came sweeping back, not all of them welcome, that Grace felt completely dismayed by this turn of events. She sat for a long time letting her emotions sway to-and-fro, re-living the turmoil of those distant, but still not dimmed, early years, until eventually her thoughts came back to the letter and the question of Margaret. Obviously, she would have to be told about the family in the Isle of Man because she had to know why this offer was being made to her. Just how much needed to be told about the attitude taken by the Corkish family, was the problem. Margaret was expected home that weekend and Grace knew she must have come to a decision by then.

'Can I come and talk to you, Jessie?' Grace said on the telephone the next morning.

'Of course, come for a cup of tea after surgery. It sounds important, do you want to talk to Jim as well?'

'Not especially, I know he has his rounds. You can tell him later. I'll see you at eleven o'clock then.'

Grace arrived just after Jim had left and Jessie made a pot of coffee then sat down looking serious.

'I hope it's not bad news, Grace.'

'Oh no, nothing like that, but it is rather shocking, well to me at any rate. I've heard – quite out of the blue – from John's mother.'

'Good heavens!' Jessie could understand the shock.

'She wants to meet Margaret, after all this time! Apparently, she is not in good health now as she is getting older, and she has asked me to take Margaret over to the island.'

'Are you going to?'

'I don't know yet. I've talked to Elizabeth of course, and she thinks the same as I do, that it has to be Margaret's decision. The thing is, Jessie, I have never really told anyone about John's family. Elizabeth knows very little and I don't think Margaret knows anything other than that Robert and I were both born on the Isle of Man.'

'Elizabeth did once mention that Robert's father's family was quite well off but that you had not had much to do with them.' Jessie hoped she was not breaking a confidence.

'That's right, they didn't approve of John marrying me. His father cut off all financial support and even contact with the family, then when John died so soon after Robert was born, it made the estrangement even greater. I think his mother might have done more if she had not been so influenced by his father, but he was unrelenting. There has been no acknowledgement of me or my family since, but her husband is dead now and the old lady seems to be regretting it. I'm struggling to decide what to do and I needed to talk to someone who was not personally involved, to get a more balanced opinion. How am I going to handle this? Margaret will be home tomorrow and I need to know what I am going to tell her without portraying John's family unfairly. I shall have to be careful not to influence her but it's not going to be easy.'

'It's not, but knowing you, Grace, you will be as even handed as anyone could expect, and possibly more than they deserve. Don't be afraid to tell Margaret how you felt at the time. She'll need to know what happened if she is to make her own decision. It's all water under the bridge now, isn't it?'

'Except that the water has changed course and is now flowing back. I didn't expect that.'

Grace knew that the way in which she told Margaret would have an influence on the way in which she received the news. Of course, Margaret was old enough to make up her own mind, but with no prior knowledge of her great grandmother on the Isle of Man, she would be looking to Grace for information and it had to be presented as honestly and in as unbiased a way as possible.

It took a long time to tell. After all, it was a large slice of her own story that she was telling and she left out the part about the house until the end, then she described it as best she could from her own limited knowledge. She could see Margaret was impressed.

'Gosh, it sounds enormous, Gran. I'd no idea we were posh,' she laughed excitedly. Then Grace showed her the letter from her great-grandmother and the laughter faded as she took in the words.

'She's leaving the house to me? That grand house you've just told me about? I can't believe it.'

'The important thing at the moment, Margaret, is whether or not you want to go to see her. If you do, you'll notice that she asks us to make it fairly soon, so what do you want to do? I will go with you, of course.'

'Oh, I'll go, I can't really refuse. I'd like to see her, and besides, I'd love to look at the house. I can go any time. We've finished all our exams and I've just got to wait for the results, but we will be back before then, won't we?'

'Right, I'll make the ferry booking. Shall I leave it to you to tell your mother? She knows I was going to talk to you about it and I'm sure she won't have any objection, but tell her I'll be with you, to look after you.'

Margaret laughed. 'I think it should be me looking after you, Gran. All the same I am glad you will be there. It will feel strange to meet her for the first time.'

* * *

It was not a smooth crossing. Rain and wind kept them below in the saloon for the whole journey so that they had reached the island before Grace could go on deck to greet her old home. There had been a lot of new building along the seafront as Douglas had developed into a popular holiday resort and much had changed, but Grace still felt a thrill as she looked down on the green water and golden sandy shore that had been part of her childhood.

She had booked a hotel for two nights, not knowing what would come of the meeting, and they went there first to leave their suitcases and freshen up. The Corkish house was over a mile away, so they took a cab. Grace had written to say when they would be calling, and as they pulled up in front of the house, the double doors opened and a middle-aged man stood waiting to greet them. He came down the steps and held out his hand to Grace.

'Hello. It's lovely to meet you. I am Isobel's nephew, Philip Corkish.'

'It is nice to meet you too. I'm Grace and this is my granddaughter, Margaret.' She brought Margaret forward.

'Margaret.' He smiled as he took her hand. 'I am your grandfather's cousin. I do hope you will call me Cousin Philip – or Uncle Philip if you prefer.'

'Cousin Philip sounds fine.' Margaret liked him at once and relaxed a little at the thought of another comforting presence by her side when she first faced her great-grandmother.

Philip showed them into a large comfortable sitting room. 'What about refreshments, can I get you anything?'

Grace thought a cup of tea would give them a moment to relax before what she considered might be an ordeal. The housekeeper brought tea and scones, still warm from the oven, and Margaret and Grace tried to look round surreptitiously as they ate and drank.

Philip told them he knew all about the letter, he was the one who had written it for his aunt. He explained that he had been running the mine long before his uncle had died and left it to him, but the house and a substantial amount of money had been left to Isobel Corkish, and it was that which she was passing on to Margaret.

'But how did she know where to find us?' asked Grace.

'Ah, I'm afraid my aunt has been keeping a watch on you. She engaged a private detective and he has been reporting back on your whereabouts over the years.'

'I see.' So, all this time John's mother had known about the family's fortunes and misfortunes, about Robert's death, yet had still not made contact until now, when she was nearing the end of her life. Grace felt the old bitterness again.

'My son, Peter, helps me with the mine,' Philip chatted on. 'You'll meet him later. He is my only son.' He glanced at their empty plates. 'May I pass you another scone, or more tea?' They both declined and looked across at each other – the moment had come.

Philip showed them up to Mrs Corkish's room. She was not in bed, as they had expected, but was sitting in a large wingback chair by the window and she was dressed. Grace would not have known her if she had passed her in the street. Age had withered her. Unexpectedly, the sight of the frail old lady stirred a deep sympathy in her, wiping out any bitterness, and she went forward, bent down to John's mother and took her hand.

'I've brought Margaret to see you,' she said gently.

Margaret moved forward to stand in front of the great-grandmother she had never known. Mrs Corkish put her head on one side and peered at the young girl for a moment.

'I see something of John in her,' she said. 'It's in the eyes.'

'Yes, both she and her father, Robert, inherited John's blue eyes, something they all got from you, I think. I can see you still have that bright colour.'

Mrs Corkish smiled. 'That is very kind of you.' She pointed towards two chairs. 'Thank you for coming. It is very important to me that you did, but I would have understood had you decided not to. We wronged you, my dear, and I am sorry for it.'

'It was a long time ago now.' Grace sat down and indicated for Margaret to sit in the nearest chair.

Margaret leaned forward. 'We both wanted to come. I've been very excited about meeting you and seeing where my grandfather was born. It's a beautiful house.'

'I'm glad you like it, Margaret, though you won't have seen all of it yet.' Isobel turned her head rather stiffly. 'Philip, would you show Grace the papers while I have a little talk with my great-granddaughter?'

Grace's eyes filled with tears as she heard Margaret finally acknowledged as a member of the family. All she had ever wanted was for John's bloodline to be back where it should be. The money, the house and the way of life, although so much a part of what John should have inherited, were not her main concern. It was the recognition that had always mattered. Even though they had always had the family name, John's father had not been able to deny them that, it had not meant they were part of the family. Now Margaret was.

Philip showed Grace down to the study and produced a copy of the letter from Mrs Corkish to her solicitor, requesting the house and the money be put in Margaret's name. It only needed Margaret's signature once she turned twenty-one to complete the legalities.

'Why does she want the house to be signed over now?' Grace asked. 'Why not just leave it to her in her will?'

'I think there are two reasons. Firstly, she thought this would be a good way to get to know Margaret, and secondly, she wants to try to persuade her to come and live in the house, make it her home. She would very much like to think of it staying in the family and I think that's probably what she is talking to Margaret about now.'

'So, there are conditions attached?' Grace was wary.

'No, no — she wouldn't make any conditions. That is why she wanted to see Margaret for herself, to let her understand what she has inherited and to tell her a bit about the family in which she should have been raised.' He looked at Grace and shrugged his shoulders slightly. 'I don't think she ever got over losing John and it made her retreat behind a façade. But I know she has always regretted not knowing Robert and she doesn't want to take any more regrets to her grave.'

'Is she dying?'

'Not in the immediate future, as far as we know, but she is slowly growing weaker and less able. Her heart is not as strong as it was, but she is well looked after and we hope to have her with us for a while longer yet.'

They were interrupted by a knock on the door. Philip put the letter back in the folder and called, 'Come in.'

'I'm not disturbing you, am I?' A fair-haired young man popped his head round the door.

'Peter, come in, we've just finished. Come and meet our cousin. Mrs Corkish, this is my son, Peter. He lives here with Aunt Isobel. It's too quiet for him where I live out near the mine. He likes to be nearer to his friends here in Douglas.'

Peter held out his hand. 'It's lovely to meet you, Mrs Corkish.'

'Oh please, both of you call me Grace,' she laughed as she shook Peter's hand. 'I mean, it's going to get a bit confusing if we keep it formal since we all have the same surname.'

Grace looked at the handsome young man in front of her. Here was another tall, fair-haired, blue-eyed member of the family.

'I have been really looking forward to meeting you,' said Peter. 'I was excited to find we had family I didn't know about. I hope we'll get to know one another better now that you are staying here.'

'Oh, but we are staying at a hotel,' Grace told him. 'We have booked provisionally for two nights since we didn't know quite how long we would be here.'

'Then there has been a mistake somewhere,' Philip said quickly. 'We all assumed you would be staying here. There's plenty of space and two rooms have been prepared for you. We thought it would be a good chance for you to get to know the house as well as Aunt Isobel.'

'We can cancel your booking,' offered Peter, 'and I can collect your cases. We can't let you disappear so soon after meeting you. Dad has arranged to stay the night here as well so that we can all have a good family gossip after dinner.'

'That is unless you'd rather not?' Philip was allowing her a choice.

Just then Margaret was shown into the room by the housekeeper.

'Margaret, come and say hello to my son Peter.' Philip went over and took her arm.

'I am taking your grandmother's tip and just using first names, since we all have the same family name. Margaret – Peter. Peter – Margaret.'

The two young people said hello and shook hands, smiled at each other rather awkwardly, then Margaret turned back to Grace, and Peter to Philip. That fell a bit flat, thought Grace in surprise, and Philip obviously thought the same because he hurriedly picked up the conversation from where they had left it.

'We were just discussing where you will be staying.' he said quickly. 'We took it for granted that you would be staying here and we are hoping to persuade your grandmother to cancel the hotel.'

Margaret looked at Grace for guidance but Grace, having misgivings due to the unenthusiastic greeting between her granddaughter and Peter, was now wondering what to do for the best.

'I'm not sure.' She hesitated. 'Perhaps it might be best if we…'

Margaret cut in. 'Great-grandma Isobel is expecting us to stay here. We had a talk, but she gets tired very quickly, so she asked if we would stay for the whole week – can we?'

Now that Grace knew what Margaret wanted it was easy to say yes, and Peter set off straight away to cancel their booking, collect their luggage and settle the hotel bill. Philip said they had time to rest before dinner and he called the housekeeper to show them to their rooms. They were surprised at how big they both were, each had a double bed and they were connected by a shared bathroom. The windows overlooked the back of the house and they saw a neat circular lawn surrounded by deep borders full of colourful flowering shrubs. Through a wooden arch they could see an area that seemed to be an orchard, judging by the fruit they could see on the trees, and they looked forward to exploring. Margaret was impressed.

'Good heavens, Grandma, I think we've landed in the lap of luxury.'

Bathed and changed, Grace was ready to rest before dinner, but Margaret was refreshed by her warm bath and keen to be off finding her way round the house. Grace had hoped to hear what Mrs Corkish had said to Margaret, but it could wait, and she would be glad of a rest. She lay on the bed, leaned back against soft downy pillows, closed her tired eyes and soon dozed off.

Margaret went down the big staircase and found her way back to the sitting-room where they had had tea. There was no one there, but the fire was glowing and its light flickered around the room reflecting in a glass fronted bookcase. Margaret went across to look at the titles. There were rows of beautiful leather-bound books and she recognised some of the authors, Dickens, Shakespeare, Hardy, Austen; the poets Keats, Browning, Yeats, Wordsworth, but there were many more she had never heard of, as well as some very large volumes of botanical and geographical subjects.

She touched the glass with a finger, wallowing in possessive anticipation. One day this would all be hers. She could spend many a wet afternoon here –then she flushed with shame as she remembered the old lady who was still alive upstairs. On a sideboard, a green glass vase held a mass of white sweet peas. Their gorgeous scent drifted across and Margaret wandered over to sniff them. It was a beautiful room. Floral curtains matched the cushions on the sofa and the armchairs were covered in faded shades of soft rose pink, all set off perfectly by the pale green walls. Out of the window, she could see a gravel drive curving up to the front door between two symmetrically laid out rose beds. Although it formed a neat approach to the house, Margaret was not keen on the formal style. She preferred to see loose swathes of flowers swaying freely in the wind, like the large fuchsia hedge on the other side of the house. This was in glorious bloom, dangling its crimson tassels over the path and spilling into pools of scarlet where the wilted blossoms had fallen to the ground. Margaret couldn't prevent herself from gloating again. If this house was really going to belong to her – then again, she stopped guiltily. She turned to move away from the window and jerked back, startled.

'Oh, sorry, I didn't mean to scare you.' Peter had come up behind her. 'I was just going to say hello when you turned around, you made me jump too. How do you like the house?'

'I love it, every bit that I have seen so far anyway. It's beautiful.'

They eyed each other. Very much alike in looks, they were both tall, fair-haired, glowing with health and with the same distinctive bright blue eyes. It was easy to see that they were related.

'We have half an hour before dinner, would you like to see more of the house, or would you like to look at the garden?'

'Oh, the garden I think please, before it gets dark.'

All awkwardness had gone and they went outside chatting like old friends. It was the back garden where they walked, and Margaret found that through the arch was the orchard they had glimpsed from their windows. Apple and pear trees had scattered their petals across the grass like confetti. There was just one cherry tree, which Peter told her hardly ever gave them any fruit because the birds always got to it first. 'But we don't mind, there is plenty of other fruit for us.'

Margaret liked that, allowing wild creatures to share the garden. It was just how she felt. They talked eagerly, anxious to find out as much about each other as they could cram into this first time alone, and when they entered the dining room later, both Grace and Philip found a completely different granddaughter and son than the rather uncomfortable pair who had been introduced to each other earlier.

The visit lasted the week and Margaret spent as much time as she could with great-grandma Isobel. She told Grace, the old lady was giving her all the guidance she would need to run the house, as well as telling her about the family she had not known. Most pleasing of all to Margaret, were the stories about her grandfather, John, although as she listened, she became aware of the injustice he had received from his father, and in turn, of the injustice done to her own father, Robert. It appeared that Isobel had not been strong enough either to persuade or defy her husband. All she could do was what she *was* doing now – handing over to Margaret what was in her power to give.

Resentment had festered for a moment as Margaret heard the details, but when she looked at the frail old lady, and saw the sadness in her eyes, she could harbour no real anger. It was just as Isobel had said, done and not to be undone, only to try to make amends for.

At the end of the week both Grace and Margaret were reluctant to leave. Grace had taken the opportunity to visit her sister Ellen and her brother Thomas, who both still lived in Douglas. Charlie now lived at Ramsey but was at sea working as part of a fishing crew, so Grace had to make do with a letter to him. The visit to the island itself, as well as contact with her family, had aroused unexpected emotions in Grace, and she realised the pull of her homeland was stronger than she had thought. To be back again where she had been born, seeing the familiar sights and walking the familiar shore, evoked fond childhood memories that were with her strongly all that week. Seeing and talking to Isobel had evoked memories that were not so pleasant, but Grace refused to dwell on the humiliation of those years. She would welcome only those memories when, as a little child, she had known the comfort of her family home, and the beauty of her island.

She looked out across the water as they boarded the ferry to take them back to Fleetwood, and reflected that the sea between the island and the mainland didn't separate them, it joined them. The same waters of the Irish Sea washed the sands at Douglas and at Blackpool. Snaefell, and the island's other inland hills, mirrored the fells of the Pennine Range in Lancashire. They were neighbours. The sea she had once so dreaded was now nothing more than a watery path.

'I'm glad we made this trip.' she said to Margaret, as they stood at the rail to watch as the boat left the island. 'I don't know why it took me so long to come home.'

'Is that how you feel, Gran? That you have come home?'

'I didn't know I felt that way, but yes, I really do. I love Blackpool, of course, and I've had a happy life there on the whole, but this is my island and it stirs my Manx blood.'

As Margaret leaned close with her head on her grandma's shoulder, Grace had the strong feeling that her granddaughter felt much the same way.

CHAPTER TWENTY

GRACE and Margaret made two more visits to the island that year. The last visit was to attend the funeral of Isobel Corkish, who died from pneumonia at the age of eighty-six. A lot of progress had been made during the first two visits, and although Margaret had spent long hours with the old lady, she had also managed to spend a great deal of time with Peter.

'I can't believe we've never met before,' said Peter. 'I feel as if I have known you all my life, yet we didn't even know each other existed until a few months ago, did we?'

'I certainly had no idea I had family living on the Isle of Man.' Margaret answered. 'What are we? Second cousins once removed, or what?'

'Or third or fourth, all I know is that we have the same name.'

'Grandma Isobel is the link between us, I wonder why she kept us a secret?'

'I've no idea, but you are here now, and that's all that matters.'

Everyone could see that romance was in the air, therefore no one was surprised when, just before they were due to return on the last day of their third visit, Peter proposed to Margaret and they announced their engagement.

'Well, I was hoping our two young people would get along, but I didn't expect it to turn out like this. It's been like an express train rushing through,' Philip said.

'I know, and yet when they first met, I actually thought they didn't like each other,' Grace admitted.

'I think it was because they *did* like each other so much that they were both taken by surprise, and they needed to get their breath back. I can't tell you how delighted I am, and I only hope Margaret's mother will feel the same.'

'Well, I can't speak for Elizabeth, of course, but I do know Margaret has confided in her. I'm pretty sure she will be as pleased as we are.'

'We must arrange to meet quite soon, there's a lot to discuss. Where the wedding will be held, for one thing. Do you think…?'

'Stop right there, Philip.' Grace held up her hand. 'You are talking to the wrong person. I shall be a guest, pure and simple. Any planning will be done between Elizabeth and Margaret, and you and Peter, but definitely not me. I intend to just turn up and enjoy the day.'

Grace looked across the garden to where the two lovers were walking hand in hand. If only John and Robert were here to see this happy day, she thought wistfully. Then, aware that she was in danger of growing morbid, she deliberately chased the thought away and took hold of Philip's arm.

'Come on, let's go and prise them apart. My granddaughter and I have a boat to catch.'

* * *

It was to be a big wedding since the Corkish family was well known in the community, and it had been agreed that it would take place in Douglas as that would be Margaret's new home.

Ellen was the only one of Grace's birth family to accept an invitation. Charlie was still away at sea and Ellen had explained that Thomas would not feel comfortable being in the close presence of the family he had once worked for as a humble miner. Grace understood.

Later, sitting next to her sister in church, waiting for the bride to arrive, Grace suddenly saw herself as a young girl, walking with John out of the little chapel where they had exchanged vows, eagerly looking forward to the rest of her life and proudly carrying inside her the child they had created. They had both been full of hope. They had not known then how immovable his father would prove to be and how those hopes would be shattered. At times the path had seemed bleak, but as today showed, everything passes eventually.

The organ burst into the first chords for the bridal entry and everyone stood to greet Margaret on the arm of her stepfather, Harry. Grace felt Ellen nudge her.

'Who would ever have believed this could happen to us, Grace?' she whispered.

Grace smiled. 'I don't think it *is* happening to us Ellen – it's happening to Margaret. We are just lucky enough to be a part of it.'

The newlyweds went to Paris for their honeymoon and on the boat, sailing back to their new home, they stood at the rail watching for the first faint outline of the island which had brought them together.

'We will fly next time,' Peter promised. 'How would you like your own personal pilot? I'm thinking of learning to fly.'

'Oh yes,' Margaret clapped her hands. 'That would be wonderful – then you can teach me!' She grinned up at him.

'Steady on, you can't even drive a car yet.'

'There it is!' Margaret was the first to see the blue smudge on the horizon. 'We are nearly home.'

Philip was waiting to collect them from the harbour and he drove them to their house before returning to his own home near the mine. Mrs Murray, the housekeeper, had prepared a roast dinner for them and after serving it, she left them alone before a blazing fire to share their first meal as husband and wife in their own home. Margaret looked across at Peter.

'I can't believe how lucky I have been. I could never have dreamed of a life like this a year ago.'

'It is your birth-right, Darling.' Peter lifted his glass in a toast. 'Here's to my beautiful wife – and the rest of our life!'

'To my lovely husband,' Margaret laughed and raised her glass. 'It's no good, I can't think of a matching rhyme, so it is just – to you, my love, and thank you.'

CHAPTER TWENTY-ONE

FOR the first few months, Margaret was totally absorbed in exploring the house and getting to know the staff they employed. Since the days when Grace had carried the laundry to-and-fro in the little cart, there had been many changes. Although it was still a large house, it was no longer the grand place it had been. After the war, former servants no longer wanted to work long hours for low pay. Many of the men, who had joined the armed forces, had not come back, and the girls who had trained as bus drivers, or machine operators in factories, had discovered an independence that would not allow them to go back to being at the beck and call of what they called 'the idle rich.'

Margaret found she had inherited a house run by one housekeeper, Mrs Murray, one daily cleaner and an elderly cook who came in two mornings a week to make the bread, plus one gardener helped by a young boy. It was a reduced but very well organised household that ran itself. Since Mrs Corkish had no longer entertained, this staff had been enough for her needs. There was not a lot for Margaret to do.

After exploring the house from top to bottom and becoming acquainted with the garden, she began to look for other things to keep her busy. The saloon car had stood unused in the garage since Isobel had died, so Margaret decided to learn to drive and was soon able to drive herself round to visit her new friends and explore the island. To someone used to using her brain however, boredom soon set in and she talked to Peter about it.

'I'm thinking of applying for a teaching post. I really ought to make use of my qualification. What do you think?'

'I understand how you feel. I've got my job to keep me busy and I suppose if I didn't have that, I would definitely have looked for something which needed my full attention. Neither of us look for an easy ride, do we?'

'Shall I follow it up then?'

'Have a good think first. Weigh up all the pros and cons before you decide.'

Margaret sat down to think. She thought about the women in her family. Her mother, Elizabeth, who had taken on the role of breadwinner when her husband had been killed in the war; Gran, busy buying and renting out property, something for which she had had no training but had made a success of regardless; then there was Jessie, combining her role as a nurse with bringing up Christopher; and, of course, Mrs Thomas, who had spent years taking in lodgers and building a good reputation. All of them were strong women who had made something of their lives. So, what was her own interest, what did she enjoy doing? There was no getting away from it, teaching was what she had wanted to do before her life had taken such a dramatic turn, and teaching was what she still wanted to do.

A month later she took up a post teaching Geography and French at a private boys' school. It was a twenty-minute drive away and she was out of the house almost as much as Peter but she was so animated and involved in the job, that their relationship benefitted and their first year of marriage was blissful.

Starting a family had always been part of their plans, though because Margaret was still so young, they had felt they could bide their time. When their second anniversary came and went, Peter broached the subject and together they agreed that the time was right and they happily made plans for the next stage in their lives. Because they were both so fit and healthy, they were somewhat surprised when six months slipped by with no results. Plenty of time, they told each other, but by the time their third anniversary came around doubts were beginning to cloud their hopes.

Clouds were also beginning to gather on the world stage. War was threatening in Europe again. Margaret was speaking to her mother on the telephone on the Sunday morning that Britain declared war against Germany and they both wept. Not again, not so soon, was the general feeling, especially among the older people who remembered the last war and its devastation. This time no one predicted it would be over by Christmas. The government had already taken steps to prepare for conflict by arranging for children from London and other industrial towns to be evacuated to safe areas. As one of these, Blackpool became a centre for evacuees and a training base for the R.A.F. The peaceful days had gone.

Although like Blackpool, the Isle of Man was regarded a safe area, Margaret realised that from now on, trips to and from the island would be restricted at best, and she felt isolated. That was not the worst of it – Peter told her he was joining the RAF.

'I am a qualified pilot, Margaret. I can be useful.'

'You are not qualified to fly armed planes!' She was frightened. 'What about the mine?'

'The mine is virtually closed down now anyway, and Dad can manage. They need people like me, Margaret, besides I want to go.' He faced her, half-apologetic, half-defiant, and Margaret knew she must accept his decision. She even managed to put on a brave face when they said goodbye six weeks later, joking that she knew why he had wanted to join the RAF. With his blond hair and blue eyes, the uniform suited him perfectly.

Many of the male teachers at her school also enlisted so Margaret was busily involved in rearranging a new timetable to enable the school to run smoothly, and she began to spend more and more time at work. It kept her mind from dwelling on the dangers facing Peter and warded off the disappointment that they had not been able to start a family before he went away.

The island itself had a role to play. Douglas became a communication post as well as housing an internment camp for those people of foreign descent who had already been living in Britain, but hailed from countries which were now the enemy. They were to be kept in confinement for the duration of the war. Nearly all the hotels and guest houses along the seafront were commandeered to house the aliens, many of whom were Italian, and huge wire enclosures were erected round the buildings. Margaret's house was partly taken over as a billet for the RAF instructors on signal training courses.

She still had her own bedroom and the small breakfast room to herself, but there was no real privacy with a houseful of men coming and going. Mrs Murray was in her glory however, and the old cook came in every morning to help with the meals. The garden was turned over to the production of vegetables, and that, along with the fruit from the orchard, made a huge difference to the quantity of produce they were able to provide. Joe, the gardener, was asked to take on two of the Italian internees as extra help, which would increase their output and help with the island's food shortage.

Weekends were the biggest problem. The men and Margaret were all out during the week, but at weekends she felt confined with just her two rooms, especially since there was no longer a private garden to wander around. After her last visit Grace had bought a little cottage on the cliff north of Douglas, intending to spend the summer months back on her beloved island, but the war had put an end to her plans. It was still there unused so Margaret wrote to ask if she might stay there at the weekends.

'Yes of course, darling, please use it as often as you like,' Grace had replied. 'I shall be glad to have it lived in.'

Margaret began the routine of driving to the cottage every Friday evening and spending the weekends there, taking long walks on the beach and tending to the little garden. Had the war not been on, and Peter away flying, she would have said this was a satisfying time, totally occupied by her school work and able to do exactly as she pleased with her weekends.

The war, however, was never far away and she thought that her greatest fear had been realised when a dreaded telegram arrived. Margaret stared at it for a few minutes before forcing herself to open it. Her fingers trembled and she struggled to read the black letters. She had to read it over again to be sure she had understood. It informed her that Peter had been shot down over Germany and was now a prisoner of war. Her first terror turned to relief and she shook uncontrollably. Mrs Murray brought her a brandy and made her sit down in the big armchair.

'At least he is alive, dear, and once you know exactly where he is. You'll be able to write through the Red Cross.'

'Yes, I know, Mrs Murray, but I have been dreading something like this, and now it's happened it's such a shock.' She sipped the brandy. 'But he's not dead, is he? He is alive thank God!'

Mrs Murray provided numerous cups of tea, and by the time she went to bed, Margaret had begun to be thankful that it was not as bad as it might have been. If this war ever ended, Peter would come home.

The next day, she wrote to Elizabeth and Grace and was able to put on a brave face so that they would not worry about her. Of course, they did worry. Very much. One of the things which crossed the minds of both of them, was that now there was no chance of a much longed for child, at least not for the foreseeable future.

Margaret spent their fifth wedding anniversary on her own at Grace's little house. She took a long walk on the beach, bringing her alongside the wire compounds where the internees sat sunbathing, and she received some appreciative wolf-whistles. She waved, then turned her back and walked towards the sea, before heading back to the house which had become her haven. Compared with many others, she knew she was lucky, but that night in bed, the loneliness and sadness at their failure to start a family overwhelmed her, and she wept as she had never needed to do in her life before.

* * *

The apples were ready for picking, and one weekend, Margaret offered to help Joe, the gardener. It had been a mild spring so the blossom had not been blown by the wind before it could fully flower and there was a glut of fruit. Joe's young assistant had reached the age for enlistment in the forces and he had gone eagerly to train for the Navy, so Joe was glad of her help as well as that of the two Italians who were sent from the camp as part of a work detail.

On Saturday they picked all day and Mrs Murray brought sandwiches and tea out to the orchard. They were having an Indian summer and in the blazing heat of the day, Margaret slipped off her blouse and wore just a little yellow vest, showing off the lovely golden tan she had acquired. She noticed one of the men, Alfredo, looking at her admiringly and she smiled back, amused at the attention. It was nice to have an admirer, even if she had no intention of encouraging him. Neither Italian spoke much English so there was not a lot of chatter, but she gathered that they both felt very lucky to have been sent to work in her garden. Joe and Mrs Murray had made them so welcome they looked forward to coming to the house each day. It made Margaret realise how hard it was for people who had lived peaceably in England before the war, to now find they were facing animosity because of their nationality. They were caught up in a situation which was not of their own making. But then they were all facing a situation not of their own making, weren't they? It was called, war.

Hot and sweaty, and with an aching back, Margaret stooped to pick up the last basket of apples she had filled.

'Please, let me help.' Bruno, the other Italian, reached to take the basket and Margaret was more than glad to let him.

'Oh, thank you. Goodness, I didn't realise how unfit I am, I'm aching all over.'

'It is very hard work. You are not used to pick apples all day, I think.'

Margaret laughed, 'No I'm not, although I am on my feet all day at school and I thought that was hard work.'

They walked to the shed where the apples would be stored. Joe was pleased with the crop. 'We can start on the pears tomorrow,' he said.

'I think you might have to count me out.' Margaret buttoned her blouse. 'Apart from the fact that I might not be able move, I have a lot of marking to get through, sorry.'

'I am sorry too.' Bruno's smile was wistful.

The next weekend Margaret went to the cottage again. The tiny garden needed to be cleared of the gone over summer plants and the wallflowers she had raised from seed, had to be planted ready for spring. Although she had written regularly, sending letters through the Red Cross, she had not heard from Peter for many weeks and it was becoming harder to write to him. All she could think to tell him about was her work at school. Not much else was happening in her life. Other than the worry about Peter and the dreadful war news she heard on the wireless bulletins, she was in a stagnant routine which seemed to be a world apart from the life she had planned as a newly-wed twenty-one-year-old. Her recent twenty-eighth birthday had brought on a very blue mood. She was growing older and what was worse, she *felt* older. It was hard not to feel bitter about the wasted years, even though she knew how selfish that was when so many people were suffering the loss of loved ones and, if the reports were true, enduring unspeakable horrors on the Continent. If she had known what was ahead of them, she would have volunteered for one of the forces as Peter had done. Then at least she would have been playing a part in the desperate struggle. Teaching, once so important to her, had now become part of her stagnant routine, and combined with the restriction of her accommodation in her own home, she felt like a caged bird. She was finding it hard to remember her life with Peter, he was slipping further into a past that was becoming more and more hazy. Margaret was sensible enough to try to analyse what was happening and she came to the conclusion that she was suffering the weariness of a long ongoing war, but she couldn't shake it off.

There were some potatoes in the cupboard that had been grown in the garden at the big house, and Margaret put two large ones into the oven to bake. She would have them with some cheese and a dab of margarine later, filling and easy to cook, and giving her time to have a quick brisk walk along the sands. It had been another hot day and the cool evening breeze was welcome. The sand was still warm and dry, waiting for the incoming tide, and she took off her sandals and walked barefooted, carefully avoiding the sharp shells and hard stones.

She walked as fast as she could, but her heels sank into the soft sand making it an effort to stride out and her calf muscles began to ache. She pushed on, determined to dispel her gloomy mood, and only when water trickled over her toes did she look up and realise that the tide had swirled in ahead of her, and when she glanced back she could see that it had already covered a large spread of the beach behind. Knowing how quickly the incoming tide could flow she decided she had better head straight towards the promenade where there was still a stretch of sand that the water had not yet reached. She was in no danger, but it meant that she would have to walk back along the promenade, which would take longer.

For someone who had lived by the sea all her life, she was annoyed with her stupidity in not keeping a closer look out. Now the potatoes might burn and she would have to eat them anyway, no one could afford to waste food these days.

She sat down on a seat on the promenade to put her sandals back on and was surprised to hear someone call her name. Looking up she saw that she was in front of one of the hotels where the internees were billeted. She saw Alfredo waving.

'Ciao, Margaret. You going for a swim maybe?' he called.

'I very nearly did.' Margaret laughed and waved back to him. 'Now I have a long walk back and I've left my dinner in the oven so it will probably be burnt, serves me right for daydreaming.'

'We see you tomorrow, then.' he called, and at that moment she saw that Bruno was also standing there. He was smiling and, unaccountably, she felt a little quiver run through her. Giving another brief wave, she stood and set off towards the cottage with a spring in her step and a lightness of heart that she thought she had lost long ago.

CHAPTER TWENTY-TWO

A TREMENDOUS blast violently shook the whole house and Grace was jerked awake and pitched to the bottom of her bed. An ear-piercing crack like a pistol shot came as the windows rattled. The explosion seemed to have happened right there in her room. Stunned and deafened, she realised a bomb had dropped. After a terrified minute or two she carefully moved her arms and legs to check if she was hurt. She didn't seem to be injured but her heart was thumping so fast she was afraid she might pass out, and she tried to calm herself so she could think rationally. Peering round in the darkness she couldn't make out very much but so far as she could tell, the room seemed to still have four walls and a ceiling.

She knew the safest place was downstairs and that she must get there quickly in case anything crashed down from overhead, but she didn't know how safe the staircase was. She edged out of bed, feeling gingerly along the floor with her toes in case the windows had broken and there was glass on the floor, and was glad when she found her slippers and slipped her feet safely inside. Unable to see very much because of the blacked-out windows, she groped for the bedside lamp and was about to switch it on when she stopped, unsure of the safety. Shaking and teeth chattering, she shuffled across to where she hoped the chair was and felt for her dressing gown pulling it quickly round her for some warmth. Her ears were ringing so much from the blast she could hear nothing else.

Terrified of what she might find, she opened the door slowly and waited a moment before cautiously reaching for the banister rail, clinging to it when it felt solid, and taking one tentative step at a time, she began creeping downstairs. She had just made it to the foot of the stairs when a loud banging at the front door made her jump. It was Mr Butler, the Air Raid Warden, shouting to check if she was all right. She'd just opened the inner door to call back and say she was unhurt when the siren began to wail.

'Stay inside. I'll come back when I know what's happening,' he shouted.

So at least she knew the house was still standing. Grace made her way to the kitchen and into the pantry under the stairs that she had prepared as a shelter. All her neighbours had done the same, as they had been advised to do, never expecting to have to use it. She found the candles and matches she kept stored on the shelf just by the door, and when her trembling hands finally managed to light a flame, she took a deep breath, comforted by the flickering light. She held the candle high and looked around. So far as she could see there didn't seem to be any obvious damage. Thanks to the crisscrossing of gummed paper strips, no windows had been blown in despite the huge blast, so under the stairs seemed to be the best place to be.

She sat down on the little seat she had put at the back of the pantry and tried to stop shaking. The bomb had obviously not been a direct hit so it must have been further up the street – in sudden panic she remembered Jessie and Jim and Christopher. She pulled herself up and hurried to the front door, struggling with the bolt, and when she finally managed to open it, she found her next-door neighbour climbing over the low wall which divided their small front gardens.

'Are you all right?' Mary asked, clearly frightened. 'You're not hurt or anything?' She grabbed Grace's hand.

'No, not at all, but where did it fall, Mary?' They both looked up the street and saw the red glow of flames over the rooftops and heard the bells of the fire engines.

'Bill has gone to see if he can do anything to help. He said to stay inside but I wanted to make sure you were all right.'

'Thank you, Mary. I'm fine, but I am so worried about Jessie and Jim. It looks to be quite near them.' Both ladies were shivering and trying to stop their teeth from chattering.

'Come in to me, don't stop on your own. I'll make us a cup of tea.'

'No, I won't come in, Mary, I'll be all right and I need to be here in case Jim and Jessie need me, if they are all right that is. Oh God, I do hope so.' She began to cry.

'I'll bring you a cup of tea in a minute, then. Go back under the stairs for now and I'll let you know what Bill says when he comes back.'

Grace made her way back to her makeshift shelter and an unfamiliar prayer came to her lips. *Please, please keep them safe, dear Lord.*

When Mary brought the tea, she told her Bill had come back and said that the bomb had fallen on a small street near North Station. He had passed Jim's house and it was undamaged. He said people were being asked to keep away so that the fire, ambulance and police crews could deal with the horrific situation and, although she was worried, Grace did as she was told, knowing that there was nothing she could do to help, but her heart ached for those poor people who had gone to bed that night totally unaware of the disaster that awaited them.

* * *

Around the corner, Jessie and Jim had climbed into bed exhausted. It had been a busy day for both of them, and Christopher had begged to stay up late to listen to Arthur Askey in his hit programme ITMA on the wireless, but at last everyone was safely tucked up for the night.

The boom from a sudden massive explosion seemed to lift the house from its foundations, Jessie and Jim were flung half in and half out of their bed as it was catapulted across the floor. Vibration raked through their bodies, the bang had deafened them and for a few moments they lay as they were, stunned and unable to move, then fear penetrated the shock.

'Christ, it's a bomb!' Jim tried to pull Jessie back on to the bed. 'I think we've been hit.'

'Christopher!' Jessie gasped. Terrified, she and Jim raced to his room. He was still in his bed, under the blankets, but so far as Jim could tell, unharmed. Still stunned, Jim couldn't think for a few minutes. Jessie and Christopher were safe, that was all that registered at first, but then he realised that, although the roof and walls of their bedrooms were still there, it didn't mean the rest of the house was standing. He would have to find out. Jessie was sitting on Christopher's bed, holding him tight.

'Stay there, Jessie, while I see how much damage there is.'

'Don't Jim, please. If we are the ones who have been hit someone will be here soon, just wait'.

'I've got to look in case anything is likely to come down on us – listen, there's a fire engine, it's going past so it's not us.' They listened as another engine raced past, bell clanging. 'Get our gas masks, Jessie, while I see if it's safe to go downstairs.'

Making sure each step was safe, he led the way down to the under the stairs shelter. Jessie switched on a torch and shone the light on white faces. They were all shaking with shock. Once they were as safe as they were able to make themselves, Jim's professional training replaced his terror and he tried to think clearly.

'I don't think the bomb landed very close to us, I think we got the reverberation of an almighty explosion, but somewhere near here has definitely been hit. I'm going to see if I can help.'

Jessie could still feel the shock waves vibrating though her body and she was still half stunned, but she didn't try to stop him. He was right, perhaps he could be of some help. Christopher was shaking with shock.

'Are you all right, love? Do you hurt anywhere?' He shook his head.

She took down the biscuit tin and offered it to him, the sweetness would help with his shock, but although he took one, he made no effort to eat it.

Jim came back looking strained. 'It's at the top of the street,' he said. 'There are houses down and people injured. The firemen and police are there, and the ambulances, but it is dangerous and they are not letting anyone near. I talked to the warden, and I've offered to provide a stop off centre for those people who are having to leave their homes but are un-injured, apart from shock or minor injury. The ambulances will deal with the serious cases, there are bound to be fatalities…' He stopped and took a deep breath.

Jessie looked at Christopher, still shivering, and decided to take him into the living room where there was a warm glow from the banked down fire, and enough heat to warm him up to help with the shock. She put a large cob of coal on the fire and a few sparks flew out as the blaze took hold, then she tucked a crocheted cover round him and settled him on the settee. Chris would be better here, and since she would be needed by Jim's side, she could keep an eye on him from the surgery. As he began to warm up, Christopher's eyes closed and he fell asleep. Jessie sat trembling beside him, waiting. When the front door opened, she turned, expecting to see Jim, but instead Harry rushed in. He went straight across to check on Christopher, then hugged Jessie.

'Harry.' Jessie could manage no more. She had to swallow hard to stop the tears from coming.

'I saw Jim outside,' Harry said, 'He says the warden is directing anyone here who only needs checking over before they go on to temporary accommodation in the church hall. It will be shock, mainly, perhaps some slight cuts or burns but Jim will take a look at them first. We'll need lots of sweet tea. I can do that, and I'll keep my eye on Christopher, while you two are busy.'

'Thank you for coming, Harry.' Jessie went into the surgery and began to prepare for the type of patient they would be receiving.

For the rest of the night they were all busy. As well as tending to the people the wardens sent to them, they provided a relief base for some of the firemen and policemen who needed to take a break from their dangerous work. Between them they dished out plasters for small cuts and grazes, lots of sweet tea, and as much reassurance as it was possible to give. Harry borrowed extra milk and sugar from willing neighbours and kept the kettle boiling all night. One very elderly couple arrived numb with shock and they spilt most of their tea down their clothes as they tried to drink with trembling hands. Harry helped them.

'What a bloody mess.' he muttered through clenched jaws. 'Just look at these poor old souls…' He couldn't say any more.

* * *

By the time the all-clear rang out everyone was exhausted. Jessie wandered through from the surgery, desperate for a cup of tea, and Harry said he would go down to check on Grace.

'I came straight here because I saw the warden and he told me she was all right, but she will be very worried about you all.'

'Tell her we are safe. Tell her not to worry.' Jessie drank her tea quickly and poured a cup to take to Jim. One of the firemen was lying on the surgery bed, having suffered a nasty bang on the head, and Jim wanted to keep an eye on him. It had taken quite a bit of firm talking to prevent him from going back to re-join his crew.

Jessie began to clean the soiled equipment they had been using and to wipe down surfaces that were contaminated with the smell of smoke. There was a strong whiff of burning in the air. She crossed over to her husband, put her arms round his neck, and laid her cheek on the top of his head. He lifted a hand and clasped one of hers. Neither one of them spoke. They knew this would live with them for a long time to come. It was the most traumatic experience of their lives.

* * *

As soon as she heard the all-clear, Grace opened the front door and went to the gate, looking anxiously up the street. Harry was coming down towards her and she could tell by the way he was walking that he was not bringing bad news.

'Grace, I'm sorry I couldn't get here sooner,' he said.

'Are they all right?'

'Yes, they are fine. Jim and Jessie were busy all night helping out since they were so near. There were a few small cuts and slight burns to deal with, nothing serious. I went there as soon as we heard where the bomb had dropped and stayed to do what I could. I knew you were safe, I saw the ARP warden, or I would have come sooner, but I was needed there.' He put his hand to his head for a moment and Grace could see the strain he had been under.

'Of course, you were, and I was perfectly all right. Mary and Bill look out for me, you know that. Oh, Harry, I'm just so relieved they are all safe. How on earth could it happen here. We are supposed to be a safe area.'

'As far as I know, they think it was a single plane gone off course, possibly after a raid on the Barrow shipyard, and he was making his way to the sea. He must have seen the railway line and unloaded the last of his bombs but he missed and hit Seed Street. What a bloody tragedy!'

It was the first time Harry had ever sworn in front of Grace, and she realised that he was so distressed he didn't even notice.

CHAPTER TWENTY-THREE

MARGARET sat at her dressing table stroking cream onto her face. She could feel the moisture sinking in, softening the tight drying effect the salt wind always had on her fine skin. A white towel was wrapped round her wet hair and she was warm after her bath. Hopefully sleep would come early tonight. Just lately there had been many nights when she had been still awake well into the early hours, and the lack of sleep was taking its toll. She could see shadows under her eyes and lines crinkled her forehead – tension lines – but what could she expect? After all, she was getting older. Only a few weeks ago she had turned twenty-nine, and what had she got to show for it? She was still in the same place she had been eight years ago, married but childless.

Through the mirror her bleak face looked back at her and tears welled. She pulled the towel from her head, dabbed her eyes, and with her hair still damp, got into bed and pulled the blanket high. To sleep or not to sleep – she would soon find out.

When she stirred later, her hair was dry and the clock showed her it was half-past five, still early morning, but at least she had slept for a full six hours. A seagull was calling outside, so close she knew it was perched on the roof just above her window, and the raucous squawk reminded her of the gulls on the beach when she had been nearly cut off by the tide, and that thought led on to Alfredo and Bruno, and that odd little thrill shot through her again.

She rolled onto her back. She was wide awake but there was no point in getting up just yet. Mrs Murray would be busy getting breakfast for the men then she and Margaret would eat theirs together. That gave her thinking time and Margaret knew perfectly well what she needed to think about. Bruno, and her undeniable attraction to him. They had exchanged no more than a few words and she knew nothing about him. How old he was, for instance, whether or not he was married, educated, or even if he shared the attraction. Apart from that little thrill there was nothing at all to base any rational thought on, but there *was* that little thrill and it did not seem to be going away. She decided the best thing to do was to wait and see.

She heard Mrs Murray clattering pots in the kitchen as she washed up after the men had left, it was time to get up. Last night had been the longest sleep she had had for weeks and the morning face she saw in the mirror was relaxed for the first time in months. By inwardly acknowledging her attraction to Bruno, some of the unhappiness she had been feeling had been erased, even though it would inevitably cause complications. The new term at school was keeping everyone busy and she didn't see anyone at the house, other than Mrs Murray and the old cook, for the rest of the week, but at the weekend she drove to the cottage again.

On Saturday she walked on the beach, but purposefully turned north, the opposite direction to the internment camp. On Sunday she walked straight out to the edge of the sea, which was at low tide, and stopped to paddle. Little crabs scuttled about her feet and the water was cold. She kicked a few splashes at the crabs then turned and deliberately headed for the camp, ready to see what might transpire. Alfredo was sunbathing as usual, and he called to her.

'Margaret, 'ow are you. I've missed you.'

'I'm fine, but I've been very busy at work.' There was no sign of Bruno and she pondered whether or not to ask after him, then decided not to. That would be going against her wait and see strategy. 'I'll probably see you next week, though.' She waved and set off back to the cottage.

In a way she was pleased that Bruno had not been there, so that there had been no reinforcement of that foolish embryonic thrill, giving her the chance to draw back and let it go. This was what loneliness did, what the war did, it pushed people into clutching at any bit of excitement in a grim, frightening world. She was no exception.

The next week was quieter at school and she left early one afternoon after struggling with a headache all day. She had heard about the bombing in Blackpool from her mother and although she knew they were all safe, it had given her a sleepless night. Mrs Murray made her a cup of tea and gave her an aspirin.

'You ought to go and lie down for a while, try to nap if you can. There is some lavender still in bloom by the gate, a few sprigs under your pillow will help.'

'I'll go and pick some, anything to get rid of this awful headache.'

Margaret held her hand over her eyes to keep away the bright light, so she didn't see Bruno until he spoke.

'Hello.'

Her hand dropped and as she looked up the sun flashed into her eyes and a searing pain raked across her temples. Bruno heard her gasp as she quickly covered her eyes again and he was instantly beside her, his hand under her elbow. 'Are you all right?'

'I've got a terrible headache. I just came out to pick some lavender before I lie down. Mrs Murray thinks some under my pillow will help.'

'She is right. Let me get it for you please.'

He picked several flower heads and handed them to her. Their hands touched and Margaret gave up all pretence of dabbling with the thrill of a summer flirtation. She knew exactly what was happening, she was falling in love.

'Can I help more? Take my arm. Let me see you to the door.' He offered his arm and Margaret took her hand from her eyes and put it on the rough twill of his sleeve. She could feel the warmth of his arm even through the thick material, and as she glanced up at him the world stopped its spinning and their eyes held each other's in a strange suspension of time. She had felt this instant attraction once before, with Peter, yet this time was different. With Peter, they had fitted together like a pair of gloves, ready to go through life hand in hand, cosy and warm. With Bruno, she felt that from somewhere, completely unexpectedly, had come a fusing with her soul. This was the love of her life, nothing would ever change that, but she had no idea what could become of it.

There was no touching of hands as he left her at the door, although he was obviously concerned for her, but it seemed as if they had both known in that one moment and without a word being spoken, that they had moved to a level beyond the tentative exploration of a new love. It was as though she had loved him forever and had just been waiting for him to find her. Back in her room she placed the lavender under her pillow, closed her eyes and slept.

* * *

They met whenever they could throughout that golden autumn and Margaret discovered heights of passion she had never found with Peter. Because of Bruno's curfew, time had to be stolen from the working day, and Margaret stopped staying late at school so that they could snatch time together before he left for the roll call. Early on Alfredo guessed their secret, and he became their watch dog, keeping a close eye on Joe, who was in charge of them, and he arranged a special warning signal. Whenever the old gardener wandered in their direction, he would sing a lullaby that he and Bruno knew well from their childhood.

It was the old summer house where they met, tucked away in a secluded part of the garden at the end of a winding path, and far enough away from the vegetable patch to be reasonably safe. Bruno told her before they made love for the first time that he was married. He also told her that as a Catholic he could never divorce.

'We are both married, Bruno,' Margaret answered. 'We knew what was happening and we still let it happen.'

'I didn't *let* it happen, mio cara, it had happened before we even met. You were out there somewhere – I was out there –and we found each other.'

In the dusty semi-darkness of the summer house, they made love again.

If Mrs Murray had any suspicion, she gave no sign of it, but Margaret often waited for her to comment on the changed appearance of her young mistress, for it was glaringly obvious. The tension lines had disappeared from her forehead, her eyes shone and even her hair had a brighter gloss. She looked like the young bride who had come to the house eight years ago.

Of course, there was guilt alongside the joy. Guilt about her broken vow to Peter, guilt about deceiving Philip when she went to visit, and guilt because of the secret she was keeping from her mother, and more especially from her grandmother, who had been so pleased when her granddaughter, and so in a way John himself, had at last been brought into the Corkish family. At times Margaret felt as though she was in a maze that had no way out, and that all she could do at those times was to go back to her strategy of wait and see.

Bruno did not carry any guilt. He told Margaret that his marriage had been over even before he came to England to find work. His wife had not shown any love towards him once they had married and he had been very unhappy. So long as he had sent money back to her, she had expressed no desire to join him or to wish for his return.

'But I am still her husband, even though you are more wife to me than she ever was,' he said.

'It was different with me and Peter,' said Margaret. 'I loved him, I still love him, but not at all like this. We were happy as friends are happy, I didn't know there was more.'

Neither of them talked about the inevitable time when the war would end and Peter would come home. That time hung somewhere in a hazy future they had yet to face.

Margaret's monthly cycle had always been regular, so when she was two weeks late, she knew at once that she might be pregnant. She waited another six weeks then went to see the doctor. He was the Corkish family doctor and knew them all well, so of course he knew that Peter was a POW in Germany. Margaret decided she had to be totally honest with him.

He listened quietly then examined her, and when he confirmed that she was certainly with child, he was neither approving nor disapproving. He arranged future appointments and discussed birth arrangements in a totally professional way, reminding her gently that as an older mother facing her first delivery, she must take good care of herself.

Bruno wept when she told him.

'I never thought I could be happier than to have you, but now, I am also to be papa.' He buried his face against her neck, wetting it with tears. She pulled him closer and it was the first time that they had been pressed together, body to body, without desire flaring up, but now there was simply an exquisite tenderness between them and it was just as satisfying.

For the first six months Margaret managed to hide her growing bump, although Alfredo guessed. She wore an old jumper of Peter's and a full skirt, and because it was winter no one commented, but inevitably the day came when she could no longer conceal her new shape and she handed in her notice at school.

* * *

That May, after six years of desperate fighting and horrific loss of life, the Allied Army finally defeated the enemy in Europe and the peace bells rang, though the total victory the Allies were hoping for seemed to be moving farther away as, in the Far East, desperate Japanese forces fought to the death rather than surrender. In order to save the lives of its own soldiers and to end the futile defiance, America sent planes to drop atomic bombs on two cities in Japan, and the catastrophic carnage brought the war to an end – but at a terrible price. Weary people everywhere faced a world changed beyond recognition.

With the war over, although food was still rationed, the lights were on again and families began to welcome the troops home. The men billeted with Margaret left for demobilisation on the mainland and she began to reclaim the parts of the house they had occupied. It was obvious that a lot of work would be needed to make the rooms habitable again. Scuffs and knocks had damaged the woodwork and there were cigarette burns on some of the window ledges as well as wear and tear on the carpets. As she gradually turned the house into a home again, she longed to take Bruno into her bedroom so they could lie together without the need for secrecy, but she could not risk offending Mrs Murray. Even though Margaret felt sure she must have some suspicion by now, suspicion was one thing, being faced with the truth was quite another.

If you looked at the stark facts, Margaret knew that most people would see their love as a sordid hole-in-the-corner affair, and she accepted that it might seem that way, but when she and Bruno lay together on the dusty rugs in the gloom of the old wooden summerhouse, there was nothing sordid about their joyous lovemaking. They were beyond the boundaries of society's uncompromising codes, cocooned in a world of their own which they were not yet ready to leave. Margaret's pregnancy was progressing well, the baby was moving and the doctor was happy with them both. He was still the only other person, apart from Alfredo, who knew about the baby.

Then a short letter arrived from Peter. Margaret knew what it would tell her. He was to be repatriated soon and now she faced taking the action she could no longer put off, she had to tell him about Bruno and the baby. She was very aware of the devastating blow she would be inflicting, especially on top of his years as a prisoner of war. No decision making was involved, that had been made months ago, but she was racked by the torments of guilt, blame, and morality; the enormity of what she was about to do was like a pierce to the heart because, besides Peter, there were a lot of people who loved her and whose lives she was about to shatter.

Without Bruno she could not have found the strength to face these feelings, but he was there to listen and console her, and wise enough not to interfere. Margaret, falling back on her 'wait and see' policy, decided to delay a few more weeks until the baby arrived before telling anyone, apart from Peter who was her top priority. She hoped, rightly or wrongly, that the arrival of a baby would be a buffer against the shock her family would suffer. Surely a tiny baby would soften anyone's heart and help her family to accept the situation, because then nothing could be changed or done about it – but telling everyone, especially Peter, would be the hardest thing she had ever done.

Quite unexpectedly, a letter arrived from Grace. Although there was still some risk of mines in the Irish Sea, a route had been cleared for shipping and she had managed to get a passage on the ferry. She would be coming to see Margaret the following week. It could not have been worse. Margaret could have faced either Peter or her mother, less painfully than Grace. Just when she had braced herself to deal with the after effects of the baby's arrival, now she had to steel herself to watch her beloved grandmother's face as she inflicted a wound that would wipe away all the happiness with which Grace had welcomed her granddaughter's acceptance into the Corkish family. One of the moments Margaret had been dreading was now here.

Grace went to her own little cottage first, but after opening all the curtains, she left her case unpacked and hurried off, unable to wait to see Margaret. When Mrs Murray answered the door, Grace was a little disappointed, she had expected it to be her granddaughter, but she was even more disappointed when she was shown into the drawing room and asked to wait a moment, as is she was a casual caller. As soon as the door opened, Grace jumped up, excited, and her heart leapt with brief joy when Margaret turned round, her granddaughter was heavily pregnant. Then the reality of the situation hit home and she flopped back on the sofa dismayed. This child could not be Peter's. She stared at the pale face of the girl she adored.

'Hello, Gran.' Margaret was calm, 'Did you have a good crossing?'

Grace couldn't speak. Margaret came slowly over and sat down heavily beside her.

'I'm sorry to shock you, Gran, but I couldn't let you know, not by phone or letter, anyway.'

Grace struggled to find her voice. 'Margaret – I don't know what to say, I can't think. What's happened?'

'It's obvious what has happened. I'm having a baby. We both know it isn't Peter's, and I'm not sure I want to tell you any more at the moment.'

Her shortness, on top of the shock, affronted Grace and irritation pricked. 'You don't think you owe your family an explanation? You don't think we deserve to be told whose baby this is?'

'Not until I have told Peter,' Margaret said firmly. 'I have heard from him and he is hoping to be repatriated soon. I need to tell him before then.'

There was a long silence. Grace was completely shattered. All she wanted to do was get out of the room. She got to her feet. 'Margaret, I don't know what to do or say to you at the moment, I've got to go.' Then, aware of the tension between them, she added, 'I'll come back again tomorrow, if that is all right?'

'Yes, I'll be in all day.'

They looked at each other like strangers meeting for the first time. Never before in their lives had they been together without affection spilling over between them. Grace picked up her bag and left.

That first night in her cottage should have been one of joy, she had so looked forward to it, but now, sitting by the window looking out across the sea until the moon rose, the pretty room held no comfort. This house was meant to be her safe haven, but now it felt violated. She spent a sleepless night trying to make sense of what had happened.

By the time she visited Margaret the next day she had at least decided what questions she wanted answered. She had also realised that this was a pivotal moment in their future relationship and she must be careful not to alienate her granddaughter.

She managed a smile as she greeted Margaret and saw at once how relieved the girl was at this relaxing of tension. Margaret waited until they were seated with a cup of coffee, before opening the subject.

'I'm very sorry I have upset you, Grandma. It's the last thing I wanted to do.'

'It doesn't matter about me, Margaret, it's you I'm worried about, and your mother.'

'I'll telephone Mum now that you know.'

'It'll be a shock to her, just as it was to me, but we will both want to help you, Margaret, you know that.'

'Gran, I don't need any help, there is nothing you can do, either of you.'

'But you can't cope on your own,' protested Grace. 'There is so much to sort out. There's the birth for one thing, and then there's Peter…' she came to a stop. How Margaret was going to tell Peter she couldn't even begin to imagine.

'I have already sorted everything out, except for Peter, but I know I need to do that as soon as possible, and I will.'

'The baby must be due very soon now and you'll need someone here with you. You need someone to talk to, perhaps go over whatever you have arranged in case you are not thinking clearly at the moment. Your mother and I will be glad to help. What happens between you and Peter we can only leave to you, but maybe things are not quite as bad as you imagine them to be.'

'You don't understand, Grandma.' Margaret used the formal address again, distancing herself from the little girl who had always called her Gran.

'Things are *not* bad. Apart from upsetting you and Mum and Peter, everything is exactly as I want it to be.' She put her cup down and clasped her hands together. 'Maybe I do owe you an explanation, anyway you need to understand. The baby's father is Italian. He is one of the internees who were sent here to help Mr Simmons in the garden. The authorities bought some of our produce and two of them came to work here three days a week. It meant we increased our production. Well, I don't need to go into details, but when I met Bruno it was like finding the rainbow's end. We were both absolutely swept away by our feelings. It has been going on for a while, we couldn't stop.'

Grace was stunned. At the back of her mind she had assumed that a mistake had been made, a one-time fling, and that Margaret bitterly regretted it. Now it appeared it was a love child in every sense of the word.

'What are you going to do?'

'Bruno is married. He has a wife back in Italy and he is a Catholic so he can't get a divorce. We have decided there is only one thing we can do. We are going away after the baby is born.'

'He would leave his family?' Grace felt shame.

'He hasn't seen his wife for over ten years, and they have no children. Bruno was working in England before the war and for a long time now he has had very little contact with her.'

'He is still married!' Grace had to say.

'I know – and so am I!' Margaret retorted. 'We both know the enormity of what we are doing but we can't live without each other. It was never like this with Peter. Of course, I loved him, I still do, but compared with this it is as if he were a dear brother. I can't change anything. I want this baby and I want Bruno. I'm sorry but there is nothing more I can say.'

Mrs Murray came in with tea and sandwiches and Grace waited till she had left the room before she spoke again.

'You said you were going away. Where will you go?'

'Australia.'

Australia! The other side of the world. Grace silently absorbed another shock. There was no point in going over things again, Margaret had obviously made her decision. There was nothing she could say which would help the situation except to offer support, yet somehow, Grace felt unable to do that at this moment.

They both made an effort to eat, but Grace couldn't think further than this day and the fact that nothing was how she had expected it to be. How thrilled she would have been if only the baby had been Peter's. That fleeting moment of joy when she saw that Margaret was pregnant had been exquisite, but then the swift jolt of realisation had swept that joy away, leaving a raw pain that was not fleeting. Now dismay weighed heavily on her, like a sack of coal. Margaret told her she would spend the afternoon writing a long and difficult letter to Peter, so with no more to be done and desperate to think, Grace left.

Back in her cottage again, Grace sat once more looking out to sea, going over each detail of their conversation. She felt utterly helpless. There was nothing at all that she could do. Nothing at all would make any difference now. All the delight she had felt when Margaret had been finally acknowledged by Isobel was wiped out in one cruel blow. She felt betrayed, not only for herself but also for John and Robert. They were the channels through which the inheritance had finally been given, so it was as if their legacy and their memory had been slighted. She felt washed out, she was too old to cope with the trauma, and that was the only word for it, even if Margaret did think of it differently. Poor Elizabeth, she would know by now. What must she be feeling? Suddenly she knew she wanted to go back home and be with the one person who would be feeling this upset as keenly as she did. She wrote a brief note to Margaret and took the next available boat.

* * *

Margaret lay down on the sofa after Grace had gone and gave way to the tears she had struggled to hold back. Facing her grandma had been just as hard as she had expected it to be. It had brought to the surface all the guilt she felt, not only about Peter, but about letting down Grace. She remembered all the joy and satisfaction that Grace had felt at Isobel's decision. Now she had ruined the long-held hope that Grace had never quite given up on, that of seeing the descendants of John, her first husband, finally accepted into the family fold. She had also let down Isobel who had tried to right the wrong that had been done to John, and who had known contentment in her final days, concerning the future of the family. Then there was the guilt that now the child she carried would, in his turn, be denied a place in the family because she could not go on living in a house where she had ruined so much hope. The only amends she could make would be to sign the deeds over to Peter so that the house remained in the family, perhaps not quite in direct line as Isobel had wished but, as her great nephew, Peter was still close family. She felt she owed that much to both him and Isobel.

She got up from the sofa and went to her bureau to begin the difficult letter to her husband. Then she must telephone Philip. Although they had spoken on the phone, she had not met up with him for three months, pleading pressure of work, so that the last time she had seen him she had been able to conceal her pregnancy. She knew she would break his heart too.

Making the decision to move to Australia was one of the hardest she had ever made. To leave her family behind, not knowing when she would see them again, was painful, and it was because of this that she had held Grace at a distance when they met. She knew that if she had allowed too much emotion to show she might start to waver. The strong ties to her family, especially Grace, pulled her in many directions, but strongest of all was the pull of Bruno and her baby. She must not let her grandma's love tug her back. Now she had the birth of her child to prepare for and then the start of the new life she planned with Bruno. It would take all her strength.

* * *

It was only a few days later when Elizabeth called round at George Street. Jessie knew at once that something was wrong, but even she couldn't have begun to guess what

Elizabeth was about to tell her. Margaret had had an affair with one of the Italians who had been working in her garden and she was expecting his baby.

'Oh my God!' Jessie put her hand across her mouth and stared at her friend.

'Grace has come back heartbroken.'

'Elizabeth, I don't know what to say, this is terrible.'

'The thing is,' went on Elizabeth, 'according to Grace, Margaret is quite happy about it.'

'Quite happy about it — how can she be?' Jessie was stung to reply before checking herself. The situation was hard enough for Elizabeth, she must not add censure to her stress.

'Apparently, he is the one she wants to spend the rest of her life with, and the child will be welcome. She's written to Peter,' Elizabeth stopped, lips trembling.

Jessie went to her and folded her arms round her friend and they stood close, sharing the shock. Later, sitting down with a cup of tea, Elizabeth filled in more details. The baby was due very soon and Margaret had intended waiting until it was born before telling everyone, in the hope that, being presented with a baby girl or boy rather than a pregnancy, it might somehow mitigate the circumstances.

'As if it could,' Elizabeth sighed. 'Poor Peter and Philip, how must they be feeling?'

'Just the same as you, I would think.'

'No, Jessie, not quite the same. I wouldn't say this to anyone else, not even to Harry, but I feel ashamed on behalf of Margaret, although Grace said she shows no sign of it herself.'

'I can understand how you feel, I would too in your place, but this sort of thing has happened before and will happen again. That sounds like a cliché, but you know it's true. If Margaret is determined, you can only make the best of it. She is still your daughter, isn't she?'

'Of course, she is, and I have already decided I'm going to stay with her for the birth. I don't know how else I can handle it.'

'She may be putting on a brave face.' said Jessie. 'She will need you now more than ever. She'll need your blessing if you can give it.'

'I'll know that when I get there.'

Elizabeth could give no better answer.

Jim was more philosophical when Jessie told him everything that night in bed. His observation was that the same scenario was happening all over the country, a consequence of the long absences couples had had to endure. He pointed out that human nature being what it was, there were stronger and weaker among us, just as there were good and bad. Jessie could see the sense in that but, because it was her dear friend Elizabeth who was so affected and because she shared her feelings, she turned over and kept her thoughts to herself.

* * *

Elizabeth spoke to Margaret several times after that first bombshell of a telephone call, and once the initial shock had subsided, her reaction was less extreme than Grace's had been. Always a placid, practical person, she had never attached the same importance to Margaret's acceptance by Isobel Corkish that Grace had done. She knew very little about the Corkishes or about John, Robert's father, and since Robert had not had any contact, the family history had not mattered much to him either. What mattered to her was that she was to become a grandmother, and that her daughter would be giving birth at the age of thirty-one, rather late for a first pregnancy. Leaving Harry behind, feeling this was between her and her daughter, she went to the island prepared to stay until the baby arrived.

Two weeks later, when she gave birth, Margaret was glad of her mother's presence. It was a girl, a beautiful dark-haired, dark-eyed girl. Elizabeth was standing by Margaret's bed in the nursing home, holding the baby, when she met the father. Bruno arrived carrying a bunch of flowers, and he had eyes only for Margaret and the child. Elizabeth handed the little bundle to him then stood back to take a good look at the man who had up ended their lives. He was about forty years of age, dark in the Italian way but not, to Elizabeth's eyes, particularly good looking. What was in no doubt was his open love for her daughter. Elizabeth could not dislike him.

'This is Bruno, Mum,' Margaret said.

'Hello, Bruno,' Elizabeth smiled.

Bruno smiled back rather diffidently. He couldn't shake hands because he was holding the baby in both arms, so he gave a slight bow. 'I am honoured to meet you.'

'The baby is beautiful. Congratulations.'

'Thank you.' He hesitated for a moment, then said quietly. 'I am sorry to have caused pain.'

'We were surprised, of course, but Margaret has told me what happened and it is not for me to judge. I can see my daughter is happy and that is enough for me.'

Elizabeth kissed Margaret and the baby then left them alone.

Margaret proved to be a natural mother so by the time Elizabeth returned home a few days later, she was feeling far happier than when she had left.

During the course of many phone calls, Margaret told her of her plans. She had signed the house over to Peter, so that it would stay in the family as Isobel had wished. Peter's reaction to the letter telling him about Bruno had been far more accepting than Margaret had expected or felt she deserved, but one of the results was that he had gone to Canada after repatriation, to stay with friends he had made during his training. While there, he had started divorce proceedings and this meant that by the time he finally returned to the island, Margaret and Bruno, together with the baby they had named Lisa, would already be in Australia.

* * *

On the day that they left, Elizabeth went round to Jessie's to cry on her shoulder. Jessie had shared those early days of Margaret's babyhood and she had been there when Robert had been killed, and she shared Elizabeth's distress now. They wept together. But although Jessie shared the heartache, she couldn't help thinking that this move was for the best. A baby should always be welcome, and she felt it was a shame that this little girl had arrived to mixed reactions. A new life in a new country would give the child the best start, as well as providing a new future for her parents.

'I wonder what makes people behave as they do?' she said later, lying in bed with Jim.

'What makes them go against their normal moral character? Is there some inherited gene that has just been waiting to assert itself unexpectedly?'

'I've no idea.'

'But suppose we could go back in time and actually meet our ancestors face to face. Would we see something or ourselves in them, or they in us. Would we like them do you think?'

Jim yawned. 'Nothing can change what has happened so let's get some rest now.'

'Or do you think we have developed characteristics they wouldn't recognise, with the world having changed so much that we have had to change with it?'

When he didn't answer she leaned across and nudged him. 'Jim?'

Jim sighed, turned over and pulled the blanket over his ears. 'Go to sleep,' he said.

* * *

Grace had not seen the baby before they set sail for Australia, and she was very aware that she had been unable to welcome it as she ought. Now she finally understood something of John's father's attitude to his son's marriage, because wasn't she reacting in just the same way, even though her response would not have the dire effect on Margaret's life that his had had on John's?

Grace's ingrained working-class sense of decency meant she could not condone what was, to her, a betrayal of the sanctity of marriage. It seemed there was a side to her character that had lain dormant until it had been exposed by this situation, an unwillingness to accept a challenge to her own values, because she was displaying a stubborn prejudice that she had not known existed.

She thought of John's mother who had never met her grandson, but who had, towards her end, sought out and made her great-granddaughter her heir. What would Isobel have thought of the events which had ended her hopes for the future of the family? Would she have seen it as the disaster it seemed to Grace? It was mainly Margaret's betrayal of Peter that had prevented a different response. She could not understand how anyone could build their happiness on the shattered dreams and hopes of someone else, though she had to admit that the world was changing and that marriage was no longer the binding commitment it had once been, and which it still was to someone of her generation. There was more selfishness about, a feeling that grabbing what one wanted was a given right. 'Life is too short,' was the saying. The war had brought about a lot of changes.

Looking back on a life of mixed blessings, Grace could have wished for parts of it to have been different. Margaret, for instance, was her only precious remaining link to John and Robert. Her birth had brought such deep happiness yet now she had taken herself out of Grace's life. She would certainly have changed that if she could. Then she thought of Elizabeth and Harry; of Jessie and Jim and Christopher; of Mrs Thomas; her sister Ellen and her brothers Thomas and Charlie, that small unchanged group who were all so very dear to her and with whom she had been blessed. There are only ever a few people who stay close to you for much of your life, she realised. Most cross your path briefly and pass on; some keep you company till the tide turns, then drift away; others take their leave at a crossroad; but a few, the precious ones, walk beside you to the end.

For a long time, Grace leaned back in her chair, letting her thoughts wander. She was sixty-six, where did she go from here? The cottage in Douglas was still there, as were Ellen and her family, and the Irish Sea was nothing more than a shining path between them. The water between her and Margaret, though, was more than just a path. Vast oceans separated them, reaching to the other side of the world, but that was where her heart lay.

She wondered if Isobel Corkish had felt the same tug between her loyalty to her husband and his firmly held principles, and her love for her son. At the time, Grace had decided that Isobel Corkish was a woman in whom the maternal instinct was weak if not absent. But then she had met her, and seen a different person from the one she had created in her mind. Once she had the power, Isobel had done what she could for her son's grandchild. She had brought Margaret back into the family, and what an impact it had had on their lives. I suppose we all leave our mark, Grace reflected. Everybody leaves some sign that they were once here, no matter how deep or shallow the imprint. Each of us is just another set of footsteps, walking in a long line, all linked to each other. At different times and in different surroundings, someone will have felt the same emotions that we do now, felt the same pain, laughed with the same joy, and in the end we're all headed towards the same destination. It's how we use the time that it takes us to reach our destination that makes the difference between us, and we have that choice.

Grace sat up straight. She knew how to use her time now. These could be her golden days, if it was not for that one self-inflicted and still bleeding wound – Margaret. But she held the healing right there, in her own hands.

She sat down to write a long, heartfelt letter to Australia.

CHAPTER TWENTY-FOUR

'I'VE had a letter from Margaret.' Grace took the cup of coffee Elizabeth was offering.

'Yes, I had one too,' Elizabeth handed a cup to Harry then sat down with them. 'Did she tell you about Lisa? I can't believe I have a granddaughter old enough to go to university.'

'I can't believe I have a great-granddaughter old enough to go to university! It makes me feel ancient, but I am so proud of her.' Grace looked at the photograph of Lisa, which Elizabeth had placed in pride of place on the mantelpiece. What a beautiful young woman she had become. She had inherited her father's dark, Italian looks, and how proud he would have been if he had lived to see his daughter about to study art at university.

Bruno had died from a heart attack when Lisa was twelve. Elizabeth, anxious to be with her daughter and granddaughter, had bravely made the long flight to Sydney on her own to spend six weeks doing what she could to help. She had got to meet the granddaughter she had last seen as a tiny baby and to hold her daughter in her arms again. Her love had helped them both through the difficult time, and when she came home Grace had wanted every tiny detail of her stay, she couldn't hear enough. It was a link to Margaret and Lisa which letters didn't provide, no matter how frequent and loving, but Elizabeth had come back with a promise from Margaret that she would come to visit as soon as she could and Grace held on to that thought.

Meanwhile, Grace had made changes to her life. Elizabeth had persuaded her to move into an apartment in a large converted house just across the road from her and Harry.

'Come and have a look at it, Grace,' she had urged, 'It is really nice, and we would see so much more of you.'

Grace had been to see it, liked it, and was still at the deciding stage when Jessie and Jim announced that they were retiring and moving to a bungalow near Stanley Park where they were members of the golf club. This changed Grace's circumstances and helped her to make up her mind. Six months ago, Mrs Thomas had passed away at the grand old age of ninety-three while at her sister's home, still loved and still missed, so with Jessie and Jim now also moving away, the little house where she had made a new life for herself all those years ago, would seem lonely. It was time to leave. She had not regretted it especially since she was not having to make another new life, she was simply transplanting herself.

Other changes involved selling all her properties, including the cottage in Douglas. Ellen's family had long ago grown up and left home, leaving a bedroom available for Grace, so the cottage was no longer needed. The two sisters visited each other every year, catching up with family news, so Grace knew that the mine had closed and that Philip now lived in the big house with Peter. Sometimes she wondered whether to contact them when she was on the island, but then she convinced herself that they would not welcome a reminder of what had been a very difficult period in their lives. Also, she was not sure whether Margaret would approve. None of them had had any contact with Peter or Philip since the house was signed over, initially due to guilt at the unhappiness caused, and later due to awkwardness, but as she grew older, there were times when Grace missed them.

* * *

She came face to face with Philip on one of her visits to Ellen. She walked into the bank where she kept an account, and there he was. Incredibly their paths had never crossed before, even though Douglas was not a big town, but now they had and they were both surprised. Philip spoke first.

'Grace! What a long time it has been. I'm very pleased to see you.'

At once her awkwardness vanished. Dear Philip, thought Grace, as charming and courteous as ever, she ought to have known that he would be.

'Philip, I can't believe we have finally bumped into each other. I've often thought about you.'

'Are you living on the island now?'

'No, just visiting my sister Ellen. I come over at least once a year. I've often thought about trying to contact you, but the situation being what it was, I was not sure if an approach would be welcome.'

'Enough time has passed now to do away with any ill-feeling or awkwardness, Grace. We've all moved on with our lives. It would be lovely to hear how all your family are – have you time for a cup of tea?'

'I have. Just let me cash this cheque and I will be with you.'

There was so much to say they interrupted and even talked over one another in their eagerness to find out how everyone, on both sides, had fared over the years. One thing they both commented on was the fact that Margaret and Peter had each gone on to have a child with a new partner yet had found it difficult to start a family when they were together.

'I'd like to talk to you about that, Grace,' Philip said. 'Not here and not now, but when we can have a longer conversation. Can we meet for dinner one evening before you go home? Perhaps on Wednesday?'

'Wednesday suits me very well. Is it something important? Should I be worried?'

'No, not all. It's important to me but definitely nothing for you to worry about.'

He suggested one of the hotels on the promenade and they agreed a time.

Grace was glad to renew their friendship and relieved at how easy he had made this first contact. The food was good and Grace really enjoyed Philip's company. His quiet courtesy reminded her so much of Richard, both of them natural gentlemen, and he made her feel as elegant and special as Richard had done. They had dinner then went through to the lounge for coffee and found a quiet corner where they could talk privately.

'Now, would you like a liqueur?'

'Will I need it?' Grace raised her eyebrows.

'I'm not sure, maybe. What would you like?'

'Just a small dry sherry, please.'

As they waited for the waiter to bring their drinks, the atmosphere suddenly became rather tense, and Grace became nervous. She took a large swallow of the sherry to fortify herself as soon as it was placed before her.

'It's something that I want to share it with you, Grace, since it does concern you to some extent.' Philip drank his whisky. 'Where to begin? Well, after Peter was repatriated, he went to Canada and while he was there, he remarried and had a son. As you know, Margaret signed the house over to him and at his request, I moved in to make it ready for when he decided to come home. There were still some personal items remaining that he wanted taken out – you understand what I mean?'

Grace nodded. She knew they would be reminders of Margaret.

'I went through all the cupboards, drawers and cabinets, clearing and sorting stuff out, and in one of the cupboards, I found a box full of old bills and receipts. Among them was an envelope, not addressed to anyone and not sealed, so I opened it. It was this letter.'

He pulled out an old envelope, removed some sheets of paper and handed them to her. They were slightly yellowed and covered with the copperplate handwriting of the Victorian era. There was no date and no introduction. Grace glanced at the end of the page and saw a signature – Isobel Corkish.

She gave Philip a puzzled look.

'Read it.' Philip poured them both another coffee.

It wasn't easy to read because some parts were faded and the paper had worn away along the creases where it had been folded for decades, but it very soon became apparent that she was reading a confession. Isobel was confessing to brief affair she had had with a Stephen Corkish soon after she had arrived on the island to visit an invalid friend. Stephen was that friend's husband.

Grace looked up, rather shocked. 'Are you sure you want me to read this?'

'Just read on.'

It was such an extraordinary moment. Not only was this a voice from the past, but actually the words of John's mother. It was the story of an innocent young girl, caught up in a situation beyond her limited experience of life. Grace felt uncomfortable reading it, but as she read on, things became more serious – Isobel had become pregnant. Now Grace couldn't take her eyes from the page.

On pretext of a holiday, Stephen had sent her to friends in Ireland, where she had given birth to a son. At first, Grace felt anger as she read of the way Isobel seemed to have been shipped off across the sea, as though discarded, then the anger turned to dismay when it dawned on her that this baby must have been John.

But she was wrong.

The baby had indeed been a boy, the son Stephen had always longed for, and he had let it be known that he was adopting the orphaned child of a colleague. Unable to have a baby of her own, his wife had also welcomed a son, unaware of the true circumstances of his birth.

They had named him Philip.

Grace gasped and stared at Philip.

'But – that's you!'

'Yes.'

'But –' She tried to understand what she had just read. 'Then Isobel was your mother!'

'Yes.'

'What about John? How does he come into this?'

'Finish the letter, Grace, it explains everything far better than I can do.'

Grace turned back to the page. When Stephen's older brother Robert proposed to her shortly after her return, Isobel accepted, and soon after their marriage gave birth to another son, John. Grace's thoughts were racing. It was hard to take it all in. So, Philip was John's brother. She stared at him, puzzled by how relaxed he seemed about all this, until she remembered that this was not new to him as it was to her, he had known about the letter for some time.

'Then you and John were brothers?'

'Half-brothers, but we were very close. Although we were brought up as cousins, we loved each other like brothers, probably because we were each an only child, or so we thought.'

'It must have been such a shock to you. I'm shaking, and it will have been far more traumatic for you.'

'It was. At first, I couldn't believe it but then it began to make sense. Aunt Isobel always behaved in a more loving fashion towards me than an ordinary aunt would have done, and I had assumed it was probably because my mother was a semi-invalid with restricted mobility that she always included me in any activities with her and John. But now I understand why.'

'So, neither you nor John knew about this? Did you never have any suspicions?'

Philip shook his head. 'I didn't and I'm pretty sure John didn't, or he would have told me. So far as I know, and that's just from what I have read, only Isobel, Stephen, and the couple she stayed with in Ireland, knew. What happened between her and my father after I was born and she married Uncle Robert, I have no idea, but they must have agreed on some sort of compromise. As a child I didn't see anything other than a normal family relationship between my mother and father, Sarah and Stephen, and my aunt and uncle, Isobel and Robert. I have done a lot of thinking since I found the letter, as you can imagine, and there is a great deal I don't suppose we will ever know, but it was obviously written before John drowned. When he did, we were all completely devastated, but I doubly struggled because I carried guilt as well as grief. I was the one who had written to Uncle William in Liverpool to ask him to help John. Like you and John, I was only young at the time and in no position to give any practical help myself, so I did what I thought was best. I remember vowing, that when I was older and more independent, I would seek out my cousin and make amends. Then there was that dreadful tragedy and his death poleaxed me. My father had told me not to interfere and he had been right. If it had not been for me John would not have been on that ship, so you can imagine how wretched I felt.'

Philip took a large gulp of whisky and Grace could see that he was affected by what he was reliving.

'You may wonder why I didn't help you, Grace, later after John's death, but remember, I didn't know you personally then. I could only go by what Uncle Robert told me, that you were the daughter of two of his former servants, and I'm ashamed to say that I allowed the snobbish rules of class division that held sway at the time, to influence me. Whereas I would certainly have helped John, I did nothing for you, and I can't tell you how much I regretted that when I first met you at Aunt Isobel's and realised how very wrong an impression of you I had formed, or should I say, had been given.'

Grace tried to be understanding but could only think how desperate she had been in those early days and how much difference some friendly contact from the family would have made. Her own mother, one of the servants he had just, perhaps unwittingly, disparaged had stood by her daughter making Isobel's one and only offer of money, useful though it had been, seem cold compared with that of her mother's unstinting practical support. The woman who had so much had given little, while the woman who had little had given everything. But none of this could be blamed on Philip. As he said, he was too young at the time and what good would it have done if he himself had been shunned by the uncle who was also his employer? Given that this was the man who had ruthlessly rejected his own son, it was highly likely that he would have been treated in the same way if he had crossed him.

'It was a long time ago,' she said, 'yet how come Isobel didn't tell you after John died? Surely, that would have been the time to acknowledge you as her son, when you were all she had left?'

'Don't forget, my mother, Sarah, was still alive, and even after both she and my father died, Uncle Robert was still with us, so she had to keep her secret. He died only shortly before she contacted you and Margaret, and I think at that point, she felt it would be too complicated to try to reorganise the family. As you know, Uncle Robert signed the mine over to me. I had been running it for him for many years and, as his only nephew, he wanted to keep it in the family, then when my father died, I inherited a large sum of money, so Isobel knew that I was well provided for. This was her first opportunity to do something for John's family, and she took it as soon as she could.'

'Actually, it wasn't her first opportunity,' said Grace. 'She gave me a sum of money secretly, just after John died, and that enabled me to give Robert a nest egg when he married, but when I heard no more from her, I'm afraid I wasn't as grateful as I might have been. I desperately wanted Robert to be acknowledged by the family and when he wasn't, I was very resentful.'

'Would it have made any difference if you had known then, that she was unable to do more to help you?'

'I think perhaps it would. There was a lot of bitterness inside me in those years and it set me on a defiant course to try to raise Robert according to what I assumed would be Corkish standards, just to show them I could, but I took on a very hard challenge and paid a high price for that struggle, before it finally dawned on me that it was not the way to happiness.'

'But you are happy now?'

'Very.' They sat silently with their own thoughts for a moment or two.

'One thing that did occur to me, the more I read the letter, concerned Peter and Margaret,' Philip continued.

'Concerned Margaret and Peter how?'

'Well, if John and I were half-brothers because of Isobel, as well as being first cousins because our fathers were brothers, that means Peter and your son Robert were first cousins and also second cousins. So, Margaret and Peter were much more closely related than any of us realised. I now wonder if that explains the instant attraction you and I witnessed, that strong magnetic attraction of shared genes that they thought was romance. It could also be the reason they were unable to start a family, even though as we now know, they were both clearly capable of having a child. The more I thought about it the more it made sense. They were too closely related.'

Grace's thoughts were tumbling one after the other as she tried to process all the information Philip had just presented her with.

'Have you told Peter?'

'Yes, after he came back to the island from Canada, but since both he and Margaret were living new lives, we decided to leave well alone. Perhaps we were wrong, but there seemed to be enough going on at the time. We were turning the house into a hotel for one thing, and Margaret was far away in Australia, then Peter's wife, Clare, became ill, so we did what we thought was best.' Philip poured more coffee. 'The reason I told you now was because I wanted to put our relationship on a better footing. When we met in the bank, you seemed to be feeling awkward, and perhaps even guilty, about the decision Margaret made, but now that we know of the much smaller gene pool – perhaps Mother Nature knew best after all?'

Grace let that remark sink in. She knew what Philip was implying and maybe he was right, but there were still a lot of questions that would never be answered. The main people to be affected would have been Philip and John. Things would definitely have changed for them, but with Isobel and John both dead, and Margaret and Peter divorced, Philip was right – what good would it do now to open that can of worms? Things were best left as they were, at least for the time being.

'Would you like another sherry?'

'Yes please. I asked you earlier if I needed it and I most definitely do now.'

'I'm sorry, Grace, I didn't want to upset you, but I thought it might help you to let go of the embarrassment you seemed to be feeling. Now that you and I have made contact perhaps we might be able to bring our families together again. But in the meantime – have you realised that I am your brother-in-law?'

'So you are.'

* * *

Now that the air had been cleared, Grace and Philip kept in touch. He was able to tell her a lot about his childhood with John and it was a great comfort to know how happy her husband had been in those days. They talked again about Margaret and Peter.

'After all the initial trauma, the outcome has not been as bad as we thought it was at the time, has it?' said Grace. 'Look at how well everyone has got on with their lives, and that includes you and me, Philip. We have survived, haven't we?'

'We have, and the fact that we all got there by a route different from the one we planned, hasn't meant the end of the family, has it? We've both got grandchildren to keep the line going, even a great-grandchild in your case.'

As she thought about the photograph of Lisa that she kept by her bed, it occurred to Grace that on her side of the family, the forget-me-not blue eyes of the Corkish genes had now probably disappeared. Lisa, with her beautiful but very dark looks, would never be taken for a Corkish, but strangely, for all the obsessive importance Grace had attached to inheritance in the past, it did not matter to her anymore. Lisa was making her own life in Australia and just to know she was well and happy was enough. From the moment she had seen the first photograph of the girl, Grace's love had been instant, as though an umbilical cord linked her to her great-granddaughter. Blue eyes or not, she carried Manx blood, Grace's blood.

So now it would be left to Isobel's other son, Philip, to pass on that distinctive Corkish gene. He had told her that Peter's son was the image of his dad, but who knew what sons and daughters of other nations might, in the future, add to the gene pool? Already there were Italian and Canadian genes in the mix and so long as love was the link, all would be well.

* * *

Grace was very happy in her flat and becoming content to take things at a slower pace. Perhaps I am now ready to be put out to grass she thought, smiling as she remembered Mrs Thomas's wise words. Birthdays came and went, adding to her years, but she was still in good health and she hoped to add a few more yet. The younger members of the family were all busy with their lives and she wanted to be around to hear more of their stories, even if she no longer helped to write them. She saw Elizabeth every day, spoke to Ellen every week on the phone, and Margaret wrote regularly, keeping her up to date on Lisa's life at university. Life was sliding by very peacefully.

* * *

Jessie called round at Elizabeth's for a cup of tea. They had something important to discuss.

'Right, what are we going to do about Grace's birthday?' Jessie asked, 'We need to do something special since it is a special one.'

'I've thought about that.' Elizabeth said. 'What about a big party here? I'm going to ask Ellen to come over, but I'm afraid Philip is not able to travel now, which is a shame. I'll invite some of her neighbours from the flats and all the family of course, and I'll make an eightieth birthday cake so that just leaves the rest of the food. What about a buffet?'

'Lovely, and champagne, but we still need that extra special something.'

'I've thought about that as well, but leave it with me for now. Let's plan the food.'

Elizabeth and Jessie were determined this was going to be the best birthday ever and they worked hard to produce a buffet that was more of a banquet. On the day the table looked beautiful. Jessie had arranged eight small bowls of pink roses and their scent filled the room. There were so many dishes of food on the long table that they completely hid the white starched tablecloth. In the centre, in place of honour, stood a magnificent pink iced cake which Elizabeth had managed to stud with eighty pink candles, a challenge for whoever was to light them. Harry and Jim were in charge of drinks and the sideboard gleamed with glass. They were ready. When everyone had gathered, Harry went across the road to escort Grace, and as they waited for her to arrive, Elizabeth and Jessie were fizzing with excitement. They couldn't stop giggling.

Before she walked through the door, Elizabeth told Grace to close her eyes. 'Now open them,' she said, as champagne corks popped.

Grace opened her eyes, and when she saw who stood there, the thought which overwhelmed her was, "My cup runneth over."

She held out her arms – 'Margaret!'

Grace stirred as a warm breeze from the open window fanned softly across her face, gently ruffling her hair. She sat up and slowly stretched her neck and arched her back to ease the stiffness of sitting. Margaret would be here soon and they would share a pot of tea together. They had six blessed weeks to enjoy.

She sank against the cushions of her comfortable chair and let her thoughts wander back along the path that had brought her to where she was today. She allowed herself this little pleasure each time she awoke from her nap. It was like playing a favourite record over and over again and it always ended with the same lovely, lovely thought.

Margaret, the girl of my heart, is home at last.

PART THREE

LISA

CHAPTER TWENTY-FIVE

THE train was on time as it slowed to a stop at platform one on Preston Station, and it was obviously already full. The crowd, who had been waiting patiently, suddenly stirred into a swarm of hustling individuals all trying to get to the doors, ready to grab the seats of the departing passengers. Lisa found herself squashed in the middle of a heaving sway of bodies.

'Ouch!' A sudden sharp pain made her wince as something hard whacked her on the leg. She hopped on one leg, grabbed someone's arm for balance, and lifted her knee to rub her shin.

'Oh, I'm so sorry.' A flustered man turned around and shifted his briefcase to his other hand. 'That chap with the rucksack banged into me and knocked me off balance.' He nodded towards the back of a hefty young man elbowing his way through the throng. 'Are you all right?'

Lisa looked at her leg. 'Well, the skin isn't broken but I bet I'll have one hell of a bruise tomorrow,' she answered crossly.

'I'm so very sorry,' the man apologised again. 'Can I help you at all?'

'No, thanks.' Lisa glared at him. 'You've done quite enough already.' And she turned back to join in the pushing and shoving, just managing to squeeze herself into a small space on a seat near the door. It was not going to be a comfortable journey, she was pressed up against the arm of the seat by the very large lady next to her, but at least she didn't have to stand. The packed train pulled slowly out of the station, Blackpool next stop. She was on the last leg of her journey.

Wriggling a bit to get more elbow room, she unzipped a side pocket in her bag, found her water bottle and used a small pack of tissues to make a pad. She moistened it with the water then gingerly pressed it to her reddening skin. At first it stung sharply but gradually the cool dampness soothed the pain a little. Just her luck, she had travelled all the way from Australia with no harm done and now, just as she was practically at the end of the long journey, this had to happen. Her leg was still throbbing when the train arrived at Blackpool North station and she limped towards the barrier.

'Lisa!' She saw a hand waving from behind the gate, it was her Grandma Elizabeth.

She waved back eagerly, handed over her ticket, and rushed to greet the only face she would recognise in this part of the world.

'Oh, it's so lovely to see you.' Elizabeth held her tightly in a long hug. 'Have you had a good journey?'

'I did for most of the way.' Lisa pulled a wry face. 'But look what's just happened at Preston.' She showed Elizabeth her now very swollen leg. 'Some idiot swung his briefcase right into me – it really hurts.'

'Heavens, that is a mess, I should think it does hurt. I hope he was sorry?'

'Well, he was, but it didn't stop it hurting, though to be honest it wasn't his fault. Someone bumped into him and he lost his balance. I would have had a lot more to say to him if it had been his fault.'

'Well, the car is outside, let's get you home then you can give that leg a good soak in a warm bath. I bet you are hungry, aren't you?'

'I am, actually.'

'Everyone is waiting to meet you, but I thought it would be best for me to come on my own to give you a chance to get used to me again. It's been so long since I last saw you – you were still a girl.'

Elizabeth unlocked the car and Lisa slung her bag onto the back seat and carefully manoeuvred her sore leg, then herself, into the passenger seat. As they pulled out into the traffic she looked around at the dreary streets, wet with rain, and wondered what she had let herself in for. It was very windy, something her mother had warned her about. 'You will be in breezy Blackpool,' she had said, 'known for its bracing air which can sometimes turn into quite a strong gale. It's nearly always windy.' How right she was. Lisa could feel the wind buffeting the car until they drove further away from the town centre and along quieter streets.

'You haven't changed at all, Grandma,' said Lisa. 'I recognised you straight away.'

'You have,' Elizabeth replied. 'You have become quite the young lady.'

'That's not what my mum would call me. She thinks I'm too independent and too outspoken for my own good.' Lisa raised her eyebrows.

'There's nothing wrong with being independent, especially in this day and age, with women beginning to compete against men on equal terms, and not before time, may I add. Here we are.' She pulled into the drive of a large brick house. The lights were shining through all the windows to welcome her, and as the door opened Lisa felt a flow of much needed warm air. She had just begun to shiver.

Elizabeth led the way into the living room where a roaring fire and most of the family were waiting to welcome their Aussie relative. 'Here she is,' she announced, her arm round Lisa's shoulder, 'here's Lisa.'

Harry was the first to step forward and give her a big hug. 'Lisa, welcome to England. We've all been dying to meet you. I'm Harry, your step-grandfather, but we don't bother much with steps or halves in this family, so I'd like you to call me Granddad.'

'Of course, I will, you're the only granddad I've got. Or how about Gramps?' Lisa chose her own name with a cheeky grin.

'This is Harry's son, Jim, and his wife Jessie.' Elizabeth carried on. 'You'll meet their son Christopher any time now, he is on his way, and I'll take you to see great-grandma Grace tomorrow.'

Lisa was grabbed into more big hugs by the people who had been waiting so long to see her, and they all gathered round delighted to welcome the daughter of the woman they had last seen over twenty years before and still all missed – Margaret.

Lisa looked happily round at everyone. Not being a shy person, she was not overwhelmed and she was thrilled to meet her mother's family at last. Now they were her family too, she knew she was going to like them all.

'I'm going to take you to your room now,' said Elizabeth as Lisa finished her cup of tea, 'And run that warm bath I promised you so that you can get rid of the travel grime and bathe that sore leg.'

Lisa was more than glad to follow Elizabeth and was soon soaking in soft, scented water. The smell of hotpot wafted upstairs from the kitchen. It was Elizabeth's speciality and a family favourite, one that Lisa knew well because Margaret had carried the recipe with her to Australia and served it up regularly in their restaurant.

Although she would have liked to stay soaking for a while longer, Lisa heard the sound of a new arrival, so she heaved herself out of the water and went to dress for dinner. When she walked downstairs a little while later, everyone stared at the transformation in her. She had arrived looking dishevelled from travelling, wearing shorts, boots, a baggy top and with a beanie covering her head. Now they saw she had a mass of newly washed black hair and wore a pale green shift dress that complimented her olive skin, and the fragrance she had used wafted about her.

For a moment no one spoke, then Jessie said, 'Lisa, you look absolutely beautiful.'

Lisa looked round at the smiling faces, saw her grandma's eyes shining with pride, and had to blink very hard to keep tears away from her own.

'You haven't met my grandson yet.' Harry took her hand and gave it a little squeeze. 'Lisa, this is Chris.'

'Hello.' Chris held out his hand. 'I've been really looking forward to meeting you.'

'It's you!' Lisa's eyes widened with surprise. 'You are the one who bumped into me at Preston Station.'

'What?' Chris was astounded. 'That was you?'

'It certainly was, look, here's the evidence to prove it.' Lisa put her foot forward to display a huge dark swollen bruise on her shin.

'Oh my God, I'm so sorry, I didn't recognise you. That hat you were wearing hid most of your face.'

'Fancy meeting you like that, talk about coincidence. You couldn't put odds on it could you?'

'You certainly could not, but I feel terrible now I've seen your leg.'

'Oh, don't worry about it, I'll mend.' Lisa grinned at him.

'Come and sit down, everyone, the food is on the table.' Elizabeth called from the dining room. As they tucked in, everyone chattered away nonstop. They wanted to know all about Australia, especially about Margaret, and Lisa tried her best to fill them in, until Elizabeth, seeing that she was looking exhausted, asked them all to leave.

'She'll still be here in the morning,' she assured them, 'but I must get her to bed now.'

Lisa lay in bed in the cosy room her grandmother had lovingly prepared for her. The bed was soft and she sank into it gratefully. A bedside lamp gave a peachy glow to the room. Outside, the rain was lashing against the windowpane and she could hear the wind howling. It was a typical Blackpool stormy night, but she was snuggled warmly under the duvet, her leg had been gently soothed with ointment and she felt she could sleep forever. She closed her eyes and drifted off at once into a deep jet-lagged sleep. Elizabeth came in to turn off the lamp and looked at her sleeping granddaughter. She would take very good care of this precious child, whom her own daughter had entrusted to her for twelve months, and give her the family love she had missed as a child. Kissing her on the forehead, she turned off the lamp and quietly closed the door.

* * *

Lisa slept late the next morning but when she did finally stir, after having a quick shower and a cooked breakfast, she was ready to be off exploring. Elizabeth asked her to phone her mother first, and when Margaret answered almost at once it was obvious that she had been waiting for Lisa's call.

'Hello, love. You've arrived, then?'

'All safe and sound Mum, how are you?'

'Oh, I'm fine, but I want to hear all about the family. Who have you met so far, apart from Grandma and Harry?'

'I've met everyone except great-grandma Grace, but I am going to see her later today. They have all made me so welcome, Mum, I'm going to love it here.'

'I'm glad you are with the family. It stops me worrying about you so much. Which room has Grandma put you in?'

'The one at the back, overlooking the pond. It has a big double bed and I've slept for nearly fourteen hours.'

'You'd just had a long journey,' replied Margaret. 'I didn't know they had a pond. That's been put in since I was over for Grandma Grace's eightieth birthday in 1958, but do you know what? You are in my old room. Grandma will have planned that.'

'Oh, cool. It's a lovely room, Mum. The pond's not very big, not swimming pool size, but the garden seems to be full of roses. It poured with rain last night, just as you said it might, but it's sunny now so I want to take a look a good look round. It could be an ideal place to paint.'

'Well, I'm glad you're all right, love. I'll get off the phone now, this call must be costing a fortune, but before I go can I say a quick hello to Grandma?'

'She's right here, waiting to speak to you – I'll put her on. Bye, Mum, take care of yourself – love you.'

'Love you too, darling. Bye for now.'

Elizabeth grabbed the phone. 'Margaret? Hello?'

Lisa watched as Elizabeth talked with her daughter. She saw the joy on her face at the contact and for the first time she understood how hard it must have been for Elizabeth when Margaret had moved to Australia. It made her feel even more touched by the loving welcome she had received, especially since she knew she had been the cause of that move. When the call came to an end, she noticed that Elizabeth held on to the phone a little longer, as if to extend the brief link, and she could imagine her mother doing exactly the same in Sydney.

'Mum tells me I am in her old room, Grandma.' said Lisa.

'Yes, you are. I thought you would like that.'

'I do and so does Mum. She says the pond is new.'

'It's been there about eight years now. We keep carp in it. Harry enjoys looking after them. He can't do so much heavy gardening these days, so it is an interest for him.'

'Can I go and wander round? I'd love to look at all your lovely roses. I've brought my sketchbooks and my watercolours, and I am dying to paint some of them.'

'This is your home while you are here, Lisa, I want you to come and go as you please. You go and find yourself a nice little spot and I'll bring some coffee out to you later.'

Lisa collected her sketching pad, went into the garden and spent the next half hour inspecting every nook and cranny. She was delighted to find four pretty little brown chickens in a fairly large coop by the hedge at the bottom of the garden. When Elizabeth and Harry brought the coffee out later, they also brought Chris and his dog, Ludo, a sweet King Charles spaniel whose tail never stopped wagging. Lisa crouched down to stroke his silky head.

'Hello, beautiful boy,' she said as Ludo tried to lick her face. She smiled up at Chris. 'He's gorgeous.'

'I'm about to take him for a walk in the park, would you like to come with us?'

'That's a good idea,' said Elizabeth, 'Stanley Park is only a few minutes away. Chris can show you how to get there when we've had coffee, then you can go by yourself any time you like. There's plenty going on, I'm sure you'll find lots of things to sketch, and when you come back, we'll have lunch in the garden. Can you stay, Chris?'

'Afraid not, I have a meeting in Preston this afternoon.'

'Well, at least you have time for coffee.' They sat at a small table near the roses and Lisa sniffed the gorgeous scent which mingled with the smell of wet earth after the rain.

'I saw some chooks at the bottom of the garden, Grandma. Is that where my egg came from at breakfast?'

'It was. They belong to Harry, they're his pride and joy. We have named them Henrietta, Layla, Eglantine and Chiquita.'

After a second or two, Lisa laughed. 'I see what you've done. Very witty. We call them chooks in Australia, but I've never seen any as pretty as these.'

Harry smiled with pride. 'They are bantams, and if we ever have any chicks, I shall call one Lisa,' he said.

'And I'll be honoured,' she replied.

* * *

Lisa enjoyed the park and she enjoyed talking to Christopher. She discovered that he was a keen photographer, although it had to be just a hobby since he had a job in Preston working as a surveyor. Although he was not the professional that she was, having gained her art degree in Australia, Lisa was pleased they had a shared interest in art. Chris pointed out the different views he had already photographed which he thought might interest her. The art deco design of the tearooms particularly attracted Lisa. It was a long flat-roofed symmetrical brick building with an impressive square stone portal framing the doorway. Directly opposite, two flights of broad steps led down to an Italian style garden with a water feature. In the centre of a large pond, a fountain sprayed its jet high into the air while four smaller fountains sent arches of sparkling water splashing down into the shallows where shoals of goldfish darted about in the shade of the floating waterlily pads.

'This is a great subject.'

'I thought you would like it.' said Chris. 'I don't know whether or not you use photographs, but I've taken several shots from here. You can borrow them if you like.'

'I use anything that helps me get a result,' Lisa said. 'I'd love to look at them.'

Ludo began to whimper for the walk he had been promised, so they took him to a large grassed area where he could run freely with other dogs before heading back home.

During lunch, Elizabeth explained to Lisa about Grace's absence at the family welcome.

'She wasn't here to greet you yesterday, Lisa, because she wanted to meet you on her own rather than with all the family there. She is in her eighties now and has to take things easy and this will be a very emotional meeting for her. I don't know how much your mother has told you about past events…' Elizabeth hesitated but Lisa smiled.

'It's all right, Grandma, I know that Mum and Dad weren't married when they had me. I was told that a long time ago. I know I was the reason they moved to Australia, but surely that is all in the past.'

'It's not only that.' Elizabeth was still hesitant. 'It's Grace's reaction to your birth I'm meaning. I don't know whether your mother told you, but she took it very badly and there was a rift between them for a while. That's why she didn't see you before they left the country. She put it right later of course and got back in touch with Margaret, it's just that seeing you now might bring back old emotions.'

'Don't worry, I understand what you are saying. I'm looking forward to meeting her. I'm sure there won't be any awkwardness.'

'No, I don't think there will be, not once she sees you. I only wanted to put you in the picture.'

When they had finished lunch, Elizabeth took Lisa to Grace's home and after introducing them to each other she left them to talk.

'It's lovely to meet you, Grandma Grace,' Lisa said, sitting down next to her. 'My mother has told me a lot about you and she described you perfectly, you are exactly what I expected.'

'And you are more beautiful than I expected, even though I've looked at your photograph often enough. Elizabeth told me what a lovely young lady you had become.'

Grace took the girl's hand in both of hers and Lisa looked down at age-spotted hands adorned with expensive rings. Even in old age, her great grandma was still an elegant lady.

As they chatted, Lisa began to tell her about the way she and Chris had met at Preston.

'Talk about bumping into someone,' Lisa giggled, 'that's exactly what we did. You know, I already feel at home with everyone. I'm going to love being here.' Grace listened eagerly as Lisa went on to talk about her life in Australia, and when Elizabeth returned ten minutes later, she was delighted to see how well they were getting on.

'So, you have got to know each other, then?'

'We have, and it's just like having Margaret back,' Grace smiled. 'It is so lovely to have a grandchild here again.'

* * *

Lisa spent as much time as she could in the park, delighted to have found a subject that attracted her, the Art Deco tearoom building. She made lots of quick sketches and painted small watercolours, preparing for the final painting which she felt had the potential to be a 'goer', as she called it.

Harry took her to a local art dealer to buy oil paints and canvas, and surprised her with the gift of a portable easel which she could carry to the park. This was the first her family here would see of her work and she wanted it to be the best she could produce. She planned to give it to Elizabeth and Harry if she pulled it off.

Working nearly every day, it took Lisa over a week to finish a large watercolour of the tearoom and Italian garden but when it was done, she was so pleased with the result she decided not to carry on and produce an oil painting from it as she had planned. She had it framed and presented it to her grandparents, holding her breath as she stood it on a chair for them to view.

Elizabeth gasped in surprise. 'Oh, Lisa, that is beautiful.'

'My word, I wasn't expecting anything as good as this.' Harry was clearly impressed. 'It's very professional.'

'You like it then?'

'Of course, we do. It's wonderful, Lisa.' Elizabeth gave her a big hug.

'That's a relief. I've got to say I am quite pleased with it myself.'

'You couldn't have pleased us more. I had no idea you were so talented.' Elizabeth couldn't stop looking at it.

'Well, I have my art degree so I should be able to produce a competent piece of work, but a lot depends on the person viewing it. Not everyone likes the same painting. You take that chance.'

Harry held the picture up and looked round the room. 'Now where shall we put it?'

'Somewhere the sun can't reach it, then the colours won't fade,' suggested Lisa.

'What about here above the bureau?' Elizabeth took down the print which hung there and replaced it with Lisa's picture then stepped back to admire it.

'Perfect,' said Harry, 'Let's see if the family notice when they come on Sunday.'

'They would have to be blind not to, it transforms the room.'

Elizabeth was as proud as punch.

On Sunday Elizabeth prepared a buffet lunch and they all came round to celebrate her and Harry's thirty-second wedding anniversary. They had gathered for drinks in the garden, but the buffet was set out in the dining room and as they trooped in, Lisa noticed Elizabeth and Harry exchanging expectant looks.

Jim was the first one to comment. He stopped in front of the bureau with his plate of food.

'You've got a new picture! That is beautiful.'

'Wow.' Jessie came over to look. 'How long have you had this?' She peered into the bottom corners of the frame, looking for the signature, then turned and grinned at Lisa. 'I thought so.'

They all crowded round, embarrassing Lisa with their compliments, while Chris, the only one who had been allowed a sneak preview, stood back with a proud smile as he watched the delighted reaction.

'Chris had an input too,' Lisa told them. 'He lent me his photographs to work from so I was able to capture the details more accurately. You have two artists in the family.'

When Lisa had taken her picture to be framed, the gallery owner had been impressed and suggested she complete a series of paintings of Stanley Park. 'I'm sure you would be able to sell them. Paintings of local places go down well with the visitors. I can give you an exclusive window display if you are interested.'

Lisa toyed with the idea. She certainly hoped to sell some paintings to help fund her stay in England because, even allowing for her grandma's generosity, there were still expenses to be met but she decided that if she was going to build an exhibition it would be better to widen her scope and include the whole town of Blackpool. She asked Chris to give her a tour.

They went first to the Golden Mile with its pulsating atmosphere. Crowds milled around the kaleidoscope of colourful, brash attractions and they had to weave their way in and out of large groups of noisy visitors, all out for a good time.

When they found a moment to be able to talk, Chris grinned. 'What do you think?'

'I think it's fantastic. Mum told me a bit about this part of Blackpool, but you have to be right here in amongst it to really feel the atmosphere, don't you?'

'That's why I brought you here first. A baptism of fire.'

They carried on along the promenade going as far as the Pleasure Beach and Lisa filled her sketchbook with quick drawings but there was so much to see that she ended up asking Chris to take photos for her so that she could cram in more impressions. It was the people she was mostly interested in, those on the beach enjoying the donkey rides, the children round the Punch and Judy stalls and the ice cream stalls. There was enough material here to keep her painting for months, if not years, and she knew she would have to be selective if she was not to become overwhelmed. By the end of the day they were ready to drop and both of them had sore feet so they climbed on a tram for the return to Talbot Square. Lisa had got what she came for, an impression of the liveliness of Blackpool – except for the Tower and they had already decided that deserved a day all to itself.

After a couple of days to soothe their tired feet, Chris took time off work and they went to the Tower prepared to stay until there was no more to see, but it was the circus, the first one that Lisa had ever seen, that captivated her. As act followed act in quick fire rotation, the riot of colour, spangles, bright lights and hair-raising stunts, held her breathless and it was here she had her light-bulb moment. How about a series featuring just the circus for her first project? She loved figure work. In front of her were acrobats, jugglers, high wire acts, all these strong well-formed bodies creating superb shapes, perfect for painting. The immaculately groomed white horses with their flowing manes and long swinging tails, high stepping round the ring in perfect synchronism, would be a challenge, but one that she would relish. Then there were the slapstick stunts of the brightly painted clowns. She grew more enthusiastic the more she saw. She turned to Chris her eyes bright with excitement.

'Chris, I think I know what I want to do. What do you think about an exhibition based solely on a circus theme?'

His first reaction was, 'I think you've chosen a very hard subject,' then he thought for a moment. 'But if you are ready to tackle it, you could be on to a winner. All these acts are booked for the whole 1967 summer season so that will give you twelve weeks. Will that be enough time?'

'Plenty, and not having to travel around will help. Everything will be in one place. I know it won't be easy but it will be so exciting and hopefully sellable.'

'Then do it, but you are braver than I am.'

* * *

'I think I have just found exactly what I was looking for, Grandma,' she told Elizabeth when she got home. 'We went to the Tower Circus and I was knocked sideways by it all. What a thrill. I was holding my breath most of the time.' Lisa was still exhilarated by her visit. 'I've decided to base my exhibition round that. What do you think?'

Like Chris, Elizabeth thought it was a very ambitious project but if Lisa thought she could do it then she was all in favour. When Lisa described what she planned, Elizabeth said. 'An exhibition like that would be good publicity for the Tower. Why don't you ask the publicity manager for a complimentary pass so that you can visit whenever you like? Take some of your work to show him so that he knows it will be of a high standard.'

A fortnight later, the project was launched and Lisa had the whole summer ahead of her to work on her first public exhibition. She couldn't wait to start.

* * *

One of the acts was an Italian troupe of acrobats and Lisa chose this for her first painting. She spoke a little Italian learned from her father so was able to communicate with them and was soon on first name terms. She attended rehearsals as well as performances and her sketchbook filled quickly. One of the young men spoke fairly good English and he was the main spokesman for the act. He also took a fancy to Lisa. She was aware of this and was careful not to be anything more than friendly towards him – she had not come to England looking for romance, she had come to meet her family and to make the most of the opportunity to find a new outlet for her painting. Anything else she was happy to leave for the future.

Giovanni was so cheerful and funny, however, that they soon slipped into the habit of taking their coffee break together and Lisa found she enjoyed his company. Gio and his three brothers, sister Lucia and cousin Sophia, were keeping the family tradition going. They were all very skilled and their act was popular. When the first painting was finished, Gio wanted to see it, but Harry had made a space in the garage for Lisa to adapt as a studio where she could put the finishing touches to her on-the-spot studies and no one was allowed in. She wanted to complete the whole portfolio before anyone else would see her work, apart from the framer and Chris, who had loaned her his own shots of the Tower, and who was therefore privileged.

She chose the clowns for her next study and worked quickly, using the paint thickly and working with quick, broad brush strokes, Impressionist style, to catch all the vibrancy of their slapstick acts. She lost none of her initial tingle and her paintings reflected the buoyancy she felt as she worked.

Sometimes, she and Giovanni walked on the sands to get some fresh air. He tried to get to know her better.

'So, Lisa, tell me about your father, he was Italian, yes? Where was he from?'

'I'm afraid I don't know. He never talked about it and we didn't speak much Italian because my mother didn't speak it. They were too busy trying to become Australian I suppose. Dad died when I was twelve, so I've spent half my life without him.'

Lisa gave a little sigh and Gio impulsively leaned over and hugged her.

'Ah, I have made you sad. I am sorry. What can I do to cheer you up? I know, we'll have an ice cream.'

He went across to a nearby booth and bought them both a large cornet. Lisa laughed.

'Thank you, Gio. You always know how to make a person smile again.'

'Of course, I want you always to be smiling. There is no need to be sad when it is so much nicer to be happy.'

Lisa looked fondly at him. This was typical of his happy-go-lucky personality. He was a lovely, vivacious, charming man, a playmate but not a soulmate, at least not for her. Still, he was definitely making this summer special and, because she was so careful not to allow any seriousness to interfere with their friendship, she knew that at the end of the season they would say goodbye with no regrets.

* * *

When she finished her last picture, three months later, she was almost painted out. She sat in the garage looking at her line of canvasses and was pleased with what she had achieved. Framing would give the final touch and then she must arrange her exhibition. Elizabeth and Harry, although very curious, had strictly obeyed Lisa's request not to take a peep until the pictures were ready. They helped her load the wrapped paintings into their car to take them to the gallery for framing and they went with her to collect them, still wrapped. Chris suggested a church hall where his photographic society held their exhibitions, but Lisa wanted somewhere more central. She still had the gallery owner's offer to display her work in his window, but there was not the space for them all to be on display at the same time.

Knowing she had left it rather late, she approached a larger town centre gallery, taking two of her favourite pictures, and the curator was sufficiently impressed to agree to clear one of the side rooms for her. It would be available the following month.

With Chris's help, Lisa hurriedly began organising an opening evening and sent out invitations using a list he had compiled for her. All the family would be there of course, and Lisa also invited Gio's troupe. Chris contacted the local newspaper in the hope that they would send a reporter and a photographer, but as Lisa was unknown, he was not certain they would attend.

'What shall I wear?' asked Gio. 'Do you want us all to come in our costumes? We will be an attraction and it might help you to sell your paintings.'

'No, no, thank you, Gio.' Lisa had a vision of him turning her evening into a circus. 'Just come in your ordinary clothes, as my guests.'

Gio put his disappointed look on and slowly shook his head. 'You might just have missed a great opportunity there,' he said.

CHAPTER TWENTY-SIX

LISA met Giovanni for a drink the week before her exhibition. It was near the end of the summer season and very soon he and the rest of the troupe would be leaving to take up their next engagement on the continent. Lucia and Sophia joined them before going on to a party, both already a bit merry and in the party mood.

'We shall miss you, Lisa,' Lucia said, wrapping her arms round Lisa and giving her a big kiss. 'What will you do without us – we are like family, yes?'

'I'm going to miss all of you so much.' Lisa hugged her back' 'But who knows, perhaps you may come out to Australia one day, and we can all meet up again.'

'Australia?' Sophia put her glass down. 'I don't think I would like Australia. It is not a happy place for me.'

'Why, have you been there?' Lisa was surprised.

'Not me, no, but my Aunt Giuliana's husband, he came to England and never went back to Italy. For a long time, she waited. After the war, she thought he would come, but no – he went to Australia. My aunt never had a family, no babies, no 'usband. She did not get over that, my poor Aunt.' Sophia began to cry, dramatically and a little drunkenly.

'No tears, Sophia.' Lucia moved across and pulled her cousin to her feet. 'All long ago now. We are going to a party you must laugh not cry!'

'Yes, no tears,' Sophia sniffed. 'Besides he was no good. My aunt was better off without him. She had us to take care of her. We must not waste tears on Bruno Colletti – poof! – he is gone.' She snapped her fingers and linked arms with Lucia. 'Ciao, Lisa.' She blew her a kiss. 'Ciao, Gio.' And she lurched off, her boozy melancholy gone as quickly as it had come.

Lisa stared after them, heart thumping wildly. What had she just said – Bruno Colletti? That was her father! Surely, she can't have been talking about the same person?

'What is it, Lisa? You look upset.' Gio was concerned.

Lisa stared at him. *Her* father? Connected to Sophia and regarded as a good for nothing by the family back in Italy? There had got to be a mistake somewhere, but logic told her that his name, coupled with the move to Australia, were two undeniable coincidences.

'Are you all right?' Gio was now looking worried.

'Yes, I'm all right.' She was still staring at him, unable to cover the shock that short conversation had given her.

Gio brought her another drink. 'Drink this, Lisa. You look as if you have seen a ghost.'

'Maybe I have, in a way.' She drank the wine straight down and the strong kick calmed her fluttering stomach.

'Whatever is it? Tell me, let me help you.'

'Oh, Gio, this is awful. What Sophia just said, about her aunt, I'm sure she was talking about my father, Bruno Colletti.'

'Your father?'

'Yes. It's terrible. She was so bitter about him and I don't think it was the drink talking. It may have loosened her tongue a bit, but what she said – that must be how her family see him – Oh!' Lisa stopped suddenly as she remembered that Sophia was Gio's cousin. 'So, you must feel the same.' It came out in a whisper.

Gio took a drink of wine before he answered. 'I don't know Sophia's aunt. I have heard of her of course, but she is from the other side of Sophia's family, not mine. The name Colletti meant nothing to me, I've only heard her spoken of as Aunt Giuliana.'

'Sophia doesn't know my name is Colletti, she only knows me as Lisa. What shall I do? Should I tell her?'

'Are you sure it is him?'

'I think it must be. I know my parents never married because Dad had a wife somewhere in Italy, but I know no more than that. They didn't talk about it.'

'I need another drink, how about you?' Gio reached for her glass.

Lisa shook her head. She needed to be able to think clearly. Obviously, her father's desertion was still regarded as a family scandal, even after all this time. Although it was no fault of hers, Lisa couldn't help but feel a sense of guilt on behalf of her father.

She knew very little of the circumstances, so before she could decide how to act, she needed to find out as much as she could. Who would be the best person to ask? Would her grandmother be able to tell her anything? Would her mother *wish* to tell her anything? There was so much confusion whirling around in her head she knew she must spend some time on her own to make sense of it. At the moment she could only think of complications, not the least being that she could be distantly connected to Sophia. She must have time to think.

She told Gio she wanted to go home and asked him not to say anything until she had come to a decision. Just as surprised and puzzled as Lisa, Gio promised.

Back at Elizabeth's, Lisa lay on the bed staring at the ceiling. For the first time she almost wished she had not come to England, then this would never have happened, yet she had been so happy only a few hours ago. Lisa had none of the volatile Italian temperament in her. Taking after her father only in looks, she had inherited her mother's calm, practical nature.

She decided that the first person she would speak to would be her grandmother, then, if there was more to find out, she would ring her mother. Elizabeth was in the kitchen making pastry to pop into the fridge overnight, ready for tomorrow's pie.

'Grandma, can I ask you something?' Lisa sat down and leaned her arms on the table.

'Ask away.' Elizabeth looked up with a smile which faded slightly as she saw the disturbed look on Lisa's face.

'You might not want to talk about it – I don't know how you feel – but I have to ask you anyway.'

'Just tell me what it is, Lisa, then we'll see whether or not I want to talk about it.' She scooped out the ball of dough, wrapped it in foil and placed it in the fridge. Lisa watched her grandmother clean her baking table, and tried to decide how best to phrase her opening remark.

'Grandma, were you there when I was born?'

'Yes, I was. I went over to the Isle of Man and stayed with your mother until you arrived, and a very beautiful baby you were too.'

Lisa smiled. 'So, you knew my father, then?'

'Not well. I only met him a couple of times before you all went to Australia, and then of course he died, and I came to visit you and your mother.'

'You didn't know a lot about him, then? If he was married to someone else, for instance?'

'What's brought this on, Lisa? Your mother will have told you as much as she thinks you need to be told, I'm sure.'

'That's just it. I only know that Dad was from Italy originally and was sent to the Isle of Man when the war broke out, and that's where he met Mum. I know they were never married. Was it because he was married already?'

'Oh, dear.' Elizabeth gave a sigh. 'This is really for your mother to talk to you about, Lisa, I'm not sure what she would want me to say. Why are you asking?'

'Something happened tonight while I was having a drink with Gio. Lucia and Sophia joined us, they had both already started drinking and Sophia was a bit worse for wear. Anyway, Australia was mentioned and she said it had unhappy connections for her. She said her aunt had been deserted by a Bruno Colletti many years ago and that the family had never forgiven him. It can only be my father, the name, the fact that he went to Australia – it must be him, so I need to know what happened, because I am going to have to tell Sophia that I am his daughter.'

'You need to speak to your mother. She will tell you what she can.'

'But that's just it, Grandma, Mum obviously doesn't want to talk about it. I have asked from time to time, just wanting to know a bit more about my background, but she has always said very little, and even that only covered the time from when we arrived in Australia. I don't even know anything about the Isle of Man other than the fact that they met there, but I don't know why she was there when all the rest of the family were obviously here. I'm twenty-two, Grandma, not a little girl, and I think I need to know more about my father and how he became involved with Mum.'

'I agree with you, Lisa, but speak to your mother first, then, when we know her response, I'll tell you as much as I can. I can't say more than that at the moment.'

'I'll ring her now, if I may – no hold on, it will be about half-past five in the morning there. I'll get up early and ring her then.'

'I'll get up early too so I can have a word with her. I think this is the best way to handle it. I can't believe the sheer coincidence of you coming up against someone who might be one of your father's Italian relatives. It's bizarre, though you do hear of the most amazing coincidences happening. Nothing is impossible. Of course, you must make sure he *is* the person Sophia was talking about first, or you may be opening a can of worms quite unnecessarily.'

'Mum should be able to help us there. Oh, Grandma, I'm so sorry this has happened. I was so happy.'

'None of this is your fault, Lisa, in fact it's really nothing to do with you in any way other than that you are the result of what happened. But you are not the cause so you must not let it make you unhappy. Now I am going to make some cocoa, take it up to bed with you and try to get a good night's sleep. I'll see you in the morning.'

Elizabeth poured hot milk into three mugs, passed one to Lisa and picked up the other two to take upstairs to where Harry was already in bed waiting for her. What a bedtime story she would have to tell him tonight.

* * *

Lisa was in the kitchen making coffee when Elizabeth came downstairs at six o'clock the next morning.

'Have your coffee before you ring, Lisa, and sit down comfortably. Have you thought about what you are going to say?'

'I have, over and over again! I think it's best to tell Mum exactly what I told you and see what her response is.'

'She will be surprised to hear from you, so make sure she knows that everyone is well. I'll be just by the door if you need me. Don't forget to let me have a quick word before you ring off.'

Lisa rang the operator to put through her call. Elizabeth went outside to wait. The phone rang for a few moments before it was answered.

'Hello.'

'Mum, hi, it's Lisa.'

'Are you all right?' Instantly Margaret was anxious.

'Yes, absolutely, and so is everyone else, there's nothing to worry about. I just want to ask you something.'

'That's a relief! Right, go ahead, ask me what?'

Lisa told her exactly what she had told Elizabeth, moving quickly to the point where Sophia had mentioned the name of Bruno Colletti.

'The thing is, Mum, do you think it is Dad she was talking about? It's too much of a coincidence, isn't it, especially about him going to Australia after living over here?'

It took a while for Margaret to answer and when she did the tremor in her voice told Lisa that she was shocked.

'I can't believe this, Lisa. All the time that has passed and with all the distance between Italy, England and Australia, who could have thought that you would bump into someone with connections to him.'

'So, you think it is Dad, then?'

'Yes, it is him. Giuliana was his wife's name.'

Lisa took a deep breath. 'Can you tell me what happened, Mum? Sophia made it sound as though he had abandoned his wife and that he was regarded as an outcast by the family, even today. Her Aunt Giuliana is still alive and, according to Sophia, never remarried.'

'No, she wouldn't. She was a very devout Catholic. That is why Bruno and I didn't marry; he knew he could not be divorced. He did leave her, yes, but it was not because of me. He had left in the first place, before the war began, because he could not spend the rest of his life in a loveless marriage. I'm not going to tell you more than that Lisa, because it is Bruno's story, and Giuliana's I suppose, and I don't think it is for us to chew it over. I was also married. I don't think you knew that did you? Of the two of us I could be regarded as the most at fault because I left a marriage that had seemed perfect until I met your father and fell head over heels in love. It was not easy, there was a lot of guilt, then we found out about you and there was only one decision to be made. I never regretted it, though I did deeply regret the heartache I caused at the time.' Margaret sighed. 'How unlucky this has come about now, just when you are supposed to be having the time of your life in England.'

'I needed to know if it was him because I will have to face Sophia and tell her who I am. It sounds like she could be a sort of cousin by marriage, or a second cousin, whatever the connection is it seems to be a distant one. I don't know how she will take it, but I have to tell her.'

'It's a *very* distant one, and only through marriage, there are no blood ties involved. So, the only connection to you is your father's name. You have no need to be ashamed of your father, Lisa. He sent money regularly back to Italy, even though there were no children, and his wife seemed happy with that arrangement until he met me. Even after we moved to Australia, he still sent the money. It only stopped when he died.'

'I am not ashamed of him at all, though it did upset me to hear him described as no good. Anyway, now I know a bit more I can handle Sophia. I hope we can still be friends. I'll do my best to see that we do, but she has obviously grown up with this family opinion of Dad and it may be hard for her to come face to face with his daughter.'

'If that is what you feel you must do then do it, Lisa, but don't let anything spoil your visit and certainly not your exhibition. Whatever she says, don't get upset. love. It all happened long before either you or Sophia were born, how can it matter now?'

'Don't worry, Mum, I know what I must do, and I won't let it upset me. They are all going to the Continent soon so it will be over and done with then anyway. Thank you for telling me, and I'm sorry to have disturbed old memories.'

Lisa spent the next four days putting the finishing touches to her exhibition, pricing and titling the pictures and preparing a short introduction to her exhibition. Chris was going to help her to hang them the day before her opening evening and before then she wanted to speak to Sophia. She went to see Gio.

'I've spoken to Mum and we are fairly certain it is my father Sophia was talking about. I'm going to have to tell her and I am wondering how she will react. What do you think?'

'I think Sophia is in for a big surprise. How will she react? That is difficult to say. For us Italians, family loyalty is everything and grudges can be held for generations. I don't say that is how Sophia will react. I am not even sure how I feel myself because this is a big surprise to me also, I just say it is possible.'

'But neither of us was even born when it happened so surely it can't affect our friendship, because I do think of you all as friends now.'

'And you are our friend. We shall miss you very much.' He suddenly beamed. 'This has been a wonderful summer and it has been exciting being painted by you, so of course all will be well. How can it not be when we have had such a lovely time together?'

Gio's jauntiness reassured Lisa and she arranged to meet all the Italians later after the matinee performance when she would approach Sophia about the discovery.

When they met, Lisa made sure she was sitting next to Sophia, and she waited until they had all sat down with their coffee before she broached the subject of her father. Then she leaned forwards, chummily.

'Sophia, do you remember when we were talking about Australia the other day and you mentioned your Aunt Giuliana?'

'Oh yes, Aunt Giuliana, she has had a sad life.' Sophia rolled her eyes melodramatically.

'Well, you also mentioned the name Bruno Colletti and that surprised me because my name is Colletti.'

'No, is that so? It is a name many people have in Italy, but what a – 'ow do you call it?'

'A coincidence,' Gio volunteered.

'Yes, that's right, a coincidence,' Sophia agreed.

'Well, it is even more of a coincidence, Sophia, because Bruno Colletti was my father. I spoke to my mother in Sydney and we are sure he is the person you mentioned. So, it seems that there is some sort of connection between us, doesn't it?' Lisa smiled eagerly, hoping Sophia would be pleased at the possibility.

The look on Sophia's face disillusioned her instantly. Her stony expression wiped the smile off Lisa's face. Her eyes were hard and her mouth set, rejection was written all over her, though she had not said a word. Gio tried to help.

'We knew you were half Italian, Lisa, but we didn't know you were one of us.'

'She isn't!' Sophia snapped.

'Sophia,' Lisa began, 'you and I were not born when your Aunt Giul–'

'Please do not speak about my aunt or my family. There is no connection between us.' Sophia's voice was full of animosity and she stood up without looking at Lisa. 'Are you coming, Lucia?'

Lucia was puzzled, having understood only a little of the exchange between the two girls, but she loyally followed her cousin out of the cafe where they had all met so happily only a few minutes ago.

'I'm sorry, Lisa,' said Gio. 'It was probably just the shock. She will have heard the tale of her aunt being abandoned ever since she was a little girl.'

Lisa didn't answer. She picked up her cup of coffee and drank it quickly, hoping it would help to calm her thumping heart and dispel her utter dismay at the reaction she had received.

'She will get over it. You will see. We shall all be friends again tomorrow,' Gio tried to cast a brighter light on what had been a very awkward moment. 'Don't be upset.'

'It's all right, Gio. I wish I hadn't offended Sophia. I thought I was doing the right thing in telling her, but it all went wrong. Don't worry, I'm not upset – well, I am, but I can't let myself dwell on it. I've got my exhibition to think of and I need to keep calm for that.'

'I am looking forward to seeing your paintings,' Gio said, 'I hope you have made me look very 'andsome!'

Lisa allowed a smile to appear. 'Wait and see,' she replied.

* * *

Chris had taken the day off work to help Lisa and she could not have managed without him. She had twelve large canvasses to hang. For the first two paintings she had worked in oils, her favourite medium, but concerned that even these early pieces would still only be touch dry by the time of the exhibition, she switched to acrylics, which had a much quicker drying time, and the line of completed pictures in the garage had grown steadily.

By the end of the afternoon, both she and Chris were pleased with the display, and after a quick check to make sure that every item on the list had been completed, they headed off to Elizabeth's where they had been promised another of her specialities – fish pie. Grace was there, and Jessie and Jim, so the meal was a jolly affair and Lisa was again aware of the family love that spread itself over them all like a warm blanket. They were all excited and eager to hear as much as Lisa was willing to tell them without giving too much away. She was hoping the bold impact of the vivid paintings would impress everyone as soon as they entered the side room. She had aimed for drama and was hoping she had achieved it.

Lisa was up early the next day, as were her grandparents. They were very proud of their granddaughter and grew more and more excited as the day wore on. Margaret rang during the afternoon.

'Today's the day then, Lisa? How are you feeling?'

'Excited, Mum, and so are Granddad and Grandma. I can't do any more until this evening, so I'm trying to keep myself busy. I'm going to have a good soak in the bath and take my time getting ready. I want to look as glamorous as I can in case the press do show up, we have notified them but we will have to wait and see.'

'I wish I could be there, darling, but I'll be there in spirit, I know it will be a success.'

'I wish you could be here too, Mum. I'll write and tell you all about it once it is over. Fingers crossed!'

'Fingers *and* toes, though you won't need any of that superstitious luck. You just enjoy yourself, make the most of it. Give my love to Grandma and Harry. Congratulations on your first exhibition and don't forget to write. Love you.'

'Love you too.'

Lisa was in the bath when the phone rang again. She heard Harry answer it and a few seconds later, heard him shout for Elizabeth to take the call. Then she heard her Grandma's shocked voice. 'Is this a hoax or something? You must be joking.'

Lisa listened, concerned, then Elizabeth said, 'Wait a minute – I'll get her.'

The next minute Lisa heard her running up the stairs and knocking on the bathroom door.

'Lisa! Lisa! There is a phone call for you. It's the gallery – there has been an incident involving your paintings. Can you speak to them, love?'

Lisa was out of the bath in a flash and opened the door wrapped in a towel. 'What do you mean incident?'

'Oh, Lisa, someone has slashed all your paintings. They have no idea how it happened…' Elizabeth stopped as Lisa dashed downstairs and snatched up the phone.

'Hello? Yes, it's me, what has happened?'

The curator explained what they had found when they were closing at half past four that afternoon, just two hours before the opening of Lisa's exhibition.

'You need to come here and see for yourself. We will have to decide what we are going to do about tonight. I will wait here until you arrive.'

Lisa put the phone down. For a moment no one spoke, then Lisa asked Harry if he would get the car and drive her to the gallery.

'I'm going to phone Chris whilst you get dressed,' Elizabeth said, 'He can meet us there.'

Lisa rushed back upstairs and threw on some clothes, abandoning all thoughts of looking glamorous. By the time they arrived at the gallery, Chris was already there. The scene that greeted them was shocking. Each painting had been slashed diagonally, top to bottom, leaving the canvas gaping like an open wound, and making every picture unrestorable. Lisa slumped against Chris. This was worse than she could ever have imagined. There was absolutely no way any of her work could be saved.

Elizabeth burst into tears. The gallery's curator kept apologising and explaining that there had been nothing to arouse suspicion. The doorway had been taped across, clearly indicating that the room was not open to the public, the lights had been off and in the dark, no one had seen any sign of entry. Security was in the hands of the receptionist and the two attendants on duty that day and they had not noticed anything suspicious or unusual about any of the visitors. They were all at a loss.

'We should call the police,' the curator suggested.

'Yes, we should,' Chris answered for Lisa, who was numb with shock. 'This is an act of criminal vandalism. Why on earth would anyone do such a thing?'

'We do get some odd sorts in here from time to time, not to look at the displays but just to sit down or even have a sleep, but we have never had anything like this happen before – not wanton destruction. It's almost as though someone had a grudge.'

A grudge? Lisa looked up. Surely Sophia would not have done this. Yet the hatred had been obvious the other afternoon and she had been invited to attend the opening along with the rest of the troupe, so she knew where the venue was. Lisa tried to look for other explanations but that one possibility was increasingly offering itself to her and, although she tried to reject the horrible thought, she had to admit there were too many reasons for it to be true to dismiss it. She felt sick to her stomach, both because of the heart-breaking destruction of so much hard work and also because she now felt sure she knew who was responsible.

The police and the curator decided that someone must have come in during the late afternoon and sneaked through the tape, although no one could remember seeing anyone in particular. The police did think, however, that the cuts had been made with a razor blade rather than a knife.

'I doubt if we will find the weapon. A razor blade can easily be disposed of, easy to conceal too in a pocket or handbag. It could have been done by a man or a woman, no great strength would have been needed, just a quick slash across, probably made easier by the fact that they are all hung at the same height on the walls. It could have been done very quickly.'

'Could it have been done by someone who has a dislike of circuses?' asked Harry. 'You do hear of people who think animals shouldn't be used.'

'It's possible but not very likely. Someone like that would be more inclined to try to set the animals free or do some damage to the circus itself, not to an art exhibition. Plus, they would likely leave some claim behind so that they publicise their cause.' The policeman looked at Lisa. 'Can you think of anyone who might want to do this to you – someone you may have crossed in some way?'

Lisa looked up quickly. She couldn't tell them what she was thinking. If she mentioned Sophia, the whole story would have to come out. This disaster would surely attract the press, and she didn't want to provide the girl with an opportunity to discredit her father's name in public. Both she and her mother would suffer and nothing would be gained by it, her pictures would not be restored.

'No.' Lisa shook her head. 'I can't. I don't know many people. I have only been in this country since April. I can't believe this has happened.'

'We haven't much to go on, but we will do our best to find out who did this. We'll take statements tomorrow when the rest of the staff are here —we will be in touch.'

'What about the exhibition?' asked Harry after the police had gone. 'I suppose it's off now?'

They all looked at Lisa but it was Chris who spoke. 'I think we might be able to salvage a workable display, Lisa. None of your drawings has been damaged and you've got your watercolours at home, those can be brought in. Any that are unframed we can put in good mounts, I bet your friend who did the framing would help with that. I'm sure we can build a display round those.'

Lisa saw a ray of hope. 'I suppose we could, yes. Do you think we can do it in time?'

'We will all help,' said Elizabeth. 'And what about our picture of Stanley Park? It might not be about the circus, but it is about Blackpool and it's a wonderful picture.'

Chris saw the possibility instantly. 'I think that is just what we need. We'll put it right at the end of the room where it will have the wall to itself. It's large enough to stand alone. The drawings and watercolours can be hung along each side and your finished work will be the first picture everyone will see when they walk into the room.'

The curator joined in. 'We have a highlighter in there. We can spotlight it for dramatic effect.'

Lisa saw the display in her mind's eye. Her practical nature exerted itself. If this was going to work, they had no time to lose. 'Let's do it!'

By ten past six, having all worked flat out, they were ready and the first invited guests began to arrive. Drinks were served in the main gallery, with Lisa's room still in darkness. When she was sure they were all gathered, she asked them to follow her across the floor to where she had invited Grace to cut the tape, the cue for the curator to switch on the lights. The strong spotlight drew all eyes and the effect was exactly what she had hoped for. Someone began to clap and there was a shout of, 'Well done'. Surrounded by people who loved her, Lisa knew that in spite of everything, her evening was going to be a success.

She spotted Gio and Lucia and had begun to go over to them when she stopped in sheer amazement. There stood Sophia, either utterly brazen or completely innocent, and for a moment Lisa was not sure which, until Sophia turned, looked across at her and smiled. It was not the smile of friendship. It was a blatant malicious smirk. She actually raised her glass and saluted Lisa in a defiant, gloating gesture.

Lisa was astounded by her open spite. As she felt her temper rise, she remembered her mother's words, don't let her upset you. She calmed herself. So, it was you, and now you think you have come to watch me squirm. You think you have ruined my evening. Well, you are wrong, my girl, I'm not going to play your little game.

With the room full of her guests, there was not a great deal Lisa could do, but she could not let Sophia get away with this. She glared back and held Sophia's eyes with all the contempt she could muster until she saw Sophia's smirk fading, then she scornfully and deliberately snubbed her by turning her back. It was the most insulting gesture she felt able to show, and it was far from the reaction she would have liked to have shown, but it made her feel better.

Back at Elizabeth's later, the conversation was dominated by the dreadful vandalism.

'You must have been devastated, Lisa.' Jessie put her arm round Lisa's shoulder. 'Who would do something so mindless?'

'I don't suppose we will ever know. After all that hard work, not to mention the costs involved. Only someone deranged could do that.' said Chris. They all nodded in agreement. Lisa stayed silent with her thoughts. Someone deranged? Or someone full of hate?

CHAPTER TWENTY-SEVEN

THE circus was in its final week and Lisa and Gio went for a meal before he left the country. She had told no one about Sophia and careful manoeuvring had meant that she had not come face to face with her again. Gio was in a sombre mood and Lisa put it down to the upheaval involved in moving the troupe and its accoutrements to Spain, where they had their next engagement. He ordered champagne and when the pudding was put on the table, he proposed a toast.

'Here's to you and thank you for sharing a beautiful summer.' He leaned towards her, raising his glass.

'Here's to you, Gio!' Lisa raised her glass in response. 'It has been good, hasn't it?'

'In spite of everything.' Gio added.

Lisa hesitated, knowing he meant the exhibition. She really didn't want to bring that up.

'What happened do you think, Lisa? You must have thought about it.'

'Of course, I did, but there is no point going over it all again. It's over, finished, best to leave it there.'

'But I can't leave it there.' Gio was more serious than she had ever seen him before. 'Lisa, have you never thought who might have done it because I have, and I must speak out now. I think it was Sophia.'

Lisa wondered whether she should tell him that she had already most certainly decided that it was.

'I can tell by your face that you are not surprised. You share my thoughts, Lisa. How did you know?'

Lisa decided there was no point in denying it. She told him about the look on Sophia's face on the night of the opening and that she had known in that moment, that it was her. 'But there is no proof, Gio, so there is nothing to be done about it now.'

'I think there is proof. One of my razors was missing and it could only have been taken by someone with access to our dressing room. Who else would it be?'

Lisa knew the men shaved their body hair before each performance, so it was obvious that Gio would notice if one of his razors was missing. If she had needed proof this seemed to be it, but she didn't, she didn't want to carry on any longer with the unpleasant affair.

'Look, let's not pursue this. The exhibition is over and we managed to salvage it to a certain extent. I sold most of my sketches and some of the completed watercolours. The only person Sophia has really hurt is herself, she has to live with what she did.'

'No, she is not the only person she has hurt – she has hurt me also.' Gio placed his hand on his heart theatrically.

Lisa was puzzled. 'Hurt you, how?'

'Lisa, you must know the way I feel about you. I wanted to ask you to marry me, but how can I do that now? How can I bring you into the same family as Sophia?' He looked at her with a tragic expression.

Lisa gulped. She knew that if he *had* asked her then the answer would have been a definite no, but then she realised that this was just Gio making the most of a dramatic moment. All his hot, theatrical, Italian blood was rising to the occasion. She didn't, for a moment, believe that he had really intended proposing, but she understood that he felt safe to ask her now in the certain knowledge that she would not accept, for the very good reason he had already laid out. Sophia!

Lisa looked at the pained expression he had arranged on his face and she knew it was for her benefit. She had to play out this drama for him, he was such a lovable friend, he deserved a good performance from her so she did her best to also look woebegone. 'You are right, Gio. We could never be happy together now with this shadow hanging over us. Thank you for the lovely summer we shared, I will never forget you.' She truly meant that last part, she really had enjoyed his jolly company. She leaned across the table and gave him a farewell kiss. Gio sighed but his eyes were not sad. He had his final scene and he was satisfied. They parted cheerfully, and Lisa was aware that neither of them offered to keep in touch.

* * *

The season was almost over, autumn was upon them and Blackpool was busy with its famous Illuminations. Having painted almost non-stop during the summer months, Lisa needed to take a break, especially since her hard work had come to such a disastrous end. She toyed with the idea of going over to the Continent but decided she couldn't risk coming across Sophia again. Then she remembered the Isle of Man. With the door firmly closed on the hope of finding any trace of the Italian side of her family, perhaps she could find out more about her Manx connections.

Elizabeth was dubious when Lisa told her of her plan to visit the island. 'You've missed the best time of the year there, Lisa, there won't be much going on right now.'

'Won't the sea and the rocks still be there? Won't the glens and the hills still be there? The sun will still be setting over the sea, there will be plenty for a painter, and no crowds. I'm in a bit of a rut just now, I need fresh stimulus.'

'Don't forget, that is where you were born,' Harry said.

'Oh, yes, so I was!' Lisa turned to her grandmother, about to ask for more information, but seeing Elizabeth's concerned face, she changed her mind. It didn't alter her plans though, and with Chris's encouragement, she booked a passage on the ferry to sail to Douglas.

'I wish I could come with you.' said Chris enviously, 'But I can't take time off work at the moment.'

'I'm not sure you would want to rough it as I will be doing. I won't be staying in any posh hotels. In fact, I'll probably end up camping.'

'I can camp! I was a Boy Scout I'll have you know.'

Lisa was very fond of Chris and she knew if she could choose anyone as a companion it would be him, but painting was a solitary occupation and she needed to have complete concentration. She also needed to be on her own to put her plans into action. She was going to find the house where her mother had lived, and where she herself had lived briefly as a baby, and she was not going to tell anyone what she was doing. Not until she had something to go on.

Chris drove her to the ferry terminal and Lisa spent the journey reading through the Isle of Man guide book that she bought in the boat's gift shop. She planned to spend at least three weeks making sketches and taking photographs before returning to Blackpool and working these up into finished paintings, using the garage again as a studio. For the last two days she intended to stay in Douglas. That was where she would begin her search for her Manx roots.

She travelled around by bus, sometimes staying in bed and breakfast accommodation and sometimes camping, sleeping in the small one-man tent she had bought. With quick watercolour sketches, she captured the spectacular sunsets at Port Erin, the magnificent rocky bay at Niarbyl, the secluded beauty of the glens and the glorious views from the top of the island's only mountain, Snaefell, which she was lucky enough to visit on a day when the frequent mist was cast aside. The compactness of the Isle of Man, compared with the wide spaces of Australia, delighted her. It meant that she could visit many places in one day and she quickly got to know her way around the small island. Was it a stirring of her Manx blood or the attraction of the ancient history of the island that made her aware of a strong sense of belonging to each place she visited? As if this was somewhere that she knew and to which she had just returned. This would definitely not be her last visit before she went back to Australia.

Douglas, her last port of call, was where she hoped to find some answers to the question of the Manx side of her family. She posted her sketches and paintings back to Blackpool so that she would be free of baggage for the last important few days in the island's capital, found accommodation near to the museum, and was about to make her first visit there when it suddenly dawned on her that she would need to know her mother's married name. In Australia they had always been known as Colletti, but although she knew her mother's maiden name was Corkish, she did not know the name of the man she had married. It would not be the same as that of her grandparents, which was Thomas, so she had no choice but to ring her grandmother. Now her mission, which she had hoped to keep a secret, would have to be revealed.

'Grandma, I am trying to find the house where I was born and where Mum lived when she was on the island and I need to know her married name. For some reason it didn't occur to me that I have never known it. Can you help?'

Elizabeth sighed, but she answered her question. 'Your mother's maiden name was Corkish, and oddly enough that was also her married name because she married her second cousin.'

'Did she?' Lisa was surprised. 'How did that come about – was my mother born on the island?'

'No, she wasn't, but, Lisa, there is such a lot to tell you it really needs your mother to explain it, not me. All I can tell you is that my first husband, that's your mother's father and your grandfather, was from the Isle of Man originally, but your mother was born here in Blackpool. Look, talk to Margaret before you delve any further. How are you anyway? Your parcel has just arrived and I've put it in your room.'

Realising that her grandmother was changing the subject, Lisa chatted for a while before ringing off and sitting down to think. She had a name, now she could start her search. The museum was quiet since it was out of season and she sought out an assistant, explained what she was doing, and asked if he could help. Not only was he able to lead her through the records, but he also knew the house she was looking for. 'It's a hotel now, though,' he told her.

'It must have been a big house, then.'

'It was one of the biggest in Douglas. The Corkishes were a well to do family and the hotel is actually run by one of them now. It's not very far from here, you can get there by bus. Would you like me to copy off the details for you?'

'Yes please. Thanks a lot, you've been really helpful.'

'Well, you've got me interested now. I love it when people come here to find their Manx ancestry and it is exciting to be tracing this family. They owned one of the mines, you know. It's closed now, though.'

'Crikey!' Lisa was impressed and later, when she was looking for somewhere to have her evening meal, she decided to have it at the hotel the curator had told her about so she could have a good look round without having to reveal her real interest.

The hotel was set in its own grounds, about a five-minute walk from the bus stop, and Lisa felt a little conspicuous walking up the long drive since most customers obviously arrived by car and there were several expensive models parked by the front entrance. Still, she had not come all this way to chicken out now, so she walked confidently up the steps and into reception.

Yes, she was told, she could book an evening meal, service began at half-past six, would she like to wait in the bar? Lisa ordered a gin and tonic and settled down at a corner table where she could look through the window. There was a beautiful garden to her right and as there was still half an hour to go before the dining room opened, she finished her drink and walked back out of the big double doors and turned towards the garden.

A large fuchsia hedge bordered a gravel path leading to the rear of the building where there were two large flower beds full of roses still in bloom. She walked to a large pink bush and leaned forward to smell the gorgeous perfume that had drifted over to her as she came down the path.

'It's called Fragrant Cloud.'

Lisa turned and a tall fair-haired young man stood there, a box of runner beans in his hands. What struck Lisa instantly was the colour of his eyes, they were the same bright for-get-me-not blue as her mother's. The museum assistant had said the family ran the hotel – could this young man be a Corkish? It was quite possible. Lisa felt a tingle.

'It's well named,' she replied. 'It has the most beautiful fragrance.'

'It is one of our newer ones.'

Lisa smiled at him. 'Are you the gardener?'

'No, I'm only helping out while I'm home from university.'

'I see.' She couldn't think how to ask any more questions without disclosing her interest, and first, she must speak to her mother. She had found the house, or rather hotel, and perhaps that was as much as she could hope to achieve on this initial visit, but now she knew that the family was here, she couldn't wait to find out more.

She enjoyed an excellent meal but saw no one else who aroused her curiosity, so she took a taxi back to her small hotel and sat down to make a sketch of the boy's head and shoulders, recalling the information her artist's eye had automatically stored. It was a good likeness. She put it with the information she had got from the museum and packed her bag as far as she could, knowing she would be leaving in the morning.

* * *

'Welcome home.' Elizabeth was waiting with open arms when Lisa arrived next day. Chris had collected her from the ferry terminal, and he too had given Lisa a delighted hug when he saw her. Lisa felt that she really had come home. She felt that she was as much a part of the family as if she had lived here all her life.

On Sunday Chris came for lunch along with Jessie and Jim, and while the older ones were having coffee, he and Lisa went into the garden so she could show him the work she had produced while she had been on the island. He leafed through the sketches, commenting on some of them, and then fell silent as he looked at the one that he had just picked up. Lisa glanced across. It was the young man she had seen in the garden at the hotel. She had not realised it was with her other work.

'Oh, that was a young man I saw in the garden of a hotel where I had dinner. I thought he looked interesting, a bit like a Viking, and I just jotted down what I could remember when I got back to my room. Why – why are you looking like that?'

Chris was still holding the sketch in his hands, staring at it. He glanced at her rather puzzled. 'It's just that he reminds me of someone.'

Lisa's skin prickled. 'Who?'

'Someone I only saw about twice, years ago. It's just one of those odd things.'

'Who was it?' Lisa was holding her breath; was she about to find out a bit more about the Manx side of her family?

Chris put the sketch down and closed the large folder. 'Oh, it's only a childhood memory – I can't really remember – it just triggered something, that's all.'

'Chris, while I was in Douglas, I went to the museum to look at the records to see what I could find out about my mother's family. Grandma told me about Mum having lived there once, but she wouldn't tell me anymore; she said it was up to Mum to tell me the rest.'

'She's right. There's nothing I can tell you. I was only a youngster myself when you were born, and I never saw you as a baby.'

'But there is something you know, isn't there? Something you remembered when you saw that sketch. Chris, please tell me, I only want to know if I have any family in the island. I know my mother was married to someone else when she met my father, and I know his name was Peter Corkish, I found that out from the records. The hotel where I saw the youth was once the house where my mother lived, presumably with Peter, and it is run now by one of the family. That is as far as I have got.'

'You know more than I do then.' Chris seemed reluctant to get involved but Lisa was not prepared to let it go.

'Please tell me who he reminded you of, Chris. I'll find out eventually, you know, because I'm determined to carry on with my search.'

Chris laughed. 'You are like a dog with a bone. All right, the sketch reminded me of Peter, your Mother's first husband. Peter was older when I saw him, not as young as this chap, and don't forget I only saw him a couple of times, but there is one thing I remember – the colour of his eyes. They were the same bright blue as your mother's.'

'So were the young man's,' Lisa took a deep breath. 'They were the first thing I noticed.'

'I don't know what you hope to find out, Lisa, but Grandma is definitely right, you ought to talk to your mother. Obviously if she has not told you anything then she didn't intend you to know, but now that you are older, I think she will realise that you have a right to be told.'

'Sometimes you are so like Grandma, Chris.'

'I will take that as a definite compliment and ignore the fact that you are likening me to a lady of well over seventy.'

'A very lovely one, though,' Lisa answered.

'Amen to that,' replied Chris.

* * *

Lisa bought a thick ring binder and began to organise all the information she had collected. This was going to take up as much time as her painting and she was going to enjoy it just as much. She began with the young man. Why had she felt so strongly that there was a connection? What had struck a chord? His eyes of course! Those blue, blue eyes that she had only seen before in her mother. She asked Elizabeth about Robert, Margaret's father and her own grandfather.

'What did he look like? Do you mind talking about him? I don't want to distress you.'

'I am not distressed, a little sad perhaps, as I always am when I think of him, and I often do. Harry and I both loved him. He worked for Harry you know, and he's not forgotten by either of us. Ask what you like, I don't mind.'

'Well, it's about his eyes – were they like my mother's, that bright forget-me-not blue?'

'Yes, exactly the same and I remember Grace saying that her husband John's were the same colour and that they all got them from *his* mother, Isobel.'

'It is definitely a Corkish trait, then?' Lisa was pleased to add another link.

Elizabeth thought for a moment. 'Not really. Remember, Isobel married into the Corkish family, so the link appears to come from her maiden side, whoever they were.'

'I didn't think of that. This is going to be much harder to solve than I thought, but hey, that just makes it more of a challenge.'

'I wish I could tell you more. Why don't you ask Grace?'

Lisa went to see Grace and broached the subject carefully. She hinted at her visit to the museum in Douglas, but without mentioning the family, and watched for Grace's reaction. To her surprise, Grace's face lit up.

'You know that is where I was born, don't you?'

'Yes, Mum told me. I'd love to know more about the island and your family, if you would like to tell me, Grandma. I had a strange feeling of belonging while I was there, it was weird.'

'Not weird. That was the ancient power of the early Manx people. They can cast a spell if you allow them to, and the island itself creates a tie that will always draw you back.'

'Do you ever wish to go back, Grandma?'

'I often do, but only in memory. I'm glad you feel like that about it, Lisa, you have family history there, you know.'

'Funnily enough, that is what I wanted to ask you about. Grandma Elizabeth has told me something about my birth, but I'm really interested in the house where I spent my first few weeks as a baby. I went to visit it because it's now a hotel. I found out it is run by one of the family who owned it when it was a private house.'

Grace absorbed this bit of information for a moment before she answered. 'Lisa, there is such a lot of family connection to that house that it is impossible for me to tell you everything right now. I would need time to search my memories, and I don't feel up to making the effort it would take to write everything down for you. Your mother knows as much as I do. Ask her.'

Lisa made the phone call that same evening. She told Margaret about the hotel and seeing the young man, and about Chris's reaction to the sketch she had made.

'Do you have any objection to me finding out more, Mum? I want to go back there, but not if it would upset you.'

'You have rather taken me by surprise, Lisa, it was all so long ago. But I do understand your need to search for the

Isle of Man branch of your family, especially in view of the setback you received from the Italian girl. From what you have told me, it sounds as if it could be Peter who is now running the house as a hotel, and it's that which makes it a little bit awkward for me. I left Peter for your father, you know, and I have always felt guilty about the distress I caused. We have had no contact with each other since then. If you did make contact with him or any of his family you might have to be prepared for another rejection, although I know you would not be subjected to the bitterness you got from Sophia. It's a chance you would have to take.'

'I'm ready for that. I will just pay it by ear when I get there. Now that I know you don't mind, and nor do Grandma and Grandma Grace, I can go ahead with my plans. I can't help feeling excited, Mum, and I promise I won't be upset if things don't turn out the way I would like. I'll keep you up to date. Speak to you soon.'

CHAPTER TWENTY-EIGHT

THE next week Lisa went across to the island again and booked a five day stay at the hotel. She looked for the young man she had seen previously, but by the end of the second day she came to the conclusion that he was no longer there. Realising that she had to act quickly if she was to find out any more in the short time available, she decided to ask the receptionist about him.

'He has gone back to university now,' the girl said. 'He was only filling time by working in the garden, he's actually the son of the owner.'

'Oh, I see.' Lisa wondered how to phrase her next question without seeming too inquisitive. 'So, does the owner run the hotel himself?'

'Yes, he manages it full time. I hope you enjoy your stay with us, Miss Colletti, and if there is anything you need, please let me know.'

Lisa realised that the receptionist was ending the conversation so she moved reluctantly away.

That evening, as she sat in the dining room, a tall grey-haired man came across to ask if everything was satisfactory. Lisa looked up at a pair of bright blue eyes, the same blue eyes as the young man, the same blue eyes as her mother. This had to be the owner, Peter.

'Yes, very nice indeed thank you.'

'I hope you are enjoying your stay with us?'

'I am, and the hotel is lovely. Is it quite old?' She felt that was a reasonable question, one that would provide some information without seeming too nosey.

'I believe it was built towards the end of the last century. How did you hear about us? I understand you are from Blackpool.'

'Yes, although I am just visiting relatives there at the moment.'

He seemed to hesitate then said, 'You are Margaret's daughter, aren't you?'

Completely taken aback, Lisa simply nodded.

'I thought so.'

'How did you know?'

'The receptionist told me you had been asking about my son and then I saw your address in the guestbook – Whitegate Drive, Blackpool. I knew that was where Margaret had lived as a young girl and I put two and two together. Your Australian accent and your Italian looks helped, of course. I'm Peter.'

To her tremendous relief he smiled, and Lisa knew she had no need to be worried.

'I thought I was the one doing the detective work,' she said, smiling back at him. 'I'm hoping to find out about the Manx side of my family.'

'You're tracing your family history, are you? In that case we must do what we can to help you. Has your mother told you that she and I are second cousins?'

'Only very recently, after I arrived in Blackpool. I know I have a connection to the island, that I was born here, for instance, and I know that you and she were once married. I hope I'm not treading on any toes?'

'Not after all this time, but look, we can't talk here.

When you have finished your meal would you like to come up to our family quarters then we can speak more privately?'

'I'd love to, thank you.'

Peter produced coffee in his living room and they spent a good hour just chatting and getting to know one another. Lisa told him about Australia and Peter asked after her grandmother Elizabeth and great-grandma Grace. They skirted around Margaret's name, but when Lisa got up to go to her room, Peter suggested that she join him again the next day.

'I have some information which may interest you,' he said, 'And there are some loose ends to tie up, particularly with regard to your mother.'

* * *

Tucked up in bed that night, Lisa took out the ring binder and began to look through her notes about the Corkish family. She had made a rough attempt at creating a family tree based on further research at the museum and she looked at her entry for Peter. His father Philip and her great-grandfather John were first cousins and, according to the dates she had got from the museum, it was apparent that Philip had been in his forties when Peter was born whilst John had been only twenty-one when his son Robert was born. This accounted for the generation gap she had noticed which separated Peter and his father, whereas her great-grandfather John, had managed to fill in his branch with two generations of offspring in that same period, her grandfather Robert and her mother Margaret. How entwined family roots could be.

As she glanced over her chart, she looked more closely at the notes she had made marking out those members of the family who had inherited the same distinctive blue eyes as her mother, then looked again, puzzled, as she saw that both Peter and his son were among them. How could that be, if, as her grandmother had said, the gene had been passed down from Isobel who was a Corkish only by marriage? She placed two large question marks by the side of Peter's name, intending to ask more the next day.

Lisa was intrigued when she met Peter for tea the following afternoon. He had a box file on the table by his chair which he opened when they had finished their meal.

'My father showed a letter to me when we were clearing the house ready to turn it into a hotel,' he began. 'Did you know that this was our family home at one time?'

'Yes, I must confess I had already been to the local museum to see what I could trace from the records there and the assistant gave me a lot of information. That is how I came to book in here.'

'Good, we can get straight on with this then.' He pulled out an envelope and removed two sheets of paper.

Lisa leaned forward to get a closer look.

'Dad and I are the only two who have known about this so far but, since you are obviously researching very thoroughly, I think what you will read needs to be part of your findings.' He handed the sheets to her.

The paper was slightly yellowed and Lisa saw that it had been written by Isobel Corkish. It stated the facts very simply. She had arrived on the island to visit her invalid friend, had become pregnant by the friend's husband, Stephen Corkish, and gone to Ireland where she had given birth to an illegitimate son, Philip. Crikey, this was a bit spicy! Lisa was thrilled to discover her family had a colourful past, but when she read that Isobel had gone on to marry Stephen's brother and had given birth to a boy named John, she realised that Isobel was revealing that she was mother to both Philip and John and that they were, in fact, half-brothers.

Although she had been eager to trace her Manx family, Lisa now felt she was digging far too deeply. Did she really want to know anymore? It was as though she had gate-crashed into the private life of a family she was only just getting to know. She put the paper down. All her anticipation and exuberance had dissipated. This was not going to be the easy dip into the past that she had expected. There were muddied waters which would need a deep probe to clear.

'What did you make of it?' Peter asked.

'It was not what I was expecting. I realise I was reading about your father, so how must you have felt, knowing how he came into the world?'

'It was Dad who found the note when I was away and he decided not to show it to me since there was so much going on at the time – my divorce from your mother for one thing – but he did show it to me when we were converting the house into a hotel. We had time to talk about it before he died, and by then he had come to terms with it all. He said it was a pity it was too late to alter the relationship he had with Aunt Isobel and his cousin John, since they were both dead, because now that was how he would always think of them, as his aunt and cousin, not as his mother and half-brother which they really were. You can't change the past and his childhood had been very happy, so he decided leave it where it was, as part of the past.'

'Now I can see how that accounts for the blue eyes on both sides of the family then,' said Lisa. 'I wondered how that had come about.'

Peter looked thoughtful. 'Funnily enough, that's something I have never thought about. You are right, though, we do all have a very distinctive shade of blue eyes. Isobel left us with a unique gift as well as a secret.'

Not one inherited by me, Lisa thought.

'Dad and I decided to put the note back.' Peter held out his hand and Lisa passed the envelope to him. 'As I said, he was happy to let it lie, so it can stay in the box. It isn't exactly a secret anymore, but at least it can remain concealed as she left it.'

He poured more coffee.

'One of the results of all this that Dad pointed out to me, Lisa, is that your mother and I are genetically much more closely related than the second-cousins-once-removed that we thought we were. We are share genes, not only from Isobel herself, but from both her sons as well.'

'Goodness, that must have taken some working out,' Lisa laughed.

'Believe me it did, and that brings me to what I really want you to know. When I was in Canada I stayed with a lovely family, and despite myself, I fell in love with their daughter. There was no way I would have done anything about it at that time, and anyway I still loved Margaret, but when I got the letter telling me she too had fallen in love with someone else, I realised that our marriage had really been more of a loving friendship than anything else. So, you see, it was the solution for me – not the tragedy which everyone thought it was. When I was repatriated, I went back to Canada and of course met Clare again, and after my divorce, we married. When we eventually came back here, Margaret had already gone to Australia. I've always known I should have written to her, but my wife became very ill and it didn't happen. I don't want your mother to feel even a shred of guilt, and I want you to be sure to tell her that because I still feel affection for her as the friend she always was.'

'She will be relieved to hear that, Peter.' Lisa had tears in her eyes. 'I think I'll go home tomorrow. There's so much I need to talk about with my mother and my grandmother.'

'Please give them both my best wishes.' Peter got up and walked across to take her hand. 'It has been so very nice to meet you, Lisa. It's been special.'

'It's been special meeting you too, Peter. I do hope we'll see each other again.' Lisa reached across to give him a hug.

'You are always welcome.'

He returned the hug and Lisa smiled. Now that she had a friend and a link to her Manx family in Peter, she could begin to bring all the pieces of the family story together.

CHAPTER TWENTY-NINE

LISA couldn't wait to phone her mother when she returned to Blackpool, and Margaret reacted just as she herself had done when she read Isobel's confession.

'The poor woman, it must have been awful for her in those days. I met her you know, when she was very old, you would never have thought she was keeping such a secret. You have surprised me by what Peter had to say. I've always felt guilty about the upset I caused, or thought I had caused, so it's a relief to hear things turned out well for him and that he has no hard feelings.'

'He said he still feels affection for you and regards you as a friend.'

'Ah yes, friends, that's all we should have been.' There was a wistful note in her voice. 'Anyway, now I can look back and enjoy the happy memories – because there were plenty you know.'

Lisa heard her mother sigh. 'Oh dear, I do miss you, Lisa, I wish I was there with you all.'

'I wish you were, Mum.'

The rest of the family were surprised when she told them about her trip and meeting Peter and his disclosure of Isobel's secret.

'Only Peter and his father, Philip, have known about it until now. Peter only showed it to me because I told him I was tracing my family tree. He thought if I was making a record, it should be a true one.'

'Good heavens, Lisa, how many more surprises are you going to spring on us?' asked Elizabeth. 'First, you bump into Chris on the train, then we find out you are a gifted artist, next you tell us about your father's complicated connection to that girl at the circus and now you tell us about a family secret that the rest of us knew nothing about.'

'I knew about it.'

Grace had been sitting quietly in her chair in the corner. Now they all turned to look at her.

'What do you mean?' It was Lisa's turn to be surprised.

'I've known about the letter for quite some time. Philip told me when I met him in Douglas once. He showed me the letter and we talked about it, then we came to the same conclusion that Peter has done, it was best to leave it hidden away. Isobel had guarded her secret very well and because of that it had not impacted on the people she shared her life with at that time. It certainly saved a lot of unhappiness, and perhaps a great upheaval in the family, but her footsteps have echoed into other lives. She left complications that had to be discovered before they could be dealt with. Lisa seems to be the one who is going to do the disentangling.'

'You knew about the letter without telling any of us?' Elizabeth was shocked. 'Even Margaret?'

'Especially Margaret. She and Peter had both got over their divorce and were happy in their new lives. At that time, it seemed best to leave well alone. Obviously, Philip didn't tell Peter he had told me.'

'Were you ever going to tell anyone, Grandma?' asked Lisa.

'Oh yes, I nearly told Margaret when she came over for my birthday but it was such a lovely reunion, I didn't want to spoil everything.'

'Well,' Elizabeth looked round the room. 'If anyone else has anything to say to shock us, will they please leave it till tomorrow. I think that's more than enough for one day.'

* * *

Having been made so welcome by Peter, Lisa was eager to go back to Douglas. There was certainly a lot to organising to do if she was to piece together her family tree as well as prepare an exhibition, but she was very keen to do both. This time there was no rush. Her mother had sent her some money, both as compensation for the ruining of her Blackpool exhibition and as encouragement for her to carry on with her next, so she could take her time and perhaps even produce the masterpiece she had always aimed for, but to do that she had to be on the island so she could become steeped in its atmosphere.

'I envy you your trip, Lisa.' Chris was wistful again. They were sitting having coffee in the garden. Jessie and Jim were there and Lisa had just told them about her plans.

'Well, I shall be there for a few weeks so why don't you join me at weekends?'

Chris looked up. 'I thought you wanted to be alone while you painted?'

'I do, but I shan't be painting nonstop. I won't have the pressure of a deadline to meet as I had when I was preparing for my first exhibition, and I decided on my main subjects when I was there a few weeks ago, so I shall have time to socialise.'

'In that case,' he said, 'I'll join you.'

Lisa was pleased, more than pleased, she was happy. Not only because he would be joining her but also because, by practically inviting himself he had, quite casually, just treated her as one of the family.

* * *

She contacted Peter to say she was returning to the island and he immediately offered her accommodation at the hotel, but she explained why she needed to be alone.

'This exhibition needs to be a success so that I can put the awful memory of my first one firmly behind me. Also, to recapture the energy with which I painted in the summer, I must have the freedom to paint whenever I feel inspired. I won't be able to conform to hotel hours. I'm going to rent a flat and hire a car, but thankyou anyway. What I would appreciate, though, is a little of your time to talk over the things you told me about Isobel. If I'm going to make a family tree, I need to make it as colourful yet as truthful as I can. Details which will mean something to future generations. You say your father spoke about discovering that Isobel was his mother – I want to ask what you can remember of his words?'

'Ring me when you get here and I will give you my whole day off to question me,' Peter said. 'I'll try to make some notes first to give us a start.'

'Perfect.'

Lisa intended to tackle the family tree before she started painting because she knew that once she had the bit between her teeth, she would not be able to stop. She had the ring binder with all the information she had collected from the museum, of course, but talking with Peter might give her an insight into Philip's feelings when he had discovered that Isobel was his mother, little snippets of detail which she might be able to extract from his exact words that Peter had not picked up on. Perhaps reading the note again might give more clues about the complicated involvement Isobel had had with the two brothers. Peter would not know anything of her feelings at that time, of course, but there may be little hints in the choice of a word, or a turn of phrase. It was going to be like going on a treasure hunt.

* * *

Peter invited Lisa up to his private rooms on his day off.

'We'll have lunch brought up here so we can eat when we like. Tell me what you want to know and I'll do my best.'

They went through all the information Lisa had in her folder, adding dates, filling in backgrounds where Peter was able to, and finally Lisa broached the question she had been longing to ask.

'One of the things I would like to know, and this is a bit personal I'm afraid, is how do you think things would have been between you and Mum if you had known when you first met, how closely related you were.'

'Ah! That's a question I wasn't expecting.' Peter leaned back in his chair. 'It's not something I have ever thought about, but now you've put it into words, let me see, I think if we *had* known we might have started a close friendship rather than a romance. We were both the only child in our family, so what we felt could have been really a strong longing for a brother or a sister. We just dived in at the wrong end. I did love your mother you know, Lisa, it was never a pretence.' Peter sat up and stretched out his arms and pulled back his shoulders. 'Goodness, that was more than I had bargained for, that's taken me back.'

'I'm sorry. I'm not just being nosey. It is relevant to what I am trying to piece together because now I want to think about Philip and John's relationship. Do you think they felt the same strong attraction of shared genes and wondered why? They were so closely related do you think they ever suspected they were brothers?'

'I know that they didn't. Dad told me that because they had been brought up together, they both just accepted the relationship for what it was. Close cousins, that's all.'

'It was obviously because you and Mum were of opposite sex that you put a romantic slant on your relationship, but I wonder, if Isobel had known that you were going to get together in that way, do you think she would have told you of the tangled history you shared?'

'You really are delving deep, aren't you? You're raising issues that I've never considered and to be honest, it has made me feel very emotional. Shall we eat now. I need a glass of wine.' Peter picked up the phone and rang the kitchen.

Lisa realised that she had probed far enough for the moment. She had enough to go on but she would ask Peter to let her see the note again before she left. Maybe she would hear something of Isobel's voice behind the words if she sat quietly and let it speak to her.

It was hard not to speculate. To produce a true record, she must keep her thoughts under control, but if she had been a writer, there was a wonderful story to be written. When she had all the details she could find, Lisa put the ring binder in her suitcase. What a strange family history she had uncovered with Peter's help. There was still a lot of organising to be done but she needed a break from the poking and prying. It had not been nice. Her painting would take over now, and that she would enjoy.

* * *

Chris joined her for a long weekend a month later and they spent it walking as much of the coast as they could, Chris with his camera and Lisa with her sketchbook. When it was time for him to leave, Lisa made a suggestion.

'Chris, I've been thinking. Why don't we have a joint exhibition? You have some fabulous shots of this beautiful island and I already have the bones of what I want to produce. Your work is of such a good standard it's a pity it doesn't get a better stage. What do you think?'

Chris looked thoughtful for a moment. 'I think you have just made a very generous offer, being willing to share your limelight, but I don't think it would work.'

'Why ever not?'

'Well, for one thing, I don't think I'll be able to produce work suitable for the type of exhibition you'll be holding. I mean you have a professional standard to maintain while I am just an amateur.'

'But that is my point, you are not. Your work is brilliant. Won't you think about it, Chris? Between us we can mount a sizeable exhibition with a wider appeal. Promise me you'll at least think about it.'

'Yes, I'll think about it.'

Not having a telephone in the flat, Lisa had arranged for any important family messages to be left with Peter at the hotel and he passed on one from Chris. He had decided to take a three-month sabbatical from work and would be joining her within the next couple of weeks. She rang back immediately.

'Chris, I can't believe it. I'm so glad you've decided. Peter has asked me to tell you he can provide a room for you in the hotel, and you can always come to my flat to develop your pictures and store your work. I have found a gallery which will be suitable, but I haven't yet approached them to go into details.' She stopped to take a breath. 'I can't wait till you are here.'

'You sound as excited as my Mum.' said Chris, 'She's the one who really pushed me into this, although it was Dad who gave me the idea of taking a sabbatical. I'll let you know when I'll be arriving.'

'Don't take too long,' Lisa risked sounding like his mother again.

Chris took up Peter's offer of a room, but without meals, and he and Lisa settled into a routine, often working on the same project but not necessarily together, so that each captured a different aspect. They travelled together, ate together and planned together, spurring each other on, and after the first four weeks of working nonstop, they were ready for a short break.

'Lisa, how about joining one of those kayaking trips along the coast?' Chris suggested one weekend. 'To give us a break.'

'I didn't know you could paddle.'

'I'm not an expert but I've been on the sea at Blackpool a few times. I'm not a beginner.'

'I'm quite good actually, I kayaked at university.'

Weather was always a factor when booking trips out, but on a day when the sea was calm, the sun shining and the forecast good, they set off on a relatively short paddle, just down the east coast and back. There were seven kayaks altogether and most of the others were people who had completed one of the courses and were now ready to venture further. They headed south from Douglas with the instructor leading and Lisa and Chris at the rear.

'It's great to be on the water again.' Lisa called. 'How about you?'

'I'm using muscles that haven't been needed for ages. I'm beginning to think I'm past it.' Chris was puffing.

Lisa laughed. 'Halfway now. Keep going.'

They had turned around in a small bay, ready for the return trip, and were back in line and paddling steadily when a black cloud swept in unexpectedly from the west, hiding the sun. The temperature suddenly plummeted and the cold air brought a down pour of lashing rain as the squall hit. The sea changed from a manageable swell to choppy unpredictable waves and it was hard to keep the kayaks from swinging out of formation. The instructor called nonstop instructions to the nervous paddlers giving reassurance – the last thing he wanted was panic. Chris and Lisa were coping well, although like the others they were struggling to keep their boats in line. Used to the wide Australian waters Lisa was the more confident. An outcrop of rocks was too near now that the waves had changed and Lisa led Chris away from them and into deeper water. They were now facing directly into the wind, and it was harder to control the oars.

'Look out!' Lisa saw the big swell looming towards them. 'Paddle down hard right.'

Chris turned to look for the wave, but it caught him before he could obey. His kayak overturned tipping him into the sea. He surfaced spluttering and coughing. His oar had gone and his kayak was tossing to-and-fro being swept beyond reach. Lisa paddled quickly over to him and grabbed the strap of his lifesaver with one hand while holding on tightly to her own oar with the other. It would be the only means of them getting to safety. The instructor saw her reach Chris and pointed vigorously to the small bay. Lisa knew he had to get his other kayakers to safety before he could help them. She was now leaning over the side of her kayak holding onto Chris with a grip that was gradually loosening and she could see that he was scared.

'Hold on, Chris.' she yelled.

Then a second large wave knocked him against the rock again and he hit his head. Despite his helmet, the bang seemed to have stunned him and he lost his hold on Lisa's boat. She had to let go of her paddle so she could grab Chris with both hands but her kayak was now at the mercy of the sea and she was struggling to hold him. If she could just bring more of his weight across the bow of her boat it would help the balance but there was no way she could lift him. All she could do was hang on to his straps and not let go. They were swinging round as well as up and down but Lisa caught sight of Chris's kayak. It had been carried past the rocks and was being washed towards the shore. Her knowledge of the Australian surf came to her rescue. Waiting for a dip in the waves which took the bow down towards Chris, she gave a mighty heave, and with the help of the upsurge swell and a rush of adrenalin, she managed to drag him sufficiently onto the bow for her to be able to take a better grip on his straps. Now, so long as she kept that grip, the sea might wash them to shore. Her wet fingers gradually froze and her grip was slipping before she finally felt the kayak drag across the stones, pushed ashore by a strong wave. The sea that had threatened them, had now saved them.

Using all the strength she had, she climbed out of the boat, rolled the now unconscious Chris over onto his back then, unable to use her numb hands, put her arms under his shoulders and began to drag him up the beach as quickly as she could to get him away from the still menacing waves. Once he was as far as she could drag him in that first effort, she stopped to get her breath back, but he was still not safe. The larger waves could still reach him. Further up the beach towards the cliff Lisa could see what looked like the remains of a ruined house, not much more than a pile of stones. The wind was still blowing hard and this seemed to be the only shelter the bay had to offer. She knew how important it was act now, before she lost her strength completely, so with adrenalin helping again, she dug her heels into the sand and shuffled her bottom a few inches up the beach, holding Chris against her chest. Then she dug her heels in and shuffled again, moving only a few inches each time, but she kept at it, digging, shuffling, digging and shuffling until she reached the tumbled down stones then flopped against them letting Chris roll over onto the sand beside her. Her strength was sapped but they were safe. The stones gave enough shelter to keep the rough wind from blowing directly onto them. It was the best she could do.

The day had darkened with the squall and now the sun appeared weakly through the clouds. Although the instructor had pointed to the bay, Lisa knew he would not be sure that they had reached it safely. He wouldn't be able to give precise details to the rescue service. She had to face the possibility of spending the night there on the sand with an injured Chris, for whom she could do nothing more than try to keep him warm, but with her own body getting colder by the minute, even that was beyond her and she was bone-achingly tired.

She tried hard not to fall asleep. She needed to be awake in case Chris regained consciousness, but exhaustion was taking over and she must have dozed for a little while, because she was woken by a slight movement at her side.

'Chris?' Her voice croaked. 'Chris, its Lisa, can you hear me?'

He gave a faint moan.

'Chris, don't go to sleep again. Stay with me.' Lisa tried to pat his face but her hands were too cold. He lapsed back into unconsciousness and after that brief hope that he was coming to, to have him fall back into oblivion again, was heart sinking.

Tiredness leeched her last bit of courage. It was so cold. The waves were still pounding onto the shore and scraping the gravel as they receded. She could hear the rasping as the pebbles were dragged back and forth, but behind that – there was something else. Another sound, like a faint humming, was growing louder as it came closer until it seemed as if it was inside the little shelter with them. The same lilting melody hummed over and over. She had the strong feeling that she was not alone. Something or someone was holding her just as she was holding Chris, boosting her spirits, restoring her courage, supporting her and suddenly Chris moved again. Lisa tried to keep him roused. She knew that people could often hear even when unconscious, and she tried to join in with the humming, to send the same comforting feeling to Chris, but her throat was hoarse and all she could manage was a croak, then as gradually as it had come, the sound faded away. All she could hear was the sea. But she had been comforted, her spirits had lifted and her hope returned. Now they would wait for the rescue she knew the instructor would bring.

* * *

Chris spent nearly a week in hospital in Douglas with suspected concussion. Once he had been given the all-clear, they went home to Blackpool, putting the exhibition put on hold for the time being. Back once more surrounded by their family, Lisa described their ordeal and the rough shelter they had found on the beach in the little bay.

'It was so strange,' she said. 'It was growing dark, and I was wet and cold. Chris was unconscious and I was worried sick about him. All my strength seemed to have drained away, then, just as I thought I couldn't hold out any longer, I heard this sound, a sort of humming, almost like a lullaby. It seemed to be in the corner where we were huddled, faint at first then getting stronger. I felt as though someone was there with me, holding me, keeping me safe. Chris stirred and I tried to join in with the tune to keep him awake but my throat was raw, I had no voice, and then the humming gradually faded.'

Grace had been listening intently, now she leaned forward. 'Was it like this?' She began to hum a soft lilting tune. Lisa stared and nodded.

'Yes, exactly like that, how did you know?'

'Because I had a dream,' said Grace, 'a very vivid dream. I was back in the old cottage where John and I had lived, and I had this strong feeling that someone needed me. I couldn't see anyone, just a shadowy shape that was beyond my reach, but it was someone I had to try to save. The sea was involved in some way. I hadn't been able to save John but this time I had the chance to help. In my dream, the only way I could let them know I was there, was to sing to them. I hummed the lullaby I had crooned to comfort Robert when he was a baby, the same one that my mother had crooned to me. I hoped to bring comfort to whoever it was, to try to add my strength to theirs. That was all there was and I thought no more of it. It had been a dream, that was all.'

'But that is what I heard,' Lisa said, 'and it seemed real. I felt for a few moments as though we were not alone.'

'Goodness, that's really weird.' Elizabeth looked at Grace. 'How could you possibly have known they were in trouble? Have you got extra sensory perception?'

'Possibly.' Grace nodded her head. 'It's strange that you should have been washed into that particular cove. I wonder if I would have had that same dream if you had landed somewhere else? Perhaps blood can call to blood, or gene can call to gene, but in my dream your response, although at the time I didn't know it was you, gave me the ending I had so desperately wanted for John. Love alone had not been enough then. It had needed more and this time I had succeeded.'

Lisa sat silently for a few minutes thinking over Grace's words. That strong feeling of being held – was that Grace's love reaching out to her? Yet she must have sent love to John but it had not been enough. What Grace was saying was that perhaps the shared genes had provided the transmission of that love this time and it had been enough to help her. The extra connection that John had not shared. But surely, if you are lucky enough to be part of a loving family, then genes or no genes, you are never alone. Lisa looked around. She *was* part of a loving family and if only her mother was here, she would have all that family about her now.

She looked at Chris, safely recovered and sitting linking arms with his relieved mother, and she began to contemplate. Although she and Chris were both part of the family, it now occurred to her, thanks to her recent experience in piecing together the complicated family relationships, that the only connection they had to each other was through the marriage of their respective grandparents, Elizabeth and Harry. There was no blood link between the two of them; they were not actually related. In their case, unlike that of Philip and John, and her mother and Peter, there were no tangled genes to complicate things and no genetic magnetism to be mistaken for romance. What they shared was not a family history but a family future.

Across the room, Chris caught her eye and winked at her.

And Lisa winked back.

ACKNOWLEDGEMENTS

I AM indebted to – Editors, Gary Dalkin of tothelastword.com and Jonathan Eyers of Cornerstones, for their invaluable eagle-eyed work which brought my manuscript to publishing readiness, thank you both; Elizabeth Ashworth, my tutor on a Writing Magazine course, whose encouragement boosted me to reach my goal; Duncan Beal and his team at York Publishing Services, who produced exactly the book I envisaged.

Grateful thanks to Mark Hindle and Hannah Hindle for their patience in leading me through the technicalities of computing, rescuing me on more than one occasion; also to Mark for his expert advice on the kayaking incident; to Carole Corbett, my first reader, who gave me very perceptive and concise feedback; and lastly to you, my readers, happy reading.